JASON STRIKER MARTIAL ARTS SERIES VOLUME III

JASON STRIKER MARTIAL ARTS SERIES VOLUME III

Amazon Slaughter and Curse of the Ninja

Piers Anthony and Roberto Fuentes

Library of Congress Number: 2001119026
ISBN #: Softcover 1-4010-3353-9

This is a work of fiction. Names, characters, places and incidents either are the product of the author's imagination or are used fictitiously, and any resemblance to any actual persons, living or dead, events, or locales is entirely coincidental.

This book was printed in the United States of America.

To order additional copies of this book, contact:
Xlibris Corporation
1-888-7-XLIBRIS
www.Xlibris.com
Orders@Xlibris.com

CONTENTS

AMAZON SLAUGHTER 9

AMAZON SLAUGHTER

Chapter 1:

Feeding the Fish

They hung the captive ninja on a wooden frame in the jungle. He was stripped to the waist, his arms spread-eagled, his legs securely fastened. All he could do was scream—and he would not.

"Where is your leader?" the big bald giant demanded. He spoke in Portuguese. He was six and a half feet tall, with the physique of a weight lifter, and an ugly scar ran down his face. His neck was so thick it made his head look shrunken. His whole aspect suggested brutal and fanatical strength.

The crucified ninja did not answer.

"I hoped that would be your attitude," the interrogator said. "I've never had the chance to flay a Jap." He gestured. His assistants took small wooden mallets and pounded on the ninja's skin. This was obviously painful, but hardly excruciating, and the victim did not cry out. Instead, his face assumed an expression of repose: he had invoked his ability to turn off pain no matter what was done to him.

"Now while we undergo our preparatory massage," the giant

said with a twisted smile, "let us review the manner of our acquaintance. You will correct me when I make an error in fact or speculation?"

Still the ninja ignored him. The men pounded the captive's skin all over, methodically, going over each area again and again so as to miss no portion. After a time they took him down and rehung him so as to have access to his backside too. Then they proceeded to his legs, stripping off his remaining clothing. The job took some time, but the interrogator merely paused in his monologue to smoke an occasional cigarette and observe.

Eventually the skin had been so thoroughly pounded that it was bruised purple, with blackish glints. The small blood vessels within it had been broken. The entire body gradually became a single extensive bruise.

"First the introduction. I am Fernando Mirabal, of Spanish descent, but quite satisfied to settle here in Brazil. In fact I am a member of the Brazilian diplomatic corps, and my brother Ramiro is the Director of Pẹtrobas, the Brazilian Petroleum Company. You are an agent of the notorious Japanese outlaw Fu Antos." He paused as though expecting agreement, but the ninja gave no sign.

Now the blades came into play. The instruments used were not knives, but fine steel scalpels honed razor sharp. They sliced easily into the flesh.

"Thus it is scarcely surprising that we should meet," Mirabal continued pleasantly. "When my brother asked my help in investigating the disturbances occurring in our newly discovered oil fields, I thought at once of Fu Antos—and I am pleased to verify that your ninja chief-scoundrel thought as readily of me." He contemplated the victim, as though fascinated by every stage of the slow torture. "I understand Fu Antos is old, extremely old. Four centuries, some sources claim. Oh, yes, I have researched the matter; that is my job! And I admit to being intrigued by the supernatural, though I can't claim to be able to practice magic myself." He chuckled. "I hope Fu is not so ancient as to be an inadequate adversary. I much prefer a genuine challenge."

They started on the extremities, slitting the softened skin carefully at the ends of the fingers, proceeding down across the hands. They loosened the skin at the base of each finger and pulled toward the ends, as though removing tight gloves. Care had been taken that no bones were broken and no vital organs damaged, so that the victim would not expire prematurely. The individual cuts were shallow, performed with surgical precision, so that there would not be a disastrous amount of bleeding. It was a bit like peeling an orange without letting any juice leak.

The undersurfaces were raw, like hamburger, bleeding slowly. They applied a special mixture of salt and vinegar to slow the bleeding further, rubbing it in. The man's body writhed and strained at its restraining straps in these moments, seeming almost ready to break its bonds. The pain was evidently excruciating, despite the victim's self-control.

"But I digress. I came to the oil camp, then visited the nearby Pacifico, the pacified Indian village." He laughed. "Not pacified enough, it seems! So I made a token demonstration. The usual: shooting a few natives, taking some hostages, borrowing a couple of the prettier maidens for passing entertainment, explaining how readily such a village might burn if some accident occurred. I had hoped someone would carry word to old Fu, and it seems I was not disappointed."

After the fingers, they turned the ninja over and worked on his back, the easiest place. They tore great sheets of skin away, slowly, carefully. Then they returned to the front, flaying the chest and abdomen. They did not touch his face or neck, afraid he might die; instead they moved down. They stripped his arms and legs, finally coming to the buttocks.

"Except in this: my little welcome was intended for the old Jap himself, not his hireling. Oh, you sneaked in cleverly enough; had it not been for our special American starlight amplifiers we would not have seen you in your black suit. But I hardly expected you to be so readily deceived by the ploy of placing an aide in my own bunk. You stabbed your knife into an innocent employee!

But his death was not in vain, for we surrounded that tent, employed the floodlights, and now we have you. Beg pardon?"

For now at last the ninja screamed, as they skinned his penis and testicles, by applying a combination pull and slice.

Mirabal smiled, seeing the victim's amazing control breaking down at last. "It was touchy for a moment, I admit. You very nearly did succeed in killing yourself, after you disemboweled one of mine and split the throat of another. But again, you had not anticipated our anesthetic dart-guns. And the delay entailed in cutting off the victim's head—that was foolish. I realize old Fu has a fetish about collecting the heads of his enemies, *but you had the wrong head."* Mirabal touched his own head with a gesture of pride. "No, I'm afraid you were a disappointment to me. I expected more subtlety."

The ninja subsided as the flaying was completed. He was now a strange looking creature, but still alive and conscious.

"Now I can still kill you quickly," the torturer said. He held up his pistol, a Spanish Astra 8-shot 9mm able to fire every type of 9mm and 38 automatic round. He aimed it at the victim's head. "Your pain will be over, if you talk. Otherwise—well, I think we have several hours work, yet. There is still the head: a more delicate operation, fraught with risks to your sensory apparatus, but surely worth the effort. After that we might begin to disconnect the muscles. I have always been a student of anatomy, and there are distinct advantages in working with living material. Don't you agree?"

Suddenly an arrow swished over Mirabal's shoulder and struck the ninja in the chest. He was dead instantly; the shot was through the heart.

Mirabal whirled and dropped to the ground, pointing his Astra back the way the arrow had come. But there was nothing. His three cohorts scrambled for cover.

There was silence. "Bugger must have slipped out while his arrow was airborne," Mirabal said disgustedly. "Wonder why he didn't aim for *me?"* He got up, brushing himself off. The others rose with him.

Then one screamed and fell forward. An arrow protruded from his back. It was a very fine bamboo shaft a yard long with a stone arrowhead and black feathers. Mirabal whirled again, getting off a shot, but again there was nothing.

"Get under cover, and stay there!" Mirabal rasped. "It's an ambush, and the bastard wants to play. I'll signal the camp for reinforcements."

He reached for his walkie-talkie—and a third arrow struck it just as his hand touched it. He jerked his arm back.

"Cono!" he swore. "We're exposed here; they can pick us off at will." He reached out and snatched the third arrow. "Black obsidian head with a glasslike edge," he murmured. "Excellent craftsmanship, not local. It seems our ninja villain has arrived." Then he raised his voice: "When I give the signal, we'll make a break for better cover. Right?"

There was no answer. Irritated, he looked across, and saw the reason. His companion had an arrow sticking out of his eye. He was dead. The third man had disappeared, and was presumably dead too.

Now Mirabal was alone. He jumped up, grabbed the other man's body, and slung it over himself as a shield. He had a limp, but was so powerful that the added weight was unimportant. He ran for cover.

Panting, he flung himself behind a huge rubber tree. "Made it!" he gasped.

"Congratulations."

Mirabal whirled again, dropping his burden as he raised his gun. But all he saw was a boy. "Who the hell are you?"

"I am he whom you seek."

Mirabal's bark of laughter resounded through the jungle. "Well, then; here's death for you!" He pointed his gun—and stopped.

The boy wasn't there.

Mirabal strode forward, peering around the tree. Suddenly a

cord looped his hand, jerking the gun away. The boy stood behind him, holding the weapon. "As you have done to my man, so shall I do to you," the lad said.

The man aimed a mighty kick at him, a savage shot to the head. But suddenly the boy was gone again. The foot passed through empty air, and then the lad's hands caught the heel of the boot and pushed upwards. Mirabal, off-balance, tried to hop back, but the boy's toe snaked forward and hooked that other ankle, anchoring the foot. The torturer took a brutal fall on his back. The air whooshed out of him and for a moment his consciousness faded. When he opened his eyes, the boy was staring down at him.

"Now," the boy said, "I will question you." His eyes seemed to become huge, and his fingers moved in a disconcerting way. Suddenly Mirabal recognized the pattern: it was the notorious ninja *kuji-kiri* finger-hypnosis.

Mirabal tried to get up, but his body was frozen in place. Those eyes, those devil fingers were sapping his willpower, taking over his mind. Now he believed: this was indeed Fu Antos, lord of the ninjas!

Fernando Mirabal tried to fight. He concentrated in an effort to break the hypnotic hold. Sweat ran in rivulets down his body, and he felt he was winning. He moved his head a fraction of an inch, slowly tearing his eyes away from that devil's gaze. Now he knew his antagonist, and was on guard; once he regained his feet . . .

The sound of gunshots passed through the jungle. The distant birds became quiet, the wild animals paused. Even the river alligators and caimans seemed to listen. What was happening?

Fu Antos clenched his small fist and bared his teeth in a momentary display of fury. "I told them to wait!" he gritted.

Mirabal was abruptly freed from the compulsion. "You were going to ambush our camp, and those rascally Indians attacked prematurely!" he said gleefully. "I could have told you that would happen. Those savages have no discipline at all."

But he was speaking to air. Fu Antos was gone.

*

It galled Fu Antos to leave the butcher, but it would take time to deal with him properly, and right now he had to get to the camp and untangle the mess the Indians had made. The situation was certain to deteriorate in minutes without his guidance.

He should have used his skilled ninjas for the job, instead of the poorly organized Indians. Well, those Indians would very quickly learn the meaning of their exuberance. Firearms were tough opponents.

Meanwhile, he would have to see the chore through himself, using what he had. There was no time to fetch his ninjas, who were widely scattered on other missions. Maybe the first shock of failure would make the Indians realize the importance of timing and caution.

Too bad he had not arrived in time to save his advance scout. But of course the man had not talked, and at least he was out of his pain. Actually, he could have killed his ninja earlier, or rescued him after only partial flaying. But he could not abide carelessness or a bungled job, and so the ninja had deserved the agony he had suffered. Had the man talked, Fu Antos would have tortured him himself. And Mirabal's monologue had been of interest, as well as his skinning technique. Fu Antos possessed a superior technique, but it was good to compare styles.

He had been moving rapidly through the overflow forest, a region near the river that became seasonally flooded. Here the trees were of medium size: palms and wild rubber trees, with massive drooping vines that rooted in the ground to become new trunks. His fast passage startled a flock of macaws that flew screeching with their brightly colored plumage flashing. He breathed the ambient odor of the jungle, savoring its naturalness. Once Japan had been primitive like this, pleasant. Alas, no more.

Now he came to a bluff overlooking the camp. It was in a clearing beside the great river: a cluster of tents, with a few palm-thatched and board-sided dwellings. Separate shacks for radio and equipment stood a little apart. There was also a wooden tower for test drilling, flanked by a jeep and a heavy truck.

The Indians' wildcat attack had been repulsed. Several dead braves were sprawled about, along with two white men. Now the remaining Indians were in hiding at the edge of the forest, while the surviving government men were holed up inside the main tent. They kept up a steady rifle fire, preventing any safe approach.

No question about it: the damage had been done. What could have been an easy, virtually bloodless takeover, was now a difficult problem. The element of surprise was gone.

Yet Fu Antos smiled. The camp was vulnerable; he could redeem the situation. His eyes traveled on to the river. A boat was there, tied at an improvised dock: a fast launch guarded by two sharp-shooting crewmen.

Yes, he would put the fear of the ninja into these people! It would be long before another such party intruded in this territory.

And now two of his ninjas arrived, attracted to the commotion. They had been reconnoitering nearby, and their prompt presence showed they had been sufficiently alert. Excellent; he had need of them.

He summoned the Indian subchief. "Maintain harassment," he said in the native tongue, for he readily mastered any language he needed to. "Delegate two men to me for special instruction."

The chief frowned. "Many are already dead. We can not go against the guns."

The Indians, downtrodden for centuries, had been eager to cooperate with anyone who promised to lead them out of their repression and misery. But they hardly trusted the ninjas yet. They had been deceived and defrauded by outsiders too often. But Fu Antos was different; so far they believed in his magical-seeming powers, if not in his age or motive. And his skin was yellow, not white. So the relation between ninja and Indian was as yet jury-rigged; it needed strengthening every so often, especially at stress points. In time it would become so firm as to be unbreakable.

Fu Antos started to twine his fingers in the *kuji-kiri* pattern, but stopped. He wanted to build a more enduring affiliation, not one based on temporary compulsion. He seized the chief's wrist, and though he looked like a mere stripling his fingers were like steel pins driving in. "Do you question me?" He twisted, making the chief lean forward involuntarily. "I will lead your braves to great victory."

Cowed by the ninja lord's power, and the stares of the two other ninjas, the chief saved face by acceding. Two Indians were delegated, while the rest kept up a barrage of arrows and stones.

"You two," Fu Antos said, gesturing with one hand to his ninjas. "Go upriver, swim underwater with the current to the bottom of the boat, using hollow reeds for snorkels. Use your knives silently to make holes in the hull. Do not let the water enter. Stuff those holes immediately with this." He showed them a concoction he mixed from clay and red powder he took from a vial at his waist.

"But the water devils—" one protested.

"That substance dissolves in water," the other said.

Fu Antos gestured, compelling them as he spoke. Now his own ninjas were questioning him. "Dung of monkeys!" he swore gently in Japanese, smiling pleasantly so the Indians would not catch on. "Have I trained you these last twenty years only to have you grow feeble when there is work to be done?" But he knew what was bothering them: though they well knew of his transformation from decrepit hulk to childlike youth, they had trouble really believing that he was the same man. They had not known him in his vigorous manhood, for they lacked the secret of immediate reincarnation. So they wavered. "Smear this salve on your bodies; the water devils will not molest you. Do not be concerned about the boat: it will sink—when the time is appropriate."

They looked at him, comprehending his meaning. This was the old Fu Antos, master strategist, talking! He gestured again, and they went.

He turned to the two Indians. "Fetch arrows," he told them. "And fine cord."

Fu Antos took from another pocket a package wrapped in cloth. Very carefully he unwrapped it. Inside were several small glass vials containing an opaque substance. "Tie one vial to the shaft of each arrow," he told the arrow-Indians. "Handle them carefully—there are demons inside." Actually it was a secret ninja concoction, akin to the old Greek fire, but more virulent. The vials would break on impact, releasing and spreading their contents, and once the stuff caught fire there would be no stopping it.

Confused but amenable, the two Indians obeyed. They prepared the arrows.

Fu Antos walked down to the river. He threw in a small packet of herbs. The packet fell apart as the water suffused it, and the herbs spread through the water in a murky cloud.

Soon there was an odd rippling across the water, as though great numbers of small fish were converging. He nodded, and turned away with a small smile of satisfaction.

By this time the boat saboteurs would be completing their job. They were ninjas; no need to be concerned about their competence. In a few more minutes they would swim on downstream, leaving the boat apparently unchanged.

He returned to the bluff. Their chore completed, the two Indians looked at Fu Antos. Unconcerned, he took his bow from the Japanese quiver slung at his side. The quiver was made of ornate lacquered woven rattan, obviously a fine old possession. His bow differed from those of the Indians: its shape was peculiar to Japan, with its hand grip about a third of the way from the bottom. There was a small arc of the lower limb and a large arc of the upper limb.

The Indian arrows were not made for the ninja bow, but Fu Antos made do. He fitted one of the special arrows to the bow and loosed it, so quickly that the Indians were amazed. It flew high and far, and plunged into the roof of the larger tent. There was a loud explosion, and a fountain of white fire leaped from the point of impact, quickly igniting the canvas.

The two Indians were silent, genuinely impressed by the competence of the shot, for Fu Antos looked like a child incapable of a man's effort. And the explosion strengthened their faith in his magic. Indians knew about fire, of course, but these arrows had not been tarred or lit before being loosed. There must have been demons in the bottles, as the ninja leader had said. Impressive, yes!

Fu Antos loosed another fire arrow. It struck the radio shack, setting fire to the thatch. Smoke curled up from the roof as the blaze spread. The occupants did not realize the hazard yet, but they were doomed.

In moments he had fired the other buildings. As the flames shot up, the doors burst open. The men charged out, guns blazing.

Now they had to run the gantlet of arrows between the houses and the boat. The men made an orderly trek. But now they were exposed, while the Indians were under cover. That went far to equalize the disadvantage of bows against guns.

Fu Antos thought briefly of Fernando Mirabal, who should have arrived here by now. But of course the man would not care about his workers; he would have made directly for a larger town, seeking reinforcements. It was no sign of cowardice to stay clear of an adverse situation; Fu Antos would have done the same, in Mirabal's position. Meanwhile, the workers were leaderless, and that would only hasten their doom. The doom that Mirabal himself would be the first to confirm, as the only escapee. There always had to be an escapee, to establish exactly who was responsible, to spread the warning far more effectively than the perpetrators could.

However, the workers were better disciplined than the Indians. There were about twenty Indians against fifteen workers, but the Indians' marksmanship was appalling. Fu Antos realized that he had miscalculated: at short range the Indians could bring down a running animal unerringly, but their bows and arrows and skills were not geared for long range accuracy. The workers, perhaps aware of this, maintained their fire from their American carbines and M-2 automatic rifles, with occasional blasts from a shotgun. Even though they were firing more or less blind, the sheer volume of lead was enough to score randomly, killing several more Indians. The two ninjas could have eliminated the entire formation, but Fu Antos had wanted to test out his allies in combat. They had a long way to go.

A dozen workers made it to the boat despite the best efforts of the Indians. "Why didn't we cut it adrift!" groaned the chief.

"Because then they would not have run the gantlet," Fu Antos responded, as though he were the man and the chief the child, which was true enough in its fashion. "Had they charged the jungle, we could not have contained them."

"But now they escape!"

Fu Antos smiled. "Many will." He watched the boat's engine start. The craft nosed out into the rippling river.

Then it began to sink, as the plugs dissolved and popped out of their holes, letting the water pour in. Perfect timing!

The men tried to bail it out, but the task was useless. The launch was overloaded, and there were too many leaks.

They swam for it—and suddenly the water was alive. The men screamed and flailed madly and went under the seething surface. White froth danced above the surface. One man jumped high in the water, exposing half his torso. Already, white bones were visible where parts of his face had been. A writhing tail projected from one socket where his eyeball had been eaten.

"The water devils!" the chief exclaimed gleefully. "I have never seen them like this!"

"I summoned them," Fu Antos said. "Demons of fire, water, trees—all answer to me."

And the chief looked at him, believing.

Two men made it to shore. Small silver fish clung to them: piranha. One man's leg was a solid mass of them. He fell, unable to walk, for much of the flesh was already gone.

"Salvage those two—alive," Fu Antos said.

The chief started to protest, then reconsidered. He saw how brutally effective the ninja lord's campaign had been. Few Indians had been lost since Fu Antos took over, and the enemy had been wiped out. This man who controlled demons was a valuable ally indeed. He dispatched two warriors.

The two prisoners were brought to Fu Antos. One was unharmed except for the small bites of the piranha attack. The other had to be carried, as his leg was useless.

Fu Amos surveyed them coolly. "Your companions escaped," he said.

"They're all dead!" one of the prisoners cried. Then his mouth tightened as the implication of the ninja's words sank in. If death were escape, what was waiting for the living?

"Food for the fish," the chief murmured appreciatively.

"This is not your land," Fu Antos said to the government man.

The prisoner looked down at him. "A mere boy!" he exclaimed. "*You* directed this unprovoked massacre?"

"You do not deem the live flaying of a ninja as provocation?"

"We know nothing of that!" But it was apparent the man did know. Mirabal's expertise had not developed without practice.

"Or the flaying of the land?" Fu Antos persisted.

The man shook his head, uncomprehendingly. "We're only prospecting for oil. Setting up to drill a test well—"

"On Indian territory?"

The man looked nervous. "We have a permit!"

Fu Antos turned to the chief. "Did your people approve any permit?"

"No! We approved none of this. They come in, scare our animals off, kill the fish, take our lands, our women, our lives—"

"Not us!" the oil man cried. "We're looking for oil, nothing else. I wouldn't touch a dirty squaw."

The denial was confirmation enough. "Why oil?" Fu Antos asked.

"Why! The world is desperately short of oil. Its value has multiplied."

"So it is for money," Fu Antos said.

"More than that! Without oil, modern industry will grind to a halt. It's a vital resource."

"Modern industry," Fu Antos said. "This is what pollutes the rivers and the air, making villagers die of mercury poisoning, of cancer, of lung disease. You do this for money, so that your people may exist like emperors while the world starves."

"You're crazy!" the man exclaimed. "We *need* that oil!"

"I am sane. Your culture is crazy," Fu Antos said. "I employ my skills for moral reasons, especially my tortures. You destroy wantonly, for greed." Then, meditatively: "And if you are denied oil, your culture will collapse."

Another ninja appeared, running smoothly. The man was in full uniform: reddish-black baggy jacket and trousers, split canvas shoes, and a hood that partially masked his face.

"Master!" the newcomer cried in Japanese. "A message from Kan-Sen by carrier pigeon."

Fu Antos accepted the paper. The message was in Japanese symbols. Kan-Sen was Chinese, but the written language was the same. WEAPONS EN ROUTE BY WATER. JASON STRIKER DISPATCHED AS COURIER.

Fu Antos smiled. He needed those modern weapons, for there were limits to what spears and arrows could do, as this engagement had shown. As for Jason Striker—he had special reason to bring the man here. Kan-Sen was performing well.

Jason Striker should perform even better.

Chapter 2:

Fun in Rio

The plane started in Miami, with a stopover in Caracas, then over the great Amazon basin and very briefly over the sea again. It circled the city of Rio de Janeiro, on a bay surrounded by mountains. There was a lovely white sand beach right along the waterfront. I like white beaches; they remind me of pretty girls in bikinis.

As we came closer I could see that the sidewalks were gaily painted in stripes and patterns. I got a good view of the 130-foot statue *Christ of Corcovado* atop Hunchback Mountain, itself over 2,000 feet high. It loomed out of the shantytown that I understood housed a million people. Rio, squeezed between the ocean and the mountains, had no urban planning; it just sprawled. A solid wall of apartment houses and hotels marched right up to the sand. I had been told by tourist publicity that Rio had been founded in 1567 as a fort and naval base. It had grown!

We had to circle over the field for an hour before landing. At last I stepped down onto the tarmac of Rio's obsolescent Galeão airport. There were no enclosed ramps or other modern comforts; I was no longer in rich USA.

I caught a cab that took me right to my hotel, *"La Estrella,"* which translated as "The Star." It was right on *Avenida Atlantica,* on the beach: a huge Hilton-style edifice, with hot running water, a huge bed, and a tremendous color TV set in my room. A sight more than I had expected, after the airport.

There was a balcony on Atlantic Avenue, with a view of the Guanabara Bay, the dazzling white sand, tall buildings and clean blue sea. Just as in my fond imagination, the area was full of beautiful young women in bikinis, yet nearby were also several fishing boats getting their nets ready.

Kan-Sen, my enemy collaborator, would contact me here.

I was not familiar with Brazilian social etiquette and did not speak Portuguese, so I took the coward's way and stayed in my room. I wished I had a telescope to help view the lithe creatures of the beach. I'm not really a voyeur; there just wasn't much to do. The hotel personnel spoke English, so I was able to have supper via room service. Then I took a long steamy bath, watched parts of shows on each of the five local TV stations, and fell asleep.

Next morning I felt rested and restless. What about Kan-Sen? I had found no message, received no call. He was supposed to provide me with all the information I needed: where to go, what to do, and what my mission was. Without him I was completely in the dark, wasting my time.

I was hardly cut out to be a secretive agent, and it galled me tremendously to have to take orders, as it were, from my bitterest enemy. But Fu Antos needed me.

I couldn't stay in my room all day. That would look suspicious, and bore me to the explosion point. I should be at my dojo, teaching my judo classes. So I acted like the tourist I was beginning to wish I was, and went out on the beach.

It was early, with the dawn sun just flashing off the water, so there were not many people. And I still didn't speak their language, except in the sense that appreciation for the splendor of the sunrise is universal. I'd picked up a smattering of Spanish over the years, but Brazil is a Portuguese-speaking country. Has to do with a Papal decision, some time back: Portugal colonized to the east of a line through South America, Spain to the west. The east became Brazil.

Then I saw a language that is unfortunately as universal as beauty: violence. A buxom girl had been walking along the beach, looking for shells or something. I was dawdling nearer the water, half-hoping to run into her "accidentally." Two cars drove up and parked beyond her. Two men got out of one and approached the girl. One of them told her to come—even I could grasp that much—and she straightened up, brushing the sand off her voluptuous body. They talked briefly—I assumed at first he was a relative—but then her tone became more doubtful, his more peremptory. She started to turn away from him, and he grabbed her behind the head with one hand and pulled her in to him. That was the point my interest shifted from the casual to the concerned.

She did not appear to put up resistance, but drew in quite close to him, her bosom touching his chest. They were spectacular breasts, and he was understandably distracted as she put an arm behind his back. Suddenly she spun into a left *o goshi* hip throw, and he was flying through the air to land hard on his back.

"Beautiful!" I breathed appreciatively. To me, the elegance of a perfectly executed judo throw is the prettiest sight of all. In theory, a person thrown with the force upon his back will not be inclined to renew hostilities, and the theory became fact on this occasion.

The other man made the mistake of grabbing her from behind with arms around her waist. She bent and caught hold of one of his feet, lifting it. He had to fall on his back. She dropped heavily on his knee, breaking it. He screamed.

The first man had by now recovered somewhat. He tried to hit her with his fist, a blow to the face. She blocked it with her hand, striking the outside of his wrist and weaving her face aside. She went in behind him and put a *hadaka jime* standing naked strangle on him, bending down her face and pushing against his shoulder. Unable to believe that a mere woman could choke him out, he resisted. He was turning purple.

But then three more men from the second car charged up. One caught her with a kick to the rib cage just under her left breast. Ouch—I knew that hurt, if it hadn't broken her ribs.

By this time I was on my feet and rushing into the fray. I had not chosen to get involved before; the girl had seemed able to handle herself, and I knew nothing of the situation. But there are limits. Still, it took me a few minutes to get there. You can't make good time in loose sand when you want to.

She rolled with the kick and turned to face this new antagonist, but the next man slapped her hard across the face. Now it was three against one, and the man she had been strangling was recovering. Evidently they didn't see me, since I was between them and the sun. She fell down, and one of them kicked her hard in the buttocks.

Then I arrived. Faster than a speeding bullet, et cetera: say what you will, but a lady in distress sets me in motion about as rapidly as anything. I kicked the recently strangled man hard on the shoulder from behind, probably breaking it and putting him out for the duration. Not very sporting, but this was not a sportive matter. If the girl had thrown him just a bit harder the first time, she would have been in less trouble than she was now.

That left three active men. The one who had just kicked the prone girl's bottom tried the same on me. But I had less of a target, and I was on my feet. He came at me from the side, and I put one hand on his upper thigh, the other on the ankle, and moved up on him so that his kick did not have much force. I did a *sasae-tsuri-komi-ashi* lifting-pull throw on his supporting foot. That is, I propped my right foot against his left ankle and levered him over by his raised right foot. As he fell on his back I finished him off with a straight punch to the middle of his face that smashed his nose.

Two to go. One tried an uppercut, but I moved my head back, grabbed his hand at the wrist with both of mine, and pushed it upward. That continued its natural motion, making his effort work for me. Then I turned and put it under my armpit in the *waki-gatame* armpit hold. This is a submission lock that puts pressure on the captive elbow, and the only sensible thing for the man caught in it is to yield immediately. But the fool tried to resist, so I increased my force. In the excitement of the fray, and nervous about the last man who was charging me, I misjudged it. His arm snapped, and he screamed in agony. I let him go; that fight was through.

The third man looked like an ex-football linesman. He weighed all of three hundred pounds, and he tried a hard tackle. He rushed in low, first attempting to butt me in the stomach. It could have been most effective against an unprepared man. But I took both his arms from above and snaked my hands over his shoulders and under his chest, linking my own fingers. Then I threw myself backwards, again utilizing my opponent's impetus. My head pressed into his upper back, serving as a fulcrum, and he flew over my back to land with terrific force on the sand. Fortunately for him, he knew how to take a fall, but he had lost much of his incentive. A three-hundred-pound landing is a rough one, no matter how experienced the man is. He got up and staggered back toward the cars.

Now, for the first time, I got a good look at the girl's face—and suddenly I knew why she had seemed familiar. "Dulce!" I exclaimed.

I had visited Cuba once, in my capacity as trainer of the American judo team competing in Havana. I had met Dulce on the beach, seemingly by accident. She was a militiawoman, perhaps assigned to keep an eye on me, but she was also great company. She was fascinated by judo and judokas, and by me too, if I had not misread the signals. I knew she was a dedicated Communist, but she had never imposed her political views on me, and I liked her too. Not merely for her appearance; she was a smart, competent woman with a good personality and a flair for language. She could speak English like a native, as well as French and Spanish and Portuguese and for all I knew several others. I could see that she had also been working on her judo, for she had put it to good use. Actually, I think judo is good for any woman. Maybe some day the world will be completely safe, with no violence anywhere; meanwhile it is smart to know self-defense.

Dulce and I had not had any love affair. Perhaps it would have come to that, but our acquaintance had been abruptly terminated by events not of our making. I had not seen her again—until now.

Male that I am, I immediately saw the potential for converting my idle waiting time into real pleasure. But I approached the matter with a bit of natural caution. After all, her interest in me could have faded; my removal from the scene had been abrupt and unexplained, and she might have harbored a natural resentment. "Should we make a report to the police? An unprovoked attack like this—"

"No—no police!" she said quickly. "These men *are* the police."

My jaw dropped. *"What?"*

"I will explain another time," she said. "Now I am afraid to return to my room."

My face must have shown my too-good-to-be-true excitement, for she took my arm, laughing. "You disappeared in a street brawl, and you reappeared in one, like a genie of violence. It is coincidence, our meeting here, but how glad I am to see you! I know you would not deceive me."

"Never!" I agreed. "Our politics may differ, but—"

"I am on a private mission for my government, nothing to do with you." She glanced sidelong at me. "Unless you were sent to intercept me?"

"No," I said. "I'm here on business of my own, helping a—a friend." Fu Antos was not exactly my friend, at any rate not in the usual sense, but that was too complicated to explain. "I had no notion you were here."

"I believe you. So we trust each other."

"Yes." And I did trust her. She would not be mixed up in dirty politics—not the lying, killing kind—even though she did work for the Communist government of Cuba. She would not lie to me, because she was not that type of person. "About the manner we parted, before—"

"Do not be concerned. Fidel told me you were breaking up an international drug-smuggling operation, and could not blow your cover."

Just like that, the Communists had covered for me! But I suppose the cat will cover for the mouse, if the cat has reason. I knew Fidel would as readily send an assassin after me, if it suited his convenience. But we had no quarrel at the moment. So I took Dulce to my room. No one seemed to notice or care. And it was a real pleasure to speak English freely again.

But caution did not desert me. I knew she had a mission to accomplish, and she knew I had one too. These missions obviously could get us killed. It was just possible—not likely, but possible—that my room was bugged. I didn't know how such things were in Brazil, and could not openly inquire. So we had to pretend that this was merely a pickup: girl is mugged on beach, man who once knew her rescues her, man gets reward.

The irony was that I would gladly have settled for the script as reality, and looking at her, I knew she felt the same. We would have to do what we both desired—and thereby cheapen it distressingly. What a waste!

But she was injured. There was the saving grace. A valid pretext *not* to perform—until the time was right.

"Let me help you," I said.

"No—it is not bad," she demurred.

I drew her into the bathroom. "Come on. I'll take care of it."

The bathroom was huge, with a sunken black marble tub like a small swimming pool and a deep orange rug on the floor and a monstrous wall mirror. Last night all this opulence had embarrassed me; now I was glad for it.

"I think I got hit here," she admitted, pointing to her left breast.

"Brute kicked you; I saw it," I said. "Any ribs broken?"

"I don't think so," she said. But she winced as I touched the place. Then I saw a small stain of blood seeping through.

She stood unresisting as I undid her bathing suit. It was one of those tight one-piece affairs, so I had to peel it off her upper torso. Her breasts were exposed, and as I had strongly suspected, they were completely authentic. I favor breasts of any size, but these were classics.

The bruise was on the left side just below the breast.

"You're lucky," I said. "His foot bounced off your rib, just breaking the skin. A little higher and to the front—" I paused, for this reminded me of a real breast injury I had once seen, a broken-bottle savage, and that reminded me of Chiyako, the love that would always be with me.

I shook off that memory. I could not bring the dead back to life. I soaked a towel in hot water and sponged off the bruise. It was ugly but not bad. To clean around it sufficiently, I had to wipe off some of Dulce's breast, too, a necessary but delightful task.

She might have pulled away, expressing affront. She didn't. She made a little sound that might have been pain but wasn't. "I am here to contact the urban guerrillas," she murmured in my ear as though they were words of love.

"You don't have to tell me," I whispered back. "In fact, I don't want to know."

She shook her head, while her hands drew me down to the rug with her. I realized that she was undressing me, and it had an electrifying effect. This was hardly the ideal spot, but if that was what she wanted—! "I must tell you, for now you have helped me, and they will never believe you are not my contact."

"Mmmm," I agreed. I *had* become involved with her, in more than one sense. Apparently she did not hold my sudden prior absence against me, and was quite ready to pick up where we had left off. Marvelous!

"I brought much money—half a million American dollars," she said, indicating her handbag, that I had not noticed before.

All women had handbags; why notice them? Especially when there was so much else about a woman to notice.

"Half a *what?*" I yelped, abruptly realizing what she had said.

"Make love, not noise," she said, putting her forefinger across my lips. We were both pretty well undressed now. In one way I was surprised that she came on so warmly, so fast; in another way I wasn't. She had thought a lot of me, in Cuba, and now we would be together only briefly before our separate missions carried us away as carelessly as they had brought us together. So she was taking immediate advantage of the opportunity, as was I.

"Yes, that was what they were after," she said. "They must have ransacked my room, looking for it, then come after me directly. I was supposed to meet my contact on the beach, give him the money, help the local group get properly organized. But he was late, or maybe they got him before coming after me."

I saw it now. Pretty girl collecting shells on beach, young man strikes up conversation. Only he hadn't showed. The police, evidently tipped off by some informer, had come instead. I wasn't really sorry to see the Communist plot broken up; Latin America already had too much violence. But I had gotten involved.

"But if those were the police," I asked, "why didn't they just arrest you? These things happen all the time. International incidents, spying, deals. Don't they usually just usher the agent out quietly?"

"Perhaps. But they wanted the money. If I were dead, they could deny there ever was any money, and who should know otherwise? My government would never admit to it, of course. It is in American dollars so that they cannot be traced; they incriminate no one, and can be spent easily. So the Death Squad—"

"Death Squad?" I whispered in her delicate ear as I slid my knee along her smooth thigh. "What's that?"

Now her lips caressed my ear lobe. "You do not know about them?"

I shifted position, kissed her on the mouth *en route,* and found her other ear. If this were a game, I liked it; if it were only a cover for shop talk, I still liked it. "All I know is that five thugs attacked you, tried to kill you, or at least beat you up. You say they were police."

She smiled, stretched, winced as she felt her bruises, then slid her body across mine in amazing stages. First her leg twined over mine like the lead-in for the *yoko guruma* sacrifice throw; then her warm hips and abdomen rolled on mine in a simulated *uki-goshi* hip throw (though that is normally initiated from a vertical position!); then one breast followed the other in a pneumatic dance across my chest like a *tate shiho gatame* four-quarter holddown. At last her lips commenced their electrifying trek, kissing their way from one side of my neck to the other in the most stimulating strangle I ever experienced.

When she reached my ear, she let the rest of her body subside. My own could hardly be described as doing the same. She snuggled in for a paragraph-sized explanation. I tried—I really tried!—to pay attention. To her words.

"Here in Brazil, many people commit crimes yet escape punishment. Notorious gangsters get off because no one dares testify against them. Corrupt politicians use their leverage to cover up their foul dealings. Businessmen cheat the public and hire high-priced lawyers to keep the law off. Everyone knows these things, yet no one acts. Except the Death Squad. They—"

I heaved, unable to lie still any longer lest I burst. My mouth caught her ear as another organ found other lodging. "Vigilantes! *Now* I understand. They take the law into their own—"

But now she was moving too. Conversation ceased as our torsos interlocked ecstatically. There was an obstruction, and I had my verification that despite Dulce's proficiency and enthusiasm I was the first to proceed this far with her. She was a "Senorita," a maiden, and she had evidently saved it for me: a signal compliment, considering she could not have known whether we would ever meet again. She was so hot inside it was as though my member were burning. "Wait! Wait!" she breathed. "Not now." But it *was* now, and the barrier was down.

Her legs crossed over the small of my back as we rolled over, as if she were trying a *do-jime* scissors strangle, and her heels kicked an erotic tatoo over my kidneys. My eye caught the action in the mirror, and it was some effect.

Deeper, deeper. I buried my face in her brown hair, so silky and clean smelling, and wondered irrelevantly why she wasn't wearing her glasses. She had always worn them, in Cuba. My mind does that: summoning inconsequential distractions at times I least wish it. "I never dreamed it could be so good," she said, and I felt like a heel for my wandering thoughts.

Well, if this bathroom were bugged, I hoped the bugs were getting a good eyeful. There was nothing fake about this. "It's good, all right," I mumbled somewhat awkwardly, sounding insincere when I damn well *was* sincere.

She blinked her eyes several times, and I thought she was starting to cry. Had I blown it?

"Can you see if my contact lenses are in place?" she asked me. "I haven't used them long, and this excitement—"

So that explained the glasses. I looked into her eyes. "I see a little edge of something, transparent," I said.

"That's it. Just slipped aside." She laughed—which was quite an effect, since I had not yet withdrawn. "In all that battle with the death squad they stayed in place, but you were so energetic that—"

"All *right!*" I mumbled, embarrassed.

In due course we dressed. Dulce rang room service and ordered a meal for us both, since she spoke the language. Of course it could have been done in English, but I was sure the food would be better in Portuguese, if that makes any sense.

I was not mistaken. Dulce did it up proper. We started with a plate of Brazilian appetizers: garlicky unshelled fried shrimps, white hearts of palm, lettuce, tomatoes, black olives, Portuguese sardines and sausages. I nibbled, knowing that I could stuff myself without ever getting past the appetizers.

Then an entree of *bossa nova* crisp deep-fried chicken loaded with garlic and served with flavorful white rice and a bowl of delicious purplish black beans resting in their own souplike sauce.

There was also wine. I'm not a drinker, but at social events like this I find it hard to decline. So I accepted what Dulce offered: Portuguese *Casals Garcia Vinto Verde*, a clear, almost astringent green wine. And of course black coffee, so popular in Latin American countries.

For dessert we had guava paste with hard white cheese and some fruit I didn't recognize.

Then Dulce clapped her hand to her forehead. "I forgot the ice cream!" she cried.

I kneaded my full stomach. "Don't worry about it. I couldn't eat another bite of anything."

"That's the problem!" she said, genuinely upset. "You love ice cream, and now you can't eat any, even if I order it."

She remembered our days in Cuba, where my sinful weakness for ice cream had manifested. They had had such *good* ice cream! But it hardly seemed worth such fretting now. Then I realized what was really bothering her.

Dulce didn't say so directly, but we both knew that our impromptu date was ending. She was grateful for my help against the Death Squad thugs, and glad for the chance to entertain me her way, but she had a mission. She would have to try again to make contact with her guerrilla group. And of course I was still waiting for Kan-Sen's call. So this was it: we would finish our meal, and perhaps spend the afternoon together, but that was all. Sad, but necessary. But we couldn't talk about it openly, so we talked about ice cream. Psychologically, I believe this is called transfer.

Now I felt dejected about missing that ice cream.

Dulce got up to go to the bathroom, and abruptly sat down. "What's the matter?" I asked.

She passed her hand over her face. "Maybe I ate too much, or drank too much. We don't get wine like this in Cuba, anymore."

"Here, I'll help you," I said, standing.

Then I felt it. An incipient dizziness, not that of wine. Some sort of drug. It had hit me later than her, because I was larger; we had eaten the same meal.

There was a forceful rapping on the door.

Dulce looked at me, realizing. "The Death Squad!"

"We don't know that!" I said, moving unsteadily to the door. "Probably just a routine—"

The rapping came again, loud, peremptory. "Open up! It's the police!" a voice called.

Suddenly I was nervous. Police—Death Squad. Much the same, here.

"Don't open it!" Dulce cried, rising—and fell on her face on the table, spilling her remaining coffee.

But in my drug-muddled state I felt it better to answer the summons. If it were innocent, good; if not, I wanted to fight before I passed out. I had no weapon, and surely they were armed. I cast about, and spied a spray bottle of deodorant. Hmm—if it worked for James Bond . . . I picked it up.

I steeled myself against the drug and opened the door. I half hoped I would find Kan-Sen outside, or even Fu Antos, masquerading as police. I was disappointed.

There were four men in police uniforms. They had drawn guns. They did not stand on ceremony. "You are under arrest," one said in passable English, and grabbed my wrist. He brought out a set of handcuffs.

I was hardly in condition to resist effectively, but this did not strike me as normal procedure. They hadn't even asked my name! Then I got a look at the last man in line, and recognized him. He was huge, with a scar on his face; I had fought him once before, in New York City, and knew him for my enemy. I don't have such sharp memory for faces, ordinarily, but he was something special. The sight of him temporarily cleared my head; I knew my life was in peril.

The bracelet locked in place about my left wrist. I grabbed that wrist with my right hand, jerked it out of the man's grasp, and struck upward with my elbow. I augmented the blow by pushing against my own closed fist, transmitting extra power to the elbow. His chin received a considerable jolt.

Then I swung the loose handcuff like a flail across the second man's head, making him drop the pistol. And up against the third man's face. They had given me quite a close-quarters weapon.

Ordinarily I wouldn't try combat against armed men, knowing the odds were greatly against me. But in this case I knew I was in trouble, and the snapping of the handcuff on my wrist had caused them to relax. Thus my instant, explosive action caught them by surprise.

Now I came up against the giant, and I knew he was more formidable than the other three combined. I discovered I still held the spray bottle in my left hand; in fact I had pushed against it, not my fist. Well—

I depressed the stud on top, aiming it at the giant's face. A thin mist spurted out. In a Bond movie it would have blasted forth to blind him; with me it merely made a small sweet-smelling cloud that bothered no one. The pressure was low. Just my luck; as a weapon it was ludicrous.

The giant looked at the feeble spray. His mouth cracked open. Laughter erupted like gas from a volcano. Then he raised his gun.

I had no choice. I attacked. I feinted with the handcuff, so that he jerked the weapon out of position, then I clipped him on the chin with my open right palm. The slap was not hard enough to do him damage. That put me in position, and I did an *o soto gari* leg sweep on him. He stepped back, resisting—but he was on the landing at the top of the stairs, and his foot came down on air. He had to fall.

I had been lucky; I knew it. Probably the man had known I was drugged, and had not anticipated effective action. He would have been correct, had I not been galvanized by my sudden recognition of him.

He cracked his head on the wall as he landed, and lay still, strewn across the stairs.

My dizziness returned full force as the excitement of combat abated. I staggered along the landing. I started to fall, saw the deep well of the staircase before me, clutched at the rail. I started down, missed a step—and the giant's leg tripped me. I twisted as though brought down by a leg throw myself. But below me was no practice mat. Just a fuzzy descent.

I saw the steps come at my face. I ducked my head, taking a roll. It was an automatic reflex, a good one.

I never felt the impact.

Chapter 3:

Gift of Tongues

Dulce woke with a splitting headache. Her tongue felt so swollen that there was hardly room for it in her mouth, and there was a metallic taste. Her awareness was fuzzy, her muscles leaden, and she could not coordinate well.

A man was slapping her in the face with a wet towel, bringing her to. He was thin, pockmarked by smallpox, and wiry. His skin was very dark; he was a *Caboclo* or copper-colored mulatto derived from white, black and Indian ancestry. Probably a peasant from the interior, she judged; illiterate, come to the more progressive coast to make his fortune. And winding up as a typical Death Squad thug.

"Wake up, bitch!" the man said in Portuguese. "I want you alert and squealing for this."

She understood him. She had a certain gift of tongues, and spoke and read English, Spanish, Portuguese, French, some Japanese and some Russian. But she didn't care to advertise this ability at the moment.

She looked about. She was in a modern wooden house, on a big old wooden bed. This was evidently a domicile of the upper middle class; the room was big and airy, but a bit rundown in the furnishings. There was a window, and through it she could see the branches of a tree, so she knew she was on the second floor. No doubt this was a liberated house whose former owner had died of indigestion: a mixture of too much anti-government politics and lead. This was part of an estate; had there been near neighbors, she would have been gagged so as not to alert them.

She was in the clothing she had worn while dining with Jason, but now it was soiled and torn. A summer outfit: black skirt reaching to her knees, white off-the-shoulder blouse. Not much protection.

The thug's hands were pawing over her body, tugging at her waistband. "God, what boobs!" he panted, his breath hot upon her face, smelling of *Cachaca,* cheap rum. His intent was obvious; he meant to take what had been put in reach.

Dulce remained woozy from the drug despite her mental awareness. She lacked physical strength; she would not be able to handle him unless she could score a kick to the groin, and that was problematical because her feet were tied. A rope bound her ankles together, and another her wrists before her. It was a signal of her drugged confusion that she had not noticed this before. She was in a Death Squad stronghold, and she would be lucky if only one or two men raped her and let her live. Yet she was so dopey that all she wanted to do was go back to sleep. Every time she tried to move her head she suffered the waves of pain of a migraine headache. She could neither coordinate nor think straight.

The thug jammed one sweaty hand on her knee, forcing her legs apart. She tried to bring them together again, levering against the rope on her ankles, but he already had his knee there like a doorstop. Her reactions were so slow! If only the lingering traces of the drug weren't so debilitating!

She concentrated, trying to clear her head so that she could at least consider alternatives. There seemed to be only two: relax and accept it, or try to fight and get it the hard way. It was an even bet that this man would prefer the latter. How could she struggle, except by thrashing about, in the process making her breasts bounce and her knees spread wide and her torso move against him? He might hurt her to make her scream even if she tried to accommodate him. Or rape her, then torture her, trying to get as many kinds of kicks as he could.

Of course she could try to turn him, off by belching, blowing snot out of her nose and wetting her skirt; some anti-rape authorities (men, naturally!) recommended that. But the kind of man who would rape a drugged and bound woman would be likely to have other kinky notions, and might well be doubly excited by her incontinence. In fact, the authorities who advised such things might actually be catering to their own suppressed fantasies: the voyeurism of the printed page, the scatological image.

In which case she might do best to take it easy, letting him do with her as he would, hoping he took enough time so that her body could throw off the remaining effect of the drug. She did not want to get raped, but it was not, in the ultimate analysis, a fate worse than death. She had accommodated a masculine member before, a much better one than this lout's.

Jason, what have I brought upon you? she thought, knowing that he too had been drugged and captured. She should have cussed him out and sent him away, rather than betray him into the hands of the Death Squad like this.

"Liven it up, bitch!" the man said, shaking her again. He was frustrated because the rope that tied her hands prevented him from getting her clothes off readily. He had her blouse ripped open in the front and her skirt hiked up to her waist, but her panties and bra resisted his clumsy, overeager fingers. He yanked again at the bra, and this time it slid up so that her breasts popped out below it, making him suck in his breath in awe. "Scream! Fight! Think I want Alberto to think I'm a pantywaist, a *Maricon?"*

Unless there were after all a third alternative—

Now his sweaty fingers caught inside her panties and ripped

them open at the crotch, giving her a rasping goose in the process. Too bad she had no teeth down there, she thought. But she forced a smile to her face.

"What's your hurry, mister?" she murmured in Portuguese. "A strong, handsome man like you . . ."

The man paused. Sometimes those least deserving of praise were most susceptible to it. This ugly bastard was quite ready to believe that he was God's gift to womankind, and that every vagina longed to have his penis lodged in it. Still, he was naturally suspicious of her sincerity. "So?"

He ran one callused palm up inside her thigh. Dulce writhed and moaned in simulated pleasure. Her head was clearing nicely; she was almost ready to act. "If you would only let my arms go so I could hold you."

He brought out his hunting knife and brought it toward her hands. But then he stopped. "You think to make a fool of me!" he snapped. "You don't need arms for love. Legs, maybe, but not arms."

Scratch one ploy. If he had released her arms—but perhaps something could still be salvaged. "Legs, yes," she agreed.

But, canny still, he refused. "Just spread your knees; that is enough."

Dulce spread her knees wide. His eyes almost popped as he peered through her ripped panties. He poked his finger in as if to see whether it was real.

"Kiss me, lover," she said, beckoning him down with her eyes.

He was happy to oblige. A kiss, at least, was no risk. Now he had access to her crotch and breasts and mouth, all at once, and she was still safely tied. A rapist's dream! His beard-stubbled face dived onto hers for a hungry, smeary contact. His suddenly-heavy body almost crushed out her breath.

"Hurry it up in there, Claudio!" a voice called from outside. So there *was* another thug in range.

Prodded by that, Claudio took down his trousers and shorts and dropped down to embrace her more fully. But her bound hands got in his way, by no coincidence, half masking her breasts. He got up angrily, drawing his knife again. "You Cuban bitch, you are going to feel what a real man feels like! Your Cuban males are way overrated as lovers." And he cut the rope between her hands, freeing them.

He was of course a fool, but she could understand it. These *Macho* Brazilians were tough men who did not believe any woman could handle one of them. Obviously the ones she had fought at the beach had not wanted to lose face by admitting her combative skills; they would have laid the blame on Jason Striker, a known martial artist. So this man had no warning, and the irony was that the drug made her almost as helpless as he thought her to be. Even with her hands free, she could not resist him very effectively. He had been remarkably cautious until now, but the sheer lure of her body had overwhelmed him.

What was it about men that made them such suckers for female flesh? No woman would have acted this way. Well, at least it was an equalizing force. She would play it for all it was worth.

"Call that a kiss?" Dulce demanded as she caught her gasping breath. It was his weight, not his sex appeal, that made her breath short, but she didn't say that. "Where's your tongue?" She wrapped her weak arms about his neck.

"So you want it that way!" Claudio said. "I'll show you my tongue!" And he thrust the slimy tobacco-stained thing deep into her mouth.

Dulce's jaws closed. With all her strength she clamped her teeth down on that tongue, savagely grinding them together as though severing a chunk of raw meat. Which was exactly what she was doing.

The man screamed: a strangled, stifled sound from the depths of his body. He jerked back his head, but Dulce held fast, her fingers locked together behind his head, holding it down while she chewed remorselessly through that living morsel. His struggles only magnified his agony. Blood welled from the expanding wound, its warm and salty thickness passing into her mouth, forcing her to swallow.

Claudio grabbed her by the shoulders and rolled desperately off the bed. They both fell to the floor, but Dulce was on top of him now, still crunching away at his tongue. With her hands weak and her feet tied, it was the only effective hold she had, and she dared not let it go. Now the blood was leaking down into Claudio's own throat, choking him. He tried to scream again, but it was hardly more than a bubbly gurgle.

"Hey, do not damage her too badly," Alberto called from below. He thought the stifled screaming was Dulce's. "The boss wants to interrogate her. You'll get us both in trouble."

She would be glad to give the boss a similar turn, if she could arrange it, only hoping the boss's tongue tasted better. At last Claudio's organ severed all the way. Dulce's head snapped back as the strands of flesh parted. She spat out the tongue.

Claudio, half delirious with pain, got one hand up and hit her in the face. He was too close, and his eyes were screwed closed against his agony; he could not generate enough aim or momentum to really hurt her. He grabbed, and caught her by one elbow. He hauled her down, his eyes now opening, blazing with murder. She was still too weak and hampered to balk him. She had hoped he would lose consciousness so that she could get at his knife and cut herself loose. No such luck. He got his hands around her throat and squeezed savagely. The grip was so fierce that it cut off air and blood together; in seconds she would succumb.

She drew back her hips, bending her knees so that her heels touched her buttocks. Then she bucked her hips forward with all the force she could muster. Her bony structure smashed against his crotch. Because he was poised, now, half above her, having wrestled her around while choking her, his genitals hung forward, exposed. The impact felt like the flattening of eggs.

Claudio emitted one final scream of doubled agony and collapsed, his hands falling away from her neck. He was unconscious, finally.

His pants were draped across a chair. His gun was with them. But right now she needed the knife, to free her legs.

"You've had enough time, Claudio!" the other yelled from outside the door. "I'm coming in!"

Oh, God! If Alberto caught her now, she would be helpless! No time to get the knife and cut herself loose; she had to have that gun now.

She pushed herself to her feet and lunged for the chair. But her dazed reactions betrayed her; she forgot her feet would not separate. She crashed headlong into the chair, sending pants and gun flying. She scrambled on hands and knees, pawing through the tangle. *Where was that gun?*

The door burst open, showing a gross fat *Branco da terra,* a dark-faced mulatto. He was proud and vain, with curly black hair slicked down with perfumed pomade. He wore an open-necked shirt with a golden *Figa:* a little model of a human left hand closed into a fist, the thumb sticking up between the first and second fingers. A good-luck charm.

He blinked; it was dark in here, and the sunlight outside was bright. This was a break for her, but it would grant her only seconds. Now her fingers found the metal, but she still had to get it out of the holster, with her hands not cooperating, and then how could she aim it? She had to steady herself.

"We are down here," she called. "I have a gift for you. Right there on the floor before you."

Alberto did not know his companion was unconscious; he thought this was merely the conclusion of a love scene so violent it had finished on the floor. He stooped to pick up the object.

It was the bloody tongue.

"What is this?" he demanded, casting it aside and wiping his hand off on his shirt.

"The tongue of an ass," she said. "See, your friend is dead."

"What!" He strode forward, his eyes adjusting. He caught hold of Dulce and rolled her off Claudio's clothing, realizing the situation. "Bitch, I'll kill—"

But as she rolled, the pistol she gripped came up. She pulled the trigger. It fired. The bullet struck him in the leg, and he dropped to his knee, cursing.

She was cursing too, inwardly. Damn this inadequacy of her body! She had always been a dead shot, and now she was firing like a duffer. She fired again, and this one caught him in the thigh. He fell almost on top of her, and the third bullet plowed through his stomach. Then his collapsing weight shoved the gun out of her hands.

But the job had been done. Dulce squirmed around until she got the knife. Then she severed her ankle bonds. She stepped over the bleeding, writhing body of the mulatto to freedom.

What now? Her cover had been blown and her money was gone. Not all of it, fortunately; half a million dollars was quite a stack, even in twenty dollar bills. She had carried fifty packs of fifty bills each with her, or *$50,000.* The rest was safe with a friend who thought it was feminine baggage. But still, a formidable loss. And because of her, her friend and lover Jason Striker had been captured or killed by the Death Squad.

Dulce was not easily defeated. She did not collapse in tears. She put herself together as well as she could, putting on Claudio's pants and finding an unbloody man's shirt in the closet. Not a good fit at all, especially across the hips, but it would have to do. It wasn't as if she were in any fashion show.

The Brazilian Revolutionary Movement had never made contact with her, but she still had a backup name. Maybe that too had been betrayed to the Death Squad thugs, but she had to risk it. Why would they have saved her for interrogation, if they had all the answers already? And it was the only way she could help Jason—if it were not already too late.

She headed for an address within one of the city's *favelas,* not far from the Copacabana Beach where she had met Jason Striker. The Revolutionists had been supposed to send a representative from the urban guerrilla unit to the beach to pick her up, but the

Death Squad had stopped that. Now she would have to take the initiative, and that was less pleasant.

Brazil was a marvelous land, and Rio de Janeiro was a lovely city. But the striking contrasts in the country's geography, that ranged from the magnificent mountain peaks to the burning deserts to the rain forests of the Amazon Basin were mirrored in the stark economic contrasts of its peoples. Brazil was a country of the very rich and the very poor, and they were often in close proximity.

The *favelas* were the slums. They had begun around the turn of the century when soldiers had found themselves without employment. So they camped on a hill covered with the *favela* wildflowers. When they came to Rio, these original "flower" soldiers took over any land that wasn't occupied and settled in dense shack colonies, bringing the name with them. Through the decades, the vicissitudes of economics caused alarming growth in these slums. In some cities, half the population lived in the sprawling *favela* colonies. Even in new Brasilia, the fabulous capital city, slum shantytowns developed faster than the ultra-modern buildings. The poor workers could not afford to commute from distant suburbs to their jobs in the center cities, so had to squat wherever they could.

What Brazil needed, Dulce thought as she moved along, was a People's Revolution, as in China and Cuba. Only then would the wealth be redistributed, this abject squalor abolished. No longer would starving children beg in the streets outside churches glittering with gold. And of course this was her mission: to bring salvation to Brazil, and eventually to all Latin America. One glorious year, perhaps soon, Communism would dominate the Western Hemisphere, as it did the East.

She smiled. Of course her friend Jason Striker might have a different view. He was politically naive. So many western men were like him, basically amateur in sex and economics. She had a certain nostalgic fondness for that innocence. Well, when things were finally righted in the Colossus of the North, the U.S. of A., she would take care of Jason, and he would be happier and better informed in both areas than ever before.

But first she had to save him from the much more immediate threat posed by the ruthless contemporary capitalism. He was likely to be tortured, and probably he would not even see the connection between that and her mission: her cause would abolish torture too. (Well, all but *necessary* torture.) But it was a lesson that was all too likely to cost him his life, and she couldn't allow that. Jason was ignorant, but he was a good man.

She came to the park in the southern section of the city, appreciating its beauty. This was *Rodigo de Freitas* lake. Once this very region had supported Rio's most notorious *Favela of Catacumba,* where some five thousand poor families had lived. Twenty percent of the residents had had criminal records, half of all dope peddlers arrested lived there, and more children under one year of age died in that single slum than in all the rest of Rio. Yet many of the denizens had refrigerators and television sets. Catacumba was cleared by the authorities in 1970—but though some better housing was provided, it was up to 25 miles out of town, making it impossible for the people to get to work in the city. Thus they were unemployed, and had to be evicted, and new *favelas* replaced the old ones, sprouting up like mushrooms. Nearly a quarter of Rio's population still lived in them. The main difference was that the *favelas* were no longer along tourist routes.

Dulce shook her head. The Capitalists simply refused to admit the magnitude of the problem, or to do anything about it. It was no answer to bulldoze a slum without providing a better and realistic alternative lifestyle for the inhabitants. What was needed was an entirely new social structure, as in Cuba.

She scouted the area carefully, decided she was not being watched, and made an unobtrusive detour to her friend's house. There she picked up another $50,000 in a shopping bag. She spread some ripe fruit on top to conceal it. Her friend, having no knowledge of Dulce's mission, insisted that she get better clothing, and so she donned a conservative dress and bound her hair into an almost masculine effect. She could not afford conspicuous femininity, where she was going.

Now on to the *favela.* At first glance, from a distance, it was like a pastel-painted jewel nestled into the mountainside, an enchanted subcity; but as she got closer, the enchantment vanished. It was a densely packed mass of hovels carrying the effluvium of raw garbage. As she entered it she tried to avoid glancing up nervously to spy advance warning of the slops that were tossed out the windows. There was no sanitation here. Children played barefoot amid the rubbish, stirring up great clouds of flies. Dogs and pigs rooted through the mess, adding their dung to it. Women carried cans of water on their heads from the single pump, much as in Biblical days. Not that Dulce had any fondness for the Bible, being a good Communist atheist, and if there *were* a God, how could He have tolerated this human degradation?

"Well, now!" a voice exclaimed beside her. Dulce jumped nervously, conscious of her bag of money. It was a man leaning in a ramshackle doorway. He wore a big-brimmed hat, an oversized sport coat, and he was cleaning his nails with a gleaming knife.

It was a *Malandro,* the *favela's* special breed of sharpie. Tough, cynical, and completely unscrupulous, this type was sheer trouble.

Dulce went on without comment, affecting not to have noticed him. But she couldn't get away with that; the man stepped out, caught up, and reached one dirty arm around to block her passage. "I don't know you, pretty doll; give me a kiss."

He thought she would be flattered by his pass. Many hovel-women *were,* knowing nothing better. It would be impossible to turn him off gently.

She kicked backward, spiking his shin, then turned to catch his black hair under the hat. She hauled his head down to meet her rising knee with a hard crack. Then she shoved him back against the shack and walked on as if nothing had happened, her bag of money undisturbed. He would not follow her soon.

She'd better find her address quickly, or she'd be mobbed. Nothing like this could remain secret very long in the *favela.* She approached a little boy who was chewing on a stick as though to extract some nourishment from it.

"Please, do you know where is the house of Maria Carolina?" That was the code name for the contact, to protect her from the authorities. Not that they were likely to be fooled long.

The boy merely stared.

Dulce took out a banana from her bag and proffered it. "It is at the bottom of the hill, near the well, painted red," she said, dangling the fruit before him. "Surely you know?"

The boy snatched the fruit and pointed. Dulce thanked him and proceeded. She hoped she had enough fruit to get her there. Sometimes food was more precious than money.

She did manage to find it, thanks to the color. Maria Carolina was *a Santauro, a* female witch doctor, and her house was bright red in honor of Santa Barbara.

Dulce hailed the occupant. "Yes?" a resigned woman's voice answered. Dulce stepped through the filthy door curtain.

It was a typical slum residence: a one-room shack with a packed dirt floor and a tiny wood-burning stove in the center. Light spilled through the cracks in walls and roof. Flattened tin cans were tacked over the worst of the gaps, but this was inadequate protection from the weather. A naked child lay sleeping on a roach-infested mattress in the corner, while two others stared at the intruder. There were open sores on their legs. A bag in one corner probably contained the woman's voodoo materials. It bothered Dulce to think that money desperately needed for food for these children was going to voodoo artifacts instead, but she was not here to criticize her contacts.

"Yes?" the standing brown-skinned woman repeated. She was dressed in rags, her feet bare. She was about 60, her hair gray, steely-eyed. She had seen hard times.

Dulce could not speak at once. She had known it was bad in the slums, but this was worse than she had thought. She was reminded strongly of a remarkable literary event a decade or two before: an uneducated Negress with three children to support had made notes concerning her life. By day she rummaged in garbage for food, and cruised the streets for wastepaper to sell, while carrying her youngest child strapped on her back. By night she had compiled her manuscript of horror, using the light of a candle. Then, miraculously, her account was published, and became Brazil's best seller. It was translated into English, too, and had more effect on the *favelas* than an atomic bomb-burst. Suddenly concerned citizens eliminated the pest-hole and retrained the people. But the woman herself, unschooled in the use of her windfall income, in due course was back in the street as before.

Then, with a start, Dulce realized: of course! That was the origin of the code name: Maria Carolina, the authoress.

No, it would be pointless to give this woman, so like the ill-fated namesake, this bag of money. Money was illusion, not the real answer to this grinding poverty. Only a complete restructuring of the society . . . But first she had to save Jason.

"I came for MR-26," Dulce said.

"If you are from the government, you are dead," a man said behind her.

For a moment Dulce thought it was the *Malandro* who had accosted her on the way in. But it was another man. "I am *from,* but not *of* the government," she said. "I left two men of the Death Squad lying in their own blood. No one followed me here. And I brought—this." She reached into the bag and brought out a pack of bills.

The man looked at them. "Counterfeit!" he snarled.

Dulce shrugged, knowing they would soon verify the legitimacy of the money. "And I have information: a cache of weapons. But first you must help me."

The children were looking into the bag now, more fascinated by the fruit than the money. They were starving, literally: pipestem arms and legs, bloated bellies.

"What do you want?" the woman asked grimly.

"A jailbreak. My friend—"

The woman laughed harshly. "You dream, voluptuous foreigner! My son is in jail."

Dulce realized that this was actually an asset. If this justifiably bitter woman's son happened to be incarcerated in the same institution as Jason—for Jason *had* to be there, or she would never locate him. "Are many of your number there? Then we can free them all. With C-3 plastic explosive, machine guns, we can fill an ambulance, drive it in near the wall—"

"Where are these weapons from?" the man asked, still suspicious, but with growing interest.

"They are safe. They were captured in Cuba from CIA agents; they can be traced only back to America. Grenades, pistols, rifles—but we must act soon. Tonight." Before they torture Jason, she added mentally.

"We will alert our men, and the other groups," the man said, obviously hungry for the weapons. "But it cannot be tonight; there is no time to organize."

Dulce nodded. He was right; they dared not go into this raid unprepared, or the guards and soldiers would tear them up. "Then tomorrow—"

"No. Two days from now, when the festival is on."

She smiled, seeing his logic. They were in business.

Chapter 4:

Mirabal's Entertainments

I came to in a dungeon. That was the best description of it. It was a huge cell lined with brick walls, and the ceiling was high. My first impression was of a multitude of people, white, black, and in between, most wearing shorts or cut-off pants and nothing else. It was hot, and the ventilation was poor, and the stink of sweat and grime and urine was intense.

There was a long line of three-decker bunks. The top beds were close to the bright light bulbs, so that the men on them had to shield their heads by spreading their shorts over them.

I sat up. The lingering effects of the drug made my head swim. I was not in top condition anyway. I had taken a bad tumble down the stairs. My automatic forward roll had alleviated the effect, but there is no soft landing down a flight of steps! There were numerous abrasions on my back, and bruises on my arms.

I stood, and cracked my head on the metal structure of the bunk above mine. In my disorientation, I had not noticed it. I sat down heavily. I felt about as bad as a man can feel who isn't sick or badly injured. Probably the wine I had taken combined with the drug to give me a real hangover. Alcohol: never again! I always regretted it when I broke training.

Especially the morning after. Especially when I woke in jail.

A high-pitched torrent of Portuguese, or what I assumed was that language, emerged from the upper bunk. Two thin brown legs, barefooted and scarred, appeared over the edge. They dropped down, followed by a lean, dirty body. It was a boy, perhaps fourteen years old. It was hard to tell, as I knew many children went hungry in Brazil; he could be older with retarded growth. His sharp, wary eyes hinted as much.

The gist of his message needed no translation. I was an incompetent fool who should watch where he put his stupid head, lest he disturb the repose of his betters.

I made a gesture of conciliation. "Sorry. I don't speak Portuguese."

I didn't expect him to respond intelligently, but he did. His barrage cut off. "You—'Merican?"

Well, well! "Yes, American."

"You have dollar?"

So that was it. He begged money from tourists, so had picked up a smattering of the language—probably of many languages. I patted my pockets, finding them empty, of course. My abductors had cleaned me out. "No dollar."

"You smuggler?"

"You pickpocket?" I retorted.

He laughed. "Me thief. Hungry."

That I could believe. "Me fight. Death Squad."

His eyes went round. "Big trouble!"

I rubbed my head. "Right!" I decided to treat him as an equal, and thrust out my hand. "I'm Jason Striker, victim of circumstance."

He took it. "Filho, of the *favela.*"

"Favela?"

"My home," he said simply.

Oh. No doubt one of the residential sections of Rio.

A bell rang somewhere. The prisoners piled off their bunks and began moving. "C'mon," Filho said. "Food."

Food. I wasn't hungry, but didn't know how regular meals would be around here. "Thanks."

The boy led me out of the cell and into a central courtyard. Apparently the cells were normally locked, so this represented an extension of freedom I'd better appreciate.

We came to the end of the chow line. It was along one, as there turned out to be a number of huge cells similar to ours, each with over a hundred prisoners.

The food, when we finally got it, was bean soup, over which a thick whitish powder had been sprinkled to give it the consistency of thick gruel, ladled from a huge vat into dirty bowls. There were also a couple of pieces of some kind of white hard tuber, and a cup of thick black sugarless coffee. I tasted some and had to spit it out; Brazil might be the land of coffee, but this was too strong for me. Not a very tasty meal, and not enough; if I were to be here long, I'd better eat it all, for I'd soon be hungry.

The bathroom, it turned out, was a bricklined trench at the far end of the courtyard. The men stood or squatted over it as necessary. The stench was horrible. A single tap in the corner provided water for drinking; the prisoners took turns at it. "I get," Filho said to me. He had already gulped down his meal. He went to stand in the water line while I finished my tuber. But in a moment he was back. "You keep eye on me?" he inquired. "Some men, they—" He made a face.

I didn't know what that face signified, but could appreciate that life could be rough for a lad like this in a place like this. "I'll keep an eye on you," I agreed, and he went back.

How was I going to get out of here? I had no notion of the charges against me, assuming the Death Squad had bothered with any. I had merely been entertaining my girl friend in my room, surely no crime. No doubt in due course there would be an inquiry, since I was an American, but I doubted much would come of that soon. Bureaucracy moved slowly the world over. I was on my own for the time being, but probably not in any serious trouble. Maybe I was lucky they hadn't killed me.

The water Filho brought was dirty, and I was not that thirsty; instead I used it for washing. The other prisoners stared at me curiously, and I could fathom their thoughts: see the mad *Americano* taking his daily bath! None of *them* bothered, obviously.

In due course we were herded back into our cells for the evening. The men did not settle down right away, but milled about, conversing in Portuguese. Since I had no way to share this dialogue, I lay down on my bunk. After a time, in the night, the food I had eaten had its natural effect, and I went to the smaller hole that served as the cell's private bathroom to relieve myself. Again the men stared from their bunks; did they expect my refuse to be white, like my skin?

There was a commotion as I pulled up my pants. I looked up and saw that Filho was in trouble. Two men had grabbed him; one held his arms while the other hauled down his ragged shorts.

What were they doing? The boy was struggling and yelling in Portuguese, but the men did not seem to be actually hurting him. They were hauling him to another bunk. Then Filho's eye caught mine. "Rape!" he screamed.

Then, shocked, I understood. They were yelling in Portuguese and wrestling Filho face-down on the bunk. One of the men had bared his member and was moving in on the boy's posterior. Here in the tropics I had heard homosexuality was more common than in the colder climes, and to some men a young boy was a more tempting target than a beautiful woman. I don't claim to understand it, and am not certain it is true; I just happened to read about it once in Burton's *Arabian Nights.*

The other prisoners, amazingly, were taking no notice. Like the residents of an American city, they preferred to ignore crime—so long as it was not being practiced on *them.* To avoid involvement.

Well, *I* wasn't going to ignore it! This was blatant homosexual rape, in public yet. I charged across the cell, swung around the tier of bunks, and barreled into the trio.

First I took out the would-be rapist. I grabbed him by the shirt, forced him off-balance, blocked his right knee with the sole of my left foot, and threw him past me with a beautiful (if I do say so myself) *Hiza-guruma* knee-wheel throw. *I* knew he would not get up in a hurry. Especially since he slid across the damp floor to sprawl halfway in the privy-pit, his outflung hand involuntarily grasping a handful of that brown slush.

Then I turned on the other. He had thrown the boy aside the moment I attacked, and now faced me. He was a huge coal-black Negro with shaved head, six and a half feet tall, and weighing something like 240 pounds. No starving chronic inmate, this!

And he was ready to fight. I would have eased off once Filho was safe, but it was obvious that this man would not let me go. I was hardly in top condition, but as a fifth degree black belt in judo with additional expertise in karate and kung fu I was well able to take care of myself. So I waited for his attack, while the other prisoners forsook their sleep to form a huge spectators' circle around us. They hadn't wanted to get involved when a boy was being attacked, but now they were happy to watch the fight.

Suddenly he moved. His right foot swept up and around in hard kick. I shifted my weight to absorb it harmlessly on my left thigh; kicks are fairly easy to counter if you anticipate them. Their relative slowness is offset by their power when they score. Still, his kick was fast and sure; he was a trained fighter.

Then I became aware of pain: not the ordinary bruise of a kick, but the sharper sensation of a cut. I glanced at my hip—and saw blood flowing. The kick must have opened a sore.

Sore? Immediately I realized it was more than that. I was wearing my trousers, and the cloth had been ripped open.

Sensation and realization occurred quickly, for thought and action are almost simultaneous during combat. They have to be, if one wishes to survive.

My opponent skipped to the side and kicked again. This time

I jumped back. I caught a glimpse of the sole of his foot: small shards of broken glass were taped there.

No wonder I was hurting! He had obviously come prepared—and he was out for my blood. Literally. Any of these kicks would have wounded me grievously, had they scored cleanly.

He kicked yet again, very fast. This time I managed to hook a hand under his foot, catching him off-balance. With my free hand I grabbed his calloused toes, lifted, and shoved him back hard. The problem with kicking is that it restricts mobility at critical times, especially when the opponent knows what he is doing. He had to fall.

Thank God for the hours I had put in practicing the new Kodokan self-defense *kata*! The *katas* are like little judo plays, emulating street-fight situations. Now when I needed it, I had done it without thinking.

I did not let go of that dangerous foot. This was no amateur! And how had he arranged this trick—in prison? Surely he did not walk on broken glass all the time. This thing smelled of a set-up. So I bore down hard while I had the advantage. I twisted him onto his stomach by using the leverage of the captive leg. Then I hooked my own leg over his knee and tilted forward, putting pressure on his leg and knee with my chest, using a forbidden (in contest judo) *Kawaishi* submission hold, *Hiza-hishigi*. "Had enough?" I inquired as I leaned into it.

But he was tough. He tried to escape. I increased the pressure, knowing the agony would have to make him capitulate. I wasn't doing this from sadism; I wanted to know why he had girded himself for such combat and made a scene that would surely draw me in. If he were an agent of the Death Squad sent to kill me, why hadn't he simply done the job while I was still unconscious? It seemed to make no sense to do it this way.

Unless the Death Squad wanted its hands to appear clean . . .

Now there was a commotion. Prison guards, conspicuously absent until I gained the advantage, charged in. Not eager to be caught fighting, for surely there were rules, against it, I started to ease up. But a guard slammed into me, hurling me forward. That impetus translated into pressure on the black man's knee, and it snapped as I fell.

Then the guards laid hands on me, and I knew better than to resist. The black man was writhing in agony; screams of pure anguish wrenching out of him. There is no worse pain than that of a broken knee. It would be long before he fought again.

I was surely in for it now! How could I convince the guards I had stepped in only to rescue a youthful friend from rape? Especially when I didn't speak the language?

The boy! "Filho!" I called. "Tell them—"

Filho appeared. He spouted a fluid stream of Portuguese. Thank God I had a witness!

The guard-captain turned on me. "So you try to rape this poor child, and beat up his friends who help him!"

What? "No, no! *I* tried to help him!"

But then I saw the boy's expression. His accusing finger pointed directly at me. He was part of this ugly little trap. He was the shill.

I looked desperately around at the other prisoners. They had all been witnesses. But they had somehow returned to their bunks and were sound asleep; obviously none of them wasted any love on the Gringo, and they would not speak on my behalf.

I had been had. No doubt of it. But *why?*

Too late I saw the rifle butt coming at my head. I tried to duck out of the way, but there was solid contact. The lights went out.

*

This time my awakening was less gentle than before. A bucket of icewater drenched my head, making me choke. I was sitting in a chair with my hands tied behind me and my ankles hobbled with a short length of rope. I could tell by the feel that I was expertly restrained; no use straining against the bonds.

A face loomed before me. It had a dramatic scar running down from the short stiff crew-cut to the bull-massive neck. The man had icy blue eyes and a big, reddish, square strong face, thick lips, a bullet-shaped head, an irregularly set nose, a cauliflower ear, big hamlike fists—in short he reminded me of a Nazi pugilist.

It was the man I had encountered on the stairs, the leader of the Death Squad. But more than that, it was the man I had fought in the Brazilian embassy in New York, when Hiroshi and I had come to recover our diamonds. He was as tough as they come, but I had bashed him pretty badly. Now he had me in his power, and he wanted revenge.

"I see you know me, Jason Striker," he said. "By sight, at least. I am Don Fernando Mirabal, Colonel of Army Intelligence. You may call me Colonel. And it seems you are in trouble with the law, now."

I didn't answer. It had already been apparent that the Death Squad had connections with the police. They had been after Dulce, and my involvement was coincidental—but I *had* given this man Mirabal some lumps, and he certainly wasn't going to let me off gently now.

"Why didn't you kill me?" I asked. It was not bravado so much as resignation—and apart from everything else, I *was* curious.

"I had thought you would be more intelligent," Mirabal said with satisfaction. "But I shall explain. We caught you in our net, but unlike the girl, you are an American citizen, of some repute. In fact, we anticipate demands for your release from both your country and the girl's."

Why would Cuba demand my release? I had done Fidel a favor once, through no particular choice of my own, and apparently he had a long memory and good information. Better than his cigars, certainly. Of course I had helped Dulce this time, and she was on a mission for her country. Well, that was a complication that was hardly going to do me much good here.

"But we had no reason to hold you. You had broken no law here. Yet it was necessary *to* hold you." Mirabal smiled. "So we turned you loose in temporary detention—and it seems you attempted a beastly act and provoked a near riot. *That* is against the laws of Brazil! Now we can keep you, and no other government can object. You really were very foolish; did you not know we frown on the raping of small boys?"

So that was it. I *had* been foolish; I should have smelled a rat, and stayed out of trouble.

"Very clever," I agreed morosely.

"Now I would like the answers to certain questions, some very simple questions," Mirabal continued. "But I hope you won't provide them right away. I really would like to get to know you better first. I am very curious to discover, for example, your tolerance to pain. But I am a fair man; I will first give you a chance to answer."

I believed him: he'd rather have me balky, so he had a pretext to torture me. Now that he could legally do so. Or maybe it wasn't legal, technically, but I was sure he had ways to get around such technicalities. I was already branded a troublemaker and a homosexual rapist in prison, thanks to his cute little trap, so my interrogation could be called legitimate. If I hadn't fallen into that snare, there would have been something else; Mirabal was not about to let me slip through unscathed.

"What mission brings you to Brazil?" he inquired politely.

I kept my mouth closed. I was not free to tell him my real mission for Fu Antos, and the truth was, I had never found out what that mission was. Thanks to Mirabal himself, I had gone to jail before Kan-Sen had contacted me. Mirabal would never believe that, though. So it was pointless even to try explaining. In addition, the longer I kept him guessing, the better it would be for Dulce, who I was sure was also in his power. Let him conjecture at what complexities we were engaged in.

"You are silent," Mirabal observed mildly. "Good, good. I am not disappointed." He rubbed his knee, the one I had crippled in New York. He had evidently had surgery to repair the torn meniscus ligament, for there was a big scar there, but the leg seemed to be about as good as ever. He still limped a bit. "We have so much to do together, you and I." He paused, considering. "But first, a little tour. I know you will enjoy this."

He put out one hand and lifted me to my feet. I am not a

small man, but he hefted my weight as if I were a child. What tremendous power! My bindings were really not unduly confining, but the moment I was on my feet I felt woozy. The drug followed by that crack on the head—I was in no condition to put up a fight at this stage.

We walked to another cell. Here a pretty young woman in a tight red print dress was strapped to what looked like a dentist's chair, her head tied back to the headrest, clamped between metal clamps, immobile, so that her mouth tried to pull open. Nevertheless she kept it tightly shut. Beside her was a tray of metal instruments. I did not like the look of this.

"Do you know her?" Mirabal inquired. Obviously he thought I did. That gave me a clue: she must be a captive member of the group Dulce was supposed to contact. If I had been associated with them, I would probably have met her. It could have been a nice meeting. She looked about eighteen and had a rather appealing figure. Slender, but with well developed breasts and thighs, and thick curly red hair falling down behind the chair. Her face was quite freckled, and there was a gold Star of David hanging from her neck. I concluded she was Jewish, perhaps a student who had gotten involved with the Communist Revolutionary movement that Dulce was trying to contact. What attraction did Communism have for these pretty girls?

"Never saw her before in my life," I said honestly. And felt like a liar, for I knew he would not believe me. Maybe I should have shut my mouth grimly and refused to answer, so as to lead my interrogator on a false trail. But that, too, would have been in effect a lie. Too bad I wasn't a philosopher, to unravel these fine points of ethics.

"Then you will not object to what happens," Mirabal said. He made a gesture, and a man came forward. "One extraction for Ester, for now," Mirabal told him. Then, to me. again: "Make yourself comfortable."

Some humor! There was no other chair in the room, and if there had been, I would have been hard put to it to sit without assistance. Mirabal was not about to offer help, and I was not about to ask for it.

The other man put on a white apron like a dentist's smock. He picked up a pair of fancy pliers from the table. He moved to the girl.

Then I caught on. "Now wait," I said. "You're not going to—?"

"So you *do* know the Jewess?" Mirabal inquired.

"I *don't* know her! But that doesn't mean I want to see her—" I broke off, afraid I was only putting notions in his head, though obviously Mirabal had plenty of notions on his own. His resemblance to a Nazi now seemed stronger, for he even proposed to torture a Jew. I didn't have to be Jewish to consider that an abomination.

"Proceed, Laureano," Mirabal said to the man. The assistant was a cadaverous but evidently wiry-strong fanatic. His skin had been burned by the sun to a leathery texture. I was sure he was a virtual arm of Mirabal, never questioning his master's will.

Laureano put his left hand over the girl's mouth, pressing with thumb and forefinger on the nerve complex on either side of her bunched jaw. The immediate pain of that pressure forced her mouth open. He then inserted the pliers into that open mouth, placing his left hand against her forehead. Now she whimpered, knowing what was coming, but unable to move. I saw the muscles of her arms tighten, and the nipples of her breasts quivered under the taut dress with her ragged breathing.

Laureano took hold of one of her back teeth and pulled. Ester screamed piercingly, for of course she had had no anesthetic. Dentistry is enough of a torture in the best of circumstances, and this was the worst. A healthy tooth.

The muscles of the man's arms strained, hauling brutally at that tooth, and the sound from the woman was appalling. The tendons of her neck stood out and the force of her futile struggles caused her dress to half-tear and pull open and drop down, exposing her right breast. The purple nipple became big and bright against the white. Her whole torso shook with the force of her agony.

I launched myself at the beast—but Mirabal intercepted me with a football-type straight-arm push that hurled me over against the wall. My head cracked back, and for a moment I saw a field of twinkling stars. My head still hurt from the bruise the gun butt had made, and this aggravated it.

But the continued screaming of the girl brought me alert again quickly. I tried again to reach her, but Mirabal's powerful fingers caught my hair and twisted my head painfully, bringing me down once more against the wall. Oh, the butcher was enjoying this, yet I was helpless.

Then Laureano gave a final heave and jerked out the tooth. Triumphantly he brought it up, blood dripping from its surface.

"Loosen her head, fool!" Mirabal snapped. "We don't want her to choke on her own blood!"

No personal concern, this. He was just making certain the poor girl didn't die before he was through torturing her. It was also for my benefit, for he had spoken in English so I would be sure to understand.

Her head was released and pulled forward. Blood and saliva drooled from her lips and over her chin, to drip onto her pale right breast. Her screams had stopped; now she was merely sobbing. No, not even that; she had, mercifully, lost consciousness.

I sobbed for her, inside. This whole brutal scene had been unnecessary, pointless, since I knew nothing that could benefit Mirabal and the girl had not even been questioned. If Mirabal had sought to show me that he was ruthless and depraved, he had succeeded admirably.

"You see, that was not so bad," Mirabal said in a conversational tone. "She still has twenty-seven teeth left."

I would have killed him in that moment, had I been able. But I kept my face straight, refusing to give him the satisfaction of my impotent rage.

"Now we shall visit with another anonymous outlaw," Mirabal said, drawing me along with one hand. I had to move as he urged, or fall on my face.

In the next chamber was an old man, naked, bound face up on a table. He was shaking with fear; the girl's screams would have been loud and clear here. As Mirabal had surely planned; he obviously was expert at his specialty of torture, both physical and psychological.

"Another stranger?" Mirabal inquired, shoving me up for a good view. The man was around sixty, with well-manicured, long-fingered pianist hands: evidently a white-collar worker, a cultured man, one of the intellectuals one might expect to find supporting the opposition to tyranny. I'm no Communist and never will be, but if anyone offered me a way to fight tyrants like Mirabal, I'd ask few questions.

Communism thrives where there is poverty and repression, and it is easy to see why. What have the downtrodden masses got to lose? Abolish the Mirabals and the Laureanos, and you are halfway to abolishing Communism. Or so it seems to me.

I contemplated the white hair growing out from the once-shaved head of the victim, and his silver whiskers. He had a strong intelligent face, though his body was thin. Was there any way I could spare this victim whatever torture was planned? Only if I could convince Mirabal of the truth: that I knew nothing of the prisoner. And how could I do that? "Does it make any difference?" I asked.

"He looks thirsty," Mirabal said. He turned to Laureano, who had followed us in. "Give the poor man a drink."

A drink? What kind of torture was that?

Laureano smiled, showing a row of gold teeth. The effect was startling: on the one hand it suggested incredible poverty or debauchery to have cost him all his natural teeth, and on the other hand it showed equally incredible wealth to have them replaced in gold. The man with the golden mouth.

He brought out a gallon jug of water and a kind of funnel. He put the funnel in the prisoner's mouth and poured. The man choked and spluttered, but the water kept coming; he had to swallow or drown.

When about a quart was down, the torturer eased up enough to let the victim catch his breath. "I think he is still thirsty," Mirabal remarked.

Back went the funnel. This time the victim tried to clench his teeth, but Laureano hit him in the belly and jammed the funnel in as his mouth popped open to gasp. Then the victim tried to refuse to swallow, but Laureano pinched his nostrils until he had to breathe through his mouth—and then the water choked him again. He had to swallow. The water was mercilessly forced, until the man's stomach bulged like an unholy pregnancy. I had no idea how much water the human torso could accommodate, but evidently it was considerable, if health and survival was no consideration.

But soon no more would go; it just poured out of his mouth as fast as it went in. It was evident the man was full; he was physically unable to take any more, though he drown in the attempt. His stomach was distended grotesquely, as though ready to burst like a pricked balloon. I could not even contemplate what was happening to his internal tissues and vital organs.

"Strange," Mirabal remarked as the torturer looked at him for instructions. "I am sure he is not yet satisfied. Let us try another aperture."

They released the clamps that held the prisoner's arms and legs to the table and levered him over onto his stomach. I thought the pressure of his own body on that distended stomach would kill him, but somehow he was still breathing. Laureano attached a longer segment of hose to a water tap, then forced the end into the man's rectum and ran it far into the body, so that neither sphincter nor stomach muscle could stop it or force it out again. Then he opened the valve, letting the city water pressure ram the fluid into the victim's posterior. There was no way to tell how much it was; I could only watch with mounting horror. But at last the limit came; water squirted out and around the tube and no more would go.

Laureano jerked out the tube. The poor man was like a paper water bomb. He belched fluid weakly from his mouth, and it squirted out of his anus with every shallow, shuddering breath he took. The sheer compression of his lungs and innards could kill him at any moment. The water torture was not as dramatic as the tooth pulling, but actually it was worse.

Then he shuddered. His muscles strained as though he were making a superhuman effort to break free of his restraints, though at this stage the pressure within was far worse than that without. But this was no conscious effort; he was going into convulsions. The water that leaked from him now was turning red; it had burst his intestinal wall, and he was dying.

"Shall we see the next?" Mirabal inquired with a pleasant smile.

I stared at him. He was completely unmoved by this horrible death. What punishment, in this world or the next, could possibly atone for the things he had done? But expression of my sentiment was pointless. "You're wasting your time," I said. "I don't know any of these people. I don't know anyone in Brazil. I can't tell you anything."

"Now you know that is not true," he said. "I can name three people you know. I am one, and Miss Planas is another."

Dulce! Oh, no! They had her too, and I knew this monster was saving her for last. What would I do when he started pulling her teeth and filling her gut with water?

"You will really appreciate the third room," Mirabal said.

The sadist!

But the next room was empty. What did this mean?

"Have a seat," Mirabal suggested, ever the perfect host.

Then I understood. *I* was the third person I knew in Brazil. This torture was for me.

Such was my mood, I was actually relieved. *They weren't going to torture Dulce.*

But they could still torture her anytime. Maybe they would

make her watch me, and when that didn't work, I'd have to watch her. Yet there was nothing I could do.

Mirabal was watching me closely. He had certainly softened me for this. I now had no shadow of a doubt that he would work me over until he was satisfied, and that would mean a fiendish death. And I had no way out.

"You think I am stupid," Mirabal said. "That I do this merely to repay you for our prior encounter, or to wrest information from you about connections you do not know."

"Yes," I agreed.

"But you *do* know the third person—the one whose place is here in this chair." Now his face twisted into a grimace of hate. "Fu Antos, boy master of ninjas."

My mouth dropped open. I had indeed underestimated Mirabal; I had been sure he knew nothing of Fu Antos and wasn't searching for such information.

"Tell me where he can be found, and you are spared this."

Fu Antos—who had cured me of the effect of the delayed-action death blow, and thus saved my life when no one else could. Who now required my service. Was I to betray him? I had no notion where the Black Castle was, but if I gave away the nature of my expected contact, Mirabal might be able to use that to trace down the ninja master.

I hobbled over to the chair and tipped myself into it. My aim was off, but Mirabal, still gracious, caught me and set me down gently. No, he didn't want me getting bruised or knocked out on my own; he had to do it *his* way. My only satisfaction was that I hadn't groveled; I had taken the seat myself, or tried to.

Mirabal did not remonstrate with me. He was not about to plead with a helpless victim for information. He was certain that his technique would bring it spewing forth. And I was not at all certain he was mistaken; I'm not good at this sort of thing. Once Kan-Sen had tortured me with a thumbscrew—that same Kan-Sen who was now my ally, to my shame.

They stripped off my shirt. This was some job, since they

wouldn't untie me—a nice compliment to my defensive skills—they had to cut it away with a sharp knife. Then Laureano trundled in a squat machine. It seemed to consist of a series of standard automobile batteries, with wires running to a generator. There was a black control box with dials on it, and long cords and clips attached. The thing gave me the shivers.

"Are you sure you will not tell us what we wish to know?"

"You already know what I think of you." I had a little gas in my bowel, and I forced it out with a loud ripping noise to emphasize my point.

"If you maintain that attitude half an hour from now, I shall be surprised," Mirabal said mildly.

That gave me a new set of shivers. He was so certain, and he was not the kind to bluff. But even if I told him what little I knew, he would still torture me. As he had candidly said, he had a grudge, and didn't want me to capitulate too rapidly. And I would not betray Fu Antos—I hoped.

Laureano put little metal discs on the nipples of my chest. Wires trailed to the machine. He taped the disks in place so they would stay. Then he turned a dial.

I lurched, straining against my bonds. A terrible electric current was passing from one terminal to the other, wracking my chest.

"I see the system is operative," Mirabal said. "Now do you care to talk?"

Talk? I could hardly get my breath! I slumped, gasping, as the current abated. What appalling pain!

"Turn it up a notch," Mirabal told Laureano. "And hold it for a few more seconds."

The agony wracked me again. I jumped like a bucking bronco, straining against my bonds. A hoarse scream tore from my throat. My chest was on fire, my lungs fast becoming paralyzed. Like a red-hot rod, the current seared through me. Could tooth extraction be worse than this? Water torture?

"You respond very well," Mirabal remarked as the power subsided again. "I shall be most interested to see how far your threshold extends. We'll just try another intensification."

I couldn't take much more of this. Had the electrodes been attached to some more vital region of my body, the surges would have knocked me unconscious or even killed me, and it would have been over. But Mirabal's torturer knew his business; this machine merely caused intolerable pain.

Yet I had no choice. I had to endure this torture, or somehow escape it. And *not* by turning traitor to Fu Antos.

"Perhaps we should attach an electrode to his genital," Mirabal said musingly. "This has always been effective in the past."

God, no! I remembered now. I had heard of this. Pulverizing shocks run through the victim's privates, not only wracking him with ultimate pain but destroying his masculinity forever. No, that was probably an exaggeration. The awful beauty of this electric torture was that it left no telltale signs, no raw tooth-sockets or ruptured guts. There would be no proof that I had been tortured. No proof except my word—the word of an accused pederast. Electric interrogation was a Latin American specialty.

But the bastard was only teasing me. He made no motion to strip me further. Maybe he didn't want to abort my masculinity until he had made me watch what he did to Dulce. It was enough for the present that I realized the possibilities, and knew what *would* be employed—at his convenience. Psychological torture augmenting the physical torture, again, and a very effective job of it.

I had to get out of this! But *how?*

Then I remembered a way.

I could not escape physically—but I had mental resources that Mirabal was hardly in a position to comprehend. I could control the pain my body suffered, to a certain extent. Pain, after all, is self-generated; it is the system's warning that the body is being damaged, and it is a strong inducement to stop. But when the damage cannot be stopped, pain is superfluous, a counterproductive effort. Then it has to be blocked out.

The current flowed again. I stiffened. But I fought to achieve dominance of mind over matter. *I can not feel it!* I told myself. *It is only an irritation.*

It didn't work. I *knew* the pain was real. Anything else was a delusion. Yet I still had to resist it somehow.

Then I remembered the *ki,* that mysterious force that lay within my body, more powerful than anything else I knew. It was not under my conscious control, but was there when I needed it.

I needed it now! I willed it forth, hoping it would come. The torture current flowed again. The pain was excruciating; they had stepped it up another notch or two. I tried to scream, but my chest muscles were knotted, cutting off my very breath.

Then the *ki* cut in. From my *hara,* my abdomen, the seat of my being, it expanded—and where it went, pain abated. It crossed the area of the electrodes on my chest, and the muscles relaxed. I could breathe again, and my head was clear. It did not completely eliminate the pain, but it was as though a powerful sedative had been administered. Now I could tolerate it, as I did the pain of a back wrenched in judo practice.

"Something's wrong," Mirabal said. "The current's not—"

Laureano checked. "It *is* going through; see the dials."

"I see *him.* He's not suffering. Look how he's relaxed."

"Maybe he is dead."

"No. He's breathing normally. Check the generator."

"I tell you, the current is there! Check it yourself."

Mirabal was evidently from Missouri, in the United States of Brazil: he had to be shown. He put his hand on my chest, letting the fingers touch the two taped terminals. He jerked it away, cursing as the current pulsed through. He shook his hand. "It's there, all right!"

Now he glared at me. I gave him a level gaze back. "Give it up, Mirabal," I said. "You can't hurt me."

"Turn it up to maximum!" he snapped.

Laureano turned up the dial. I was aware of the increased power, but it passed through me harmlessly. My *ki* had nullified it. Not completely, but enough so I could stand it, smiling.

Mirabal stared at me, baffled. "He must have lost his feeling! No one could withstand that current."

I shook my head, affecting sorrow. "I *feel* it; I just don't *suffer* from it. Too bad you can't understand. You should meet my friend Fu Antos; he really knows about *ki.*"

"Fu Antos!" Mirabal grated. "So you *do* know him, just as I suspected! You're one of his minions!"

Oh-oh! I had really spilled the beans, right when I thought I'd won. Treachery of overconfidence. I had to distract Mirabal, before he found a way to pry what little I knew of the ninja's situation out of me. So I pursed my lips and wafted a shimmering globule of spit at him.

It scored, right in the middle of his gloatingly open mouth.

Mirabal lost control, just as I had hoped he would. His fist lashed out to strike my cheek. The blow didn't hurt me, for the *ki* made me well-nigh invulnerable. But he had carelessly let his other arm brush against the metal frame of the machine, and as his fist made contact with me the current grounded through his body. For a moment he stood transfixed as the full power of his devil machine paralyzed him, his eyes staring in agony. Physical strength is no hedge against electricity. Then the contact was broken, and he fell back.

Quickly, horrified, Laureano turned off the machine. "Colonel, are you all right?"

Mirabal had to maintain a front; I understood that, without having to like the man at all. "I'm all right!" he snapped. "Get him out of here!"

And so my siege of torture ended, thanks to the *ki.* I was hardly conscious of being led back to the main prison cell, to be stared at by my fellow inmates. The *ki* had drained from me when the threat ended, and I was virtually unconscious on my feet.

They unbound me, and I fell on my bunk, too weak to do more.

Chapter 5:

Spear in the Rear

The forest of the Amazon basin in South America is one of the largest in the world, and it covers almost half of Brazil. The trees grow close together: chestnut, mahogany, cedar, rosewood, kapok, wild rubber trees, many varieties of palm, and of course Brazil nuts. Hundreds of species can be found within a few square miles, and many trees are over two hundred feet tall. They are overgrown with lichens and vines, so that the deep jungle becomes a tangled mass.

Through it all twines the Amazon River, largest (not longest) in the world, with its myriad tributaries. It is the only feasible access to much of the backwoods. Roads can quickly be overgrown by the living carpet of foliage, so only the water remains clear. Thus a watch on the rivers gives an insight into much of the human activity of the region.

It was technically illegal to molest the jungle natives of Brazil, but few of the authorities paid attention to this. If the Indians had land that "civilized" men wanted, it was a simple matter to kill or drive off the primitives. Professional Indian-killers were available for hire at reasonable rates.

But this time the Indians, stirred up by intruders from Japan, had had the audacity to strike back. A prospector's camp had been wiped out, and Fernando Mirabal himself had barely escaped with his life. Such a demonstration had to be dealt with.

Actually, Mirabal was sure the ninja camp was not here; Fu Antos was too smart to give away his location so readily. But with luck a ninja might be captured, and then perhaps truth serum or a lie detector would bring forth the necessary information. No more crudities like flaying; that took too much time, and was too risky. Torture was ineffective against ninjas. But drugs—maybe. Possibly some of the Indians knew where the ninjas were; for them torture would be in order.

Colonel Mirabal himself was not along on this expedition; he had business in Rio de Janeiro, following up another lead. But he had given the task force leader specific instructions. The job would be accomplished.

There were about 50 policemen collected from all the towns of the neighborhood, and about a hundred volunteers. It was an ill-matched, motley crew, in it strictly for the money and the chance to indulge in a little harmless bloodletting. But they were well armed and eager to collect the bounty on every dead Indian, plus whatever pillage was available for free enterprise.

On the way upstream they had a little practice mission, nothing serious. They encountered a small village of *pacifico,* pacified Indians. About 25 old men, women and children were taking their morning bath in the shallow waters. They stared at the convoy, not knowing its purpose.

The lead craft went on upstream, machine-gunned some tapirs drinking at the edge, hacked them into great chunks and threw the bloody pieces into the center current. The blood suffused the water, arousing the crocodiles and piranhas. Then a small party went ashore and cut behind the Indian village.

When all was ready, a couple of launches came close and sprayed the Indians with rock salt from sawed-off shotguns. The stuff did not kill outright, but made numerous small wounds that bled and hurt.

The Indians scrambled for the shore, terrified, uncomprehending, helpless—and were met by the machine guns of the land party. They could not escape, so had to stay in the water, and now the killer fish attacked savagely, incited to a frenzy by the new blood.

The two prettiest Indian women were hauled onto the boats, mass-raped, and tossed back in for the crocodiles.

Temporarily sated, the men re-formed their convoy and pressed onward. It had been fun, but it wasn't as though they had killed any real men. The hunters' appetite, like that of the piranha fish, had only been whetted for the real mayhem.

But Fu Antos, Lord of the Ninjas, had profited from his experience with the oil-prospecting camp. He knew that the presence of men from the coast meant trouble. Had they been content to leave him alone, he would not have fought them; but he could not tolerate a direct invasion of his territory, and he had promised the Indians protection. So he kept his spies out, though this meant slowed construction of the Black Castle, and he was well informed of this expedition. The village massacre had caught him by surprise; he had thought the Indians would be ignored. But the episode had given him time to prepare, and a ninja did not need *much* time, ever.

The lead boat was a modern police launch. It passed a bend in the river near where the prior oil group had its doom, and entered a narrow section. Suddenly it shuddered and halted, and began to sink. Its bottom had been ripped open by submerged stakes, sharply pointed and angled to pierce the hull of a fast-moving craft. Overloaded by the number of men on its deck, it was helpless. Men dived off from either side.

Immediately there was a stir in the water. From one side electric eels approached, released from underwater cages by the shock of the boat's collision with the stakes. From the other converged caimans, reptiles related to the crocodile. The action was violent.

The second launch rounded the bend in time to see the last of the first. It slowed, its .30 caliber machine gun coming to life, raking the shore on either side. But there was only silence from the jungle.

Then something arced high over the trees and fell on the deck of the boat. It exploded into flame. It was a homemade thermite bomb, a ninja formula like Greek fire. It spread across the deck, burning relentlessly. The men dipped buckets of water from the river to douse it, but the flame only spread faster. In moments it had eaten through the deck and was taking over the boat, its terrible heat driving back the men.

The remainder of the expedition now arrived. Six smaller boats, bristling with armed men. Too many to nail with the thermite catapult, they moved to the banks of the river, firing at anything. They did not dare remain exposed on the water, and the caimans prevented swimming. But they could take over the shores, and now they knew the enemy was near. This was what they had come for!

There was no resistance. All the boats beached without loss. A hundred and twenty men spread out, beating the brush, firing up into the trees, making sure there were no men in the area.

Then someone screamed. He had been bitten by a tarantula, the huge hairy tropical spider. Such bites are seldom fatal, but attack by such creatures can be terrifying. And suddenly there were spiders all around, dropping silently from the trees. Not only tarantulas, but also black spiders, larger than the black widow and with a more poisonous bite. They had been cleverly anesthetized, awakened by the commotion below, still too drugged to hide. So they attacked.

The men charged screaming from the area, losing all semblance of discipline. And as they dispersed, and became separated from each other, and lost sight of their boats and officers, the silent arrows began to fly. One by one the men fell, firing wildly into the brush before their struggles were ended by well-placed ninja arrows, nooses and spears. Some put their feet into miniature covered pits filled with sharpened sticks smeared with human excrement. Painful, disgusting, but not serious wounds, except that the chance of serious infection was excellent. Others tripped over cords stretched near the ground, releasing sprung saplings that hurled spears forward. Or were caught in loops that lifted them high into the air where they were easy targets. One man, lifted by such a snare, whipped out his hunting knife and cut the rope—only to land on his head, splitting his skull open.

Fu Antos was unsatisfied. He had organized the ambush so that no ninja would be seen, and none killed. That caution had prevented him from carrying through the eradication of the invading party. The secret of the Black Castle was in danger of becoming known, and therefore was in peril of complete destruction; secrecy and security were virtually identical. He had to take immediate steps to stop future excursions. Simple defense of the jungle area would no longer suffice.

*

He was very high up in Petrobas, the Brazilian Oil Company, literally. He was on the thirtieth floor of the modern skyscraper that housed the oil bureaucracy in Brasilia, the futuristic capital of the United States of Brazil. He was a highly paid executive in charge of locating potential oil fields in the central Amazonian wilderness. He was one of the few really intelligent bureaucrats. Given the mere hint of oil in a given region, he would sniff it out relentlessly. And he had the hint: special purchases of equipment, shipped up the Amazon River. Someone was drilling for oil—not a mere test well, but a producing one. Somewhere in the jungle of the Amazon.

There were other evidences. An oil prospecting unit had been attacked and wiped out by formerly acquiescent Indians. That suggested that some private enterprise was operating in that region, stirring up the natives with promises of wealth or whatever, acting to keep their discovery secret. Fernando Mirabal, brother to the Director himself, had narrowly missed being killed in that action. The Mirabals were bad enemies to have; those Indians would be sorry.

If he, Gal Costa, could locate that strike and verify it, he could arrange to expropriate the site for the government petroleum company. There were certain complexities involved, but that was his business: to comprehend and manipulate the jungle of economics and regulations so as to bring maximum profit to his company. He did the brainwork, then turned the matter over to Ramiro Mirabal, the Director, for the action. It was a good working arrangement.

Fu Antos, hidden in his half-built, largely underground Black Castle in the jungle, thought so too. There was much dead-wood in Petrobas, as there was in any government enterprise. But some branches were live wood. It was necessary to prune those branches, so as to render the giant oil company inactive, at least as far as new oil fields research went. So a few select assassinations would alleviate the problem with minimum fuss; there need be no more bloody excursions up the river. The Mirabal brothers had proved more formidable than anticipated. Fu Antos had hoped to nab Fernando during the police raid up the tributary, but the man, wary of such traps, had not come. It had been a bad mistake to let that man live after their first encounter. But the lesser actions could not wait; if he held them up pending the death of Mirabal, he could lose the war.

This sort of thing was far from the mind of the executive Gal Costa, high in his air-conditioned office in the capital city. Never in his life had he been physically threatened. His concern, as he stood hands linked behind him looking out the immense picture window at the magnificent skyline, the almost purple sky above the red earth beyond the modern building—his concern was only with the evidence on paper. No one else had fathomed the pattern; no one but he knew where the secret oil field was. There were elaborate maps on his wall, and hefty tomes of statistics on his shelf. By a process of perceptive elimination he had narrowed down the possibilities to three, and two of these were questionable for devious but convincing reasons. In the third there was probably an extremely rich oil field awaiting exploitation. Now it was time to make his report, significant not so much for its factual information but, like a lawyer's summation, for its clear rationale and the specific thrust of its recommendations. Costa was in his fashion a creative artist; he could perceive and document that obvious possibility that all others missed. Ramiro Mirabal would read this report, act on it, and strike oil, and there would be a new world power nexus right here in Brazil. This was potentially more significant than the Mexican strike. And Costa would be well rewarded. Ramiro was very good about things like that; he helped those who helped him, so long as they were loyal.

Costa buzzed for his secretary. She entered, carrying her notepad. She was a *Meztiza,* half-Indian—a small mousy-looking girl, dark of skin and hair. No office ornament; he had chosen her for her discretion, competence, and loyalty. She was an excellent stenographer, and never spoke of company matters outside the office. She lived in one of the *favelas* near the city, supporting her aging parents and feebleminded brother. She was not well paid, for then she might have become independent; as it was, she knew that only absolute loyalty to the company would preserve her job and therefore her livelihood. For if she were fired, she would be blackballed, and her half-caste family would starve unless she turned to drug traffic or prostitution—and she lacked the nerve for the first and the figure for the second. Costa knew his employees well.

"Put a hold on all incoming calls, Candelaria," Costa snapped. "Notify the switchboard that I am not to be disturbed for any reason for the next two hours. Lock the door. I'm ready to dictate."

She returned to her desk to make the necessary calls. But the first one was to an outside number. The phone was lifted at the other end, but no one answered. "Time," she said, and broke the connection. Then she took care of the other matters and returned to her employer.

For an hour she took dictation. Then Costa grew hungry, as he generally did when in the throes of creativity. "Fetch me a candy bar," he said. "Quickly." It was not that his hunger was that urgent, it was that he wanted the surge of food energy to guarantee the continued high output of his brain, so that he could birth the brilliant report at one sitting. Every minute's delay threatened to dull the fine cutting edge.

Candelaria unlocked the door, went into her office and thence to the hall with money from the petty change box. A man stepped silently forward to meet her. He handed her a wooden box. She accepted it with hardly a pause and carried it on down to the candy machine, feeling a slight vibration within it. Perhaps it was merely her nervousness.

The man stood waiting for the elevator down to the ground floor. Modern as this building was, it still suffered delays. The indicator showed the elevator was stationary on the second floor; something was holding it up. After a moment the man moved to the stairwell and started down. Thirty stories was a long way, but he preferred not to wait.

Candelaria carried box and Hershey bar into her office. She brought both all the way into the executive's office. She handed him the candy, went back to the door, set down the box and opened it.

"Candelaria!" Costa said, irritated. "What are you doing?"

"It will only take a minute," she said, drawing out a plastic bag filled with something that quivered and hummed.

"I'm in the middle of dictation!" he protested.

"Dictate to *this,*" she said, flinging the bag toward him. It burst open, releasing a dark cloud that buzzed angrily. She stepped quickly out the door, slammed it shut, and locked it.

"What on earth—" Costa exclaimed, furious at this unexpected insolence. That girl had just lost her livelihood! Then he saw the cloud and recognized it. "Bees?"

Years before, an enterprising beekeeper had imported small honeybees from Africa, in order to crossbreed them with local, strains and develop superior honey producers. The African bees made half again as much honey as American bees. But they were also ten times as fierce. The individual sting of a bee was no worse than average, but these Africans were much more eager to sting. Where a person might blunder into a nest and receive two or three stings ordinarily, he would receive twenty or thirty from an African swarm in the same time, and when he ran, they would follow for as much as a mile.

In 1957 some of these killer bees were accidentally let loose near the city of São Paulo, Brazil. Since then they had spread relentlessly, killing or mating with local queen bees. Their vitality and aggressiveness gave them a competitive edge against the natives. Every year they increased the radius of their territory another hundred miles or so, until they covered all South America. The North Americans were viewing the approaching invasion of their continent with growing alarm, unable to do much about it. As with the stinging fire-ants, that flourished despite all the efforts of modern technology, the bees progressed.

All this flashed through the executive's mind in an instant, for he well knew the history and nature of the bees. It would take perhaps 500 stings to be lethal to a man—but this confined swarm could deliver that. There was no other living target in the room.

He hurdled the bag and charged for the door—and found it locked. Fernando Mirabal could have bashed it down with his mighty shoulder; he was a fantastic brute of a man. But not Costa; he was soft and paunchy from years of desk work.

Now the bees were on him, striking like miniature dive-bombers. Sting! Sting! Sting! Faster than he could perceive, let alone avoid, they scored on his bare arms and face and neck. He shut his eyes, but they stung through his eyelids. He screamed—and they stung his lips and tongue. They were all over him, in his clothing, crawling up inside the legs of his pants, through the sleeves to his armpits, from his shirt collar down his back, stinging everywhere.

Maddened by the continuing pain, he picked up his heavy swivel chair with hysterical strength and smashed it through the picture window. Now there was an escape! He flung himself out through the jagged gap and sailed through the air, knowing that relief was at hand at last.

Costa's descent was more efficient than that of the ninja who had brought the bees. By the time the ninja reached the ground floor, a guard was there. The building was already being sealed off, with all occupants suspect. "Stop!" the guard cried, aiming his handgun.

The ninja walked quickly up to him. His lips parted lightly, revealing a small wooden tube. From this tiny blowgun emerged a poison-tipped needle, *Fukumi-Bari* , a special ninja dart. It pierced the guard's right eyeball, carrying its serum directly into his brain, and the man fell dead.

The ninja departed the building and the city swiftly, mission accomplished. If Candelaria were lucky, she too would escape to find sanctuary at the Black Castle; but even if she failed, she had the satisfaction of avenging her situation.

*

The dwarf-ninja stood only three and a half feet tall, but size was no indication of his prowess. He was, after all, one of the original Japanese minions of Fu Antos.

He moved down the river in his miniature canoe, paddling swiftly and silently until he spied the night lights of the town. This was where the oil company troops were garrisoned. The town itself had a population of about 5,000, and was the nearest substantial settlement to the ninja camp: useful for minor supplies and contacts. So normally the ninjas had left it alone. Now it had become a liability, to an extent. The capitalist forces were moving in, and it was necessary to blunt their encroachment by selective pruning, as at Brasilia.

The dwarf beached his boat silently and tied it within the high foliage of a tall overhanging tree: the last place a soldier would think to look. In addition he left a band of poison on the handle of its paddle, just in case a stranger did discover it and try to use it. Stealing ninja equipment was hazardous business.

Now he slunk around the backs of the buildings, seeking the army unit's temporary barracks. A battalion of troops had arrived in the past week, some five hundred men under the command of Major Albuquerque Lima.

The major was not the run-of-the-mill army man. He was Nordic, of German lineage, his parents having settled in Brazil and changed their name after World War II. His father had been a career officer in the German military machine, one of the thoroughly professional soldiers that had made the Wehrmacht the finest fighting force in the world despite Nazi interference. He was tough, fair, and tactically brilliant, prevented from rising to higher rank solely by the conspiring jealousy of his less-qualified colleagues. He had made a specialty of jungle warfare and felt quite capable of handling a band of renegade Indians and any outside collaborators who were stirring them up.

Fu Antos concurred with that assessment. Major Lima was dangerous, and would become more dangerous as his successes in the field forced his unwilling superiors to yield him increasing authority. Without him, his battalion was merely another unit, its guiding genius gone.

The town, like many in the central Brazilian wilderness, was fairly new. It was near the river but not on it; instead it perched on a small rise of the ground, built there because of the periodic river floods. There were no paved streets; yellow dirt roads and crude wooden houses served the people adequately. Few people lived in central Brazil from preference; could they but afford it, virtually all would inhabit the pleasure city of Rio.

The normal police post was small, about fifty men augmented in times of crisis by volunteers. However, the local police had been wiped out in the prior excursion upstream, and the army camp had been constructed on the outskirts of town.

It was patrolled by armed guards, of course, but passing through this perimeter was child's play to the ninja dwarf. He skirted the main barracks, going instead to the *Letrina.* This was a simple wooden housing constructed over a big hole in the ground. The army was efficient about such things; no fooling with expensive and water-wasteful flush toilet facilities. When the hole was filled, dirt would be shoveled over the refuse and the shit-house moved to a new pit.

There were two sections: one for officers, the other for men. The dwarf observed the privy for some time, waiting until it was empty, then entered the men's room. Here there was a board-seat with four holes. A thin partition separated this from the officers' facility.

He donned his tekaki, metal claws fastened to both hands and feet, enabling him to climb vertical surfaces. He arranged a rope and little screw-in hooks about his body for ready access, and fastened his specialized weapons on his back. Then he mounted the seat nearest to the officers' partition, put his hands down on either side, lifted up his feet, and swung them back and down into the hole. He let his body drop silently, performing an acrobatic feat that would have been impossible for a larger or flabbier man.

The pit was deep, but even in a few days a battalion of five hundred men can generate a lot of fecal matter. There was only four feet clearance between the seat-board and the semi-liquid mass of substance below. Since the seats were raised two and a half feet above ground level, the pit was getting full, and the structure would have to be moved in a few more days. The stench was intense.

The ninja clung to the wooden ceiling by means of his *tekaki,* moving like a human fly toward the officers' section. One mis-hold and he would fall, suffering a fate a good deal worse than cleanliness. The partition extended down part way, terminating at ground level, eighteen inches above the smelly stew. The dwarf descended this, then froze as two enlisted men entered their section. He watched, clinging to the wall as their meaty posteriors plunked down on the seats and disgorged their contents.

The troopers, their rounds expended, departed. The ninja resumed his journey. He brought his head down beneath the partition, so that he could see up into the officers' twin-holed evacuation center. All was clear. He passed one arm through and jabbed his claws into the wood, then followed with the other arm. Like a snake, he completed the contortion, his forepart ascending the wall while his hindpart descended on the far side. Somehow he performed the maneuver noiselessly and faultlessly, never touching the refuse below.

Now he mounted to the seat-board. There were fewer officers than men, so that the twin seats represented much more adequate accommodations than the four. But officers always had the best of it; that was what they were paid for, even though their refuse stank as bad as that of the common herd.

The ninja emplaced himself between the two holes, which were more widely spaced as though to accommodate broader beams. He hooked on firmly with both feet and one hand, then used the free hand to bring up one of his screw-hooks. Carefully, laboriously, he drove this into the wood. Silence was more important than speed. Then he screwed in a second hook, and strung his *musubinawa*, a special rope fashioned from woman's hair, between them. At last he rested his back within the loop of this fine, light, strong rope, and let go with his other hand. He unlimbered his small, sharp, barbed spear and held it in his right hand. Now at last he was ready for business.

This procedure had taken well over an hour, and it was now two in the morning. He had a prospective wait of several hours. No normal man could have stood it, suspended uncomfortably above a pit full of shit—but this was a ninja. In perfect silence he waited. The atmosphere infused his being and caused him an imperative need to defecate—and, ironically, he was in no position to do so.

Reveille sounded just before dawn, and the army camp came abruptly to life. The troops piled into the men's section, dropping an irregular avalanche of manure into the four mouths of the privy and letting loose an exuberant fusillage of wind. In minutes the level of odor rose appreciably, slopping under the partition in slow waves to displace the lesser offerings of the officers. As though to combat this intrusion, an officer came to make his own discharge.

Now came the ticklish part. The dwarf had placed himself so that he could cover either hole, since he could not anticipate which one his prey might use. But there were a number of officers, and only one—Major Lima—was his assignment. There would be no second chance; he had to be sure he scored on the major, not a lesser man.

He had to look. The posterior that covered the right hole gave no clues as to the rank of its owner. From this vantage, all men were equal. Well, not precisely equal; General Napoleon of France had spent so long wrestling with an evacuation complicated by piles that he had been unable to commence the battle of Waterloo advantageously. More of history was written in the outhouse than all the texts cared to admit. At any rate, the ninja had a problem. Had he been able to study photographs of the major's rear, he could have identified it now, but there was little light, and no such pictures had been available. Too bad that anal divination was not a contemporary practice, like palmistry or forehead divination. So he had to risk a peek through the left-hand hole.

He did this cautiously, not poking his head through but angling his body so that he could glance slantwise through it and up at the officer's insignia of rank. To do this he had to slide his legs almost directly under the occupied hole—and they were quickly soaked by the flowing urine. He paid no attention. His gaze traveled up the sleeve, up the arm to the shoulder as he twisted about in his sling, to command a view of the insignia of rank on the collar.

At last he saw it: a simple single star of a second lieutenant. Not his man. He swung smoothly back to his hiding place between the holes as the stream abated and the man stood up, not offering any solids to the pot this time.

A few minutes later a second officer entered. This one took the left seat, and the dwarf swung the other way to spy his rank.

There it was: the three five-pointed stars, one with golden

sunbursts between the points. The major!

Now the dwarf hefted his spear, braced himself, and aimed it at the anus opening like a black flower. Gas blasted out from that orifice, like the firing of a blank—and the point of the barbed spear thrust directly into that fart and up into the intestine, driven by all the convulsed power of trained ninja muscles. The major lurched up, but the shaft followed, and as gravity brought the torso down again the tip pierced the beating heart and killed him. The man slumped on the seat, his career over. The dwarf snapped off the protruding shaft of the spear, leaving no visible cause of death, not even flowing blood, then proceeded to make his getaway, mission accomplished.

He clung to the seat-board with his claws, unhooked the support cord, unscrewed the hooks, and let go. He dropped straight into the septic pool below. As he slowly sank into the brown slush, he placed a hollow reed in his mouth. Then he moved his arms and legs to draw himself down under the surface. Soon only the tip of the reed projected above, as the thick lumpy stew closed in.

It was several minutes before another officer entered the privy. Then there was a commotion, audible to the dwarf despite the insulation of substance. He was sure the leaderless troops would not suspect the cause of the major's demise—not until the surgical post-mortem was performed. By that time it would be night again, and the ninja would silently emerge from his camouflage and make his way to the river.

Quite possibly the soldiers would never catch on to the precise mechanism of the assassination.

Ass-ass-in. Under his mask of shit, the dwarf smiled briefly, for he knew the term for his act in many languages. An ass had received a spear in the ass.

But he had reckoned without knowing the cadre of officers and noncoms the major had assembled. In minutes these superior men had deduced the nature and timing of the event. Preferring not to wait on the tedious and uncertain process of formal justice, they took direct and immediate action. A sergeant made a charge out of three blocks of eight-pound military TNT, equivalent to over fifty pounds of commercial dynamite. He cut off a five-second length of fuse, dropped the mass through the privy-hole like a huge turd, and ran outside.

There followed a spectacularly ugly and smelly scene. The explosion blew the privy apart, followed by a rain of wood, dirt, urine, feces, and fragments of the dwarf ninja.

*

Fu Antos learned of this vengeance very quickly. It made him angry, for the dwarf had been one of the most valuable of his agents. It also suggested that this army battalion was more formidable than anticipated, for the cadre had reacted with very nearly the insight and decision of a ninja. Simple elimination of its commander would not suffice; the entire unit had to be destroyed.

But the battalion was now fully alert. Soldiers patrolled the perimeter of the entire town, challenging all strangers, and troops occupied many of the houses. The town was now under martial law. The dwarf's canoe had been found and burned; machine-gun nests now overlooked the river. There was no way to infiltrate this area without the risk of substantial losses, and the ninjas could not afford further casualties.

Fu Antos chose a subtler approach. He waited until the major's corpse had been put aboard a police craft with its honor guard for transport to civilization, then sent another ninja to swim the river. All eyes were dutifully on the funeral craft, making it easy; but the ninja stroked well beneath the muddy surface anyway, breathing through a tube to the air. The projecting part was concealed by a small tangle of floating debris. There were many such items in the river, so even the soldiers whose eyes strayed were not suspicious. At the appropriate point the ninja held his breath and swam underwater to the big pipe inlet where the river water was drawn into the town's supply system. Well water was not good in this swampy area, so the river was the cleanest source, bad as it was. The water was pumped to a big tank where it was allowed to stand, so that much of the sediment settled out and floating particles could be skimmed off the top. It was passed through filters and piped to the army camp and many of the houses, now fairly clean and safe to drink.

The swimming ninja opened a packet of powder, carefully kneading it so that it mixed with the water as it emerged. This solution was sucked into the supply pipe.

The action took only a few seconds. The ninja swam back to his drifting debris, now further downstream, and applied his mouth to the tube embedded there. He continued on down the river unobserved, following the major.

There was no immediate result of this mission. But the deed was done. The powder was a secret ninja formula derived from crushed mushrooms: a hallucinogen similar to LSD but more potent because there were no safety standards. In short, a drug of madness.

All day the dissolved drug sat in the tank, spreading through the water. It was so powerful that even diluted thousands of times it still was dangerously potent. It neither floated nor settled out; it permeated the tank, being further thinned by incoming replacement water. Its effect was thus diminishing, and would vanish in a few days without trace. But that one day would be all that was necessary.

Hallucinogenic mushrooms such as peyote have been used in many parts of the world. In some cases their essence passes through the human system without chemical change. Thus the shaman or medicine man may take a potent dosage, and the tribesmen drink his urine and suffer similar effects.

The ninja drug intensified the natural, usually-suppressed propensities of people. A moody person would become so depressed as to sink into catatonia or commit suicide. A violent one would become a raving maniac, destroying everything around him. A strongly sexed one would become a literal satyr, indulging in repeated and grotesque sexual acts, raping women and buggering men.

A few hours after the ninja's passage, it began. Not all the people drank from the tank; many poorer ones had to dip directly from the river, and wealthier ones drank milk, wines and fruit juices in lieu of water. But they were in the minority, and because there were so many armed soldiers in the town, in such an atmosphere of alarm, the sane people were swamped in the rising tide of madness.

No ninjas or other outsiders were near to report on that awful night. In the morning a river boat discovered the town burned to the ground, its inhabitants strewn all about: some shot, some stabbed to death, many strangled or clubbed. The women lay naked, evidently sexually molested, and many children too. The few survivors could offer no explanation; inexplicable madness had suddenly descended on the population, and the town had become a gruesome battlefield.

Only the sergeant who had blown up the privy had a reasonable insight into the rationale of that destruction—and he had not been there. He had been a member of the major's honor guard, cruising down the river as the ninja swam in.

Chapter 6:

Wrath of the God

I don't know how long I slept. Maybe a couple of days, for when I finally came to I was ravenous. In fact, it was the dinner bell that woke me. I needed no shill of a boy to guide me to the chow line this time, which was just as well, because Filho was gone.

I fell in at the end of the long queue; it had taken me just enough time to get my bearings to make the last. My shoes were gone, and I was now in baggy prison pants with no belt, so that I had to hold them up with one hand. So when I made it to the front, I'd have trouble holding my meal.

But the man on the end protested. He spoke no English, but pointed toward the head of the line. *"Por favor. Almoco."*

"Uh-uh," I said. "I don't believe in crashing. I'll wait my turn."

But now others saw me. Two men came back toward me. I thought it was going to be more trouble, but they were smiling. "Please, Mr. Jason," one said in recognizable English. "I am Honorio Chagas. No one will eat until you do."

My brow wrinkled. "What's this all about?"

"It is all over the prison. How they put you under the shock treatment, and you just laughed and told them nothing. And the butcher Mirabal got burned by his own machine and had to have a doctor come. And you never betrayed your comrades even though they were tortured before your eyes."

"I had no comrades," I said. "Those were innocent strangers." But I wished he hadn't reminded me of that lovely girl and that poor old man, so brutally treated because of me. Mirabal *was* a butcher!

"Just so," Honorio agreed approvingly. "You had no comrades, and so the lives of many in the movement were saved. It is unfortunate that brave old Carlos died, but at least he did not talk. And you beat up the informers. Here is your food." For he had brought me to the head of the line, and they were serving me. I decided to go along with this; they were determined and I was hungry.

But now I had another problem. I couldn't take the food without letting go of my baggy pants, and then they would fall, and after what had happened before I was damned if I was going to bare my rear. Accused of pederasty, indeed!

My new friend saw the problem. "Here—some string," he said. He looped the twine about my waist and tied it with a bow.

"Thanks," I mumbled, accepting the food. It was a special treat, my friend informed me: *Picadinho,* or ground meat with okra and pimentos. *Inpame* and *Xuxu,* a pale green squash. *Jilo,* a delicate variety of eggplant. And so on, an astonishing variety for prison fare, I thought. Of course not everyone had every type; there was not enough. But the fact that there was any choice at all was remarkable. "What's the occasion?" I asked.

"Did you not know? It is the Carnival," he explained. "Even in prison, we must celebrate, and we honor you especially, for your courage."

"I was only trying to stop Filho from getting raped," I said. I don't like rape, and the involvement of a child or young person makes it worse, and homosexual rape of a boy—but it had all been a setup, unreal. Someone had figured my reactions very carefully! "Why didn't anyone speak up then? You all saw what happened."

"We did not trust you, sir," he explained. "We thought you were another shill, that we would only betray ourselves by speaking out. As for the boy—" and here he spat eloquently to the side— "impossible to rape that kind."

That set me back. The clear implication was that Filho was himself a homosexual, used to the act. A male whore. I had heard somewhere that boys of a certain age were highly prized for this purpose; indeed, that they had erotic nerves in the anus that—or maybe it was a conditioned response—and I had charged to this one's rescue! No wonder the other prisoners had been suspicious!

"I see you did not know," Honorio said. "We Latins hate sodomy worse than you do, but this was a trap, and it smelled. We are sorry we misjudged you; we apologize."

"First you thought I was a shill," I said. "Now you think I'm one of the urban guerrillas. I'm neither. I really did not know those poor people who were tortured. If I *had* known them, I probably would have admitted it, to save them from—you know what Mirabal *did* to them?"

"We know," Honorio said. He opened his mouth wide, to show two teeth missing. "But even if you know nothing, you are still Jason Striker. You would not come here to betray us."

Was he trying to pump me for information about my mission? I could not afford to trust him. "I didn't want to come to Brazil at all," I said. "As soon as I get out of here, I'm going straight home."

He nodded, not questioning me further. I finished my meal. It wasn't enough; it left me still hungry. But I knew I had a generous portion, and I was not about to complain.

The whole of the prison had changed. Now everyone was friendly. I went for a drink of water at the lone tap, and someone warned me to beware of the worms. I had not been able to read the sign, in Portuguese. I didn't know what kind of worms were in that water, but I was good and thirsty this time, and there was nothing else. I drank.

I returned to my bunk, feeling better. The long rest had done me good, and the improved mood of my fellow prisoners helped a lot. I lay down to rest some more.

Several gunshots woke me. Honorio was with me almost immediately. "Down, friend!" he exclaimed. "Take cover." We cowered down by the bunk.

Then all hell broke loose. There was a terrific explosion, and all the prisoners started running around and screaming. It was an instant, full-scale riot!

Honorió grabbed my hand. "Follow me, Striker; it is for you they come."

"What?" I was confused.

"The MR-26 blew up the wall of the infirmary. Now we all escape, but especially you."

Still I resisted. "I don't know anything about the Mister Twenty Six! It has to be a mistake!" Later I was to learn that it had been no mistake. Dulce had escaped, made contact with the Communist MR-26 Revolutionary Movement, organized them together with the MR-8 and several other similar groups, and planned a full-scale attack on the jail—all to free me. It was quite an irony, these Communist revolutionary groups coming to spring a complete capitalist like me.

They had filled a fake ambulance with C-3 plastic explosive and TNT and driven it to the prison infirmary, telling the guards they were coming to pick up a sick prisoner. The guards, celebrating the carnival by imbibing 100-proof *Cachaca*, the colorless alcohol that was Brazil's national drink, had not been suspicious, and had let the ambulance into the inner courtyard, separated from the prisoners' court by a fence of iron bars. The plan was to explode the ambulance there, then charge in with a panel truck filled with men and wipe out the surviving guards. Then they would pick me up and their friends and scorch rubber getting out.

But, as with so many straightforward efforts, the actual attempt had complications. The two men driving the ambulance had faked papers; the idea was for them to enter the prisoners' courtyard so that they would not be harmed when the ambulance exploded in the guard's court. But one man lost his nerve and started running when a guard challenged him. That had triggered the exchange of shots that woke me. Then another guard had tried to open the back of the ambulance. Booby-trapped, it had exploded far more violently than the guerrillas, unsophisticated in such matters, had anticipated. The bombing was heard all over Rio, and a huge black cloud of smoke rose into the air above the prison, signaling the location plainly. This meant that help for the guards would be on the way much sooner than planned. The panel truck, charging in, rammed into the wall and got stuck in the gate. It was out of commission; and now it was every man for himself. The MR-26 people tried to rescue their own number from the cells, and the MR-8 theirs, forgetting any unified effort.

This was the chaos I now found myself in. No wonder I balked!

"Dulce," Honorio said.

Then I decided to go along. How she could have become involved in any of this I could not guess, then, but no one in this prison should know of my connection with her, unless she had told him. Maybe this was another trap—but she did have something to do with the guerrillas, and the explosion and riot were real enough.

Honorio led me to the gate between the prisoners' and the guards' compounds. Acrid smoke filled the area, and there was a wrecked panel truck to the side, partially blocking the way. Bodies were lying around. The explosion had blown the gate off its hinges, but some guards had rallied and were trying to stem the breakout. In the confusion we made it through the bedlam to the infirmary. There was a smoking hole in the wall. Guards were trying to close it off, but were held back by snipers firing from the buildings beyond.

"We can't go there!" I protested. "We'll be shot too!" Honorio raised his hand and yelled something in Portuguese. Prisoners turned to look at him. Then they charged the guards near the wall. There was shooting and a brief struggle; then the guards were dead or unconscious. I was astonished at the number of homemade weapons I saw the prisoners use. The helpless guards were literally hacked to death by spoons honed razor-sharp, fragments of broken glass, razor blades embedded in potatoes, homemade blackjacks, even knives fashioned from metal from the bunks.

"Come!" Honorio called to me.

"What did you *say* to them?" I demanded, hanging back.

"I said, 'Here is Jason Striker whom you let go to the torture on a false charge, and now his friends from the MR-26 Movement have come to free him, and all of you can go too—if you only get rid of those guards. This man whom you wronged so villainously forgives you and gives you your freedom, for this one small favor!'"

"You didn't!" I said, aghast.

He smiled. "No. I said 'Kill the bastards and get the hell out before the army comes!'"

I saw the girl Ester, her of the lost tooth, running with several other female prisoners, apparently quite recovered from her ordeal. Her plump buttocks jiggled with every stride she took. I was glad to know she was free. Too bad the old man had died.

And then I wondered: how had Honorio known about the death? Surely Mirabal would not have advertised the news over the loudspeaker. But there was no time to conjecture about such moot points.

Now we passed on through the hole. I was afraid the underground Revolution snipers would fire on us, but they didn't. Instead someone called: "Jason!"

I looked up-and there on the roof of the building across from the prison was Dulce, waving. What a wonderful sight! She had already been freed. That made my day complete—or so I thought.

I charged down the street and around the corner of the building, hoping to meet her at the entrance. But I was one of a ragtag band of hundreds of escapees. The other prisoners, wisely, were eager to get as far away from the prison as possible, with no delay. My bare feet were vulnerable; I had to watch my step, lest my tender toes get trampled in the stampede. And my damned pants kept falling down; somewhere in the rush the string had snapped and been lost. I had no underpants, and—well, it was awkward.

So we swept pell-mell around the corner—and suddenly the crowd was ten times the size. We were like a rivulet joining a stream, our impetus merged with the larger body. A stream? Nay, this crowd was the mighty Amazon! I tried to get to the door of the building, but it was upstream and manifestly impossible in my present state. I was carried along the opposite way, down the street amidst the crocodiles, I mean the cheering throng.

What *was* this? It seemed as though the entire population of Rio had disgorged into this one channel. Furthermore, the people weren't walking, they were dancing, despite the press of bodies, and they had a tremendous variety of weird costumes. Had the city gone crazy? No, of course it was the Carnival.

I finally fought my way to the fringe and flattened myself against a building, letting the main current flow past me. Then I gripped myself, especially my sagging trousers, and forged up-stream toward the key building. I took advantage of momentary eddies in the human stream, and clung to the wall when the tide became too strong, making erratic but inevitable progress. Soon I would recover Dulce!

But abruptly I stopped.

Because I saw two real predators on my trail, as crocodilian as men could get: Laureano the torturer and the three-hundred-pound football linesman of the original Death Squad that I had flipped on the beach when I rescued Dulce.

I was in trouble. I might ambush them and knock them out, but I couldn't be sure how the crowd would react. They might turn against me, as had the prisoners during the homo episode. Sure, the prisoners had had reason to be suspicious, but maybe this crowd did, too. I was hardly a promising looking specimen, with my sprouting beard stubble, sagging pants and bare feet. I might be mistaken for a mugger or killer. Anyway, the last thing I wanted was to make a big scene. Better simply to lose them. One thing I dared not do was lead them toward Dulce; maybe that was what they really wanted.

So I merged with the flowing crowd again, this time drifting with the current, ducking my head to reduce my height. I was taller than most of the natives, and it was a distinct disadvantage now.

My strategy seemed to work. Not because I had any real expertise at losing a tail, but because the surging and varied crowd made keeping track of anyone practically impossible. I lost the Death Squadders—but I also lost myself. Yes, I *know* that would never happen to James Bond—but I was stuck. Wherever I looked, there was a sea of gyrating bodies, gaudy costumes, smiling faces. What an extravaganza! It was like being caught in an ocean storm, as though I had now been washed all the way out to sea, with dancing human flesh in lieu of the raging elements.

I fought my way to the fringe of the crowd again. And grabbed for my pants again. Too late. They dropped down to my knees, and passersby chuckled at my bare buttocks. If only the bastards hadn't taken my belt, and if only I hadn't lost Honorio's string.

I bent over to get hold of my pants, and someone pinched my buttock. I whirled around, but I couldn't tell who in that mass of jiggling people had done it. What really got me was the fact that the only ones within range were women. I guess the ladies like to turn the tables when they have the chance. Can't really blame them. But I got my pants back up in a hurry.

I struggled into a broad central avenue. Here there was a snarl of traffic, and I do mean a snarl, because I saw what had to be the mechanized units of the Brazilian Army on their way up the street. Stalled. Several tanks were unable to move through the jam, and just had to wait, while their crews smiled and waved at the passing people and watched the slow-moving floats. No doubt these units had been summoned to deal with the prison break. Fat lot of good they'd do.

It was the carnival, all right. I saw floats very much like those in American pageants, filled with pretty girls—and let me tell you, the pretty girls of Brazil are just as shapely as anywhere else. I'm sort of a voyeur; I admit it. In fact I'm even a bit proud of it. One striking exhibit was like a giant beer bottle, with an almost-naked girl sitting on the neck, and others dancing all around it to Latin rhythms. I really enjoy this sort of thing, but would have liked it even better if I weren't a hunted prisoner.

One strange thing I observed: there were quite a number of men dressed up as women. There was no question of their sex; some were big and muscular, and one had a mustache. After my recent homosexual accusation—I just couldn't get that indignity off my mind!—I found this transvestitism a queasy matter. Did these men have repressed homosexual desires? I saw no, er, hanky-panky going on, though. Well, it wasn't anything I understood.

I forgot to hang on, and my pants dropped again. Damn! I grabbed for them—and leaped as I felt a sudden burst of extreme coldness, as if I'd sat down bare in a snowbank. Someone had squirted a shot of ether between my legs, the rapid evaporation making it icy. Another damned practical joke!

Actually, this was evidently the season of pranks. I saw people pelting each other with confetti, serpentines, rotten eggs, flour from bags, and something I learned later was called *bombitas de peo*, literally translated as "little fart bombs"—filled, of course, with the most appalling stench.

The afternoon was wearing on, and I was wearing out. The scant prison lunch seemed far in the past, and my stomach was growling. I felt like a fart bomb myself. I stumbled into an alcove where, oddly, there were no people, and paused, getting my bearings.

I saw a little roadside shrine, evidently a monument to one of the voodoo gods. It was a lump of brownish stone or clay or packed dirt streaked with grease, formed into the shape of a grotesque head whose eyes and mouth were formed with small seashells. A parody, surely, a joke, like a gargoyle; it reminded me of the time years ago when both Huntley and Brinkley broke down in chuckles on the evening news, telling how people were sending gargoyles to friends for Saint Valentine's Day. Yet somehow this was real and malignant, unnerving. Probably it was my guilty conscience stirring for what I was about to do. The thing was on some sort of wooden platform, covered by a cloth, with burning candles set around it, and several big, beautiful conch shells, and some dried-out pieces of coconut.

I had heard something about these. (I have a lot of funny bits of information jumbled about in my head.) People left offerings of food and clothing, much as they burned candles to saints. Apparently the food just sat there until it spoiled, or some hungry animal got to it.

Well, *I* was a hungry animal! I hoped the voodoo god would not strike me down for my sacrilege, but hunger would certainly get me otherwise. I picked up a huge banana and peeled it, or tried to. I was so weak I had trouble even with that; the thing resisted my efforts as though possessed. By the god, maybe. I finally tore it open and took a bite—and it was so hard and fibrous I had to spit it out.

No wonder. This was no banana, it was a plantain. The huge cousin to the banana, so tough it had to be cooked. Served me right.

I ate some stale bread, and an overripe mango, and they really were good. There was also a little bottle of *Cachaca*, the ubiquitous alcoholic beverage of Brazil. I was thirsty, so I picked it up, considered the pale liquid inside, remembered my inevitable regrets over alcohol, felt a redoubled thirst, opened it and took a swig. And fired it back out in a blast like that of a blowtorch. It seemed like almost pure alcohol. If the voodoo god drank that firewater, no wonder he was such a grouch! I recapped it with my eyes streaming and put it back. Instead I pocketed the handkerchief full of black American pennies that also sat there. No kidding; they were genuine Lincoln-heads, anomalous here in Brazil. Genuine money, and I might need it. Not merely for money, but for self-defense. The fact is, a stocking filled with coins is one of the best blackjacks available. Hoods used this kind, and when the police search all they find is loose change. I dare say it would be a dandy way to dispose of a weapon, too: drop the stocking in the trash, spend the money, and how would it ever be recovered or identified? For that matter, a sack full of sand is pretty good too. Anyone can arm himself if he really wants to. Anyway, there were seventy-seven pennies—yes, I counted them as I ate—and I presumed this was a magic number. A good mass.

There was a large floppy battered peasant hat beside the food, another offering. I put it on my head. Finally I took a long red scarf and wrapped it around my waist. That served in lieu of a belt, and was a godsend. A voodoo godsend. Now I could keep my white rear hidden as well as my face. "Thank you, voodoo god," I said sincerely. "If I ever have a chance to return the favor . . ." And it seemed to me that there was a momentary glint in the eye of the grim statue. I shuddered.

I started to rejoin the throng, then had another thought; I picked up the bottle of *Cachaca* and held it in my left hand. I had no intention of drinking it, but it would do nicely for camouflage. Now I looked just like a peasant on a spree; the Death Squad would never identify me.

Well, there was one other thing. I squatted, scooped up a handful of dirt, and smeared it over my hands and arms. This darkened my skin and gave me that unwashed look of the illiterate farmer. For good measure I put some in my hair too. Now at last my costume was complete.

I merged with the crowd again, feeling better. I had little reason, for I had no idea where I was. Even if I found my way back to the hotel, I would not be safe, for the Death Squad thugs would surely be watching it. That meant I had no way to get Kan-Sen's message, and could not proceed with my mission. Dulce was my only hope—and where was she now?

Somehow I would just have to get some more money and locate the airport and take a plane home. Then I could check directly with Kan-Sen, and start over.

Only two or three things wrong with that notion. First, how

could I locate the airport, let alone obtain the money for passage? Seventy-seven cents would hardly cover it. Second, where would that leave Dulce? Alone and hungry in these teeming streets? Third, with no proper clothing and no identification, how could I get back into my country? And wouldn't the Death Squad be watching the airport and the other routes out of the country?

In short, I was nowhere. So why the hell did I feel so good?

I looked about, more or less free now from the pangs of hunger, embarrassment over my bare-assment, and apprehension about the pursuing Squad. So I could better assimilate my surroundings. And they were impressive.

Brazil I had heard was as large and populous as all the other South American countries combined. I could believe it! I had never seen so many people, so packed, so hurried, going nowhere I could fathom, but going there fast. Cars plunged through the multitude: Volkswagens, Simcas, Mercedes, and big American cars, zooming by each other, through red lights, squealing around corners while the pedestrians drew aside just barely enough to avoid disaster.

Why hadn't I been aware of this suicidal streak in the natives? Maybe prison had sharpened my sensitivities. Or, riding a taxi and dining with Dulce, I hadn't paid proper attention.

Dulce, somewhere in this incredible city. I'd never find her!

A group of blue-faced, white-nosed—and I mean poster-paint white, baboon-bottom blue!—black-foreheaded clowns went by. They had huge bouffants of orange fuzz in lieu of hair. There was a jangle of music, one might say tintinnabulation, as the pace of frolic intensified. Children paraded by, their bare feet dancing in the dust in rapid-Samba patterns. They carried drums, whistles, musical triangles, and the *cuica,* a weird wheezing instrument. Many adults wore brightly colored masks.

There were also elaborate costumes emulating the colonial rule of the past: fancy laces, expensive satins, powdered curly wigs, billowing hoop-skirts. Many outfits looked quite expensive, and I wondered how the poor people could afford them. In contrast,

ANTH

there were also a number of formal European suits, and near-naked young women. And Egyptian slaves in short white tunics and silver chains. Alpine peasants in thin white blouses and brief green shorts. Sultans' concubines in gold brassieres and flimsy silk trousers through which the panties showed. And so on; myriad and delightful were the ways in which the girls showed off their unquestionable charms. Anything, it seemed, went.

I passed a girl dancing on a bandstand. *"Oba! Oba!"* she squealed as she gyrated. This was one of the words I was catching on to; it meant "Wow!"

And suddenly I realized: the jailbreak must have been timed for this carnival-time, so that the escaping prisoners *could* lose themselves in the milling throng, just as I had done. Those army tanks, bogged down in the mire of holiday traffic—beautiful!

Now the crowd parted to let a parade squeeze by with its accompanying band and costumed dancers. They seemed tireless, like the Oba-girl I had passed before, but my bare feet were hurting. I wedged back against a shop window with its big sign saying LIQUIDACAO—apparently a big sale.

A blowzy woman clutched my arm. *"Boa tarde!"* she cried exuberantly. Evidently a salutation.

I looked at her, repelled by her fat, flushed, coarse face, and tried to pull away. "I don't speak Portu—"

"Seu nome?" she inquired, tightening her hold.

Nome? Ah: Name. "Jason," I said. "But I don't—"

"Nao compreendo," she said. *"Voce doente?"*

I glanced back—and saw Mr. 300-lb. Football Linesman cruising down the wide street, peering this way and that through the crowd. I couldn't stay here; I was right in his path. Those Death Squadders sure were after me.

I tried again to draw away from the woman, but she held my arm in a grip like that of a wrestler. Suddenly I realized I was going at it wrong; I could use her for camouflage. My pursuers obviously were searching for a tall lone foreigner.

"Have a drink!" I said, offering her the bottle of *Cachaca.*

Her eyes lighted, and that was a good trick, considering how bloodshot they were. She grabbed the bottle and popped the cork with her teeth. She was obviously expert at this sort of thing; I had twisted it off like a screw-on cap, in my ignorance. She tilted the bottle to her mouth and gulped the firewater down. Then she paused, with a half-glazed look of contentment, politely proffering it to me.

Her slobber was on the rim, and I didn't want to touch any more of that paint-dissolver anyway. But the Squad player was closer yet, and now he seemed to have a couple of henchmen. I became very uncertain of my camouflage; how could dirt and a hat convert me into a native? So I had to do it: the smell of liquor on my breath would be the finishing touch, for they surely knew I didn't drink. I gulped a gulp, knowing that this time I had to swallow, not spit.

And gulped. A river of fire coursed down my throat. I coughed, my eyes smarting. The woman whacked me on the back helpfully. *"Oba!"* I gasped.

When my eyes cleared and normal breathing was restored, I spied the Squad leader almost on top of us. I had to hide my face. I took the woman in my arms as though she were my girlfriend. She giggled, pleased, jiggling all the way from her double chin to her double kneecaps, while the D.S. man squinted suspiciously. Did he recognize me? I had flipped him on the beach, and that's the sort of thing a man remembers.

The woman was fifty years old, dirty, and sweaty from her dancing. Not that I was in any position to comment, with my own dirt and sweat and feet. Her hair straggled in sodden banks, looking like a frizzy fright-wig. From her mouth came a strong, bad odor; in fact her teeth were no more than rotten stumps. Her breasts must have been marvels in her time, but now resembled cow udders. She was some sort of mulatto with dark bronze skin, a huge waist and a very wide mouth. But the Squadder was still watching. So I nerved myself and kissed her. I had to squat down somewhat to embrace her, as she barely came to my collarbone; this added awkwardness to indignity.

Her lips were like liquor-spiked mush. Her huge breasts and belly shoved into me like inflated cushions, reminding me distressingly of the water-tortured man. What brutish things people did to their own bodies, in the name of uncontrolled appetite! I heard demonic laughter, and imagined for a moment it was that of the voodoo god whose chapel I had robbed, but it was the D.S. man, as he turned away. He couldn't see why anyone would want to kiss such a monstrosity. If only he knew!

The crisis was over. I came up for air, and tried once more to disengage, but now the bitch was hauling me into an alley. With the sausage-thick fingers of one hand she was unbuttoning her blouse, showing her ponderous mammaries jiggling on her barrel-belly.

Good God—she wanted the finale!

I remembered what Hiroshi had told me of Fu Antos's early days: how he had made love to an ugly feebleminded woman, before an audience. But I was not Fu Antos, and I had had enough. I had to apply a simple wrist lock to free myself of her hold, and even then she resisted determinedly. I broke away, dragging her roughly forward in the process. She fell to elbows and knees, her exposed breasts almost dragging in the dirt.

Her manner changed abruptly. She cursed me in Portuguese—I could tell it was profanity by the pistol-shot explosion of syllables—and swept up a broken fragment of a brick.

I turned and ran. The brick caught me between the shoulder blades and fell down, split in half. What aim that woman had! Then I was out in the crowd again, and safe; I would have a bruise, but nothing bad.

The *Oba* girl was still dancing. I made my way toward her merely because she served as an attractive landmark. She was petite with a plump face, lovely red lips, and jet-black hair reaching down to her buttocks. Her waist and hips were small but well formed. Her handsome thighs flashed under her skirt and her necklace of seashells bounced on her bosom. She had half the age of my alley-bitch, but ten times the sex appeal; it was fun to watch her. I really had nothing better to do.

Abruptly the girl stumbled and pitched forward off her stand. I dived to catch her before she hit the pavement. I made it; she landed neatly in my arms. A lithe, light morsel.

"You're okay, I think," I murmured, setting her on her feet. "Just tired. Take a rest."

But she stared wildly around. "Umbanda!" she exclaimed.

"I'm sorry. I don't speak—"

"*Umbanda!*" she repeated. She started to walk, and stumbled again. A second time I caught her. It was not a chore I objected to.

"Look—your legs are dead," I said. "Don't get me wrong—they're beautiful legs! But how long have you been dancing here? Two hours? You can't go-go forever. You've got to rest."

She looked at me with seeming comprehension, while the crowd cruised by obliviously. Then she gestured toward the row of shops fronting the street. *"Umbanda!"*

It must be a place, I decided. Maybe a hotel where she was staying. She wanted to go there so she could rest and eat. "Okay, I'll take you there," I said. Fickle as I am, I'll do anything for a young pretty woman, and nothing for an old ugly one.

I picked her up by knees and shoulders and carried her through the throng like a bride. It took time and effort, but every wave of the crowd shoved that pleasant torso against me, and that was fine. We made it to the edge, and I followed her gestures until we came to the place she wanted.

It was a little shop with the word UMBANDA. A family business?

We entered. The shop was crowded with statues of Catholic saints as well as voodoo replicas. The shelves were full of a variety of herbs, powders, lotions, essences—as well as more modern aerosol cans with printed labels.

The proprietor came forward. He was an old Negro at least seventy, bowed down with those years, with frizzled white hair.

The girl spoke unintelligibly, and he nodded. He went to a shelf and brought down a small package of powder.

I looked around and saw a voodoo statue just like the one in the alcove whose offerings I had borrowed. This was a voodoo store!

The shell-eyes of the figurine seemed to be watching me. I had taken its offerings; did it mean to punish me?

The proprietor said something, the girl answered—and I became aware that something was amiss between them. Something to do with the purchase. Haggling over the price?

The girl turned to me. *"Por favor,"* she said pleadingly.

So she was out of cash. Inflation was rampant here, I knew; prices could double in a few months. But of course that could happen back home too. If I could put a strangle on inflation and wipe it out—but no judo hold could do that, unfortunately.

I turned out my pocket and produced the seventy-seven black pennies. "That's all I have—but if it'll help . . ."

The proprietor shook his head. Not enough. Not surprising.

The girl gave a little sigh of resignation. She picked up her money, returned my pennies to me, and turned to go.

"*Esperar*!" the proprietor said. He held out the package. He was agreeing to the price after all.

We paid our money and accepted the package. On the way out, my eye caught that of the idol again, and it gave me the shivers all over again. I was acutely conscious of the source of my limited wealth. The voodoo god *did* know!

The girl saw my glance, and nodded knowingly. "*Umbanda*," she repeated.

Oh. Maybe that was the name of the voodoo god, my benefactor. Ah, well. "Umbanda," I agreed. "Where to now, Oba?" I expected her to return to her bandstand. It had been a pleasant little interlude, and I was glad to have helped her, but I had other concerns to attend to. Such as finding Dulce before the D.S. found *me*.

The girl gave a start and glanced at me as if I'd goosed her. She stood at the edge of the throng, looking across it at her stand. I saw that another girl had taken it over. She looked down at her package, then again at me. She shrugged, making a decision. "*Vir,*" she said, taking my hand.

It looked as though she had adopted me. Well . . .

We sidled along between the stores and the crowd. Now it was dusk, and the lights were coming on. I had spent the whole afternoon in my wandering.

The carnival showed no sign of abating. If anything, it intensified into a seeming frenzy as the darkness enveloped the city. Colored lanterns bobbed in bright waves, swung by dancers. Many were on tall poles, and looked heavy, so the dancers had to be strong and skilled. Down the street was a whole group of lights, an organized band of dancers twirling them. Each person had a sort of leather belt like an apron, with a place to catch the bottom of the pole, and they swung it with their hands to make it twirl and wave. Very pretty, singly and in concert. Despite my predicament, I was getting to like Rio. But now my Oba-girl seemed to have lost interest.

She led me through side streets, out of the noise of the crowd, and finally into a dark building. I thought I was in for a private tryst, and I was not loath. I'm a bit like the man in the musical *Finian's Rainbow* who sings: "When I'm not near the girl I love, I love the girl I'm near." I realize this makes me seem less heroic than I'd like, but I'm really *not* a hero, just a judo instructor gone astray, never cut out for the high life. Only one girl ever evoked my outright love, and she died, and no woman since was able to touch me deeply. It would have dishonored the memory of Chiyako for me to love another woman, or so it seemed. So I took love where I found it, not wanting any more lasting commitment. In judo I was a *yudanshai,* a master; in love a *mudansha,* a dilettante. I followed her into a gloomy passage, then into a dimly illuminated room crowded with people. Not a tryst, but a meeting—or a mass orgy.

I looked around the circle of faces, actually an oblong of faces, as the people sat on benches near the walls. They were mixed, ranging from white to black, and solemn: neither hostile nor happy. They shared a common passive intensity, as though in meditation. Many wore gaudily colored medals with mystic inscriptions, and bright plastic-beaded necklaces of the sort I had seen at the store. Some wore jewelry made of shells, animal teeth, tusks and ornately carved wood.

Pottery burners set around the room contained fragrant incense; some of it merely charred, but some of it sported color-changing flames.

Now I became aware of sound: weird chanting with an indefinable melody and strong tom-tom beat. It was soft, not loud, but the base harmonies had a compelling effect, like the massed heartbeat of a sleeping giant. I spied the source of it: an old-fashioned phonograph. Was this a fancy dance, after all?

Around the room, set in alcoves, and on tables in the center, were painted plaster figurines—many strange, some shockingly familiar. I recognized St. George on a white horse, a Buddha, and Jesus Christ himself. But then I remembered: modern Latin mysticism combined voodoo with Roman Catholicism, using the Saints and conventions of both.

I had been brought to something very like a Black Mass.

Oba led me around the edge to a gap in the seating, and we sat down on the end of a bench. Now I saw hooded objects in the center, on the tables, hazy behind smoking incense. These shapes were somehow menacing in their somber outlines, like malignant ghosts. I don't consider myself superstitious, but there are times when I get distinctly nervous about the supernatural, and this was such a time. *Something* was brooding, menacing, unnatural, in this room.

I don't know how long we sat there, with me trying to get up nerve to walk out and never quite making it. Probably only a few minutes, though even that was far too long for comfort. Why had Oba brought me here? I had only tried to help her when she fell. That damned music kept insinuating itself into the crevices in my civilized armor, undermining my certainty that black magic had gone out with the onset of the twentieth century. My eyes darted guiltily around as if seeking some escape. Now it seemed that we sat in some kind of pavilion, with hand-hewn poles supporting a palm-thatched canopy. I had not noticed that when we entered, but it must have been here, perhaps concealed by the gloom. It now seemed as though we were in an isolated jungle temple rather than a city building. I was reminded vaguely of Halloween. I counted some fifty or sixty people and knew there were more I could not see without making myself too obvious. All silent, all somber.

The music stopped. Apparently that had been merely the introductory piece; now the live show was to begin. A figure entered and marched to the center. It was obviously the man in charge. He wore a white suit, white shoes, white socks, white hat, and looked like a businessman, except for the multiple rattling bone and shell necklaces he sported. He was dark-skinned. Actually, three quarters of the people in Brazil were some shade of dark, ranging from off-white to solid black. He had short, dark, greasy hair that looked as though it wanted to curl but couldn't. His face was pockmarked from acne or smallpox and he had a gold tooth in front, but his eyes were bright and compelling. He was neither tall nor young, being forty-five or fifty and standing about five-two, and he was thin—yet he had the subtle mannerisms of good breeding and education. I was struck again by the contrast the largest necklace made: it had a large crystal bead, followed by white, blue, red, yellow, black, green and brown beads. Tasteless—I thought then.

The man spoke, and now seven young women traipsed in, scantily clad in robes of many colors. So there was after all to be entertainment of some sort; every time I thought I had it straight, something happened to change the picture.

The girls formed a circle around the man. He went to the tables and struck a wooden match. The sulfurous flare of light was eye-stabbing in the gloom, making me wince. The master-of-ceremonies touched it to a candle on the main table, pronouncing strange-sounding words. I mean these didn't even sound like Portuguese, but some litany from the hidden heart of the Dark Continent. Then he brought out from a cabinet below another hooded object and set it on the table beside the candle. He took a small pitcher of water and poured some on the floor before the table, three times.

Suddenly the candle was snuffed out as if by an unseen hand. I jumped, though of course this was merely some magic trick or a random draft of air. There was a general murmur of alarm; evidently the spectators did not view this as coincidence.

The man lit the candle again, bowed his head reverently before the covered figure, and spoke in that strange tongue again: *Ala le ele cupache ago meco Eleggua ake boro ake boye, tori toru la ya fi yoroure.* Or something like that; I really did not catch it.

And the candle went out again.

Now there was a fair commotion in the room. Something was definitely wrong.

The master-of-ceremonies seemed to realize it too. He whipped off the hood—and there was the cement head of the god whose offerings I had raided.

"Eleggua," the girl beside me murmured.

So that was the name of the god, my nemesis. I had misunderstood when she said "Umbanda" before; the one was the *cult,* the other the *god.* This was no entertainment, it was a genuine voodoo ceremony. And why did that make me so nervous?

The witch doctor—for so I knew him to be now, despite his mostly modern dress—spoke to the idol. He brought out a fat cigar, lit it, puffed, and blew the smoke at the head. No insult, I realized; evidently the god liked good cigars, and this was its way of experiencing them. Then the man set the cigar still burning, down beside the image as an offering.

Once more he lit the candle. But somehow his sleeve caught it, and the candle tipped over to fail against the head. The grease flared up, producing copious smoke, while the witch doctor stepped back in alarm. Ignorant as I was, I knew that this was entirely unorthodox, in fact, a sacrilege.

The blazing head exploded. Fragments of pottery, cement and hard dirt fell to the floor. And underneath that heat-shattered visage was revealed—a human skull.

"Exu!" many voices cried, shocked. And somehow I understood that this was a new and terrible aspect of the god. This was, in fact, Satan.

And the awful square hollows of those two eye-sockets stared straight at me.

The witch doctor was quick to notice this fact. He pointed to me. "Who are you?" he cried, whether in Portuguese, African or English I could not tell in my confusion, but I understood him well enough. "Who are you who has enraged our God?"

Now Oba was staring at me with horror. She had never suspected she was harboring such a criminal.

There was nothing for it but to face the music. I stood up. "I am Jason Striker of America. I took food and clothing and money from this god's shrine in the city because I needed them. I faced death otherwise, and did not know he would object so strongly." I was really saying I did not know I would get caught.

Now all the people were staring at me as though I had broken wind in church—as perhaps I had.

Suddenly I was on trial. Yet the witch doctor was fair. "Evidently you do not know our customs," he said in English. "You have insulted the most savage aspect of one of our most powerful gods, and he will have his reckoning. Thieves are legion in Rio; nothing is safe, especially during the carnival. But no one, *no one* steals from the gods! Especially not savage Exu." And he looked grim.

So that was why those items had remained untouched beside the idol. I should have known that anything stealable would have been stolen long before I got there. I looked around, bracing myself for action, going down instinctively into a basic defensive position: legs slightly spread for good balance, one arm high and the other low for defense or attack. I was sorry I had offended these people, but I wasn't going to submit myself to primitive voodoo vengeance without a fight. I had already had my fill of Brazilian custom in prison.

"Peace," the witch doctor said. "We shall not hurt you. Exu himself will secure his reckoning in his own fashion. You cannot escape it."

Oh. They *believed*, of course. Primitivism extended right into the present, here in Brazil. Yet I was nervous. The way the god had seemed to reject the offering, and changed its aspect to orient on me—the witch doctor could *not* have known beforehand.

"I must ask the god what he wishes," the witch doctor said. "We cannot proceed with our mass without the *despacho*, the ritual offering to Exu. He must accept it, or we are lost. We must appease him."

I didn't want any more trouble if I could avoid it. There were too many people here for me to overcome; certainly I could not escape without hurting someone. Besides that, I was in the wrong. If the witch doctor was willing to be reasonable, I would have to go along.

"I shall use the shells," he said. "The Table of Ifa is infallible."

He took sixteen small shells in both hands, rubbed them together, then threw them on a straw mat. He studied the configuration, then threw them again. Some landed on their "top", sides, the serrations like little mouths, while others showed their hollows. I was reminded of the *I Ching* of the Chinese, in which yarrow sticks are thrown into patterns and interpreted by the books; my friend Kobi Chija had used that method on occasion. Kobi, the father of Chiyako, my lost fiancee.

That memory was painful, as always, and I concentrated on what the witch doctor was doing. He threw the shells four times, then looked at me.

"On the first throw of the *caracoles* only two shells were upright," he said. "This would be Exu speaking, and the proverb he invokes is 'There is an arrow between brothers.' It is possible that this is a warning, a curse he has placed on you, fomenting trouble between you and—"

"I have no brother," I said.

"Or one close to you. The god does not choose to express his sentiment in a single phrase, and we would not understand it if he did, for we are merely mortals. The second throw showed nine shells upright; this is a clarification by one of the other gods: 'Your best friend is your worst enemy.' This strengthens the first warning."

"If that's the curse, it's a bad one," I agreed, uncertain how to react. The man seemed perfectly sincere, explaining this to me as I would explain a fundamental judo point to a new student. Why did he bother? He could hardly have any good feeling for me. Later I was to learn that in fact *Santerios,* as they are known in Spanish, often do maintain a doctor-patient relationship, having genuine interest in the welfare of their clients. A few are avaricious and some are frauds, as with any profession, but most are honest and competent. So this was in character for the man. This adventure was to give me a lot more respect for the witch doctor. Once I would have sneered at the very notion of voodoo. Not any more.

"You could not have chosen a worse god to offend," he agreed. "I have been *pai-de-Santo* for many years, and I have never before seen Exu so angry. We must resolve this crisis, or there will be terrible trouble."

"For you as well as me?" I inquired, perplexed. I had the growing feeling that I was dealing with a sincere man; he had a manner about him that compelled respect.

"For us all," he said. "Your offense was from ignorance, but it can be no accident that you came here. Exu summoned you, to call you to account. Therefore we are obliged to work with you, to help you expiate his anger. If we fail, that wrath. will fall on *us,* for we are *not* ignorant."

I felt more and more like a heel. At the same time I wondered: Oba had fallen at precisely the time I was there to catch her; could the god have stricken her at his convenience? Then Oba had changed her mind, as though guided by some voice in her head, and brought me here, and that decision had happened under the eye of the god, in the store. I preferred to call my presence coincidence, but I had to admit there was a pretty strong case to be made the other way. The way Eleggua had refused the candle and manifested as Exu—well, there's a bit of the primitive in every man, and the primitive in me was ready to believe. "I don't suppose just apologizing and giving back the things I took would suffice?"

"I do not know," he said. "But I suspect it would not suffice, for then others might have the notion that they could take Exu's things and return them only when challenged. More likely he seeks to make an example of you, so that never again will his chapels be profaned. Exu may even have directed your initial offense with that in mind; we can not yet know." If this complication upset him, he gave no sign. "The third throw showed eleven shells upright. This is Exu speaking again: 'Be distrustful; carry water in a straw basket.'"

"Can't carry much water that way," I remarked. "Even *I* know that!"

"Precisely. Do not depend on what you see, for it will slip away like water through straw. The fourth throw showed twelve shells upright: 'You are defeated through your own fault.'"

"But why should Exu curse me?" I asked. "I'm ready to make amends. In fact, I planned to return the things when I had a chance; I'm sure I said as much at the time. I never sought any quarrel with him. It doesn't make much sense."

"Not immediately; not to you," he said. "Let us see whether Exu's ire has abated."

I sat down again, and the ceremony resumed. This time there were no hitches. Exu accepted the cigar and candy. There was a sigh of relief through the hail. My own sigh was among the others.

Now the three drums started, making an intricate syncopation. The seven girls danced. Their movements were symbolic, not erotic; I soon felt myself swept up in the ascending beat of it. My feet moved; my hands tapped. But I kept my seat, not wanting any more trouble. Oba, beside me, had relaxed; I was no longer an albatross.

On and on it went, the beat louder, more insistent, the girls moving faster, their beads and shell-necklaces rattling rhythmically. The others in the mass were as rapt as I. Voodoo this might be, but it had its compulsion.

Suddenly one of the girls screamed and fell. She writhed on the floor, but the others kept on dancing, as if hypnotized by the drums. The fallen one wore black, and her necklace had triplets of red beads alternating with triplets of black ones. From her mouth poured a chanting stream of unintelligible sounds, out of which leaped the electrifying words "Jason Striker!"

The witch doctor—or more correctly, *pai-de-Santo*— when in Brazil, speak as the Brazilians do, I always say—listened intently. I realized that the dancer had been possessed by the god she represented, Exu, and that that god was not finished with me. And in the throbbing pulse of the dance and the flow of the girl's words, I felt an awful chill. I had entered this place an innocent skeptic; now I was becoming a guilty believer. What a mouthful the god had to say about me!

At last it stopped. The girl lay still for perhaps thirty seconds, then climbed to her feet a bit shakily and resumed her dance. I was sorry for her, for the brutish possession she had had to suffer on my account; it had surely not been pleasant for her. Now flecks of blood were on her costume where the spittle of her seizure had landed.

The *pai-de-Santo* came to me, frowning. "It is very bad," he said. "Exu accepted the *dispacho* only to enable the ceremony to proceed, that he might make his ire properly known."

"Uh-oh," I said, and I was not being facetious.

"He has put a terrible curse on you. You will be slain by your best friend, at the time you least suspect. Exu has spoken, and will not be appeased."

So it was only a voodoo curse, by a god I didn't believe in. Nothing to alarm me, yet I *was* alarmed. The drums, the dance, the divination by shells, the speaking with tongues—there was an authenticity and authority about all this that forced my unwilling acceptance. I knew voodoo had an appalling hold over illiterate superstitious peasants, yet this was a bustling big city, and many in the audience wore expensive clothing. This *Umbanda* evidently had an aducated clientele. *They* believed, but I was a more civilized modern man—*wasn't* I?

"You may not believe," the *pai-de-Santo* said without rancor. "But Exu is all-powerful. He can strike you anywhere in Brazil; only by returning quickly to your homeland, where your own god is strong, can you hope to escape him."

"I'd like to," I said. "But I couldn't *stay* out of Brazil. I have a mission here."

"Then perform it quickly, if you value your life," he said. "Dead men accomplish few missions."

"I can't promise to do it quickly," I said. "I'll just have to take my chances."

"Chance is not a factor, with Exu," he warned. "He will manifest his will despite all you can do."

I shrugged. "I appreciate your sincerity. But I must do what I must do." Even though I had no idea what I had to do.

He shook his head. "You are like the man who does not believe a car can hurt him, so he walks without regard to traffic. He is a fool."

"I'd like nothing better than to leave Brazil forever," I said, nettled. "But I have unfinished business, people I can not abandon. I have never run from anybody, and I'm not starting now." Not quite true, as I was fleeing from the Death Squad—but that was a special situation. I could have doubled back and ambushed the Squad any time—but what point, more killing?

He shook his head. "I admire your courage."

A small man came over. "Pardon my interruption," he said in a husky voice. "But are you not, under all that dirt, Jason Striker, who broke from prison?"

Trouble already! I tensed, ready to move the moment he did. "Yes. And I know the Death Squad is after me. And now Exu has cursed me, but I'm going to hell in my own fashion, if you please."

But he broke into a smile. "Do you not recognize me?" He removed his hat—and lo, it was a girl, with a freckled face and thick curly red hair. In fact, it was—

"Ester Behar, whom you tried to help," she said, poking one finger into her mouth to draw the lip aside and reveal the clotted socket of the back tooth that had been extracted. "I saw you when Mirabal the butcher tried to make you recognize me, and I heard you fight him and get knocked down. I heard your screams as they tortured you, and when they stopped I thought you were dead, and I was very sorry. Then the explosion, and my friends from MR-8 came to free me, and I learned it was because of you. I owe you my freedom, perhaps even my life. I came here to seek peace for my soul, and only now entered the mass. I am Jewish, but so many of my friends come here that I—" She paused, embarrassed. I understood that her rabbi would frown on her attendance here, but she had been through a truly horrible experience, and perhaps her faith had been shaken. In times of severe stress, beliefs can change. I knew! "And lo, you are here, as if the gods summoned you," she concluded. "Now maybe I can repay you personally."

"Thanks," I said, relieved. "It's enough that you're free. But I doubt you can do much about a god's curse."

"So? I regret I was not on hand to see what happened. Which god—?"

"Exu," I said. "My best friend will kill me, because I robbed the god's offerings."

Ester made a silent whistle. "Exu's like that! He is Satan in our pantheon, you know. The literal devil. Another god might have shrugged it off, comprehending your need, but not Exu. He'll have your hide, if not your very soul."

"So I'm told. But I was hungry, and my pants were falling down. The things were just going to waste, or so it seemed at the time. I used the money to help this girl buy something at a voodoo store, and she brought me here." I spread my hands.

Now Oba spoke in Portuguese. Apparently she had grasped enough of the exchange so that she was able to verify my story.

The *pai-de-Santo* nodded. "She says she lost strength suddenly after dancing six hours, and you helped her, and then she bought an elixir of strength so as to dance some more, but was moved instead to bring you here. She does not know why she decided this, but it is evident the god cast his net for you. Does this not seem beyond coincidence, even to a skeptic?"

"The god could have punished me better by poisoning the food I took," I said.

"Strange that Exu should punish this man," Ester remarked to the *pai-de-Santo.* "We know that sometimes ignorant foreigners rob the gods, especially with things of value for their museums, yet they are not punished."

"They are punished by being foreigners," the *pai-de-Santo* said.

Ester nodded dubiously. "This man has already been punished much. He is marked, because he resisted the torture and helped us all get free. He is a friend to the freedom fighters and an enemy to Mirabal the butcher. He did not mean to insult the god. We were all so desperate to get away before the army came—"

The *pai-de-Santo* raised his hands in a gesture of mock surrender—curiously modern, in this setting—and nodded. "Enough. It is evident that Exu's wrath is poorly chosen. Perhaps another god will abate the spell."

He gave directions, and the dance changed. Six of the girls retired to the sidelines, and one took the floor alone. She wore white, with white beads, and carried a little white cotton flag, and to my eyes was the most elegant of the group.

Ester sat down beside me on the right, while Oba remained on the left, seemingly oblivious to our dialogue. The *pai-de-Santo* moved back to the center tables.

"That is the dancer for Oxala, called Obatala in the Spanish-language regions," she said. "I was raised across the border, and this really isn't my religion, so sometimes I get the forms confused, but the essence is the same." She hardly needed to make such apology; I would never know the difference, and I was glad to have her explanations. "Oxala is the chief of the gods, and his color is white, signifying purity. If he helps you, you are saved, for he alone is stronger than Exu."

"*I* had no idea there was such a hierarchy," I murmured. "It's almost like an ancient religion."

She snorted. "*Almost?* Umbanda is a *modern* religion! It's one of the Brazilian forms of *Santeria,* which is an amalgam of Black African voodoo and Roman Catholicism." As I had recollected on my own—but she evidently had much more specific information. "The very term 'Santeria' means the worship of Saints. The voodoo gods are really the same as the Saints. Santeria as a whole has more actual devotees than any other religion in the Western Hemisphere. Many people *profess* Christianity, but they *practice* Santeria." She said this with a certain smug emphasis. She, of Jewish background, could afford to sneer at the Christian foibles, of course. Yet she herself was a kind of devotee, and she had evidently studied this Santeria, or Umbanda, more than merely casually.

"But black magic—" I protested, upset that someone as intelligent as Ester was should believe such nonsense.

"It is more than magic," she assured me. Then: "Look—Oxala has rejected the appeal. It is not wise to express skepticism when making such an appeal for help from the god."

Good point! Either I wanted voodoo help, or I didn't. A bad attitude would get me nowhere. I couldn't see that any signal had been made by the god, but maybe that was the point. No action on an appeal is the same as negative action. Had I thrown away my best chance?

Now the second dancer came forth. Her gown was red, and her necklace was red and white. While Oxala's girl had been serene and pure, this one was passionate. She carried a small double-edged axe in her right hand, and she waved it about with such animation that I was afraid it would fly loose and hurt someone.

"That's Xango," Ester said. "Known in Spanish as Chango, the most popular and colorful god of fire and thunder. There are many fascinating legends about him; he is quite a lady's god, with one wife and two mistresses for a start, and a roving eye. Perhaps that is why he is known in the Catholic system as Saint Barbara."

"Saint Barbara!" I exclaimed. "A *female* saint?"

"Xango sometimes dresses as a woman," Ester said with a smile. "It is to honor his sister and mistress Oya, who saved him from prison. Actually, a number of men dress as women during festivals. Haven't you seen them?"

I had, but that was not my immediate concern. "But a legitimate Catholic saint," I protested. "And female, at that! Is nothing sacred?"

"All is sacred," she assured me. "Haven't you noticed that Saint Barbara has a small castle at her feet, and in her hands holds a sword and cup? All these objects are sacred to Xango. And red is the color of both saint and god. They say the castle is where Saint Barbara was killed for her Christian belief, but still—"

"But a *saint*—" the enormity of it overwhelmed me.

"I see you still do not understand. The gods of Santeria came with the slaves from Africa. At first these were suppressed by the Christian masters, but then the slaves recognized behind the facades of the saints their true identities, the ancient and venerable voodoo pantheon of gods. And so their faith was restored, stronger than before. They had the best of both religions. Is it any wonder they have such conviction?"

"I suppose not," I said, shaking my head. Voodoo and Catholic saints! Then something else occurred to me. "A castle." For I remembered the Black Castle that Fu Antos was building deep in the Amazon jungle; my mission was surely intimately linked with this. Xango—Saint Barbara—Fu Antos—I knew so little, yet already the network of intrigue embraced gods and saints.

The sound of the drums rolled forth like thunder, deafening in this hall, and the candles flared high like flickers of lightning. God of thunder, yes!

But like a storm that passes over with no more than gusts of cold air, the dance crescendoed without response from the god. Xango would not help.

The third girl came out, garbed in green with a brown and black beaded necklace. She wore bright metal bracelets, anklets, and headdress, with a polished steel girdle. Knives flashed in her hands. The first dancer had been serene, the second passionate; this one was militant, like an Amazon in her armor.

"Oggun, god of war and metals, especially iron," Ester said. "He is Saint Peter in the Catholic pantheon. Very powerful in the hunt. But he is a very close friend of Elegguo, whose aspect Exu you angered."

"So he won't help me either," I said, disappointed.

"That is not certain. He is a bitter enemy of Xango, who took away his wife Oya to be a concubine, and was not even faithful to her. Thus his metal iron is a constant target of Xango's lightning bolts."

"You really have these things worked out!" I exclaimed. "Adultery and quarrels between gods."

But Oggun, too, declined to help. No one, it seemed, wanted to go against the terrible Exu. Not for a mere gringo. I was getting worried. Sure I was a skeptic, but I didn't want that curse hanging over my head if I could avoid it.

The dancer retired, and the next came forth. She wore a yellow and green costume with a golden necklace. She carried a mirror in one hand and an elegant comb made of shells in the other, and as she danced she ran that comb constantly through her flowing blond tresses.

"Oshun, goddess of love, marriage, and gold—your Venus," Ester murmured. "She controls river waters, so if you plan to sail on fresh water, her blessing would be invaluable. She loves to dance, and is always much fun."

I could believe it. Despite her manifest vanity, preening and combing her hair and constantly checking her face in the mirror, this dancer exuded pure sex appeal. She had hips of perfect rondure and she flung them about in a manner calculated to inflame the masculine passion. Her large breasts seemed about to pop out of her halter, and her gaze, seemed to fix directly on me with a "come hither" appeal. She flirted shamelessly with the audience.

"Do not expect too much of her," Ester warned me. "She is Xango's sister and his mistress. She once freed Xango from confinement by flirting with the skeleton that stood guard. While she aroused it, Xango escaped."

"She aroused a skeleton? Sex—uh, romantically?"

"That she did. She is remarkably desirable. But she is terrible when angry."

"Women are," I agreed, remembering certain experiences.

"She is the goddess of money and all things yellow. If you need money, do not eat a pumpkin, for that is sacred to Oshun. She made the first lamp by hollowing out a pumpkin and placing a candle inside it."

"A jack-o-lantern!" I exclaimed.

She shrugged. "At any rate, she also declines."

"Too bad," I agreed as the dancer retired. I was really disappointed, and not just because of her beauty. My inconsequential remarks were only glossing over my deepening conviction that there was, indeed, something to this voodoo. Those people were too serious, their ceremonies too well worked out. Their gods were too—human.

The next dancer wore green and yellow, and her beads were the same. She was neither serene nor passionate, neither warlike nor sexy. She was intense, with staring eyes that seemed to see entirely through me. My nervousness increased.

"Orunla, god of divination," Ester said. "Master of the past, present, and future, owner of the Table of Ifa."

"The Table of Ifa," I repeated. "The shells—"

"Yes, the *caracoles* apply to the Table of Ifa. Orunla governs all time. He alone can tell you your fate, and thereby enable you to ameliorate the curse."

"Orunla, give me a sign!" I breathed prayerfully.

"That is the first step," Ester said approvingly. "When you begin to believe in the gods, the gods begin to believe in you.

Perhaps it is your North American arrogance of skepticism that really bothers Exu. When he has humbled you, he will be merciful."

"In a pig's eye!" I snapped, abruptly revolted at my descent into superstition.

And the dancer returned, without any signal of aid. And I felt sudden loss, as though salvation had been near at hand, but lost because of my foolish obstinacy.

"Exu will never forgive you now," Ester said sadly. "When will you Americans learn? There is more to life than hot dogs and big new cars. The almighty dollar is powerless against the wrath of a god."

"Sorry," I said contritely. This was these people's religion, and I owed it the same respect I had for any religion. A little respect could certainly do me no harm.

The sixth dancer came forth. She wore a blue robe, with a blue and white necklace. She was older than the others, mature, yet possessed of such sheer beauty and aplomb that all the others seemed like mere children in comparison. They were girls; this was a woman.

"Yemanja," Ester said appreciatively. "Goddess of the moon, and of the sea. See how she moves her canoe."

Indeed, the dancer's hips swayed like rolling waves, the blue of her costume rippling with a frill of white, like whitecaps. She was a stately queen.

"Pray to her," Ester suggested. "In your heart as well as your head. Abase yourself before her. She is your last hope; the minor gods can not help you against Exu."

And I believed her. "Help me, Queen-Goddess Yemanja!" I whispered.

The dance continued, and I knew with a sinking certainty that my plea had not been heard. There was no way to balk the curse of Exu. But it was almost worth a curse to watch the unearthly beauty of Yemanja's ritual.

Then something dark crept out from under the table. It was a huge black roach. It moved toward the dancing woman.

I lurched to my feet with an inarticulate cry like a *kiai!* yell. I dived for that roach as if it were Mirabal himself, seeking to crush it before it brought its hideous ugliness to soil the elegance of the Queen. But the thing skittered sidewise, perhaps blown by the force of my rush, and I rolled ignominiously on the floor. I was aware that my antic had probably wiped out my last chance for godly aid; I heard the shocked murmuring of the crowd. At that moment the drums stopped.

In the sudden silence I lay on my back, looking up. It was quite an experience, for my head was almost under the dancer's skirts where she stood frozen, and I saw her marvelously well-formed legs right up to their juncture, and that wondrous bush of golden curls. I stiffened—and I don't mean sexually, though maybe that was also the cause—for the roach was now climbing her left leg.

She stooped, reached around and under with one hand, and caught the roach neatly between her fingers. She brought it struggling to her round face, peered at it with her large, long-lashed eyes—and popped it into her expressive mouth. She chewed, savoring it.

There was a gasp from the audience. "It is the sign!" the *pai-de-Santo* cried, in what language I knew not, cared not. "Yemanja grants her favor!"

Suddenly the drums resumed. The dancer stepped out again. I rolled giddily to my feet, my mind's eye still seeing that lovely mouth consuming that horrible cockroach, but also seeing those magnificent thighs beneath the skirt—no panties. What horror melded to what bliss!

"The cockroach is sacred to the goddess, you see," Ester explained as I approached the bench. She acted as if nothing special had happened, which should have given me pause for thought. Just what did they expect at these shindigs? "A person possessed by the goddess will consume any roaches she finds, and they are considered to be messengers."

The dancer whirled and gestured, and swooped near to me as

I started to sit, a bit dazed. She wiggled her fingers in a little "Come hither" gesture, and I had to respond. I stepped toward her again, and now the beat caught hold of my soul as though I had stepped into the strong central current of a deep river, not a river of carnival celebrants, but something much more vital and subtle. I danced too, spinning and raising my bare feet in a crude approximation of her movements. I could not help myself, though a part of me felt like a complete buffoon. In her devious, horrible fashion a goddess had smiled on me, showing me heaven where I expected hell and vice versa, and I had to worship her.

Yet it was only the beginning. There was a cry, and the girl I had dubbed Oba jumped to her feet, chanting. After her followed others, until it seemed the whole congregation was dancing to that compelling beat. Like the ponderous waves of the ocean it swelled and faded, making us twitch in harmony with its devious syncopations. On and on we danced, tirelessly, now in silence, now crying out.

Again, how much later I do not know, the drums stopped. The dance subsided. The *pai-de-Santo* occupied the center of the floor. "Yemanja, mother of gods, shows her favor to this man," he announced. "But we must ascertain the nature of that favor."

He brought out the divination shells again, and cast them. After several throws he announced. "Yemanja will accept sacrifice. But we must learn what type."

He brought out a coconut, set it on the table, and broke the hard shell with one strike of a special hammer. There was no milk; the coconut had evidently been dried so that the pulp was hard and white. He broke it into four equal parts, inspected them carefully, washed them in water, and tore seven bits off each. He sprinkled these bits over the image of Our Lady of Regla.

"Seven bits, to invoke Yemanja," Ester explained. "It is different for each god."

How nice: like dialing a telephone. Each god had his number.

The *pai-de-Santo* chanted strange words as he did this. Talking to the operator? Then he held the four pieces of coconut in his left hand. With his right hand he touched the floor three times, and the image three times. Then he prayed, and the congregation spoke in unison at certain intervals, as in a responsive reading. He made the sign of the cross and finished the invocation. Finally he threw the four pieces on the floor.

Each piece was white on the inside and brown outside, so when they fell they showed white or brown. In this case, three were brown and one white.

There was an immediate reaction among the spectators. All around, people pulled at the lobes of their ears and opened their eyes wide.

"*Ocana-Sode*, that cast is called, where I come from," Ester said. "In any language, it means evil for you. The people are trying to dispel that evil—but this is a bad sign." And she pulled delicately at her own lobe.

"The goddess changed her mind?" I asked worriedly, and caught my own hand going to my ear.

"Perhaps. Or maybe she is powerless to abate the spell of Exu, who is stronger than she."

The *pai-de-Santo* looked up. "We must now make sacrifice," he said. "Only this can bring us help."

Now he fetched a live duck from an adjacent room. My skin tightened, for I suspected what was coming and did not like it. But Ester put a restraining hand on my arm. "It is necessary," she said. "Do not, in your ignorance, insult another god."

Good advice! I kept silent.

The *pai-de-Santo* smeared honey and lard over the hapless bird, then poured rum over it. He then used the coconut fragments to inquire whether the goddess required the actual blood of the duck. I chewed on my tongue, hoping she would decline, but the fall of the throw was one brown and three white: a qualified yes. He verified it with another throw.

Now he got a good grip on the duck's head, took out the sacrificial knife, and cut that head off with a violent slash. I felt as if my own head were coming loose. As a judo instructor I deal in violence, but also in fair play; the notion of an innocent bird giving its life without even a chance to fight back appalled me. Was I myself a similar victim?

"Oggun killed it!" he stated loudly.

"Now that's a lie," I protested.

Again Ester restrained me. "Part of the ritual. All killing is done in the name of the god of war, so that no blame will attach for the act. Oggun doesn't mind, and it saves a lot of trouble."

I shut up. After all, I was the cause of all this.

The *pai-de-Santo* held the bleeding carcass before the image, letting the blood drip to the floor. Then he wiped it up with a handful of the bird's own feathers. Finally he placed the bird in a burner and started it roasting. I thought of the ovens of Nazi Germany, cremating innocents.

The dance resumed, and while it continued the fire consumed the body of the sacrificial duck, until it was nothing but ashes.

And then, as if it were an instant, it was morning. The beat stopped and the congregation dispersed. Ester had disappeared, somewhat to my disappointment; she must have figured she had thanked me enough by explaining everything. We had danced all night!

The *pai-de-Santo* caught me aside for a private conference. "You may not have understood everything," he said. "Exu laid a curse on you, and Yemanja has abated it, but she could not nullify it entirely. So she sends her daughter to protect you; as long as she is with you, the thrust of the spell will be blunted. But if she becomes separated from you, only the willing sacrifice of a loved one will save you from death at the hands of your friend, and even then, it is not certain. This is as far as the goddess can go."

"Tell her thank you," I said, and I meant it. I was too tired to be very expressive. Then my brow furrowed. "Her daughter?"

"Goddess of an African river and wife of Xango," he explained. "You have found favor with her—I do not profess to know why—and so she cooperates with her mother to animate a human body, and to guard you from evil." He winked. "Do not be concerned about her married state; Xango has nothing to do with her, instead preferring her sisters Oya and Oshun. He will not be jealous."

"Oshun?" I repeated. "Isn't she—?"

"Yes, she is the goddess of love and gold, whose dance you saw. Perhaps it is because she turned you down that her sister helps you. Oba was always jealous of her husband's mistresses, and perhaps wishes to give him a certain taste of his own medicine."

Oshun—Miss Sex Appeal! I could see why a god would prefer her to his homebody wife, and why that wife would be resentful. Then I did a doubletake. *"Who?"*

"Oba," he repeated, gesturing. And now the girl I had called Oba came forward and took my hand, leading me out of the building.

Stunned but hardly dismayed, I went with her.

Chapter 7:

March on the Black Castle

"Well, my dear," Mirabal said, smiling like Frankenstein's monster, "you caused us much trouble. You made so neat an escape from our private detention center that I am surprised we recaptured you so readily. Why didn't you vacate the area immediately, once you saw the prison break was successful?"

Dulce didn't answer. This was her first meeting with this man, and she was apprehensive. The leader of the Death Squads—what could she expect at his hands but torture?

"It could not be that you are stupid, for you are not," he continued imperturbably. "You are one of the most brilliant and talented of the Horse's spies." This was an unsubtle slur on the head of the government of her own country; Fidel Castro was said by his enemies—and some of his friends—to smell like a sweaty horse, owing to his laxity about personal hygiene. But Dulce did not react. "Yet I doubt it could be a plot to assassinate me or any high ranking member of our government, for you are known to us, and would never be given the chance to act. Of course you are very capable with your bare hands, but you would require more than that to overcome me."

Still she did not reply. Mirabal so far had been completely accurate; Dulce was a trained fighter, but so was he, and he had monstrous layers of muscle she lacked, as well as being completely ruthless. Few, very few human beings could overcome Fernando Mirabal in honest barehanded combat, and he was not one to confine himself to honest methods.

"You could not have had anything to do with certain recent assassinations," he continued. "You had already been taken into custody when they occurred, and they were far away. Do bees mean anything to you? Spiders? Privies?" Her gaze was blank. "No, I thought not. So it would appear you have no connection to those activities. You are a leftist agent, not a ninja."

He walked around the room, pondering aloud. "I always like to know the truth," he said. "Illusion can be costly to those engaged in counterespionage. We have already lost an entire town by underestimating our opposition. So I ask myself why this luscious Cuban plum, so difficult to grasp and hold, should now fall so easily into my hand, and I must have an answer. Why should you merely wait in a building facing the prison, until it was too late to escape the tightening police cordon? One might postulate all manner of reasons, but overcomplexity is treacherous. Better to explore the simplest: that it was an accident, unintentional on your part. Then why should you be so careless? And I have only one answer: love."

Now her pert nose wrinkled as she made an inaudible sniff of derision. She was absolutely lovely in that pose, though her hands and feet were tied.

"Ah, my dear, do not disdain that tender passion," he chided her, his soft words incongruous, coming from so huge and brutal a man. "For the love of one man you roused the revolutionary groups to attack the prison, and actually succeeded in freeing him. Jason Striker—yes, I see it in your eyes! You would do anything to save him from torture or death. Anything at all! Yet you dare not express it openly, for El Caballo would not approve." He chuckled. El Caballo meant "The Top" in Spanish. In Cuba it was a term of respect for Fidel, but Mirabal used it derisively. "I must admit the Horse has good taste in some matters. And so you waited, heedless of your own safety, waited to meet the gringo, lest he become lost in the great city, and be recaptured because of his ignorance of our custom and language. But he was swept into the festival crowd, his pants falling down, and he was victim of that same distraction you so prettily planned for the prison authorities, and could not get back to you, and so it was my men who completed your liaison instead. Such irony, that the prisoner goes free, while his rescuer is made captive! Normally it is the prince who frees the lady at great peril to himself, not the other way around."

Dulce made no sound, but her lips formed a word in Portuguese: *"Puerco,"* pig.

"You will be pleased to know that Striker remains free," Mirabal said. "You need not have troubled yourself about him; I was about to release him anyway."

Now at last she reacted overtly. "Liar!" she snapped.

"Why should I lie to you?" he inquired. "You are powerless. I inform you only that you may understand what I wish you to understand—when the time comes. You shall quite possibly be of inestimable service to me." He paused, but she had no comment. "I interrogated the American, and learned that he was on a mission for Fu Antos, the chief of the Japanese ninjas, an old time warrior cult who have recently infiltrated our inland forest region. Striker's meeting with you was coincidence; that led me astray for a time, for I thought it had to be by design. Since it is important to me to locate and eliminate the ninja villain, I decided to allow Striker to 'escape,' aided by one of my agents within the prison, then watch where he went. If he led me to the Black Castle and its oil strike . . ." He shook his head. "Alas, Fu Antos outsmarted me. I could have sworn from his actions and reactions that Striker was just a bumbling fool possessing no information of value. Therefore I was sure he was a courier of vital news. And lo, he fooled me completely, by being exactly what he seemed to be. He was merely an ignorant decoy. While I wasted my attention tracing his aimless wanderings through the city, the ninja was receiving a vast shipment of weapons via the river." He shook his head in grudging admiration. "Who would have thought a martial artist of Striker's reputation would come all the way to Brazil merely to serve as a distraction! I could not anticipate that, and but for chance, that ploy would have been successful. But now I have no further need of the American."

Dulce could no longer feign indifference. "You lie again. You hate Jason. You are holding me to lure him into a trap."

"I do hate him. He injured me in our prior encounter in New York, and for that his life is forfeit. Which is the beauty of it: the ninja knew I would focus on Striker immediately, and so run the risk of overlooking more important matters. So—"

"But it will not work. Jason will never do your bidding from fear of my torture."

"Torture you?" Mirabal inquired, raising an eyebrow. It was a minor gesture, but it displayed the type of bodily control that made him a formidable fighter. Whether twitching a brow or hammering with a fist, his coordination was perfect. "No, my dear, you shall not be tortured. I would not have one bit of you disfigured. And you are right: Striker would not be moved. He loves you less than you love him, and neither knows nor cares where you are. He is with a lithe young girl he met in the streets, a seamstress and dancer, and now he sleeps off his night's endeavors in her apartment." Dulce's eyes flared, but she did not dignify his taunt by giving it the lie.

"Striker has in any event become superfluous," Mirabal said. "I shall allow one of my squads to obtain the practice of the chase this afternoon, after the American is suitably rested. There is no sport like the pursuit of live prey! The men shall gain invaluable experience as they track him down and make their kill, and the unfit among them will no doubt be destroyed. Striker has a certain talent in the rough and tumble; it makes up for what he lacks in wit." And he rubbed the back of one knee reflectively, again remembering his own initial encounter with the subject. Then he returned to Dulce: "No, my dear, you need have no fears. You shall have the very best, until I have need of you." And he shaped his huge gnarl-calloused hands around the rope between her wrists, tensed his astonishing muscles, and snapped it like so much string. Then he did the same for her feet, freeing her. More than ever, he resembled Frankenstein's monster, except that the monster had been, at heart, innocent.

"You should have left me tied!" she cried. "You'll have to take me by force! I'll never submit voluntarily."

"You misunderstand, my voluptuous beauty," he said. "I have no personal desire for your body." But he loosened his belt and dropped his trousers, uncovering his phenomenally muscled legs. Dulce might have attacked him at that moment, while his ankles were temporarily hobbled, but she knew he was alert and would give her no chance. He could kill her with one blow of his horny fist, literally, and *would.*

He removed his undershorts, revealing his elephantine genital dangling like a python. Suddenly his left hand shot out, catching her elbow. He hauled her into him, and like, a bird caught in the coils of a deadly snake she suffered herself to be enfolded without resistance. He drew her up, running his right hand over her breasts, squeezing them through the cloth of her dress, inserting his fingers into her cleavage. Then the hand traveled down over her abdomen, across her swelling hip, and around to enclose her buttocks in a firm pinch. His head tilted down; he lifted her by the buttocks as though hoisting a child, and kissed her lips.

"No, my dear, I shall not place my tongue between your pearly teeth," he murmured, giving her posterior a final penetrating goose. Then he let her go and stood back.

His naked penis remained completely limp.

He had proved his point. He was physically unmoved by her sex appeal.

"What do you want with me?" Dulce asked, half relieved, half insulted. "I know nothing of Fu Antos."

"I am aware of that. We have virtually located the Black Castle. I have maintained surveillance of all unusual traffic on the tributaries of the Amazon River, a Herculean task. My agents pinpointed the freighter carrying the weapons as soon as they were loaded on it near Key West, and we have monitored its radio calls. We moved in at the time of transfer to the smaller boats, but never hindered the procedure. Thus we have located our quarry: a convoy of small boats carrying weapons for the ninja. Already my men, posing as itinerant workers, have eliminated the ninja representatives, quietly; my own personnel now man the crafts. Thus we shall have safe access to the Black Castle of the Ninjas, trusting them to guide us in. Is it not beautiful?"

Dulce had no knowledge of the Black Castle or the ninjas, but she was interested in another aspect. "Then I am of no use to you," she said, hoping he would let her go. She might yet be able to warn Jason.

"On the contrary, you are my insurance," Mirabal said. "In my researches into the history of the ninja cult—I always study my enemy carefully—I came upon a truly remarkable coincidence." He studied her for a moment. "Yes, you are perfect. The gods have truly smiled on me this day."

Then he left her, carrying his trousers in one hand, his limp member still proclaiming its disinterest.

"*Maricon!*" she exclaimed in her native tongue, with amazed realization. "He is a homosexual!" Or at any rate, a sexually indifferent man. Some were like that.

Still, she was unable to fathom the meaning of his other words. For what was she perfect, if not for information or love? Yet she had a gnawing certainty that she would not like the answer when it finally came clear.

*

The captain of the lead boat kept his eyes open as the river narrowed. He was on his own; Mirabal would not join the party or indicate his involvement in any other way until the battle was joined, lest his arrival by helicopter tip off the ninjas. No word of this mission had been allowed out; even the troops did not know where they were going or why. In fact, no one knew; there had been neither time nor privacy to torture the prior captain for information about the precise landing or identification codes. Probably the man hadn't known anyway; the ninjas would intercept the convoy at their convenience. That was when it would get hairy. Was it really possible to outfox the foxes?

It was night. Slowly the boats moved on upriver, using only those lights required for safety. There was no signal from the shore.

Then a voice spoke from the gloom of the dark cabin. "Captain."

A chill ran down the captain's spine. He turned. He could barely make out a hooded figure. How it had come aboard the boat without detection he could not guess, but its very presence was all the evidence necessary. This was a living ninja!

"Yes," the captain said. If there were a secret password, he would soon be dead, but he was under orders to take that gamble and he knew better than to disobey. He had seen a few of the victims of Fernando Mirabal's displeasure.

"To the right. Dock," the ninja said in bad Portuguese. The captain turned the wheel. The boats behind followed. There was a small, dilapidated-looking wooden pier half-concealed by the jungle. It was just like a thousand others scattered along the Amazon River system. The pilings were rotten and the planking was overgrown by vegetation. But underneath it was strong, braced by new timber, the exterior carefully preserved as a facade. It was, in a sense, invisible: no one would have thought to use it or even approach it, ordinarily.

A number of Indians were on hand with mules to help unload

the shipment. Many of the cases were small but heavy, containing disassembled machine guns, bazookas, ammunition and grenades. Many were sealed in oil drums or wrapped in tarpaulins. They were not hard for one or two men to handle.

But soon the Indians grew suspicious. Certain code-signals were not forthcoming. Hands went for weapons.

And there was a barrage of fire from the boats. "Get the ninja!" the captain cried—and fell, a knife in his back. The men charged, but already he was dead, the ninja gone. Obviously the ninja had realized before that this was not the original crew, but had allowed the unloading to proceed so that his people could ambush the troops and recover the supplies. The less sophisticated Indians had blown the whistle prematurely, and perhaps that had been fortunate.

A crewman used a radio. "They're on to us," he said. "We killed the Indians, but the ninja got away. Move up the second convoy fast; no more point in secrecy."

For a few miles back there was another and larger expedition. That one carried mechanized equipment the ninjas had never ordered. Now it would see action.

Under the overhanging trees of the jungle a road had been made. It was cleverly covered over by green turf and even a thin layer of standing water in places, but underneath it was solid. Someone had put a lot of work into this secret highway.

The armored column was on its way, using the ninjas' own jungle turnpike. There was no longer any attempt at concealment; the battle had in effect been joined. Without the prepared road, it would have been impossible. This was the very heart of the continental forest. The trees were large and close together, rising one hundred, one hundred and fifty, and even two hundred feet above the floor. Their upper foliage was luxuriant and interlaced with vines and parasitic growth so that sunlight could not penetrate to the level of the trail. There was therefore hardly any undergrowth, except in occasional grassy gaps in the forest cover. This was the forest primeval.

This was in fact a battalion of the Brazilian army, with eight hundred men accompanied by select armored units. Unlike North American troops, most of the men used their feet instead of riding. There were five light old armored cars, carrying .30 and .50 caliber machine guns, and eight half-tracked personnel carriers bearing the most privileged troops. Five jeeps handled the officers. A tank led the column, and another terminated it, with men riding on each. The convoy moved at the pace of the foot-soldiers, however, slow but sure.

Suddenly the lead tank bogged down. The road had taken a hidden turn under the marshy terrain, and without a ninja guide the machine had blundered off the built-up support. The other vehicles halted, and the men got out, poking about to locate the road. This was only a delay, not a setback.

Then the arrows started flying. Each was tipped with deadly nerve poison; the slightest scratch meant death. A dozen men were dead before the others realized what was happening. Then the cry went up: "Ambush!"

The men dived for cover of their vehicles. The turret of the stalled tank spun about, its machine gun raking the jungle in a semicircle. But it seemed to have no effect.

The arrows continued to fly. They were few but highly selective; virtually every shaft scored on a soldier. The effect was disproportionate to the damage: these weapons made no sound, so the first evidence of their presence was the mortal strike. When the men faced about and watched for the source, the arrows stopped, only to rise silently from the obscurity again when attention wavered. Some shot high into the morning sky, to plummet down on those people taking refuge behind what little natural cover there was.

"And we waited till morning to start our march!" a sergeant gritted. He had known that was folly, but had been overruled by the officers. He was Genaro Cabral, a leader of men, formerly of Major Lima's battalion. He had dropped the TNT bomb into the privy, destroying the dwarf ninja. "Well, we'll stop *that!* First pla-

ANTH

toon, face out in a circle, watch the horizon, fire on the level through the brush when and only when you see an arrow rise. We're bound to nail some of them!" He hoped. This brushy clearing had evidently been chosen by the ninjas because of the cover it provided them; they were probably dug in.

The men of his platoon obeyed with alacrity. A sergeant is the core of any army unit; when crisis comes, he *acts.*

No more arrows came. "All right," the sergeant bawled. "Second Platoon, hitch a chain to that stalled tank and haul it; back onto the road." Strictly speaking, he lacked the authority to give such directives, but no one challenged him.

Now the disciplined troops began to function. The arrow-ambush had seemed devastating at first, but there were actually only twenty casualties, and the psychological effect was being dissipated. Still, the spasms of the dying men had been unnerving; the poison threw one big cramp, and some suffered broken spines, writhing and screaming before their hearts failed. So there was horror in the ranks, but a few primitively armed warriors could not, it seemed, successfully oppose a modern army.

The tank was brought back to the road. Now soldiers went ahead with poles, tapping the ground under the marsh, locating the firm foundation. The convoy moved ahead again.

Unfortunately, the men now fell into the traps laid for the vehicles. There were a lot of traps; evidently the ninjas had worked all night, as the sergeant had feared they would. He had learned something from his experience with the dwarf ninja, but he was the only one here to whom that experience was firsthand. The others thought the stories of the ninjas were exaggerated. Now they were learning the hard way. Five of them dropped into a huge pit, to be speared on the sharpened stakes below. But at least their sacrifice saved the tank. Another masked pit contained a dozen poisonous snakes, who quickly bit the unfortunates who dropped in to visit. Trees had been felled across the road, their surfaces covered with poison so that those who moved them suffered terrible burns and lingering death. Further along, a huge tree toppled right on top of one of the personnel carriers, ruining it; the tree had been cut and propped so that a slight push would bring it down. This sort of thing kept progress slow.

The column entered a thickly wooded section, where the trees were smaller but so close together it was impossible to see far. Here the ground was firm throughout. The vehicles picked up speed.

Then more arrows came—this time spearing the tires of the jeeps. The tanks and halftracks were impervious, but the officers weren't in them. The column slowed to a halt.

"Keep moving!" the sergeant yelled. "It's another ambush!" He knew that it was possible to drive on flat tires, and that this was much safer than stopping exactly where the ninjas wanted them to stop. "Push for that hill! Make a circle at the top! We can defend that better."

His leather-lunged volume made itself felt. The officers, concerned for their health, kept their mouths shut and let the man on the spot handle it. It was not that they were timid or inferior men; they merely yielded to the exigencies of the situation.

The jeeps lunged up the hill, their deflated tires flapping and bumping, while the troops clung tightly to the accompanying vehicles. They lurched into a rough circle at the top, and the men poked their rifles out.

Nothing happened. A crew got out to start fixing the tires, and then a few arrows drove them back. "They're nickel-and-diming us to death!" the sergeant observed in his own vernacular.

The officer in charge thought so too. Small but steady attrition could bring them down in time; it was a tactic used in many parts of the world, even humbling the mighty U S of A in Asia. "Cabral, take a company and clear the area," he ordered. "We'll take some casualties, but it's better than being struck sitting like ducks for their arrows."

And so Sergeant Cabral moved out with his men, alert and wary. They carried Garand M-l rifles at the ready, and some M-3 submachine guns shooting at anything that moved. They encountered no resistance. They did not realize yet that they were entering the mouth of hell.

"Come out and fight like men!" the sergeant bawled. He was a tough old veteran whose words were mainly to keep up morale. He knew the ninjas would never attempt to match the firepower of conventional troops in the open, but if he made them look like cowards, his own men would gain confidence. As Major Lima had stressed (and what a loss his death had been!): the key to success in the jungle was not in the rifle but in the mind.

Amazingly, his challenge was answered. Abruptly green and brown-splotched ninjas showed from behind trees, like so many apparitions. Each loosed a deadly arrow. One of the arrows brought down the bold sergeant; the others took out the remaining non-coms of the company. The nervous soldiers let off a volley of shots—but, confused by the number of targets and trying to duck the incoming arrows, they missed. The figures disappeared; not one had been hit.

Now the company was leaderless. But, aware that there was no way out, the men dropped to the ground and aimed at the trees. There had actually been no more than a score of ninjas, and almost two hundred soldiers remained. "Try that again, why don't you!" one yelled.

And the ninjas did. They manifested before their trees like spirits of the wood. This time the troopers aimed more carefully. Their rifles fired, and the bullets sang around each ninja.

Yet not one of the robed figures fell. Like ghosts they advanced upon the soldiers. Ghosts with bows, for the arrows winged into the faces of the prone men.

"It can't be!" one soldier cried, firing first at one figure, then another. He knew himself to be a dead shot, yet his efforts had no effect.

Now the ninjas opened their hoods—and gaunt skulls were revealed. It was only paint, but it had demoralizing effect, for many of the troops were superstitious. The shots stopped, giving the ninjas time to close the gap.

The ninjas were upon the soldiers. The bows had disappeared; other weapons took their place. Some were *katanas,* the Japanese *Samurai* warrior swords. On the ground, in close quarters, the troops were at a disadvantage. The swords slashed down, cutting arms, legs and heads in half. The men raised their rifles as shields, unable to take effective aim at such close range. But the finely tempered swords sliced right through the metal barrels, rendering the rifles useless even for this.

The soldiers, with the courage of desperation, rose up to grapple their adversaries. But the ninjas were demons in close combat. Their weapons moved devastatingly: spears, halberds, war clubs, maces, *tetsubi* iron bars, a *naginata* like a spear with a blade in the end, chained sickles—each ninja had his favorite death dealer. The weapons were lacquered in black so as not to reflect light. But soon a more deadly aspect manifested: the blades and clubs, like the arrows, were poisoned. The slightest break of skin allowed that potent coating to enter the body, and death followed in seconds. Thus the ninjas were doubly dangerous, despite being outnumbered ten to one. They spread a wide swath of death, merely by nicking as many soldiers as possible. The two hundred became a hundred and forty, then one hundred, and the odds were reduced to five to one.

Among the ninjas was a small man, really a boy, who nevertheless wielded two swords: one long, one short. Yet those two blades were the most devastating of all. For this was Fu Antos, Lord of the Ninjas. He had come late upon the scene, having been occupied with the fortification of the Black Castle and the development of the first oil well. But this subversion of his arms shipment during his inattention had caused him to take a personal interest in rectifying the situation, and to seek a bit of exercise in combat.

Fu Antos whirled this way and that, a dervish of death. Here he lopped off the face of a gaping man; half that face went flying away. There he brought his blade down straight, cleaving a head in twain like split wood. Another he decapitated with a single stroke; the corpse stood there a moment spouting blood. Fu Antos was a miniature berserker of slaughter, never tiring; his *ki* gave him the strength of several grown men.

Now three men pressed in on him. With incredible power, the ninja master brought his two swords together in truncated arcs, cutting the two side men in half at the waist and meeting in the torso of the center man. For an instant the tableau remained; three surprised soldiers staring at the little ninja. Then the two side bodies toppled, rolling apart, and the third sank down with a kind of squish.

Another soldier was leveling his rifle at Fu Antos' head. The ninja's two swords whirled. The short one lopped off the tip of the rifle; the long one swished by the front of the soldier's face. The man's nose flew off. A flick of the wrist, and Fu Antos speared that nose in the tip of his short sword. Then he returned it to the man, pinning it to his face by means of the blade. Ungrateful for this cosmetic favor, the man collapsed and died.

The numerical odds were down to four to one. "Run!" someone cried. The soldiers panicked. In a mass the survivors rose up and charged through the jungle toward their convoy.

The ninjas did not follow. Instead they brought out their bows again and loosed a shower of arrows at the fleeing body of men. And by the time the troops made it back to the trucks, only twenty remained.

"Ghosts with swords!" they gasped. "They cannot be killed! Our bullets won't touch them!"

"Bullshit!" a lieutenant snapped. "They must be wearing bullet-proof cloaks. All you have to do is grapple with them, smother them in their own folds." But he looked nervous.

Meanwhile, the tires had not been fixed, and the convoy remained stalled. It had a good defensive position, and the machine guns and tank-mounted cannon could destroy ninjas no matter what they were wearing.

"Radio for reinforcements," the officer said. "We need special equipment to deal with this. Flame throwers, bazookas. We'll clean them out, all right."

Again, Fu Antos agreed. The elimination of Major Lima had blunted the Brazilian army's jungle-fighting capacity, but here and there competent officers remained, and they tended to surface at awkward moments. The bulk of the convoy sat tight; the battle had only begun. Those six hundred soldiers could overrun the Black Castle's incomplete ramparts, and there were reinforcements coming for the army, none for the ninjas. They had to be stopped here in the jungle. It was necessary to destroy the personnel, not the equipment, so that the ninjas could use the weapons they had expected to obtain.

The ninja leader, contemplating the convoy from his forest cover, smiled. The infiltration of the ninja's own shipment by the soldiers had been a brilliant tactical stroke. He should have anticipated it and taken precautions, but he had been so busy with the construction of the castle and related matters that he had not paid proper attention to the opposition, and could blame no one but himself. Once this youthful body grew to manhood, he would make fewer such mistakes. And he had to give credit to the leader of the opposition: Fernando Mirabal. That was the man who stood most in need of assassination—and Fu Antos had let him go free after having him in his power. Calamitous misjudgment!

Well, perhaps he would get another chance at Mirabal. If the man showed up anywhere near the Black Castle, and he was bound to. He would not escape the reckoning of the ninja. Though in a way it was too bad, for in certain respects Mirabal had a mind that was worthy of respect. In a curious way, that mind was similar to Fu Antos's own.

But at the moment there was more urgent business: to wipe out this formidable force before it came within range of the castle. The cannon, mortars and bazookas could devastate the stoneworks, once they oriented on a clear target. But they would be equally potent in defense of the castle, if they could be captured intact. Yet the soldiers might well blow up their own equipment rather than turn it over. So a proper strategy was called for, to separate men from equipment without damage to the latter.

It was time to initiate the sequence of the elements: Air, Earth, Fire and Water. Air was gentle; it would accomplish this critical separation. The other elements were more brutal, and would have to wait upon the defense of the castle itself.

Fu Antos raised his hand in a signal: AIR. And a ninja runner moved quickly to the ninja smoke-expert, who even now had prepared a wagonful of fine, dry wood shavings. He would move his wagon directly upwind from the convoy and proceed.

Soon it began, for the ninjas were always efficient. The flame crackled up, then dampened as special potions were poured into it. This infusion of Water into Fire had its effect on Air; the smoke thickened, too heavy to gain much altitude. Instead it rolled like a bloated python across the landscape, through the forest toward the convoy. The wind shoved it along, making twists in the snake's giant torso, but the thing kept growing from the muted fire. The ninjas, alert to their own devices, gave that dark vapor a wide berth.

The head of it crossed the convoy: perfect aim. The long torso slithered by, infiltrating the trucks and tanks, curling around the soldiers. It had a sweet, tangy flavor, not unpleasant.

But the officer caught on. "Gas!" he cried.

He was right: this was a ninja form of nerve gas. Many of the same mushrooms that had polluted the town's water supply, bringing madness, were in this smoke. To breathe it was at first exhilarating, but that was the onset of disaster.

There were few gas masks, for this tactic had not been anticipated. Major Lima would have come prepared, but Major Lima had been removed for that very reason. The officers and tank crews had masks, but not the soldiers. A sergeant had a better alternative: "Run!" he bawled. "Get out of the gas! Hold your breath—don't breathe it!"

The men needed little urging. The tank and crews and officers donned their masks; the others fled into the forest.

Then hell broke loose. Vicious animals charged among the

soldiers: wolflike dogs, jaguars, and boars. The beasts looked rabid, for several of them foamed at the mouths. This terrified the soldiers, who did not know that the ninjas had carefully squirted foam into the animals' mouths as they were released. The men fired wildly, but the creatures were already in their midst, and the shots only brought down other soldiers. In addition, several men had inhaled too much of the smoke, and now were enjoying themselves firing right at the handiest targets: their associates. The animals themselves slashed randomly with their tusks, teeth, and claws, seeming to exist only to kill. It was a thorough melee.

Small bags flew through the air to burst at the feet of the men. Small poisonous snakes emerged. They slithered around the feet and legs of the men and started biting. Other bags loosed little wasps, scorpions and stinging flies, with similar effect.

Then monstrous bat-forms swooped down from the trees. They were ninjas, employing gliding kites. In moments they too were among the panicked soldiers, slashing, hitting and mauling. Then they were gone again, leaving many more soldiers dead.

Now only the gas-masked men remained with the convoy. The ninjas ran toward it, and the vicious animals let them pass because they wore a special repellent.

The turrets of the two tanks swung about as the ninjas approached. But it was difficult for the men to orient well while wearing gas masks, and vision from inside a tank is seldom ideal anyway. The ninjas gestured at the tanks, drawing their fire, then dropped out of sight before the aim could be adjusted.

But even a confused tank is dangerous. The lead one charged forward, its treads crunching the ground where the ninjas had disappeared, grinding up the turf. The ninjas could no longer be secure in their invisibility; they had to scramble out of the way. One was too slow, and the tank crushed his legs. Destroyed but not dead, the ninja reached inside his uniform, grabbed a packet of poison, and popped it into his mouth. Then he died, satisfied that he could not be interrogated.

Meanwhile, Fu Antos quickly got in under the guns and clambered onto the moving tank. He emptied a bag of itching powder into the vent.

Like all ninja products, it was superior grade. The men inside went wild as the fine material sifted down into their uniforms, aggravating the skin intolerably. If there is anything worse than ants in the pants, it is itching powder in a tank. In moments the tank, too, was vacant, the masks off.

The second tank was orienting its cannon on Fu Antos. He jumped down and used the other vehicles of the convoy as cover, so that it could not fire. The other ninjas had already dispatched the officers in the jeeps, but the tank crew could not know that. Then he skated two *tonki,* little throwing knives, in through the forward apertures of the tank. No other man could have made such accurate throws.

The tank hesitated, while the crewmen inside shifted places, the living and the dead. Fu Antos mounted it during that hesitation, and poured liquid Greek Fire down the vent. Flame erupted. Now the tank was dead.

Fu Antos's mighty *ki* protected him from the narcotic smoke, but even he was not entirety immune. He moved out of it before it affected his mind.

The battle still raged in the jungle. The soldiers, mobbing the outnumbered ninjas, had at last brought down several. One ninja was struck amidships by a bazooka shot, and simply disintegrated. Another was caught close-range in the stream of bullets from an M-3 machine gun. Though his cloak protected him somewhat, the sheer impact knocked him over. Two other men emptied their guns into him at point blank range. Each bullet hit close upon the last, so that the effect was cumulative, and he was battered to death without ever suffering perforation.

With ninja casualties mounting, it was time to break off. Fu Antos made a signal, and abruptly the ninjas departed.

But now the wind shifted. The awful smoke rolled toward the remaining men. Again they ran. But that meant the smoke no longer covered the convoy.

The ninjas reappeared. They climbed into the deserted vehicles. But they were not able to operate the tanks or personnel carriers, lacking the knowledge. So they planted explosives and blew them up after unloading the cases of weapons and ammunition.

Hidden in the forest, they opened the cases, so as to transfer the supplies to more convenient carrying form. And they received a shock. The first case, marked GRENADES, contained a jack-in-the-box with a face like Mirabal's, its tongue sticking out. And a note saying "Congratulations! You have just become the proud owner of this box of rocks." And the rest was—stone.

Mirabal had outsmarted the ninja after all.

So far.

Chapter 8:

The Love of Oba

Now Oba took me to her apartment. Actually it was both more and less than that. It was in a big two-story house in one of the poorer sections of town, that had been partitioned into small rooms, each occupied by a person, couple, or family. We passed into a central courtyard, with a communal laundry, and thence up to her room.

She opened a round red can of guava paste labeled *Conchita,* cutting out some pieces and putting them on hard soda crackers from a big square box. I didn't know what it was, so she put one in my mouth. I chewed dutifully, and it was delicious. I gulped some cool water, and that was delicious too. In fact, I was feeling very good, riding an ebbing wave of euphoria. Then she showed me her bed, and suddenly my day and night of action caught up with me, and I lay on that bed like a felled tree.

It was late afternoon when I woke. Oba was gone. I was not worried; I knew she had other things to do besides watch me snore. She had left some more food on the table where I would find it: a pot of black coffee, more crackers and paste, and some tasty soft white cheese. Simple fare, but good. I checked the little ice chest, but there seemed to be no milk. That's the difference between me and the Brazilians: I'm a milk drinker. Ah, well: coffee, then, and fresh-baked bread.

She had also left two big crumpled dirty blue and red 10-cruzeiro notes for me. I was especially touched by this gesture; this was probably all she could spare, though it was only about two and a half dollars in American money. Well, I would repay her. I pocketed the money.

I ate quickly, then cleaned up. God, I was filthy! I had forgotten about the dirt I had smeared over myself yesterday. I must have been a real spectacle, dancing in that black mass in my bare feet and caked dirt. I found a razor and shaved, aware that the instrument's normal use would have been on the legs of a pretty girl. Odd that so many women shave their legs to silken smoothness, but not their arms. Just which limbs do they expect to bear the closest scrutiny?

There was a bidet in the room. You know, one of those strange female saddle-shaped urinals they use in Europe. What the hell: I straddled it as well as I could and relieved my bladder. I had encountered one of those things when I attended the martial-arts tournament in Nicaragua, and it really set me back. It conjured all sorts of half-obscene visions—bare distaff posteriors squirting fluid, that sort of thing—well, I never claimed to be sexually sophisticated. I got a kind of kick out of using it, and had to finish up quickly before getting a masculine reaction. If I ever write my memoirs, that sort of detail won't be in them, though. Don't we all have thoughts we are ashamed of!

I looked around the room. I had been oblivious to its detail, yesterday—actually this morning, but it *seemed* like yesterday—but now I was rested and had idle time. The windows had heavy red drapes, and from one of them I could see the big Maracana Stadium. There was a radio but no TV, a big dresser with a mirror, the table with its two chairs—and that was about it for furniture, apart from the bed. Oba was obviously not rich. There were pictures of Saint Lazarus, a leper with two dogs, and Saint Barbara with a sword in one hand and a small castle behind her. That of course reminded me of my remarkable evening.

There was an old Singer sewing machine, one of the non-electric pedal jobs, and a clothing dummy, and bolts of cloth, patterns, spools of thread and such like. She was evidently a seamstress in her spare time, or maybe that was her main occupation. There was a picture of a man, a rather handsome mulatto with curly short black hair and a powerful jawline. Her boyfriend? Then why had she been willing to pick me up? Could be she was merely helpful, a nice girl; best not to presume too much.

Still Oba didn't reappear. What did I know of her, anyway? Maybe she had gone to fetch the Death Squad. No, I had to have some faith; I had tried to help her, and maybe she had a small yen for me, so she helped me back. She'd be home in due course.

What the hell. I was no pimp, to lie around being served by a woman. I needed money to buy my passage home, and to repay Oba for her kindness. I had to go out and see how I could earn it.

I found a pencil and printed a note on some of the bread-wrapper: OBA—I WILL RETURN. J.S. That should reassure her.

I went out and down the stairs to the central patio. There were a number of people around, and they stared at me, no doubt taking me for Oba's lover. Well, let them take! I made my way to the street and on to a broad avenue going by the stadium. I was careful to note the address so I could find it again.

Soon I was back in the crowd. Again I rode the wave of it knowing it would bring me to where the action was.

And it took me to a major martial arts festival.

Suddenly I knew how to get out of Brazil. Martial arts is my bailiwick.

I entered a large open space. Further along were huge tents, like a circus, and I could hear sideshow barkers calling. But what interested me was up close: a trained fighting bear, and a sign with the figure one thousand cruzeiros. Obviously anyone who could beat the bear would win that prize.

I paused to do some crude calculations: 1,000 cruzeiros—I had to refrain from thinking of them as "crud-zeroes"—would translate into about one hundred and thirty dollars, if I had my exchange ratio straight. An airplane ticket to America would cost me about four hundred dollars—so it wasn't enough. Also, I would need clothing, so the Death Squad spies wouldn't recognize me at the airport, which they surely had staked out. Good Brazilian businessman clothes, probably at least another hundred dollars. Plus some for bribes—hell with that! So I needed a stake of five hundred dollars, and I surely was not going to steal any of it from any voodoo idols. This bear prize could be a start toward that total.

I approached more closely. Actually there were two animal matches; the more popular one was a chimpanzee. It was the chimp who paid one thousand cruz; the bear paid five thousand. That was more like it; I could win my grubstake outright, over six hundred dollars.

But first I watched the chimp. He wore red boxing pants and red boxing gloves, and was much smaller than a man. But the animal was tough. Many men tried it, paying the entry fee of ten cruz—and the chimp beat them all easily. Chimpanzees, like all apes, are much stronger than men.

No one dared even attempt the bear. I knew the odds were much worse for it, but the prize was much bigger too. So I paid the entry fee of twenty cruz—praise the voodoo god for Oba's generosity!—and took the ring against the ursine champion. It was a European black bear, six feet tall and over four hundred pounds. Its claws were clipped and it was muzzled, but it remained a monster. Had I not been desperate . . .

I came in fast with a *tai otoshi* body drop, hauling the bear over my leg. It staggered but did not fall; its hind legs were too short and its gravity too low for this to be effective.

It reared again on its two hind feet and tried to grab me in a bear-hug. This time I went in deep with a *ko-soto-gake* small outside hook, going into *sutemi* by throwing myself down along with the bear, carrying it across my hooking leg. This worked; it rolled on its back. However, merely throwing it was not enough, in this match; I actually had to subdue it. So I put *a kesagatame* scarf hold on it, my arm circling its neck, holding it down. But again it was too strong for me, and shaped wrong. I changed to another holddown, *katagatame,* but still it was getting away. So at last I went into a modified *hadaka jime* strangle from behind. In addition to the pressure of my arms around its neck, I crossed my legs around its waist in an illegal (in contest judo—but this was hardly that!) scissors hold and squeezed as hard as I could. This was a hold not even a bear could break readily, though it certainly tried. I knew it was losing consciousness.

Then a bell clanged. Oh, no! The owner had called the end of the round, and would not let me continue the strangle. I got up. Now I realized that there had been some small print in the terms, that I had not been able to read anyway, so that the bout had to be finished within a short round. I could take my winnings of 1,000 cruz for lasting one round, or go for a second round. And I knew the bear would not allow itself to be caught in that strangle again.

With ill grace I accepted my winnings. A few more seconds and I would have won the full prize, but one fifth of a loaf was better than none. I should have known that the rules would be set up to favor the entrepreneur, not the client.

I continued on down the street to the big tents. There was a sign at the largest one, printed in three languages: Portuguese, Japanese, and English. It was a Sumo tournament and exhibition, Japanese wrestling. Anyone could enter by paying the fee, but in this case I knew the rules. Few were entering, for a professional sumo wrestler is an impressive hunk of man, huge and fat and strong.

I needed more money than the truncated bear purse had provided, and that sort of cash was available for the sumo winners. Judo is an excellent all-around martial art, overlapping the techniques of karate, kung fu, aikido and wrestling. Many serious judokas will study other martial arts, to increase proficiency in judo. I had done the same, and one of the arts I had dabbled in was sumo. In fact, one of the things I did in my own dojo was to have my young students strip off their jackets and do sumo. It was good exercise, it made for variety, and it was fun; the kids loved it.

Of course I would be at a disadvantage against a classical sumo wrestler in his own specialty. But I knew there would be no top-ranked *sumotori* here. Brazil had a sizable colony of Japanese settlers, the largest in Latin America, about half a million, but this was hardly Japan itself. So I figured I had a reasonable chance for the purse.

Actually, I could make my money without reaching the finals. Betting was legal here; all I had to do was bet on myself and win a couple, and I'd have my money. Or, playing it safe, bet *half* my money, or five hundred cruzeiros. That way if I lost, I'd still have a stake. The five hundred cruz would be about sixty-five dollars, if I won three times and doubled it each time, that would come to, let's see, five hundred and twenty dollars. Just about right, without even risking my other half of the bear winnings. That would be reserved to repay Oba.

So I entered. What did I really have to lose? If I *didn't* enter, I would be stuck here anyway.

The tournament was inside the big tent, on a raised platform marked with a circle. All around the edges of the tent were hawkers' booths and little sideshows; maybe I would have a chance to look into some of them after the tournament. I'm a sucker for such entertainments, and I was also hungry. The first thing I'd do after this was buy some good ice cream.

But now my first match came up. The object in sumo is to make any part of your opponent touch the ground—other than the soles of his feet, of course—or shove him out of the ring. Kicking, punching, hair-pulling and gouging are forbidden. In sumo, the "ring" really *is* a ring, about fifteen feet across, with no ropes around the edge, only a white ring on the floor marking the boundary. The platform is supposed to be made from sixteen rice bales, supported by four pillars at the four points of the compass, each painted a different color. This platform was painted, but the floor was wood, not rice. Too bad; I rather appreciated the niceties of tradition.

I had to don a *Fundoshi*, the tight-fitting black loin cloth. Around my waist was a fat cord of hemp; it was permissible to take hold of this, and it gave good leverage. My opponent wore the same. He was a veritable mountain of flesh; I judged he outweighed me by 150 pounds. No wonder the local boys weren't having much luck!

The judge, or *gyoji,* was dressed in a brocade kimono. In real sumo there is also a jury of five men, but here it was up to the lone judge.

There were normally a lot of formalities associated with sumo, and combatants could take a long time preparing for a match, though the match itself was usually short. But this was degraded sumo, and the local Brazilian entries were generally so inept that little preparation was required. My opponent had little way of knowing I was different.

The signal for the start of the match came. The sumotori rushed me, thinking to finish me off in the first hustle; after all, all he had to do was grab me and shove me out. That was his mistake; a man too intent on shortcuts is easily trapped. I grabbed his outstretched right arm, braced my left foot against his right knee, and hauled him over in a *hiza-guruma* knee-wheel throw. His forward impetus sent him flying right out of the ring. So the easy victory was mine, not his.

That trick doubled my money, at least the amount I had bet. Now I had one thousand cruzeiros, plus my Oba's-newshoes reserve. However, it had cost me the element of surprise. The other contestants were quick to recognize my martial arts ability. An amateur does not perform a perfect knee-wheel throw on a professional—not by chance. They would be alert for me now.

My second match was proof of that. It was against another man-mountain, but he did not charge me. He came in cautiously, then suddenly grabbed my neck with both hands. These big men were trained to move very quickly in the ring; never think of a sumotori as a slow hulk.

He was trying to choke me into submission, a legitimate tactic. But the strangle is fundamental to judo, as is the choke. A strangle cuts off the blood to the brain, a choke the air to the lungs. A strangle correctly applied will be effective much more rapidly than a mere choke. I had had many years practice in resisting more competent chokes than this. I tensed my neck muscles—and they were formidable, if I do say so myself—hunched my head down, and resisted his relatively crude effort. My wind was cut off, even so, for he had great strength in his hands, but it would take him two minutes to down me from asphyxiation. Meanwhile, I clamped my own hands to his neck, going for the strangle. I was ready to bet the match that I could outlast him in this particular ploy.

I was right. He lacked the tough neck for this. My thumbs sank in and put pressure on the two nerve centers at the sides of the neck over the carotid arteries. A nerve-strangle is even faster than a blood-strangle. That was it; he fell unconscious. I had my second victory.

That brought my money to two thousand cruzeiros. One more win would do it.

The sumotori of my third match neither charged nor choked. He circled me warily, then reached out, and I caught hold of his right arm. He thought I was going for another forward throw, and braced himself to counter. But I trapped his right arm in my left armpit and turned inward into a *waki-gatame* arm-lock. The sudden pain made him fall on one knee, costing him the match.

Good enough. Now I could collect my winnings and get out of here. The rapidity of my victories was not unusual; in sumo it is generally settled very quickly. It is all geared to a quick heave utilizing maximum effort, like weight lifting.

But a large hand clapped my shoulder as I walked toward the

partitioned changing-room. The strike was from behind, startling me. "Jason Striker!"

I turned. It was another sumotori, 350 pounds—but this one I recognized. He was a yokozuma, a grand champion of the art, one of the genuine masters. "Kiyokuni!" I exclaimed. "What brings *you* to Brazil?"

He lowered his eyes. "I am getting old, friend, past my prime. My rank is for life, but my body fades. The competition in Japan, the strong young ones—" He shrugged. "I had to win, for I had gambling debts. Yet I could not."

"You were in debt, yet you traveled to the Americas?" I asked, trying not to make it sound too critical.

"As an entrepreneur," he explained. "I was not ready to untie the traditional knot." He meant the knot of hair tressed on his head. A great champion, ready to quit, untied the knot in public, signifying his retirement. "My friend, the *Osensei* Hiroshi of Aikido—"

"My friend too," I interjected. I had not realized that these two knew each other—the huge sumo expert and the tiny Aikido expert. Hiroshi had gotten me into this present adventure, as a matter of fact, coming to plead Fu Antos' cause.

"Hiroshi suggested that I organize a troupe of wrestlers like me—too old or too new or recovering from indisposition." Now he meant drug addiction or alcoholism; that has happened to some very good martial artists, unfortunately. One of the greatest judokas of all time, Shiro Saigo, went that sad route. "I borrowed all I could to set it up. Now we tour the world. Though we are not the best Japan has to offer, we are better than any elsewhere. And we perform a valuable service, promoting the art of sumo and educating other people to the Japanese way. We give seminars on the courtesies of martial art and proper technique, and we offer limited instruction for those interested in sumo. Our fees are reasonable, and a man past his *competitive* prime may remain at his *teaching* prime much longer."

"That's great!" I exclaimed. "You are spreading a good knowledge."

"We like to think so," he agreed, inclining his head in a little gesture of appreciation for the compliment. There is something about the grave, automatic courtesy of the true martial artist that always touches me.

"Well, you certainly helped me," I said. "I got in trouble and lost my money, and now I have won back enough to get home again. Without this tournament I don't know what I would have done."

"But surely you are not leaving now!" he protested. "You have won three matches in fine style. Two more will bring you to the finals. Already the spectators have taken note of you, this strange North American who makes the huge wrestlers whimper! You are generating excitement, attracting people, and bringing us profit. Please, I must insist that you continue in the tournament!"

I could not very well turn down this sincere plea of my huge friend. I approved what he was doing, and I really was in no hurry, now that I had my money. I did not need to bet any more—I never gamble voluntarily anyway—and could finish out the competition for the fun of it. "I'll stay," I said.

"But you must be hungry!" he exclaimed jovially. "You are hardly more than a skeleton." Compared to him, I *was,* since I had no fat on me. "Come, we shall prepare you for the remainder." And he urged me forward into one of the smaller tents. The main tent had no sides, just a top to keep the weather away, but the smaller tents were complete.

As a matter of fact, I *was* hungry. I did not want to eat a large amount right before the vigorous exercise of a match, but something would be very good right now. So I joined him in a lovely Island repast of raw fish, fried rice balls, a bowl of black bean paste and noodles, and plenty of Japanese tea with no sugar.

Now it was time for the next match. Apparently Kiyokuni had delayed the proceedings so as not to rush me. I knew this one was going to be tougher, for my opponent treated me exactly like a professional sumotori. I could not afford to grapple him in the conventional sumo fashion, for he was much stronger and heavier than I. I had to win fast, or lose, and I rather expected to lose. The plain fact was that I was not a match for a good sumotori in his specialty.

He grabbed my belt. I cut suddenly to the side, whipping my hip sidewise and back in a *taisabaki* motion used in judo to counter a forward throw. Because I was nervous, and recharged by the good food Kiyokuni had shared, my action was extraordinarily powerful. The sumotori's wrist jerked violently.

He gave a cry of pain and let go. The judge called a halt, coming in to examine the man's hand.

Oh, no! I saw it now. The thumb was bent backward out of its socket, wrenched or broken by my thrust.

"Here, let me—" I said automatically. The judge held the sumotori's arm, and I took hold of the dislocated thumb and pulled hard. The victim grimaced with pain, but in a moment the digit settled back into its proper place. But that hand would be useless for some time.

The judge indicated the victory for me, but I didn't care about that. "I'm sorry," I told the sumotori, not certain he even understood my language. "I did not mean to hurt you."

He controlled his pain like the man he was. "That hand was weak from prior injury," he told me in English. "I was careless, and you did not know." And he made a little bow.

There was nothing else I could say. I turned away, chagrined. These things do happen; I have been injured many times in judo. But that did not make me feel much better. How would that man be able to make his way, now?

But my next match was upon me. Now I would be happy to lose, and get out of this before I caused any more trouble. Yet I had to do my best; never in my life have I thrown a match, for any reason.

The sumotori grabbed me around the waist, trying to lift me so that he could carry me out of the ring. I resisted, levering against his own mass so that he could not get me up. So he used all his strength and bulk to squeeze me and bend me backwards, literally crushing me in his embrace. Let me tell you, the press of a sumotori is no trifle; I could hardly gasp in enough breath to maintain consciousness.

Then I remembered a trick little Hiroshi had employed against a huge wrestler at the Martial Open. No doubt it was the mention of Hiroshi the Aikidoist in my discourse with Kiyokuni so recently that brought this to mind. I tried that trick now. I put one arm at the small (really a misnomer, on this monstrous man!) of his back, and the other under his nose. I pressed upward and back on his face while hauling him in from the back. The upper lip is sensitive; he had to draw back to alleviate my pressure, but could not. I kept pushing with all my might, forcing him to bend, and at last he capitulated. The match was mine.

Now, to my surprise, I had made the finals. Only one wrestler remained, and I would have to vie with him for the grand purse of ten thousand cruzeiros, or about one thousand three hundred dollars, that I didn't really want now. And—my opponent was my friend Kiyokuni, naturally a competitor himself. No doubt he saved his venture some money by winning many of the purses himself, and this was legitimate, so long as he won fairly, as I was sure he did.

I looked out over the crowd, seeing how huge it had grown, inflated like the ponderous belly of a sumotori. There was a lot of support for Japanese martial art here in Rio. Many of the spectators were of Japanese descent, but many were not. It was a credit to Kiyokuni's promotional ability.

Then I spied a too-familiar face at the fringe. It was Laureano, head torturer for Mirabal. What was *he* doing here?

What else but searching for me? The same excitement that had attracted the swelling crowd had brought him to investigate. I had in effect blown my cover, and I had to get out fast. "I have changed my mind,' I said to Kiyokuni. "I can not participate further."

He was shocked. "Jason, you can not do this! It is the final match!"

"I—I am indisposed," I said, not wanting to get him involved in my Death Squad problems. "I shall yield the match and purse to you. Please use some of it to help the man whose hand I injured."

"Indisposed?" he repeated, and I realized I had made an unfortunate choice of vocabulary. He thought I was pleading addiction to some drug. Then he shook his head, refusing to credit that. "But you have done so well! Everyone is waiting for this encounter! It is a record crowd." Then he paused. "Ah, you worry about Toshida! That is all right; we do not throw our injured troupe members into the street to die! All of on this tour have problems; all contribute to a common fund to assist those whom misfortune befalls. Do not be concerned."

"You are my friend," I said. "I cannot fight you."

He smiled with understanding. "Ah, you seek to avoid embarrassing me before this throng! I appreciate the thought, but I am a warrior. I can take my losses as well as my victories, and I would be privileged to lose to you, my friend. Come, I insist—the match must continue."

Laureano was looking my way, and I was sure he had spotted me. His eyes seemed to glitter insanely behind rimless glasses. There were four or five men with him with their shirts hanging out, covering their belts, surely concealing their weapons. Among them was the big ugly football player/thug. Trouble galore! "You misunderstand, friend. I can't hope to defeat you. It would be a mismatch."

"Now you sound like a coward, and I know you are not!" he answered. "Come, it is a fair match, and it would look strange if you suddenly withdrew now. People would think I had bribed you to forfeit, and my reputation would suffer." And he looked at me with such a pleading sincerity that it was painful.

What could I say? He was honest, well-meaning, and correct. He did not know about my problem with the Death Squad, and I did not want him to know. I had to go through with it, and made a good show for the spectators, many of whom I knew had placed sizable wagers on the outcome. All I could do now was hope to finish it quickly, one way or the other, and get out before Laureano and his hoods reached me.

Kiyokuni and I approached each other slowly. I had not been fooling when I pondered the strength of the sumotori; he might consider himself over the hill in Japan, but he had been one of the mightiest sumo wrestlers of all time, and was still a formidable opponent. In a straight judo match I think I could have taken him, for that was *my* specialty; no doubt I had better endurance, and could nail him when he tired. But I was quite unlikely to beat him in sumo, and was much more likely to lose rapidly than to win slowly. He would not fall for the tricks I had used on the lesser combatants. Furthermore, he knew me from Japan, and had seen me fight there; he was wise to my techniques.

We grappled and pushed at each other, not trying for an immediate win so much as a minor advantage that could be parlayed into a winning combination. Yet I felt the tremendous musculature under Kiyokuni's fat; he could bull me out of the circle any time and knew it, but the showman in him wanted to make it look tougher for the betting spectators, and the friend in him wanted to spare me the ignominy of too-ready defeat. He would not throw the match, of course, any more than I would, but there are kind and unkind ways to prevail. Damn his kind heart; if he beat me in five seconds and let me go, I could avoid murder or capture by Mirabal's torturer!

I heard a cry. Now the Death Squad was right up to the platform. Laureano's burning half-mad eyes were fixed on mine, his right hand stroking the bump below his hanging shirt; he had a gun there, all right. I didn't think he'd shoot me right there on stage, in full view of the crowd, but seeing the lurking insanity and lust for blood in his face, I wasn't *sure.* He'd probably do it rather than let me slip away again. And if he tried, he very well might hit my friend Kiyokuni. I had to break this off right now—but *how?*

Suddenly there was a piercing scream. My gaze turned involuntarily that way. It was Oba, right before Laureano, who was trying to push past her to regain a clear shot at me.

She screamed again, with marvelous volume. All heads turned. She gesticulated wildly, a torrent of Portuguese emerging from her pretty little mouth. She pointed at Laureano in a gesture very similar to the one the boy Filho had used on me in prison. Nearby faces scowled.

Then I knew what she was doing. She was accusing the Death Squadders of attacking her, and the crowd believed her. In truth, Laureano was innocent of this particular charge, but I wasn't going to raise my voice on his behalf. Let him have a taste of his own medicine, the false accusation and frame-up. Serve him right!

Now I had leeway. I freed my right arm, got clearance between us, and let go with a mighty uppercut to Kiyokuni's chin. It was a knockout blow—and an obvious foul.

There was an instant roar of outrage from the crowd as the judge signaled the penalty. They could not know that I might have saved Kiyokuni's life from a misplaced assassin's shot. The sumotori fell back, losing consciousness, a surprised look on his face; he had never suspected I would be capable of such a dastardly deed. The judge, too, was shocked; he was yelling something at me, but his voice was drowned out by the crowd.

Half a dozen sumotoris scrambled into the ring, furious. Instead of freeing myself from a match, I had gotten myself into a brawl! Why hadn't I simply confided in Kiyokuni and let him help hide me from the Death Squad? Sometimes I'm not very bright, sad to say. Kiyokuni was not only a fine fighter and the employer of these men, he was their friend and benefactor. I could well understand their anger and sympathize with their intent, but could not afford to wait for it! They would beat me to jelly in an instant, and if they didn't, the Death Squad would finish me off instead. My own folly!

They converged. Surrounded by the dancing whales, I prepared my escape. Fortunately they got in each other's way, being so eager to get at me. I leaped up and delivered a flying kick to the side of the face of the nearest, knocking him down. But another grabbed me from behind with both arms. I jumped, using him as leverage, and shoved with both legs at the chest of the one in front. He fell back like a monstrous tenpin, bowling over the others. Then I bent forward and gathered in the knee of the man holding me, who was staggering backward from the recoil of my shove; I encouraged that stagger with a backward kick to his abdomen that incapacitated him without injury. I was not trying to hurt these people.

What a melee it was! Oba was still screaming, the crowd was closing in on the Death Squad and on me simultaneously, the judge was appalled, sumotoris were sprawled all across the ring, angry spectators further out were starting to throw stink bombs, and one wrestler remained on his feet coming at me. Laureano's gun was now in his hand, and the other Death Squadders were reaching for theirs. I had generated a riot that might soon cost the lives of a number of people—but had I saved my own life?

Laureano's gun came up, the muzzle centering on me as the last sumotori charged me. The other wrestlers were getting up; after all, they were used to taking falls. It was now or never.

I ducked down to meet the wrestler. Fortunately he was a light one, a scant 300 pounds. I put my bowed shoulders into his midsection, caught his right leg with my right arm, braced my legs and lifted him in an unsteady *kata-guruma* shoulder whirl. When I had him up, I turned around in the "airplane spin" of the television wrestlers, letting his legs fly out to bash down the others. Then I heaved him off the platform, directly into the Death Squad, crushing them down beneath that awful weight.

I jumped off the platform, grabbed Oba's hand, and ran for it. I had no time to pick up my money or even to recover my clothes. I only hoped Kiyokuni would understand, once he thought it out.

Then I spied Laureano. The man was extricating himself from the pileup, apparently having been on the fringe. He was bent over, trying to rise despite part of the Football Player sprawled on one of his arms, and his posterior was facing me. It was an opportunity I could not resist. I broke away from Oba, jumped toward the torturer, closed my fist, and smacked him at the base of the spine right between the buttocks with an *Ippon-Ken* strike. It was an *atemi* blow, outlawed in karate competition because it could injure the spinal nerve, interfering with the function of the legs and the urinary system.

Laureano screamed and collapsed, and I knew my blow had done the trick. It would be a long time before he walked normally again, and he might lose control of his bladder. He would suffer horribly—just the way he had made countless prisoners suffer.

Now Oba and I merged with the crowd. I felt naked in my scanty *Fundoshi,* and no wonder, for it was really no more than a tough jock strap. But the milling throng didn't seem to notice; probably they assumed it was just a carnival costume. They didn't know I was the cause of the riot.

Oba took the lead, smiling sunnily. And I realized that this little goddess had indeed saved me from betrayal by a friend, voiding Exu's curse. Kiyokuni had meant only well, but he had nearly been the death of me; only Oba's timely distraction had foiled that.

There was a cry. I looked back, and there was the big Football Player, towering over the heads of the crowd, forging through like a tank. He was waving his fist at me; he wanted me to know he was back on my trail. He must have shown his badge or whatever and freed himself, and resumed the chase, heedless of the plight of Laureano. I certainly hadn't given him the slip long; he was like a damned bloodhound. There seemed to be more Squadders with him than before, too, seven or eight now. And they obviously had caught on to Oba's connection to me; that particular ploy would not work again.

"Vir," Oba said, tugging me on.

"I hope you know an escape hatch," I muttered, following her. "Those bastards mean business." And how!

She led me to a door, and we ducked in. I hoped Football hadn't seen us do it, but had no real confidence. It was some kind of an exercise hall, with students working out. Not judo or karate or Aikido; I couldn't place it at first glance, but it certainly had the aspect of a martial arts dojo. For one thing, the pupils were in armor. Did the Society for Creative Anachronisms have a Chapter here?

The Master came up. He was at least sixty years old, stood five foot six, with a substantial pot belly that brought his weight up to perhaps 180 pounds. His eyes were watery, his beard wispy, and I could see the somewhat trembly nature of his pulse. There were big dark liver spots on his hands, a sure sign of advancing age. Taken all in all, not impressive. Perhaps he had been a sharp martial artist once, but no longer. He wore a *samurai* sword, and now I recognize his martial art. This was *kendo* or *iado,* the science of swordsmanship.

Oba spoke quickly in Portuguese. The Master smiled and turned to me. "Jason Striker!" he exclaimed, though Oba had not named me.

Uh-oh. If he knew me, would he give me away to the Death Squad? No, I had to trust him; evidently Oba knew him, and anyway I had no choice.

"Fuji, kendo," the Master introduced himself simply, so I could understand. We exchanged bows.

Now I had to admire his school, for it would have been bad form to allow minor matters like a Death Squad hot on my heels to distract me from common courtesy. Chafing inside, I did so.

Most of the students were still working out. They were not actually in armor, at least not the conventional kind; that had been my error of a too-hasty glance. They wore cotton blouses and ankle-length divided skirts, with bare feet. They had helmets similar to baseball catcher's masks, with iron face grills and padded leather side flaps, the whole cushioned by a towel underneath. The breastplates consisted of bamboo slats, extended by a short leather plate to protect the crotch. Shell gauntlets covered the arms from the backs of the hands to the elbows.

Their "swords" were made of bamboo, with sixteen inches of

handle and thirty of blade—and that blade was split, tied together by an interior cord. The result was to deprive it of its striking power. But it could make a sound, and the judge could estimate the power and cleanness of the blow by that crack. More advanced students fenced without armor, and used more substantial wooden swords.

It is foolish to judge by appearances, especially in martial art. I knew that, but this time I forgot. I'm afraid my border-line contempt must have been evident to Master Fuji, and in retrospect I am keenly embarrassed. I had a lesson coming.

There was a sudden loud pounding on the door. We knew what that was. Oba spoke again, urgently. The Master gestured me to a curtain, and we hastened to hide behind it.

The curtain was semitransparent, with a coarse weave, so it was possible to see through it by putting my face up close.

Now the men of the Death Squad charged in, a brutish crew. Laureano was not among them, thanks to my knock on his posterior; the Football Linesman led them. Despite the danger I was in, my glance passed by them to the wall beyond, attracted to the display of wooden swords.

Wooden swords. Fat lot of good they would do against thugs armed with guns. And that must be a wooden sword Master Fuji was wearing too, not a real one. He was virtually unarmed.

"Move aside, old man," Football snapped arrogantly, or something like that in Portuguese; his peremptory tone raised my hackles. I never did much like bullies, and these ones were worse than most.

Master Fuji looked small and frail before these brutes, but he stood his ground, answering softly but firmly. He would not permit a search without a warrant, or whatever the formality was, and of course the Death Squad hadn't bothered with that. I appreciated his courage, but knew it was useless; they would simply shove him aside and proceed, quite possibly ransacking the premises and terrorizing the students while they were at it.

Yet the students continued their ritual postures as though

oblivious to the threat to their instructor. They surely knew he was in danger, or at least embarrassment; were they disciplined, or were they afraid? Some example for the field of martial arts! I flexed my muscles, planning combat strategy, but I knew it was hopeless. There were eight thugs, and all were armed; in one second those pistols would be in their hands and blasting away.

Football spoke again, to his men, and they spread out to circle the Master. The old man spread his hands, shaking his head. "No!" he cried. "I forbid it!"

Football's left hand thrust out, shoving the Master back. He staggered. Now the other thugs closed in for a bit of sport. They encircled him completely, vulpine smiles on their faces, reaching slowly for their guns. They wanted him to see what they were doing, to make him cry out and try to resist or get away. A frantic rabbit was always more sport than a passive one.

Now, in the Orient it used to be a crime punishable by death for a visitor to draw a weapon in the host's house. Such an action was never taken lightly; to draw was to challenge to the death. An offender could be forced to commit *seppuku,* ritual suicide, even when he was in the right.

This was Brazil, not the Orient, but a martial arts dojo is really an extension of the Orient. I knew the Master would have to act, or be shamed before his students, and therefore he would at the very least get beaten up, and perhaps die. I had to get out there and fight my own battle.

Yet this thought and this resolve were only halfway through my brain, and my body had not yet responded, when the Master exploded into the most phenomenal action I have ever seen. It was so rapid and so devastating that at first I could not believe what I saw. Only later was I able to work it out, re-creating what had happened.

Here, then, is that re-creation. The Master was ringed by the eight Death Squad thugs. Football was in front of him, the others stepping in from all sides as their hands went for their guns. Master Fuji drew his long sword from the scabbard—and lo! it was, after all, razor-sharp steel, not wood—with his left hand. He brought it up high to clear the scabbard, the hand reversed on the hilt—seemingly an impossible grip for combat. But then he brought it down and back, and stabbed the man directly behind him through the gut, piercing the liver.

Then he drew the sword out, clapped the hilt into his right hand, angled it up past his own head and whipped the blade across the two thugs farthest to his right. The first, standing upright, was slashed deeply across the chest, so that the blood and muscle blossomed out. The second, leaning forward, had his throat slit. The *katana*, having a blade as well as a point, and being slightly curved so as to facilitate slicing, was well adapted to this motion.

The thugs had not yet quite realized what had happened. Seeing is not the same as believing, not in the first instant. Not when a rabbit metamorphoses into a tiger. They were still reaching in leisurely fashion for their guns. Except for one man, the third from the Master's right, who had drawn and was just leveling his weapon. Master Fuji swung back, slicing open the skull of that man. The thug's brains slopped out from that terrible forehead gash, tumbling across his face as he fell.

Again the Master reversed his stroke, gripping the sword in the classical two-handed Japanese way. With a *kesagake* movement he opened the abdomens of the two on his left. Their entrails spewed out like garbage from burst bags, and they too collapsed, dropping their guns.

Only two remained standing at this stage. Both had their guns out, and both had now caught on to what was happening. But the sword reversed course again and severed Football's right arm, sending it flying through the air still holding the pistol. Amazed but not stupid, he turned to run, but collapsed as his blood pressure dropped, for his stump was spurting wildly. Unless he received prompt medical attention, he was likely to die from loss of blood, and such attention seemed unlikely.

The last man managed to get off one shot. It missed Master

Fuji, who took care of him with a terrible *do-giri* stroke that almost cut him in two at the level of the nipples.

Then the Master returned his *katana* to its scabbard without looking; the guard on the handle made a faint click as it struck home. The whole action had taken five seconds.

I stumbled out, unable to abort my attempt to participate though the action was over. I must have been gaping, for the Master faced me with a little smile. "Also Iado, 8th Dan," he said, completing his self-introduction.

Oh. Iado was true sword fighting—steel, not wood—and 8th Dan would be one of the highest grades in the world. No doubt about that! It was the art of the quick draw, the swordsman's equivalent to the old western American cowboy gunslinger's draw. Since the action was brief, it did not require much stamina; even an old man could be devastating, as we had just seen.

Master Fuji spoke to Oba, who was looking a bit faint. In response she took me by the hand and guided me through the classroom to a back hall, while the students came to clean up the mess. We would not be bothered any more by the Death Squad assassins!

My mind numbed, I suffered myself to be led. Oba took me to a private room in back, and closed the door behind us. Then she turned and collapsed into my arms, sobbing.

I held her, well appreciating her emotion. To see eight people so suddenly slaughtered—it horrified me too. I had looked upon the Master as a basically harmless retiree, a devotee of a martial art that never had had much impact . . .

I became strongly aware of Oba's lithe body, trembling in my arms. I felt a pang of guilt for thinking of sexual qualities in this moment of relief and horror. Yet there is a relation between opposites, whether it be male and female, or shock and acceptance, or horror and love. My emotion had been roused, and so had hers, and that extremely negative outward impression yet was a mutual experience that drew us together. I don't know whether that makes sense; I'm not much of a philosopher.

At any rate, I kissed her, and she kissed me back, fiercely. My hands slid down along her silken hair to cup her firm buttocks—and I drew back, unwilling to let her shock at the bloodshed set her up for a seduction. I am, at the root, an amorous man, but there are limits.

She stood alone, a lovely nymph. How I wished I could talk with her!

Oba suddenly remembered something, her mood changing in that mercurial way women have. She rummaged in her handbag and brought out a little wooden item, handing it to me with a smile.

I accepted, turning it over in my hand. It was a carving of a human hand, the fingers closed, thumb sticking up between the first two like a fouled-up fist. "What is it?"

"*Figa,*" she said brightly.

"Figure?"

"*Figa.*" And she strung it on a thin chain and hung it around my neck, a necklace.

"I don't understand . . ."

So she explained, by gestures, making a little play of it. There were several confusions, but gradually I came to understand.

The *Figa* was a good-luck charm, an amulet against the evil eye. (Oba made the fiercest, cutest evil eye expression I ever saw.) It symbolized passion and fertility, warded off envy and jealousy, and kept evil spirits at bay. It must never be lost, for then all the bad luck it had warded off would come crashing down on the owner's head. It had to be bought and given as a present; anyone who bought his own *Figa* would find it valueless, just an inert object causing neither good nor harm.

It was a cute figurine, and a cute notion by a cute girl. "Thank you, Oba," I said. And now my curiosity about her was aroused. Yet how could I question her, with this language barrier?

Well, why not? Maybe she would comprehend a little. "Just who are you, Oba?" I inquired. "A working girl? Secretary? Won't you be missed from your job? Oh—or are you a seamstress? I saw the cloth in your room. No wonder you dress so nicely. Or do you have some connection with the voodoo, umbanda, or whatever?"

Her black eyes glowed, and I thought she understood. And she began to dance.

It was beautiful. She had the lithe, slender dancer's body, with muscular legs and perfect coordination, and she moved with such grace I was entranced. "So you are a professional dancer," I murmured. "I should have known."

But she continued, and it was evident that she had more on her mind than showing off her form. Her gestures were stylized, repetitive, not like the voodoo dance, but like pantomime.

That was it! She was telling a story!

I watched, and gradually it came clear. Nuances of gesture and expression, and occasional spoken words, brought to life the story of the gods of voodoo.

In the beginning there was chaos, a being without definition, incomprehensible to the mortal mind. He was composed of three spirits, one of whom created the heavens and the earth and all living things, including man in his own image. But the man was vain, so the god tried to destroy him. Yet the man was immortal, and survived though all the earth was blackened by the scourge of the god's lightning. Still, after that, he stayed out of sight.

The gods—the three aspects of the One God—then had mercy on the earth, and re-created life on it. The aspect Olofi (Oba pronounced his name for me) was put in charge of this chore, while the others went away to continue creation elsewhere in the universe. Olofi, mindful of the bad example set by the first man, gave the second man eleven vital commandments: not to steal, kill (except for food and self-defense), eat human flesh, make war, covet, curse, ask too much, or fear death (but not to commit suicide); and to honor his father and mother, respect the god's laws, and teach these commandments to his children.

Poetic license, I thought: how could the first man honor his father and mother? He *had* none, by definition. But I was struck by the similarity to the Ten Commandments that our Judeo/Christian/Mohammedan God had handed down to the people following Moses: Thou Shalt Not Kill, Thou Shalt Have No Other Gods Before Me, and so on. Was there really much difference between voodoo and conventional religion?

The dance/pantomime continued: the first man was Oxala. (The first *man?* I had supposed from Ester's discourse that Oxala was a *god.* Maybe the line between mortal and immortal was fuzzy, at least in the beginning.) Olofi gave him a wife named Odd-something-or-other; it wasn't clear to my American/English-oriented mind. Anyway—and I swear I don't know exactly how she conveyed this information, unless I was picking up her mental projection, telepathy, or had it by intuitive osmosis—Oxala was represented as the original White Knight. I mean he was a tall, handsome white man, in a white cloak and white armor, on a strutting white horse. His wife Odd-etc. was a black woman, fair (if that is the appropriate word) and voluptuous with the huge breasts of maternity. The two mated—and wasn't *that* a spectacle, in this lone-dancer pantomime!—and Odd's tummy swelled grotesquely in rapid pregnancy. Then her pelvis moved forward, and she came almost into a squat, opening her legs wide. In America we think all babies must be born from a supine mother lying in a hospital bed, drugged to alleviate pain. But elsewhere in the world many babies drop into this world from the upright womb, gravity assisting the undrugged effort. I saw it all, such was the power of her suggestion.

She birthed a son, named Ag-something, and a daughter Yemanja. "Yemanja!" I exclaimed, interrupting my own morbid fascination with the dancer's pangs of parturition. "Goddess of the Moon, my patron—" But why should I be surprised? Oba was telling me her identity, as I had asked: not who she was in mundane life, but her goddess-genealogy. I already knew the river goddess was the daughter of the sea-goddess Yemanja; that was why she was here, helping to abate the curse of Exu. Now I knew that Yemanja was the daughter of the first man and woman in the voodoo pantheon.

But there was more. Yemanja was a beautiful woman whose skin was yellow. She married her brother Ag (so that's incest; and whom do you think Cain, the son of Adam, married, if not one of his sisters?) and they had a son Or-something—Orangutan? I could not keep track of all these complex names; that would have to do! When Orangutan grew up he had no sister to marry (sibling incest seemed to be the rule with these gods; better than descending to the common folk for mates, no doubt) so fell in love with his mother. Now *this* was a scandal, even among gods. Ag became ill with envy and disgust and died, and Yemanja resisted. But Orangutan was handsome, talented, strong, persistent and, it developed, ruthless. He raped her. (Hoo-boy, what a dance Oba danced!) Yemanja cursed him, and he also died. But she was already pregnant with his seed. She climbed to the top of a high mountain and killed herself.

But even this was not the end. In fact, it was the beginning. She died in one sense, but not in another, for she was immortal. This ambivalence was also typical of this pantheon. Thus the world faced the consequence of her suicide at the same time as it knew her as the continuing goddess of waters; no contradiction. The dead goddess's abdomen burst asunder, releasing the waters of the universal deluge that drowned the world. Was there a Noah's Ark in voodoo mythology? The dance didn't say. Fourteen new gods were birthed in that torrent. And the first true man and true woman—Adam and Eve in my framework—formed from Yemanja's bones.

Among these posthumous gods were Xango, Oshun and Oba. Now at last I had it straight!

And she told me about Oba herself, who I gathered is known in the Catholic framework as Our Lady of Mount Carmel. She was both sister and wife to Xango, but the god of fire and thunder had a fiery and boisterous nature and a roving eye. Oba was afraid he would take up with one of her more glamorous sisters, such as Oya. So Oba went to another sister, Oshun, to seek advice, not realizing that Oshun herself, goddess of love, was one of Xango's interests.

"Well now," Oshun told her mischievously. "I know an excellent magic spell to keep him home. All you have to do is cut off one of your pretty little ears, cook it up in a pot of okra soup—that's his favorite, you know—and serve it to him."

"But—" Oba protested, appalled, touching her ear. She didn't even think to ask how her sister was so familiar with Xango's tastes.

"Don't worry; he always comes home ravenous. He'll eat it."

"But will it have an effect on our love life?"

"It certainly will! Guaranteed." And Oshun smiled with anticipation.

So naive, dutiful Oba stiffened her shapely spine, lifted a sharp knife, and courageously cut off her left ear. She staunched the flow of blood, clenched her teeth against the pain, and made the ear/okra soup.

When Xango came home that evening, Oba put the soup before him. He sat down to eat, dipped a spoonful, then paused, looking at her. "Why are you wearing that stupid white handkerchief over your head?" he demanded.

"Please eat your soup before it clots—uh, before it gets cold," she said evasively. "Why shouldn't I wear a kerchief if I want to? It isn't as if you ever take me out anywhere where I need a hat."

Sore point! He couldn't take her out, for then she would find out about the women he made time with during the day. "But why a blood-colored rose over the ear?" he asked.

Uh-oh! She must be bleeding again, and it was soaking through the kerchief. "I have my reasons," she murmured.

Xango would have pursued the matter, but he really didn't care very much what his dull wife wore, and he was hungry. So he muttered something about feminine vanity, and ate a spoonful of the soup. And reacted. "What'd you put in this stuff?" he demanded. "Tastes meaty—almost like human flesh."

"You know it is forbidden by the Third Commandment!" Oba replied, affecting shock. But it did upset her, for she *was* tricking him into a fundamental violation. If he ever found out! Her knees felt weak, her stomach knotted. Still, his unwavering love, guaranteed by the spell, would make it all worthwhile.

"You're acting awful funny today," he muttered. But he settled down to eat, for he had a hot date with none other than Oshun, and he didn't want to be late. He slurped it all down in short order, including the ear. "That last pod of okra tastes more like an ox's hoof," he complained. "Next time pick it fresher, and wash the dirt off it."

Oba nodded dumbly, wondering how long it would take the spell to act. Xango spruced up his hair and departed, paying her no further attention.

"Sister, you'd better put out tonight," Xango said to the goddess of love when he reached her. "My wife's been acting strangely. I think she's suspicious."

"I *know* she's suspicious," Oshun said as he nibbled on her perfect neck. "But I played a really cute trick on her today."

"What are you talking about?" the god of thunder rumbled as he took hold of her classic left breast.

"I told her she could put a spell on you by feeding you her ear." And Oshun laughed, sending remarkable ripples through that breast.

But Xango tensed, crushing instead of squeezing. "You *what?*"

"The little dummy may even have believed it," Oshun continued, shifting to alleviate the pressure. "Even though she's no romantic expert, she really ought to know that it isn't a girl's *ear* a man wants to eat." And she drew his head down toward her marvelous body.

Xango was lusty but not stupid. "Her *ear!*" he ejaculated. He jerked away.

"Hey, where are you going?" Oshun cried. She wanted him coming, not going. But instead of bringing him closer to her with the good laugh she had anticipated, she had only succeeded in sending him stomping out. All she had for her effort was a hurting breast. "Maybe I should cut it off and make soup out of it," she muttered darkly, glancing down at herself.

Back home, Xango unceremoniously ripped the handkerchief off Oba's head. There was her mutilated ear. He clutched his stomach, knowing now what he had eaten. Thoroughly disgusted, he stormed out of the house.

Oba remained Xango's official wife, but he never again cohabited with her. But the scheming Oshun did not profit much either, perhaps because of her complicity. Instead, her sister, Oya, patroness of fire, Oggun's wife, became Xango's favorite mistress. Subsequently it was Oya whom Oshun had to outwit by arousing the lust of a skeleton, as Ester had already informed me.

"Now just a minute," I said. The truth is, I was burning with godlike lust, completely aroused by the force of her dancing narrative, and I was no skeleton. But there was something else. I approached her and put my hands to the sides of her head, pushing back the hair that covered her ears. I thought I had seen—but it could have been my imagination, stimulated by the pantomime.

She had a cauliflower ear. Evidently it had been bashed once, perhaps by a jealous lover. She, like the Oba she portrayed, had sacrificed one ear to a man. And would probably give everything to have that man back again. No wonder she had put so much feeling into the story!

And do you know, that only redoubled my passion? "A goddess should not go unloved," I said, certain now that it had been her need for fulfillment that had motivated her, at least subconsciously. Probably her boyfriend was a martial artist, or at least a strong, brawling man, and she had recognized certain similar qualities in me and been drawn in. At any rate, she was some girl. I have never seen anyone else dance like that.

She met me as she had before, with matching passion. Maybe her dancing catalyzed her as it had me, arousing her desire for the things she had represented. There is a technique of acting, called Method, in which the actor *becomes* his part, living it fully while on the stage. The mortal Oba had become the goddess Oba—and I had become Xango.

We kissed and kissed again, deeply. Then my mouth slid down over her neck. Her blouse fell open and I ran my lips and tongue over her firm free breast, fruit of a goddess. And she leaned over, clutching me to her, climbing me, biting and sucking at the base of my neck, and say, wasn't *that* stimulating! I got my hands down around her thighs, cupping her buttocks under the skirt, snaking in between panties and flesh, kneading those masses feverishly. She was burning hot down there, and those dancer's muscles flexed under my grip like living things—which of course they were.

Her hands also were busy. One clutched my shoulder, digging in almost painfully; the other got hold of my *Fundoshi* and twisted it around a bit to the side, uncovering what threatened to burst out anyway. She grasped my swelling member and kneaded it in rhythm with my pressure on her buttocks and mouthing of her breast. Suddenly my urgency became incipient; if I didn't act quickly, I would spurt into space.

But there was no bed in that room, and no time to fool around with clothing; the need was too imperative. I put my two hands under her arms, my thumbs pressing into the sides of her breasts, and lifted her bodily. Her legs spread wide and hooked behind me as her hot cleavage came down on my rigidity. I leaned back, supporting her whole weight, shoving aside her panties, setting her down directly on my member so that gravity forced the deepest penetration as my piston slid into that hot oiled cylinder. Then I slid my hands behind her back, pulling her upper torso in to me, burying my face in her fragrant mass of hair.

I believe the position is known as "The Tree" with the trunk of the man supporting the limbs of the woman as he stands erect in more ways than one. But for me it was more like a diesel, the maximum compression triggering the explosion.

Our climax was painful in its violence. On the one hand I had the feeling that my member, supporting her full weight, would break off; on the other, I pictured her flying up to the ceiling, propelled by my irresistible jets. It was the most intense sexual experience I ever had, yet not the most pleasant, because of the muscle-deadening exertions required.

I sank back to the floor, bending my knees to do a judo breakfall, such was my momentary exhaustion. But Oba clung to me, following me down as it were in *makikomi,* maintaining the hold by utilizing both her limber torso and her dancer's thigh muscles. It was possible, I discovered, for a woman to clasp a man without using her limbs.

"No," I said, realizing that she expected more of me than was humanly possible. But, still joined, she found my lips with hers and kissed me with all the passion of the first time.

And to my amazement, my hardness remained. Now she rode me like a horse, bouncing on me so vigorously I was afraid she would come loose and land on me crushingly. But she had excellent control. And slowly she brought me to a second climax, longer and harder but no less powerful than the first.

God, I thought. Never get involved with a goddess—or a dancer! I was prostrate on the hard floor.

Yet even now she did not relent. She continued to move on me, pressing me from outside and inside. "It's impossible!" I gasped. "This is worse than Mirabal's torture!"

I was wrong. It seemed to take a thousand years, and may actually have been half an hour, but in time her persistent stimulation roused me to a third performance. Actually I was almost completely acquiescent now; *she* did the lovemaking, drawing from my gut the last dregs of my potential. It was slow, slow, slow, like a quiet tide rising, yet in the end the volume of sensation was as great as the prior peaks.

At last she was satisfied. Yet even now she did not actually let me go. She settled on top of me, retaining my battered member within her, and we both sank into a kind of placid trance.

I'll never forget the love of Oba, but I hope never to experience it again. I'm not getting any younger, and that sort of thing takes incredible stamina. I'd rather do fifty pullups, one-handed. It was days before I was able to raise another erection; she had emptied me.

But what a way to go!

Chapter 9:

Animation of the Curse

The Black Castle was on a rise in the middle of a roundish swampy plain within an almost circular mountain valley. There was an unnatural look about the area, as if it were a moon crater overgrown by the jungle. Few trees grew here; most of the valley was open except for low brush. In the center, in contrast, was a cluster of enormous trees, and it was within this island forest that the castle was taking shape. As yet the ramparts were hardly visible above the trees. Thus it could not readily be spotted from the air.

Fu Antos looked out from the highest battlement. He had won the battle but not the campaign, as he knew; he had a few of the modern weapons, but they were only one factor, and his ninjas were not yet conversant with their use.

It had been a job rescuing those supplies from their assorted booby-traps, but ninjas had much expertise at that sort of thing. One of the boxes had contained the severed head of Candelaria, the girl who had delivered the bees to Costa of Petrobas. Unfortunate, but it showed how quick Mirabal had been to make the connection between that assassination and the ninjas.

At any rate, the ninjas now had fifty to a hundred M-3 submachine guns, fairly simple to operate: merely point and squeeze the trigger, and the guns would squirt bullets. Also a fair number of hand grenades, and some C-4 plastic explosive: white, odorless, crumbly, like dry cream cheese. The plastic had already been specially positioned, and they had only imperfect notions how to use the other devices, preferring their primitive weapons. So they were still at a disadvantage. These few ninjas could not hope to stand for long against the might of the Brazilian army. So long as Mirabal lived, the Black Castle was not secure.

Yet Fu Antos had resources. If he could trick Mirabal into committing his full force into the fray . . .

He had not long to wait. The colonel had not bothered to trace the tedious hidden road to the castle; he had sent his troops sloughing through the marshes in such numbers that the jungle animals had been routed. Human-sea tactics, suffering many casualties even before contact with the enemy. No finesse, just raw power. He had expected better of Mirabal.

Then he looked again. These were not government troops, these were Indians! Had *they* joined their enemies?

No, now he saw the army men. Their guns were trained on the Indians. The Indians were from several pacified villages, evidently rounded up by force; they had to attack the Black Castle or be shot from behind. They were armed only with bows, knives, spears and similar native weapons, no guns.

Poor Indians! They had believed the promises of the government for a better life if they adopted the ways of the white man. Now they had been rounded up like cattle and driven to the slaughter, men, women and children. The warriors were first, followed by their families; the warriors knew that if they did not attack the castle, their families would be shot down from behind.

And if they attacked, the ninjas would either have to slaughter their friends or allow the Black Castle to be swamped. Very nice ploy. Only a ruthless genius would have set this up, and only a more ruthless genius would be able to nullify it.

"Meet the Indians under a flag of truce," Fu Antos said. "Explain to them that we shall have to massacre them along with the soldiers if they come near the Black Castle. We do not wish to do this, for we regard them as our allies, and we know they are being forced to fight. But if they join us, we will help them overcome the soldiers, and many will survive."

The flag of truce was displayed, but snipers from Mirabal's side shot all the parties meeting under that flag. The ninja representative was unhurt, protected under his bullet-proof cloak, but it was obvious that no truce negotiations could take place. The Indians were obviously more frightened of the troops than of the ninjas. That was unfortunate, for it doomed them all.

Even half finished, the ramparts of the Black Castle were formidable. They could easily withstand the attack of the Indians. But the tribespeople charged across the open portion of the valley. It was pathetic, for the men could run faster than the women and children, yet hesitated to leave their families isolated on the battlefield. It would be a terrible thing to slaughter these victims of circumstance, but that was what Mirabal was counting on. If the Indians were allowed to overrun the castle, the government troops would soon wipe out the ninjas, and probably the Indians too, who would then only be in the way.

Fu Antos did not waste either ancient or modern ammunition on the Indians. He let them get to the walls and attempt to scale them with the crude ropes and wooden ladders they carried. Then the waiting ninjas dumped pots of boiling water, oil and fecal matter on their heads, along with plain old rocks. It was just like old times.

Some ladders hooked over the ramparts, which as yet had not been built very high. The ninjas simply used special hooks of their own to shove the ladders off and over, to fall on the heads of those below. The few Indians who actually made it to the top were met by trained swordsmen. The Indians' crude knives, machetes, wooden clubs, and stone-tipped spears were no match for the weapons and expertise of the ninjas. One ninja used a *kusarigama* chained sickle that he hurled through the head of one Indian, stuck into the body of the next, drew him up close and dropped him over the wall, throttled a third with the chain, and bashed in the forehead of a fourth with the steel ball on the end of the chain. That was typical of the action; it was one-sided, and the ninjas did not lose a man.

There was, however, one injury. A crafty old Indian crept over the top, lay down, and used a blowgun. The dart caught a ninja in the left eye. It was not poisonous and did not kill him, but did cost the man that eye. The ninja struck the old man's arm between the wrist and elbow with a karate blow that splintered the bone, then made a *shuto* block to the neck, breaking it. The corpse rolled off the wall.

After that the Indian women and children came up the wall. Now the ninjas did not even bother to use their weapons. They attacked with bare hands and feet, parrying the feeble efforts of the Indians and heaving them off the wall. The ninjas took some more injuries in this hand-to-hand scuffle, for the children bit them and the women had claws like tigers, but their fingers poked out eyeballs, bashed in noses, and stunned nerve complexes with devastating effectiveness.

Fu Antos looked on from his turret, seemingly aloof, but seething inside. "Now we are killing women and babies," he murmured. "For this shame there must be a penalty. Loose the animals."

Signals were made. Suddenly cleverly concealed trapdoors opened near the edge of the valley and crazed animals charged out, into the pitched tents of the army camp. Bats flew into the tents, seeking darkness—but their bodies were coated with poison that rubbed off on whatever they touched. Dozens of *capybaras,* the world's largest rodents, scooted through with small torches tied to their tails, setting the tents afire. And large snakes slithered among the troops: anacondas up to thirty feet long, and boa constrictors up to fifteen feet. They did not actually hurt many soldiers, but they created a tremendous distraction that prevented effective dousing of the flaming tents. And vicious monkeys dropped from the trees: reddish howlers and spider monkeys, with poisoned teeth and feet. And from other cages came stubby-legged bush dogs with snub noses and short tails, standing only a foot tall at the shoulders, but crazed and vicious.

In short, the government troops were suffering the same sort of harassment as the ninjas. In due course all the animals were killed or driven off, but many soldiers had been wounded, the ranks were demoralized, and the tent camp was a smoking ruin. Mirabal looked on the devastation with an expression very like that of Fu Antos watching the dying Indians. Tit for tat!

Now, at last, Mirabal committed his own troops. The Indians seemed to have fully occupied the ninja defense, so that nothing could be spared for the fresh army. The troops charged across the marsh, not even bothering to fire their rifles.

The colonel had managed to carry in and emplace half a dozen mortars: fairly simple substitutes for cannon. Each unit was merely a tube. The shell was dropped in the muzzle, and fired itself when it struck the base inside. It lacked the range and precision of major artillery, so lobbed the shells high, like a catapult. But a comparatively small and light mortar could do the job of a howitzer if appropriately emplaced and operated.

Now these mortars were set up in a line at the base of the cliffs where there was a narrow but firm ledge. The region seemed to have been made for mortars, a fatal oversight on the ninja's part. They started lobbing shells at the castle, and each shell packed an awful punch.

The first one missed the castle, overshooting it. A plume of water and dirt appeared, pretty from a distance, awful from close up. This was not bad marksmanship, but the process of zeroing in. The first shell was normally fired long, the second short, and after that bracketing the third would be right on target.

"Earth," Fu Antos said, invoking the second of his four major defense elements. The first, Air, had been used with devastating effect on the besieged army column: the narcotic smoke. A ninja waved a black flag from another high turret, a signal to an unseen associate.

Another plume manifested, short of the castle. The mortars were zeroing in. Still Fu Antos stood on the battlements, waiting.

Now a round of six mortars struck. Three missed to the side; two exploded in the castle's center court; one blasted a gaping gap in the outer wall. The stones jumped and toppled, falling on the few Indians still trying to scale that section, crushing them. But it was obvious that the castle could not withstand many more such strikes; there would be too many avenues of entry for the troops.

Now the mortar shells were pulverizing the castle with direct hits, collapsing the bunkers where the ninja women and children were sheltered. "Get to the ramparts!" one man cried in Japanese. "That's as safe as any other place, and you can fight there." So they moved out, as brave in their desperation as the families of the Indians, while the terrible shells slowly demolished the castle.

Yet Fu Antos merely watched.

Then there was a muffled noise from the mountainside behind Mirabal's army. The entire cliff shuddered and collapsed. An avalanche formed, triggered by the carefully placed plastic explosives the ninjas had captured. Rocks and dirt and trees tumbled majestically down, onto the ledge where the mortars were emplaced.

The earth had swallowed that portion of the army. Yet a single mortar escaped. It continued to bombard the castle, until a kite-flying ninja made a *kamikaze* dive at it, blowing it up with a hand grenade. Now the artillery was silent.

Still, the soldiers were committed. They plowed on toward the castle. The ninjas were now using catapults to lob grenades at the troops, but it was obvious that this was a mere nuisance to a force of this size. Once the soldier's firepower was brought to bear at close range, the men would be able to scale the half-built walls or ram through the gaps made by the mortars with virtual impunity, killing any ninjas who showed their faces.

"Fire," Fu Antos said. And now the ninjas manned huge pol-

ANTH

ished-steel mirrors that caught the sun, focused it, and speared it at the oncoming troops. Like lasers, the fierce beams bathed the soldiers, and the men screamed, their clothing bursting into flame, their ammunition exploding on their bodies like firecrackers. Grenades, heated to spontaneous ignition, blasted holes in the advancing line, until the soldiers in the front ranks had to throw all their remaining explosives away. Some were only passingly touched by the beams; they fell clutching their faces, blinded, hair singed.

But Mirabal, watching closely with his powerful field glasses, gave orders. .75mm recoilless rifles were trained on the mirrors, which were necessarily exposed. Expert snipers fired at will. One mirror was hit directly; it blew up, the fragments raining down like shrapnel. Another was put out of commission when the legs of the ninja operator were struck; man and mirror crashed to the ground. After the first shock was over, the mirrors lost much of their effect.

Still, the troops had been decimated, and were in no fit condition to storm the castle. Now Mirabal committed his reserves. Another five hundred men charged over the bodies of their comrades toward the castle. The ninjas had little left with which to oppose these.

Yet a detachment emerged from the main gate of the castle. Only a dozen men, but there was something odd about them. They were swathed in white robes and mounted on old horses, bearing lances. Strange cavalry!

The soldiers, thinking it might be a surrender mission, did not fire immediately. The horsemen approached, their clothing resembling nothing so much as tattered bandages.

Then one soldier caught on. "Lepers!" he screamed.

There was little in Latin America that carried greater horror, for less reason, than leprosy. Leprosy is one of the least contagious diseases known, but most people shun all contact with those afflicted. The soldiers panicked.

The horsemen charged among them. Their lances bore blades set lengthwise near the point that could cut open flesh without getting stuck. Indeed, the riders were so feeble that any direct strike of their lances would have unhorsed them; their gnarled hands could hardly bear their weapons. But the soldiers were not even trying to fight; they wanted only to get away, impelled by a horror worse than death itself.

Mirabal snarled another order. His sharpshooters aimed, and in seconds all the lepers fell. But it took some time to reorganize the troops for battle; the bloom was off, and the men were shaken. They would not pass anywhere near the fallen lepers.

Still, there were many more soldiers than ninjas. The last ragged charge crunched forward relentlessly. The ninjas were now out of arrows and had to use their captured rifles. Erratic as their aim with these unfamiliar pieces was, this was a net increase in their firepower. But they were so vastly outnumbered that they could not hope to stop all the troops.

Several hundred men stormed the ravaged ramparts. The defenders were out of hot oil, out of refuse, and low on ammunition. Their numbers had been thinned by inevitable casualties; only a dozen ninja men remained, and twice that number of women and children, who now were doing much of the firing. All were shaken by the mortar bombardment, many were wounded, and most were dead tired.

Fu Antos remembered almost four hundred years before, when the troops of Nobunaga, Shogun of Japan, had overwhelmed the first Black Castle and slaughtered all its brave ninjas and their families. He experienced a feeling of *déjà vu*. Those limited ninja forces had withstood the siege of the mightiest army in Japan's medieval history. Then it had been crossbows against Portuguese muskets; now it was cross-bows, against Portuguese artillery. Mirabal's army lacked the sheer numbers of Nobunaga's, but possessed many sophisticated modern weapons. So it had been a fair match and a great battle.

Certain mistakes had been made in the Japanese siege, and Fu Antos had seen to it that those mistakes were not repeated. He had prepared his defenses of Air, Earth, Fire and Water to eliminate potential weaknesses. Modern technology and an intelligent, ruthless enemy commander had strained the ninja position to the utmost. But victory was assured, because this time Fu Antos had no traitorous female within his walls to betray him to the enemy when victory was within his grasp.

Mitsuko: after centuries, that name still stirred his gut with rage and desire. Lovely treachery! The love of woman was ever the undoing of man. This time he had no woman, and his enemy Mirabal was said to be no lady's man.

But it was time to finish, lest the battle be lost while he reminisced. "Water," Fu Antos said. A pigeon was released. It winged swiftly across the valley toward the river.

The siege continued. Slowly the massed troops gained the upper hand. The ninjas were now confined to individual towers, firing from upper embrasures, while the enemy overran the center court. It seemed to be all over but the mopping up.

Then water appeared. It welled up from vents within the castle, poured out from sluices in the walls. The top blew off a center-court fountain; a geyser of water gushed up. The castle was perched atop a massive subterranean conduit, and was now rapidly flooding.

The enemy saw the trap too late. The soldiers were caught between sheer stone walls as the water rose. No way to climb out of it, not with armed ninjas on guard.

The sluices in the deep mountain reservoir had been opened; millions of gallons of water were rushing down to debouch within the castle. Yet those outside the walls were no better off, for now a giant wall of water was rushing down the valley, sweeping over everything in its path. The reason for the strange aspect of the valley was now apparent; it suffered periodic and devastating floods. There was no escape.

Many of the soldiers and Indians could not swim. They were caught by the developing current and spilled over the ramparts, carried along involuntarily. Now the water turned red, and it was lumpy with drowning bodies. Even those who could swim were at a disadvantage, because they were trying to keep their rifles clear and so could not use their hands. They had to disarm themselves in order to survive.

Still the water rose. A strong impetus carried the soldiers along toward the gap in the wall blasted by the first mortar strike. Those who somehow clung to the ramparts were picked off at leisure by the ninjas in the towers.

And of course there were now crocodiles in the lake forming around the castle. And assorted snakes, large and small, excellent swimmers. And giant electric eels.

The ninjas had won, thanks to the last of the elements, water. Only the mopping up continued as the waters subsided. Only one enemy remained with the resources and cunning to escape, and that one was Fu Antos's special prey. For it was Fernando Mirabal, instigator of the entire persecution against the ninjas. Once he was eliminated, a minimum number of judicious assassinations would preserve the secret of the Black Castle forever.

The colonel, of course, had fled the moment he saw the water rising, knowing that it was over. But he knew better than to attempt the booby-trapped ninja road alone. It was impossible to drive through the virgin jungle, and anyway the ninjas had sugared the gasoline of the remaining army vehicles and disabled the helicopter during the animal-distraction. So Mirabal moved on foot.

And Fu Antos followed. His ninja skill made the colonel's trail easy to read; the man had concentrated on speed rather than concealment. He was a powerful man, and had made excellent time, but no one could traverse wilderness as swiftly as a ninja. Steadily the gap closed.

Mirabal came at last to an old prospector's cabin. He had spotted it in his preliminary survey of the area, circling about in his helicopter, and made a mental note: just in case. Now it was the case, and he had sought it out. It was almost over-grown by the resurgent jungle: a good place to hide.

Fu Antos arrived shortly after. He too knew of this cabin, as he was conversant with the entire area. His quarry was inside, unquestionably, gun ready. But from its small window waved a white cloth.

Mirabal wanted to parlay? Fu Antos raised an eyebrow. "Very well," he called in Portuguese. "Come out unarmed. I will speak with you." He did not need to add that any attempted treachery on Mirabal's part would void the truce instantly.

The colonel came. He was gambling that the ninja would honor the truce, at least long enough for the necessary dialogue. They met under a tree before the door, an incongruous pair: the huge man and the young boy.

"I have this place so full of booby-traps you'll never get me," Mirabal said. "And I am well armed. You might get through, but the chances of saving your own life are only fifty-fifty. Is it worth it?"

"I have fire-arrows," Fu Antos said.

And the cabin was dry wood. Set afire, it would force the man out, easy prey to a ninja arrow. Mirabal did not even bother to bluff further. He knew he was virtually helpless before this unimpressive adversary, like a giant cobra before a tiny mongoose. Fu Antos parlayed merely to savor his victory; had he had any doubt at all of his command of the situation, he would have struck instantly. Only the agility of the colonel's mind could save him from the implacable vengeance he had earned, and his prepared ace-in-the-hole. "I can be more useful to you alive than dead."

Again, no verbal parrying. The hopeless buzzing of the trapped fly was music to the spider. "Continue."

"I have resources that can rebuild your castle within a month, in complete secrecy. You have mental powers and raw materials that could profit me immensely—diamonds and oil, for example. Working together, we could achieve the dreams of both."

Fu Antos raised an eyebrow inquiringly.

"You want to know how you can trust me not to betray your secrets the moment I am safe," Mirabal said. In effect he was groveling, relieving the victor of even having to put the questions. "You possess unparalleled hypnotic powers. Use them on me; verify my sincerity. If I mean to betray you, kill me now. I offer no resistance, only a new allegiance, penalty of my defeat."

The man had offered his services to the victor, in a time-honored gesture. But the ninja only shrugged slightly. The offering was insufficient.

So Mirabal played his trump. "And I have—this," he said. He reached inside his jacket, brought out a waterproof envelope, opened it, and held up the photograph inside.

Fu Antos looked, and froze. At the moment of his seeming nadir, Mirabal had struck at the ninja's most fundamental liability. "It is—her," the ninja whispered.

Mirabal bowed his head in mock surrender. "Now kill me."

The ninja was oblivious to the ploy. His intense interest had been hooked; to kill the Colonel now would be to throw away the compelling information he offered. "Tell me of her."

Mirabal had the grace not to gloat. His hook had lodged, and through it he would not only save his life, he could achieve tremendous wealth and power. Why hadn't he thought to cooperate with the ninjas before, instead of fighting them? There was no essential conflict of purpose. "She is Dulce, an agent of the Cuban intelligence network. She is highly intelligent, trained in combat, and absolutely loyal to her principles. She would foment an armed revolution to save her man. All in all, a woman worthy of the finest man."

Fu Antos hardly listened. For the image he stared at was that of Mitsuko, his beautiful wife of almost four hundred years before. The wife who had betrayed him to the enemy, bringing about the downfall of the first Black Castle. In all the intervening centuries he had cursed her, yet had been able to love no other. This was not precisely Mitsuko, for the picture depicted a Western girl, but still, the resemblance was remarkable.

"She is alive and well in my possession," Mirabal continued. "The photograph hardly does her justice. But there is one complication."

"Bring her to me," Fu Antos breathed, in those words signifying his capitulation. He was ready to trade his nascent empire for mere possession of this one woman, exactly as Mirabal had anticipated.

"This is the complication. Oh, I can bring her here an hour after I reach a telephone; she is confined in one of our offices in Brasilia, not far by air from here. But her loyalty is to another man. I would be delivering only her body; her heart would not be yours, so long as that man lives."

"I will kill that man," the ninja said with cold finality.

Mirabal raised his hands in a gesture of incapacity. "Please do not misunderstand, Lord Ninja. I do not seek to thwart you, only to clarify certain awkward aspects that may have already occurred to you. This woman Dulce is not a carbon copy of Mitsuko. Her love is not negotiable. If you killed her lover, she would seek to kill *you,* and I doubt even your hypnotic power could change her mind for long. She is a superior creature; she must be won gently, not by force, or she will be no better than your wife was. But, properly cultivated, her loyalty to you would be unflinching. She would be what Mitsuko *should* have been. It would be a mistake to—"

"Dare you preach at *me?"* Fu Antos demanded, his eyes blazing. Suddenly he had no faintest resemblance to a child, despite his size.

Mirabal bowed his head. "I apologize for my presumption. I shall have her brought directly to you."

Fu Antos was mollified. "Rephrase your thought."

"Obviously it will be necessary to eliminate her lover. But you should not do it personally. Rather you should side with her, and help her to avenge her loss. Gradually her appreciation for this support will convert to appreciation for *you.* It may take a few years, but some things are best done slowly, properly, like the maturing of fine wines and cheeses. Love must develop in its own fashion, at its own rate; only then is it deep and complete. Your body is growing yet; by the time it is ready, *she* will be ready."

Fu Antos nodded, impressed by the logic. His mind was centuries old, but his body was a stripling, really inadequate to the task of loving a voluptuous woman properly. He needed time.

"This is the first service I can perform for you," Mirabal continued. "I will kill her lover, and let her escape to you. You and I are known enemies; you will be guiltless. You will send your ninjas out to kill me, though they may not have any more success than they have in the past."

"Who is her lover?"

Now it grew ticklish again. "Jason Striker, the American judoka. I believe you know him."

"Striker!" the ninja breathed.

"I realize he has been a friend of yours, or at least has performed some small service," Mirabal said carefully. If the ninja was prepared to dispense with Striker . . ."But I can show you that he is the one she—"

"A ninja has no friends," Fu Antos said, his expression hardening. "Jason Striker must die."

Mirabal nodded, his victory complete. "I shall intercept him. He is now on his way to Brasilia, in the company of a lithesome dancer, to meet your agent."

"You are well informed," Fu Antos said dryly.

"It is my business to be informed. Striker has been intimate with her—" Mirabal paused, having a notion. "In fact, it might be best if Dulce were to have concrete proof of his infidelity, before he died. That would destroy her romance with him completely, leaving her ripe for . . ."

"If you were on hand, she would know it was false," Fu Antos pointed out. "She would suspect Striker had been framed."

"True," Mirabal said regretfully. "I did frame him before." He pondered another moment, then brightened. "But there is always an alternate method. It happens that the dancer's estranged husband is in my employ. He has shown little interest in his wife, but he has a jealous nature. He is proficient in *capoiera*, the great Brazilian fighting art. On my orders, he could help Dulce break out, he claiming to be a ninja agent with information where to meet Striker."

Fu Antos nodded, smiling.

And so it was arranged: Jason Striker's best friend in the Amazon collaborated with his worst enemy to have him slain, because of the girl who loved him, exactly as the god Exu had decreed. There was to be no escape from the voodoo curse.

Chapter 10:

City of the Future

The truck jounced along the red dirt road, northwest through the highlands of Brazil. I saw endless fields of beans and rice, orchards of coffee trees, and huge herds of cattle ranging square miles of pasture. I had not really grasped before how *big* Brazil was.

The sun was hot, but we were pleasantly cool, for huge blocks of ice surrounded the cargo: live crabs and lobsters from the coast, bound for the gourmet restaurants of the capital city. Every so often a lobster claw emerged from the slats of a crate and tried to pinch me: one of the defects in the service I had to live with.

Near the river—I had no idea *which* river—we passed a series of swampy lakes. The truck slowed to get around a wooden-wheeled cart drawn by half a dozen slow oxen, and the mosquitoes were on us in a swarm. We slapped and slapped; there was nothing else to do. I had visions of malaria and yellow fever, though really had no idea whether these were dangers this far south of the Equator.

Our transportation from Rio de Janeiro to the wilds of the continental interior had been as abrupt as the rest of this crazy adventure. Kan-Sen's message had finally come through to the hotel, delayed by I knew not what bureaucratic snafu. It had been taken by an employee who was in *Umbando* and had seen me at the mass, so he took it to the *pai-de-Santo,* who delivered it to Oba's apartment. When we returned there, after the Kendo school massacre, we discovered it: orders to go to Brasilia, where a ninja would contact me at a certain restaurant.

So here we were, Oba still protecting me from the wrath of Exu. I had tried to suggest that she had fulfilled her assignment, and that little danger for me remained now that the Death Squad had been wiped out, but the language barrier had prevented her comprehension. It had not, however, prevented her from understanding that I had to go to Brasilia. So she had arranged transport for us on this truck, that happened to be going to the very restaurant I needed. That was either one hell of a coincidence, or there really *was* something about voodoo assistance. I hoped I was not, like the lobsters I rode with, heading for hot water.

Then at last, as the dawn came over the fringe of the huge tropical forest, it hove into view: Brasilia, capital city of the future. I could not see it all from the ground, of course, but Oba drew a picture in the dust that put it into perspective like an aerial photograph. The city looked like a modern swept-wing airplane, seven miles from the golf club in its needle-nose to the railroad station dangling from its tail, with a single highway traversing its entire length like a ramrod through its metropolitan gut.

Even from the truck it was impressive, but perhaps not in quite the way intended by the architect. For there were more *favela* slums here, massive ones whose population rivaled that of the city proper. Oba had explained something about the *favelas,* by gesture and pantomime, as we had had plenty of time to exchange communications. Quite an education.

We passed the airport and entered the city from the south: the tip of its right wing. We drove three miles up the center of that wing along a broad parkway, divided with triple lanes with green gardens between.

Oba pantomimed more detail as we went: to the east, in the nose section, were the ministries, courts, and towering congressional office buildings, like the brain in the cockpit of the craft. To the left, in the tail section, were some of the entertainment facilities: the ovals of the racetrack and sports stadium. Oba made two marks with her finger, clarifying the map. Somehow those smudges in the tail reminded me of ovaries, and that suggested another kind of entertainment, more of a participant exercise than football or horse racing. But I quelled my one-track male mind. I still hadn't recovered fully from our heroic triple indulgence in the kendo school, and anyway, if I tried to make time with Oba now, that damned lobster would pinch me in the ass.

Beyond the entertainments, at the very tip of the torso, was the newspaper and printing complex. And again my unruly imagination ran rampant, as I visualized scandal sheets and propaganda being ejected from the feathered anus of this roc-like bird. I'm just a natural lowbrow, I guess, especially when I've spent two wearing days being rattled in a fish truck with an aggressive lobster and a girl who doesn't speak my language.

But Oba was acting out an episode of the city's history. It seemed there was a big contest, open to all the architects in Brazil, with a large cash prize: to design Brasilia. The leading firms of the nation spent months preparing designs and drawings and models to submit to the judges. One person who was too modest to enter was Lucio Costa, though he was known for his architectural brilliance. But his friends coerced him to enter, and finally, reluctantly, at the very last moment, he spent twenty-five cents for paper and pencils and quickly sketched his plan, just to shut them up. Well, at least it was an entry.

"Now, don't tell me, let me guess!" I said. "The winner—"

Oba smiled. Right: the Selection Committee, experts drawn from all over the world, awarded first prize unanimously, to the two-bit effort. And that selection was hailed all over the world as an innovation in city planning, imaginative yet basically simple. Costa's design became Brasilia.

I was impressed all right. We were now driving past the superblocks, each containing a dozen trees and surrounded by gardens and playgrounds. Each superblock, Oba let me know, was supposed to be virtually self-contained, with its own stores and schools. At least, that was the theory; I wasn't clear from her gestures and my observations whether it had actually worked out. If it *had,* why the *favelas?*

There was no traffic congestion, even in the high-rise center of town. Of course; we had arrived at dawn, too early for slothful government workers to be up. Later in the day it might be a different story. Cloverleaf loops and ramps made stoplights unnecessary, and the sheer geography of the layout facilitated movement.

We pulled up behind the monstrous theater and restaurant section in the heart of the city where the load of seafood was to be delivered. This was as far as our driver could take us.

We thanked him, inadequately, and moved out on foot. All the way around to the front of the restaurant, where we entered in order to make contact with the ninja.

Now I had to order a glass of fresh skim milk, and refuse to settle for anything else. Feeling stupid, I did so. The waiter spoke very little English, so there was a minor hassle, and it turned out the closest they could come was canned milk. Brazilians were not milk drinkers. I was adamant, though conscious of my seedy appearance.

Finally the waiter went for a consultation with the headwaiter. Oba was staring at me with perplexity. I was, of course, being quite unreasonable. I wondered what uproar I would have created had I emulated Hiroshi and ordered something *really* exotic like yak's milk.

The headwaiter approached, a forbidding figure of a man, and I was daunted. Where was the ninja? Had there been a foul-up in communications? "We have reserved our best private dining room for you, sir," he murmured in English.

"Oh, we can't afford that!" I protested, uncertain how much money Oba had and feeling like a pimp. I had no money, having lost it all when I fled the sumo exhibition. Kiyokuni would have given me my winnings, of course, but I had been ashamed to face him so soon after the riot, and with the urgent message from Kan-Sen. So I had taken off for Brasilia in my borrowed clothes. Oh there are many things I would do better, if only I had proper time to reflect. Half my problems stem from my own spot misjudgments.

"There will be no charge," he assured me. "Your friend will be along soon; he asks you to eat well while you wait."

My friend, Fu Antos? Or one of his ninjas? Must be. "All right," I said. I'd certainly be glad when all this mystery was through. I'm not temperamentally suited for intrigue or high living.

The private dining room was ornate, fit literally for a king. There was a couch and several easy chairs beyond the huge banquet table, and so many potted plants and even small trees that it resembled a greenhouse. The waiter attended us, then discreetly retired, giving us romantic privacy.

We were served crab cocktail with plenty of red sauce, onion soup with thick cheese floating on it, a salad of heart-of-palms, the hearts being tubular and white and probably very tasty; filet mignon with black beans, and plenty of Brazilian wine. In short, an elegant Latin American meal. I'm really no gourmet, either, how I wished for a cheap U.S.A.-American type snack! I wondered uncomfortably whether my friend the pinching lobster was buried somewhere in this repast.

That started a disconcerting chain of thought. This was too similar to the meal I had had with Dulce. Not in detail but in atmosphere: strange, delicious dishes, in private with a pretty girl. I had no reason to be suspicious, yet, when I contemplated all that fancy food, my hunger left me. Also, for no reason I could fathom, I remembered the Iado Master and the sudden slaughter of the Death Squad. All that blood and guts. Maybe I was getting paranoid, but I couldn't eat.

Oba had no such reservations. Even if I could have explained my concern to her, I wouldn't have. I knew it was just my foolishness, an overdose of suspicion; James Bond never suffered loss of appetite, did he? And this was probably the best meal she had been offered in a long time.

"Comer! Comer!" she urged me, gesturing with her fork. No mistaking her meaning: Eat, eat!

So I did something I wasn't proud of: I faked it. I shoveled bites of food into my pockets when she wasn't looking, and made chewing motions. Messy as hell, but when I get hung up, I get hung up all the way. I poured my soup into the big flowerpot beside my chair, hoping it didn't kill the plant. Same with the wine, the palm tree behind me drank that. I felt disgusted with myself.

Actually, Oba wasn't paying much attention, or I never could have gotten away with it. She ate with such gusto I wondered whether she had ever had a chance at such a repast. And my forebodings seemed less and less sensible, until I was chagrined at my foolishness. Here I was with a soggy pocket, passing up a wonderful meal.

Yet there is an ornery streak in me that sometimes just won't let go. If I ate now, I would be admitting that I had been wrong not to eat at the start, and it can be very hard to admit something like that. So the nonsense compounded itself. I had started out not to eat, and now I was perversely determined to finish out that way, going to hell and hunger in my own fashion. I knew I would regret it, for there was likely to be much work after I met the ninja representative. I had not been summoned all the way here for nothing, after all. There had to be some hugely important task, something only I could do. Perhaps I would be instructing the ninjas in special judo and karate techniques, so they could better defend their secret Black Castle from intrusions. Yes, that must be it, and I was glad to do it for Fu Antos, the unique man who had saved my life from the effects of the delayed-action deathblow, not so long ago. I owed him my life, literally. Though there were times when I wondered about the ninja master.

Oba sank onto the table. Her nose pressed into the egg custard. Startled, she jerked up, wiping her face. But then she swayed forward again.

Suddenly alarms were clanging stridently in my brain. *She had been drugged!* Just as before, the food, the drink, the same pattern. Someone knew about us and had arranged the same trap that had suckered me before; only this time my subconscious had warned me off. There are limits to how many times I will fall for the same stunt, it seems. Sometimes my unconscious mind is smarter than I am.

Who could have arranged this, except another Death Squad? Mirabal's men must have intercepted Kan-Sen's message, and eliminated the ninja assigned to meet me here. I had to get out!

But how could I get Oba free of this trap? She was an innocent girl, not involved in my mission. She had only wanted to help me.

Well, I'd make do. I stood up.

Too late. Someone was coming.

I could fight, but suppose there was a whole crew, as before? Oba would be sure to suffer, even if I got away. I couldn't desert her; she might be tortured, having her teeth pulled out, or worse.

Then I had an inspiration. I dumped my platter of food on the table near my place, knocked over my glass, and threw myself to the floor half under the table. It would look as if I had eaten half my meal, fought the drug, and succeeded only in making a mess before losing consciousness.

I kept my left hand over my face, as if accidentally, so that I could peek through my fingers, unseen. I wanted to know who my enemy was, where he was, and how he was armed, before I made my move. If it were Mirabal . . .

But it was only the headwaiter. Still, that was significant, for he evinced no surprise at what he saw. That meant he was in on it.

He spoke to the waiter behind him. That was all, just the two of them, and neither one armed. I could handle them readily.

But I waited. Surely these two men were not the conspirators. They were employees of the restaurant. They might have been bribed or threatened, but the ones I wanted hadn't shown up yet. Useless to tilt at the flunkies.

The headwaiter spoke in Portuguese. How I wished I could understand him! The two men came and dragged me out and turned me over, and I remained limp, only groaning a little as if trying to fight out of it. Too complete an unconsciousness might be suspicious, assuming this was the same drug as before; I had been able to fight it off for a while, then. Unconsciousness is not necessarily total; it only seems that way in retrospect because of memory blackouts.

They picked me up and dragged my trousers off. I didn't like this, but allowed it; obviously they had something in mind, and I doubted it was homosexual rape. Maybe they were going to dress me in something else? Why? What if they discovered my pocket full of food, already well mashed? But they didn't; they merely hauled me over to an easy chair in the corner and went to work on Oba.

They stripped her all the way naked, cleaned the custard off her face, and carried her over to me. They lifted her up, bent her knees, and set her in my lap, facing me.

What the hell? They surely knew—or thought—I was in no condition to take advantage of this opportunity. I hoped my masculine reaction would not give me away, but it was all right, because her firm buttocks rested on my thighs and concealed that region. The position brought mixed memories, though!

They propped her head on my shoulder and draped her arms and hair around me as well as possible. An unconscious girl does not hang on too well, so they had to draw me up a bit and pin one of her hands between my back and the chair. Her handsome breasts pressed against my chest, and I felt her bare abdomen swell rhythmically against mine with her breathing. What a posture!

Then the two men quickly wheeled out the table and replaced it with a fresh one. Presto, no more mess!

But what could it all mean? Eventually Oba and I would wake up, and perhaps be under the impression we had made love. But would that be so shocking? We had made love before—and how!—so there was nothing shocking about that notion. Actually Oba was as thoroughly lovable a creature as I've encountered, and I don't mean just her fine dancer's body or her pretty face. So this careful pose made little sense; left to our own devices, we just might have assumed it on our own.

The waiters set an open bottle of liquor on a little table beside us, after pouring out two glasses, half full. So it would look as if we had left our drinks in favor of more intimate entertainment. But still, that was only appearance. Unless someone else spied us.

That was it! We were being framed, just as I had been framed on the homosexual charge before. Certainly the same sort of mind had concocted this trap, the Death Squad mind.

Well, I could foil that. As soon as the waiters left, I'd get dressed and take Oba out . . . and never find out who had engineered this.

Yet if I stayed, who knew what mischief was in the offing?

Too late, again. Someday I'll have to learn to make difficult decisions fast, or I may not live to make more slow ones. The waiters ducked out, and someone else was coming down the hall. No time to get out. Well, nothing I could do now except to play it through.

A figure appeared in the doorway. Two figures.

Someone screamed. A woman.

Through slitted eyes, peering past Oba's luxuriant hair, I saw the people, and received my worst shock of the day.

Dulce!

She was staring at the two of us, so suggestively arranged, and I knew there was only one conclusion she could draw. She was the very last person I would have wanted to show up at this moment.

Beside her was a man. He looked vaguely familiar, but I couldn't place him, and of course I didn't know anyone in this city.

It hardly mattered, for he screamed and charged. Instantly I recognized the mode of the martial artist; his muscular development and the manner he moved gave it away. And there was no doubt of his intention. He was out to kill. I may be slow in some respects, but in combat I catch on quickly.

I exploded out of that chair. Or tried to. Oba was in my arms, and I had either to drop her or use her as a shield, and I balked at either. So as the man's fist came down, I turned, catching the blow on my shoulder. Then I set Oba in the chair, somewhat roughly, but speed was of the essence. I straightened, about to whirl into my antagonist, and he caught me with a hard kick to the side. It scored right under my ribs, and his calloused toes smashed in with appalling force, half stunning me. A man does not have to get struck on the point of the chin to suffer disorientation.

I pitched forward. I was not unconscious, but at this stage it was easier to take a fall than to fight the pain; in a moment I would recover from the shock of the blow and be able to function better. And it wouldn't hurt at all if he thought I was out for the count.

But as I landed, he kicked me again, in the small of the back. And again the pain blossomed. A girdle of paralysis clamped about my waist; I felt like dying. Something internal had ruptured, or maybe a nerve was crushed; I couldn't tell, but it was awful. I was really taking a beating.

A third time he kicked me. He didn't care whether I was awake or asleep; he just wanted to bash me to death. And he was pretty well succeeding. I knew then what I faced: this was a renegade *Capoiera* fighter. *Capoiera* is a Brazilian specialty, said to be the dirtiest martial art in the world. Anything goes; the glass-sharded feet of the man I'd fought in the Rio prison had been an example. This bastard would pulverize me if I remained a target.

I had no choice. I had to fight back or be demolished. I gritted my teeth against the pain in my back, and when his fourth kick came I whipped my arm about and caught his foot. That made him stagger, and I was able to get to my knees.

He cuffed me on the ear, and I let go, hoping I didn't have a cauliflower ear like Oba's now. The old schoolboy punishment of boxing the ears was a painful one. As I stood up unsteadily, he performed another *Capoiera* specialty: he fell back on one hand

and one foot, and then shot the other foot at my face. But I had anticipated this, now that I had identified his style of combat, and I countered instantly. I knocked his leg aside with my forearm, then leaped forward, onto his body.

We crashed to the floor together, him underneath. A hitting specialist is at a disadvantage when encumbered, which is one of the reasons judo is such an effective all around martial art: it includes striking *and* wrestling forms. He was like a python, whipping his body back and forth, trying to shake me loose and get his finger in my eye or his elbow in my throat or his teeth anywhere, but I whipped with him, and used his contortions to my own advantage.

First I got behind him, straddling his body, pressing him down; he countered by heaving up violently, to throw me off. But as his body cleared the floor, I hooked my left leg around his left arm, slid my right arm around, his right shoulder and up to grab my own lapel (lucky they hadn't stripped me of that, too, but actually I know plenty of "naked" techniques too), and thus had both his arms entangled from behind, with his feet out of the way. That's the secret of judo, using your opponent's own strength against him, so that the more he exerts himself the better off you are. He didn't like that position, so he tried to buck me off, and again I took advantage of his power. I took a forward roll, landing beneath him, giving him the sensation of success, but it was illusory, for I had not relinquished my control of his arms. He lay face up, his arms pinned, his head on my belly. Not uncomfortable, but not much for carrying the attack to me, either. But I had no such restriction; I shifted my right leg to control his right arm, freeing my left leg. That gave me both my left leg and left arm to work with. I grabbed his collar and pulled across his throat, putting my leg around his head for leverage. There was a *lot* of leverage in that leg, too.

Now this may sound complicated, so I'll put it in simpler terms: it was the *Jigoku-Jime,* or "Hell Strangle", so named because it is hell on the victim. His arms were entangled, his legs thrashed helplessly, and I was applying terrible leverage to his neck. Hercules himself could not have broken that hold.

Meanwhile, Dulce had gone over to Oba and hauled her out of the chair, probably intending some sort of mayhem herself. But she had discovered the girl was unconscious. Dulce was not the sort to beat up a helpless rival, no matter how angry she was. So she was contenting herself with shaking. Oba violently, waking her, still thinking it was the effects of the liquor.

Oba's eyes opened slowly; obviously the drug was still on her. I hoped there would not be a woman-woman fight; I was in no position to break it up promptly. But then Oba saw me with my strangle on the struggling man, who was almost out though resisting heroically. She made an anguished little cry and staggered to her feet, fell, and crawled toward us on hands and knees, her handsome breasts drawing down. I thought she had mistaken our position, supposing *I* was the one getting wiped out, since I was on the bottom, but it was not so. She threw herself on me, trying to wrench my leg from the man's neck. She screamed something in Portuguese.

Naturally her action was ineffective, and in a moment she collapsed across the man. He, too, had had enough; his legs stopped moving as he lost consciousness. She had succumbed again to the drug, he to my strangle; ironically they finished in each other's arms.

"Let go," Dulce snapped at me. "She said you are killing her husband."

Actually I had already eased up. A judo strangle is a controlled thing, quite safe when properly applied, and I hadn't gotten to be a fifth degree black belt without knowing how to do it right. I was subduing him, not killing him, despite his attempt to kill *me.*

"Her *husband?" I* demanded as I disengaged. Sometimes I'm slow on the uptake; I have admitted that many times. Now I knew where I'd seen this man before. The picture on Oba's dresser: him.

"He brought me to meet you. He helped me escape from

Mirabal, and here you are, like the tomcat you are, seducing his wife! No wonder he lost control!"

"Fat chance," I said, rubbing my back, trying to alleviate the continuing agony there. "The food was drugged, and we were posed. Remember when you and I dined together? That's how the Death Squad strikes."

Her eyes widened. Dulce was no dummy. "She *is* drugged. And he tried to kill you without even questioning—" She paused. "But you—why aren't *you* drugged?" And her suspicion of me was strong again.

I explained tersely. Then: "Obviously this was another trap. Someone wanted me dead, and wanted you to think I had betrayed you. Just how convenient was your escape from Mirabal, and how did you know where to find me?"

Her eyes narrowed. "*Too* convenient! This man had word from a *santerio* or something, a note telling you to be here. He told me he was a friend of the ninjas who wanted to make a deal with the MR-26 Movement, so if I would come with him and meet with Fu Antos—" She stopped, shaking her head at her own gullibility. "Obviously he's no friend of the ninjas! He must be Mirabal's agent, sent to track down the ninjas, using me and you. And his wife is in it with him."

The man was beginning to stir. "I don't think she's in on it," I said, getting into my pants. "But we'd better get out of here; she obviously still loves him." Indeed, Oba was clutching the man even in her unconsciousness.

Dulce smiled grimly. "Hurts your male ego, doesn't it."

"Yes." Better to let her think that than the truth, that Oba and I had been every bit as intimate as the pose suggested, at another time. But I certainly wanted no more to do with Oba now; I don't like adultery. Let her return to her husband, whom she still loved despite her injured ear, just like her namesake goddess. If only I had been able to understand her whole meaning, during the pantomime dance.

We moved out quickly, leaving Oba and her husband to come

to what terms they might. Maybe this time Xango would stay at home a little longer. His wife had quite a bit to offer, if he cared to try her out.

We sneaked out the back door, dodged around the building and down the street, alert for pursuit, but there was none. It seemed Mirabal hadn't figured his neatly laid trap would miss.

"So the colonel arranged to have me killed, in your presence," I said as we walked along, putting more distance between us and the restaurant. "But why?"

"Obviously so I would panic and run to the Black Castle for help, whereupon they would follow me and ascertain its location," she said. "I'm afraid I was naïve."

"You know where the Black Castle is?" I asked, surprised.

"Not exactly. But the ninjas did make an overture to the urban guerrillas. That was why I believed the *Capoeira* agent. Before we raided the prison, I learned that there was a ninja stronghold in the jungle, and I know its location to within about fifty miles. I did not know the connection to you, until Mirabal informed me. If we contact the Indians in that region, they will put us in touch."

"And we can warn Fu Antos how far Mirabal has penetrated his network," I said. "The ninjas are in terrible danger. Mirabal is savage and smart, and he has the whole resources of the government. Yes, we have to do it." Then I paused, startled, my hand at my throat. "The *Figa!*" I exclaimed. "I lost my *Figa!*"

Dulce eyed me. "Don't tell me that doll even had you wearing a native amulet!"

"It's bad luck to lose it," I said, my ears heating. "It must have come off during the fight."

"We're not going back there!" she said sharply. "That would really be bad luck."

"No, of course not," I agreed, chastened. After all, it *was* only a magic charm, of no actual value. Maybe I was upset because it had been all that remained to me of Oba, with her dancer's body and dancer's stamina.

"Here's the bus," Dulce said. "We have a long ride."

"We do?" I hadn't realized we were taking a bus. But we were, and we did. I snoozed off and on, and Dulce remarked how the land here was no good for farming, the soil being thin and poor under the seemingly luxurious canopy of trees.

And so we rode into the wilderness, heading away from the city of the future, toward the castle of the past. We got off at a tiny village, a mere cluster of huts, and walked into the dense tropical forest.

We did not suffer from hunger. Huge, heavy nuts lay on the ground under the big trees. Dulce found edible roots, and fruits that hung on little stems poking out directly from the massive trunks. I'm no nature expert, but I'm not entirely naive about the wilderness; I had been a beret in Indochina years back, and learned to forage from the land. But Dulce evidently knew more about this particular locale than I did. She had pills to purify the water and kill the liver flukes that infested it, and knew how to make a fire. She spied an armadillo, and I killed it with a karate blow to the head. I was sorry for the creature, but it was food.

We came across an abandoned patch of cultivated land where the Indians had tried to grow some fruit. There were a few tubers, plantains and mangos, guavas and avocados remaining.

I was ravenous, after my missed banquet, and afraid we might not find as much food further along, so I stuffed myself. My stomach rumbled as it encountered the roast armadillo, and all that avocado didn't help, but I didn't want to waste anything. Dulce only looked at me and shook her head. "Little boys and ice cream . . ." she murmured. It was her way of remarking on my gluttony, or perhaps she was bitter about something else. Like a slender dancer, nude, in my lap.

We walked. The floor of the deep jungle was not bushy, though there was a great deal of mossy growth. In fact, we could have ridden bicycles through it, only watching out for animal burrows and raised roots. My notion of tropical forest being dank and impenetrable was completely false. Well, not *completely*; it was indeed a tangled mass above, high in the canopy. Huge liana vines climbed the trunks of the trees and hung everywhere, just as in the Tarzan movies. We could not see the sun at all; every square foot was covered by leaves. And the jungle floor was no crawling mass of pythons, headhunters and carnivorous plants; there were animals, but we knew of their presence mainly by their sounds and traces. It really was quite peaceful.

The air was hot, for though this was the winter season in North America, it was the height of summer here in South America, and we were nearer the equator. Dulce, wiser than I, soon stripped to the buff, and made me do likewise. "The earth is antiseptic here," she said. "It is the sweat-soaked clothing that brings smell and illness. To be bare is to be healthy, only stay out of the sun."

Like Adam and Eve, I thought. Could it be that the innocence of the first man and woman was the source of their health? That when they emerged from the healthy shade of the forest and put on grime-holding clothes, they put on disease as well? Then what a paradise we lost when we gave up our nudity! I glanced sidelong at Dulce. Her unfettered beauty threatened to raise the beast in me, and I had to look away.

At night, fatigued from a long walk, we stopped in a moonlit clearing. We gathered a mound of dry leaves for a bed; if it rained, well, we were naked anyway, and would dry. It was a novel funfeeling, this Adamic and Evian repose in the forest.

However, the obvious, un-innocent thought occurred to me, actually it had been building ever since we went natural, and I made it known to Dulce. Or rather, it made itself known, when her thigh banged against it. It was a wonder she didn't get bruised, for this particular serpent was rocklike. Would it tempt her?

But first I had to confess my relationship with Oba. "We were posed, there in the restaurant, but before that, in Rio—"

"It is all right," she said coolly. "I do not own you. I am not a jealous female. I know how men are."

Cutting words! I would have preferred to have been bawled out. "She helped save me from the Death Squad," I continued lamely.

"Men are polygamous. It is unrealistic to expect otherwise. I do not have to love you to get in bed with you."

She meant that *I* did not have to love *her.* She was tightly controlled, so I had only a hint of what was suppressed inside her, but that hint was a glimpse into an awful chasm. *She* loved me, unworthy as I knew myself to be, and what could I say? For me, love was a many-fickled thing. Yet after my fiancee, Chiyako—

Dulce relented. She stroked my cheek in the dark. "I am sorry, Jason. I know you loved once, and never again. The Chinese girl."

"She's dead," I said. And winced, feeling an internal pain. But that might have been indigestion from all the unfamiliar jungle food. Brazil nuts are pretty greasy and concentrated. Avocados had a lot of fat, too. And that armadillo, well, my stomach hadn't forgiven me for that yet, it seemed.

So we made love, but it was not as good as before. After that we chatted a while, and decided that in the morning we would make up some bits of bark to be like *caracoles,* the voodoo coconut fragments, and try a throw to indicate the direction we should take to find the ninjas. It seemed Dulce was not a complete skeptic about such magic, and neither was I, now. Though the loss of my *Figa* complicated that.

*

I woke in the night. I had a pain in my right side just under the ribs. That lingering indigestion would not go away! I knew I shouldn't have stuffed myself; why had I done it?

I got up and paced about, hoping to release a little gas pressure and be done with it, but the pain only intensified. I leaned over and vomited, and that seemed to help, but only for a little while. The misery spread to my back, and became so bad I wanted to cry out.

Dulce woke. "You're sick!" she exclaimed.

"Something I ate," I muttered.

"I ate the same, and *I'm* not sick." She looked at me worriedly in the moonlight, and came to put her hand on my arm. "It can't be your conscience, because you don't *have* much."

"Well, I did get kicked in the back pretty hard in that fight," I said, ignoring her unkind dig. "I felt something go, then, but I had to keep going—"

"Lie down," she said. Obediently, I returned to the leaf-bed, though that did not alleviate my condition. This was one hell of a stomachache, not a kind I had had before.

She ran her hands over my body, squeezing here, pressing there, and there was nothing sexual about it. She must have had medical training in Cuba; she had marvelously gentle hands. I suppose the Communists are good at such things, inculcating all the necessary skills in their agents.

"I don't think it's appendicitis," she murmured as she turned me over and probed my abdomen.

"Can't be," I said. "My appendix was taken out years ago."

When she poked into my stomach on the right side, I groaned aloud. But she continued, gauging the locale by my reactions. One particular spot seemed to generate pure pain at the slightest pressure. "That's what I was afraid of," she said at last.

"What?" I gasped, relieved that she at last had some diagnosis.

"Gallstone."

"What?"

"You have a gallstone, by the signs," she said. "I have seen it before. It usually does not develop so suddenly, but your recent exertions may have accelerated it."

"Gallstone?" I repeated stupidly. "I told you I got kicked a couple of times. In the side and back. It really hurt! Maybe something was ruptured."

"Be quiet," she said, just like a nurse with a balky patient. "The liver produces bile; that neutralizes the strong acids coming into the intestine from the stomach and helps break down fat. The bile is stored in the gall bladder until it is needed. Sometimes stones form from parts of the bile that have settled out of solution, and these stones can block the duct so that the bile cannot get out.

This interrupts the digestion, and can cause the most severe pain the body can experience."

"Now she tells me," I moaned.

"It can be controlled for a while by diet and drugs."

"Here in the jungle?" I demanded.

"But the only real cure is surgery."

"Surgery!" Like most athletic men, I have a morbid fear of surgery.

"It is very simple, as these things go. Just to remove the stone, so the bile can go through. But—"

I knew: how could I undergo surgery, here in the wilds of the Amazon?

"We will get help, at the Black Castle," she said.

"Yes! Fu Antos, he cured me before. He has terrific power. He can use his *ki* to—"

"I was hoping they would have a surgeon there," she said.

"Oh, yes. But how can we get there, even if we find the way? I'm not sure I can walk far."

"I'll carry you if I have to." And she wasn't fooling! But I thought of being draped across her shoulders, all that pressure on my stomach while she staggered along, and I quailed.

"I'll make do, somehow," I said. "If only we could stop the pain."

"Your jacket!" she said, delving into our bundle of clothes.

"What?"

"The food in your pocket."

"I dumped that out. Anyway, I'm not hungry." The understatement of the night! "And it's drugged."

"Yes. It will serve as an anesthetic, in small amounts. We can scrape some from the cloth—"

"I'd rather not," I protested, remembering my prison experience. "That drug has all sorts of bad connotations. And it might aggravate my condition."

"That's true." She considered, then brightened. "I know! I saw wild coca plants growing, back a mile or so. Wait here."

"I don't care for any cup of coca, either!" I objected. "Anyway, it's pitch black. You can't—" But she was gone.

She was quite a girl, I thought. Evidently she could make her way in the dark with confidence. She was certainly one worth marrying, if I knew what was good for me. Was it really necessary that I love her? But of course there was her Communism, that I doubted she cared to give up, even for me. I had a fleeting little nightmare: Dulce standing proudly, torch raised, like the Statue of Liberty, declaiming, "I could not love thee half so much, loved I not Marx more."

Before long she returned with what felt like a handful of leaves. "Chew this," she said.

I was in no condition to argue. I don't even remember what they tasted like, and it was too dark to see them. So I chewed. And you know, in due course I began to feel better. My pain diminished, and strength returned.

"Hey, this herbal remedy is great!" I exclaimed. "What did you say it was?"

"Cocaine," she said succinctly.

I laughed. "No, I'm serious. This stuff really helps. What—"

"The coca plant. *Not* cocoa. A lot of people confuse the two. The drug cocaine is extracted from it. It is an excellent anesthetic."

"I'm an addict!" I exclaimed, appalled.

"One dose does not an addict make, not in this form. The natives chew it all their lives without much ill effect. Right now it's better than being in pain from the gallstone."

I could not debate that. I kept on chewing.

Next morning I felt much better. In fact, I felt terrific. We ate a little more fruit, then went on to discover a small stream with a nice pool. I rinsed off, then stood on the bank and watched Dulce with open appreciation as she bathed. She was like Venus. This life could not last, but what an idyllic interlude!

It ended abruptly. Indians appeared. One brought his bow

up, aimed, and loosed an arrow at me. I reacted automatically: my arm swept across and deflected the arrow just before it struck me. I could not simply let it go past; it might strike Dulce.

A second Indian aimed. I was ready; I tried to catch the arrow in midair, but only knocked it aside again. Still, I did it with a flourish, trying to make it look easy. It wasn't easy; had I not had some practice in this sort of thing, I would have been brought down.

A third Indian, a big buck, charged me with his spear, screaming. I screamed right back at him, a piercing *kiai!* yell, just as he hurled his weapon. I caught the spear, reversed it, and poked it between his legs, sending him into a jarring tumble. Then I held the point to his throat, showing how easily I could kill him.

The other Indians, amazed, came up and kneeled before me. Dulce emerged from the water. "That was beautiful, Jason," she murmured.

She faced the Indians and addressed them in Portuguese. After a brief dialogue, she turned to me. "They are headhunters, but have decided to be friendly. We are invited to visit their village."

"Headhunters!"

"They don't practice it any more. And they will send a runner to notify the ninjas. I believe we can trust them."

Just like that! I was glad I had gone out to impress them instead of really fighting them. I didn't want to lose my head, on top of my bodily problems. But of course I had known that the Indians of this area were allies of the ninjas.

The village treated us royally. I had to make another demonstration of arrow deflecting so everyone could applaud, and Dulce and I made a mat and demonstrated some judo throws. *Ippon seoi nage, o uchi gari, koshi guruma,* just the ones we could do without clothing, since we remained nude. Many of the Indians were nude too, so that didn't bother me.

That evening we feasted. Dulce tried to warn me to go easy, but I was sure she had been wrong about the gallstones, and I was feeling so good I pitched right in. The main course was some kind of meaty stew, very good. I washed it down with plenty of native beer. The water, you see, was not safe because of the flukes, and I was thirsty as hell. But along about my third helping of stew, I drew out of the pot what looked like a baby's hand. Horrified I stared at this confirmation of their cannibalistic culture, but Dulce explained it was only monkey meat. Nevertheless, I decided I had eaten enough.

And that night I had another gallstone attack that made the first seem mild. Dulce gave me more coca leaves, and warned me that if the gall bladder burst I could die, unless I had surgery very soon. I promised never to go off my diet again, and finally this attack abated.

Fortunately a ninja came in the morning to lead us to the Black Castle. I kept chewing coca leaves and made it, glad that my ordeal was almost over. Even the notion of surgery did not seem so bad, now.

*

After that my memory becomes sketchy. Perhaps it was the recurring agony of the gallstone, or the mind-affecting coca I chewed to alleviate it; more likely it was what happened next. I was entering the most awful period of my life, physically, mentally and emotionally. But that's another story, a tortuous one. I can provide only snatches, with certain retrospective interpretations, and I can not promise even these are completely accurate. So for what little it may be worth, I offer these bits:

The Black Castle seemed to be in ruins, surely that's a mistaken image, but I swear that's what I remember, with stones tumbled about. The plain around it seemed to have been flooded recently, though there was no river in sight, and there was a stench as of a recent bloody battlefield.

Inside it was bare, but that was only the surface. Below there was an incredible labyrinth of tunnels and chambers. Like an iceberg, nine-tenths of the castle was beneath the surface. The important thing was that we had made it; we were safe!

Except—another horrible vision. The boylike Fu Antos, larger than I remembered him but still a child, met me not with open arms of welcome, but with a great sword. This memory is the most nonsensical of all; it could never have happened that way! I was surely delirious. But I report the snatch as I have it. I, crippled by my physical agony and sheer astonishment, was unable to resist effectively. Those terrible hypnotic eyes of the lord of the ninjas, four hundred years old; the gleaming blade swinging at my head—

It was Dulce who threw herself between us, intercepting the sword with a wooden chair. "Stop!" she cried. "Spare him, Lord Ninja! Only let him live, and I will do as you wish."

And what could Fu Antos want of Dulce, whom he had never met before? More of my delirium, of course; I must have run a hell of a fever!

Yet I found myself alone on a crude wooden raft, drifting down the mighty Amazon River, with only a few coca leaves for sustenance. In my fevered vision, that I knew must be untrue, I had been betrayed by my best friend, Fu Antos, at the time I least suspected. With my lucky *Figa* lost, only the sacrifice of the girl who loved me, Dulce, had saved my life.

All false, of course. But one thing was not false: I was dying. For my gallstone had not been removed. My whole body was turning yellow from the jaundice of this malady. I could not survive long.

Something bit my hand, which was dragging in the water. I jerked it out. Must be piranha fishes; they would get me in the end. My whole life passed before me, as I have recorded it now. For now the pain was starting again.

I hear the cry, the raucous scream of some hungry jungle bird. It sounds like the gleeful laughter of a vengeful voodoo god. But it fades as I lose consciousness . . .

CURSE OF THE NINJA

and others

INTRODUCTION:

This volume is only half a novel. We were writing it when news came that the series was being canceled, and work abruptly stopped. The first five Chapters, of a projected ten, are virtually complete, with spot summaries of intended scenes near the end of Chapter 5, and a little bit of Chapter 6, followed by a summary of the remainder. Unfortunately it was the finale toward which we had been building for two and a half novels that was aborted. We were not pleased, but it was not our decision.

The volume has been filled out with several stories and sample projects, showing what else we would have written had there been any interest by a publisher. We trust this will have some interest for readers. This is really a collection of pieces, filling out our collaborative activity. We hope readers will enjoy it regardless.

Chapter 1:

Dream of Red and White

He was a middleweight, around 176 pounds, completely bald, standing only five feet five inches tall but with his mass filled in by solid muscle. He was in a deep defensive stance and clearly afraid of me.

Good—I needed an easy victory! I took hold of his jacket with my right hand, caught his right sleeve with my left, and whirled into a powerful *uchi—mata* inside thigh throw. It was one of my favorite techniques, and I was good at it. Very good. I hauled him up on my back, and my right leg thrust back between his thighs and up to sweep his legs into the air. He flipped completely over and came down hard on the mat in front of me.

"*Ippon!*" the referee cried, making the signal, his hand straight up. Wonderful gesture! That meant it was a clean throw, with my opponent landing with speed and force on his back: my victory.

Judo is a martial art, a system of self defense, like karate, aikido, kung fu and others. If I were attacked on the street, and threw the thug like this on the hard concrete, he would not get up again in a hurry. But of course in contest judo we don't want to hurt the opponent—not that much, anyway—so we have a mat. We are careful to use correct technique so that he falls harmlessly.

Immediately both judges got up. "*Koka*!" they cried, signaling with their hands at chest level. That meant an imperfect throw, a minor effort. An *ippon* is like a home-run in baseball with the bases loaded, or a touchdown in the final seconds in football: a game-winning score. But a *koka* is like a base hit or a first down: nice to have, but not really enough by itself.

There was a brief conference, and majority ruled: I was awarded a measly *koka* for my throw. Well, these things happen, and a good judoka does not complain. He can think his private thoughts, though; I would have rated that excellent throw better than a mere base hit.

I returned to the match and moved Uke around a bit. In judo, the man who performs a technique is always Tori, and the one who gets techniqued is always Uke. That's pronounced OO—kee, two syllables with, the accent on the first. The term derives from *ukemi*, or "fall" in Japanese. Anyone serious about judo has to learn Japanese terms and pronunciation.

Uke was still too nervous to attack me; he knew he'd been well-thrown even if the judges didn't. So I spun into another *uchi—mata*. Again he flew and landed, and again the referee signaled *ippon* intelligently. And wouldn't you know it, again the two judges overruled him. "*Yuko!*" they cried, hands slanting down.

Well, a *yuko* is like a double in baseball that knocks in a run, or a field goal in football. Enough to win, if the other team doesn't do anything, but not spectacular. I was frankly dissatisfied. I'm not nearly as good a sport *inside* as I am *outside*. But I kept my face calm.

I closed a third time. I probably should have varied my technique, but at this stage I was determined to achieve the recognition my performance deserved. I shoved Uke back, and when he resisted I hauled him abruptly forward and off-balance, and rammed into a third *uchi—mata*. It was explosive; he sailed up so high he would have been thrown clear of the mat and into the lap of a judge if I hadn't hung on to his right arm. He came down partly on his side with a crash that shook the room. In fact, my throw was so violent that I myself fell forward on my head, turning to come down partly over him.

"*Waza-ari*!" the referee cried, hand going out to the side at shoulder level. That's like a baseball triple with a couple of runs scoring, or a football touchdown with no extra point. A good, strong showing, but not enough to win outright. After twice being overruled, the referee was being more cautious. These judo-baseball-football scores are not directly comparable, of course; it's just an approximation.

Surprise! "*Ippon!*" the two judges exclaimed, grinning. It seemed I had finally put enough oomph into it to satisfy their savage tastes. The match was over; an *ippon* always terminates it right there. That's one of the ways judo differs from other sports.

But I wasn't through. Not by a long shot. The moment the first Uke bowed off the mat, a second one was bowing on. For I was not in a tournament or contest; I was running the line. I had to fight five *yodans*, or fourth degree black belts in Kodokan judo, one after the other without respite.

A *yodan* is a tough customer. A black belt in judo signifies a master grade, like a professional baseball or football player: the pick of the martial art. A *shodan* or first degree black belt could mop up any number of barehanded attackers in a street fight, though judo is called the "gentle way" of fighting. A *nidan* or second degree black belt could normally wipe out a *shodan;* only about one in three *shodans* make *nidan*. And there is a steeper ratio for each step up; one *nidan* in ten makes *sandan*, the third degree, and one *sandan* in thirty makes *yodan*, the fourth degree. So a *yodan* is one in a thousand black belts, roughly.

And I was running a line of five *yodans*. Me, Jason Striker, a fifth degree black belt, or *godan*, one in a hundred thousand. Trying for one in a million. Could I do it?

The first couple shouldn't be too bad—but as I grew tired,

those constantly fresh Ukes would become greater hurdles. And if I lost even one match, I was finished.

But I had no time to worry about that. The first Uke had been tense and stiff, knowing he was overmatched. This second one was relaxed and confident. He was a large black man with a small mustache and big belly and strong arms. He knew the odds were against him, but with one break he figured he could take me, and he was bound to try. He might not be as good as he thought he was, but then again, he *might.* Maybe he was pushing for 5 Dan status himself.

He let me grip his lapel with my right hand—then he went for *waki—gatame*, the armpit hold. This consists, basically, of clamping your opponent's arm under your own armpit and bending it backward. The pressure on the elbow-joint will force quick capitulation. But as with all armlocks, you have to be careful; too much pressure can break the captive arm. The victim will normally surrender long before that happens, so you give him a chance to tap out, to yield, and nobody gets hurt.

This bastard didn't give me that chance. He grabbed my arm and drove down to the mat, not caring whether it broke in the process. But I was not exactly a novice; I somersaulted forward in a judo roll, changing the angle and fouling up his leverage. Then I broke his hold—but he moved with me and got on top with a *yoko-shiho-gatame* side four quarter hold. His left hand circled my neck; his right gripped my left leg.

"*O-saekomi!*" the referee cried, signaling the commencement of a legitimate holddown.

Out of the frying pan . . . I had thirty seconds to get out of it, or I was lost. Fortunately the hold was not absolutely tight; they seldom are in matches, since they have to be applied despite resistance. I used what room I had to maneuver. I grabbed his jacket on the side with my right arm, then twisted, reached over his head with my left hand, and grabbed his belt. This was tough to do, for of course he was shoving me down, and time was passing. Fifteen seconds, twenty.

I bucked, my back arching high with my head and feet touching the mat. This is called bridging, and is a standard escape technique, but I had prepared for my bridge by pushing with my left hand as if to shove him off; naturally he resisted the thrust. Then as I bridged I reversed it, pushing with my right and pulling with my left, exerting a lot of torque in the same direction he had been shoving. As he pressed down hard on my torso, I added to his movement. I had a lot of strength in my arms; those hours of weight lifting I had done while training for this sure came in handy. Now for a human bench press.

I heaved him right up and over in a forward somersault, then rolled on top of him in a *yoko-shiho-gatame* of my own. Now he had to break the hold—and he couldn't. He struggled valiantly, sliding across the mat, but I stayed with him. My hold differed from his in two crucial points: it was not loose around his neck, but so tight his head was shoved up painfully so that he could not even think of bridging. And my chin dug into his chest, putting pressure on his soft breastbone and further restricting his motions. These little details make all the difference. In fact, there can be just as much strategy and action and drama in the course of a holddown as in a spectacular throw, though it is more subtle. In thirty seconds I had my *ippon* for the holddown.

Why was I doing this? Because I was going for the biggest step of my career: promotion to *Rokudan*, the sixth degree belt. This is beyond the black belt stage; the colors are red and white striped. Few men outside of Japan ever make this grade; I would be the highest ranked Caucasian in North America. Truly a status worth fighting for. 6 Dan was a worldwide elite; fewer than ten white men in the world had made this rank, in all the history of judo.

I had already done the technical questions and the three classical *katas* or stylized demonstrations. These covered the *nage* or throws, the *katame* or grappling, and the *kime* or the ancient forms of self defense. I had also done two more of my own choosing. This five—man competition accounted for sixty percent of the examination. I had to win at least three of the matches and lose none.

And these opponents were not about to lie down and play dead for me.

The third man was big and strong. He was about 35 years old and weighed perhaps 230 pounds and seemed to be of Japanese extraction. That meant mass and skill and experience—a tough combination. I was panting from the effort of overturning and holding down my last opponent; not really tired, but the edge was off.

So I tried for a quick win, much as the last had tried against me. Uke went for me with his right arm outstretched and stiff; I grabbed his sleeve with my left hand, my right hand going to his wrist. I lifted my right leg and put my foot against the top of his left leg. Then I fell back and to the side, pulling on that arm and pushing on his leg.

When we were on the mat I passed my left leg over his captive arm, over the elbow, to put pressure on it, while I bent the arm back with both my hands. But this Uke was tough; he tried to resist and pull his arm back, and he had a lot of power. He was getting away, and I had to twist onto my side to hold him and apply more pressure.

Two things happened then, both unfortunate. Our opposing forces were so great that something had to go, and it did. His arm—and my spine. I heard a tearing sound as the ligaments of his arm tore, at the same time as pain shot through the twisted muscles of my lower back. He screamed and tapped out, and I let go, the victor.

He would not be able to practice for a while, and I was sorry for that. But it had been his own fault for struggling so hard against a potentially injurious hold; he could have yielded with honor and without damage the moment I secured it. I had applied pressure slowly, giving him opportunity to do just that, and instead he had tried to fight out of it.

I had my own troubles. My wrenched back was not too bad, but I could not afford to let it rest, and it would weaken my attempts at throws in the two remaining matches and make me look worse than I was. With good luck I would not aggravate it too much; with bad luck, I could wind up with a serious injury and lose my promotion to boot.

It takes a moment for one contestant to clear the mat and the next to come on, for everything is formal in judo. In that moment my eyes surveyed my surroundings. We were in a large *dojo*, or judo exercise hall, with bleacher seats tiered in a huge oblong, filled with spectators avidly watching the action. They were not paying fans, but the friends and relatives of the judo players who had come to participate in the tournament and the promotions. Judo is one of the few sports where the players pay and the spectators come free. Not always, but true in this particular case.

Crowded up as close to the demonstration area as allowed were a number of my own students and associates. There was Illunga, an almost-handsome, no, almost-beautiful black woman who instructed karate at my *dojo*. And a tall, copper—bronze haired slender woman, a brown belt, watching intently, one of my best students. And of course a number of my friends and judo associates, here to watch me try for the big one.

The next man was a giant, even bigger and stronger than the last. He must have weighed 300 pounds, no fat. He took off his glasses just before he stepped out, and peered myopically at me. Some very powerful men have weak eyesight, but judo is hand-to-hand combat, so it hardly matters. A blind man could be a good judoka; some blind men are. This one had a beaked nose and white-flecked hair, and seemed Italian. He would have power to burn, while I struggled along on my tiring system and hurt back. This was going to be bad.

We closed, took hold, pushed each other around a bit, feeling it out. Then I leaped in for a *morote seoi nage* shoulder throw. My right arm bent at the elbow and angled across his chest, heaving up as I rotated to draw him up over my back. But my back gave a stab of pain as I took the load, making me hesitate fractionally—and Uke used that moment to recover his broken balance and stand firm. His left foot swept forward as he hauled me backward, going into a counter—throw.

I danced out of the way. But he followed up his advantage, dropping into a left *tai otoshi* body drop throw, seeking to augment my spinout right into a fall. However, avoiding such traps was second nature to me. I jumped over his outstretched leg and tried to counter him myself; a failed technique in judo is a golden opportunity to initiate a counter technique. But he had the jump on me and was carrying through a continuous attack. He was already winding into a *soto makikomi* wraparound throw, passing his right arm over my head and throwing himself to the mat, carrying me along with him. It was a *sutemi*, or sacrifice technique, doubly powerful because Uke's deliberate loss of balance was transmitted to my body, bringing it down. When a heavy man does this, there's an awful lot of pull. I was unable to resist it, but I did foul it up so that the throw was imperfect.

"*Yuko*!" the referee called. It was a good call; the bastard *had* taken me down. No doubt Uke thought it had been an *ippon*, but now those hard—nosed judges were on my side.

Well, that put me behind, but not by much. This man was a demon on his feet, but maybe not so tough on the mat. *I*, however, *was* tough on the mat. It was part of being an all-around judoka. Even as I fell, I wasn't just messing up his throw, I was setting up for my own next technique. I twisted and hooked one leg over his belly, gained leverage with that leg, reached around him and literally climbed on the back of the giant. He got on his hands and knees, trying to stand up. You aren't permitted to retain a mat—hold once your opponent stands up, and wouldn't want to; he could drop you hard, falling backwards and crushing you beneath his weight. Remember that image of the concrete pavement: no hold is worthwhile if in real life combat you'd get your brains beat out while maintaining it. But naturally I acted to keep him down. I rode his back as though he were a horse, and pushed with my stomach and with my legs on his thighs so that he sprawled on his belly; my weight and position would not permit him to get his legs under him.

Then I slid my right hand around his neck, grabbing deep inside his left collar. My left hand passed the opposite way, grabbing his right collar. Then I pulled back, drawing the cutting edge of my right wrist into his neck, shifting a bit to nudge the muscles over the carotid arteries aside. It was the *okuri-eri-jime* strangle.

But Uke had a strong neck. He ducked his head down, his chin blocking my wrists, and tried to buck me off. My hold slipped a trifle, but I reapplied it immediately. Then he got his hands up and pulled hard on my fingers when the referee wasn't looking. This was an illegal tactic, and it hurt my fingers. But then the referee looked, and gave the man a *chui* or half point penalty. I tried to complete my strangle, but could not, and finally time ran out.

Uke had a *yuko* for him and a *chui* against him. The penalty was stronger than the positive score, and so he lost. My victory, but hardly a proud one. And now I had a wrenched middle finger. And one match to go.

Well, it wasn't the first time I'd fought in an adverse situation. Back at the Martial Open, when top representatives of seven major martial arts had competed against each other for a kind of world championship, I had gone up against a devastating karateka, my hand injured. I had been marked for death—but my *ki* had saved me.

The *ki*—that mysterious inner force that emerged sporadically to tide me through my worst crises. I had no real control over it, and could not summon it at will, but it was terrific when it came. But of course I would not use it in an ordinary judo situation like this. It was my skill that was at issue here, not my paranormal powers.

The last Uke was comparatively small, about 150 pounds, and fast. Oh, was he fast! I reached for him but could not get my grip; he avoided me, and there is no rule in judo saying you have to let your opponent take hold. He was fighting me edgewise. I stepped around, seeking a better position—and he caught my descending foot with a *de ashi barai* foot sweep. It was like stepping on a banana peel; my foot went out from under, and I went down. I tried to turn out, to void the throw, but succeeded only partially; Uke had been too fast, his timing perfect.

"*Waza—ari*!" the referee cried, and the judges concurred. And so did I; it had been a very nice technique. But it boded ill for me; I needed at least a tie, and so far I was losing.

Naturally I had no chance to bring him into matwork; he was lightning on his feet, and not about to let me slow him down with my grappling technique.

I was in trouble. The smallest man in the line had thrown me. All he had to do was stay away from me for the rest of the match and he would win. I had to catch him.

Easier decided than accomplished. I stepped in—and he tagged me again with *de ashi barai*. I didn't go down this time; I learn such lessons very quickly. But his motion was so neat that I did stumble, clinging to him momentarily for support. Here his strategy worked against him; he should have swung into another technique while he had the advantage, perhaps finishing the match with another *waza-ari*. Two such scores are the same as one *ippon*. But he was geared to strike and withdraw, avoiding any countertechnique. He was too defensive, and so he missed his opportunity.

There was *my* opportunity. I had less than a minute to go in the match, but my greater experience was already translating into a tactical advantage. He wanted to be defensive—let's encourage him!

I feinted, trying for a big technique, and he drew his legs back. I tried for a shoulder throw, and he ducked his head and shoulders down, moving fast. I shoved him further down, reached my right hand over his shoulder, grabbed his belt, and leaned hard on him. As he tried to come up, I put my left foot between his legs, sat down, and boosted him over my body in a *sumi-gaeshi* takedown.

For some reason referees don't score this kind of throw high; all I got was a *koka*. But now I had him down on the mat.

I never let him go. I rolled on top of him as he came down, still gripping his belt, and applied the *kuzure kami-shiho-gatame* holddown, a variant of the upper four quarter hold, a good one. Now he was mine; no matter how he jumped, he could not get away. Ten seconds, fifteen, twenty, twenty—five—

Uke gave a sudden terriffic wrench, throwing his feet up and over my head, jerking his whole body in a kind of back somersault. There was no warning; he caught me counting seconds instead of concentrating on the business at hand. His head slipped free and he was loose.

Time was called. The match was over. I had been so close, so close . . .

But then I remembered: twenty five seconds on a holddown constitutes a *waza-ari*, matching his prior score. And I had made a *koka* on my takedown.

I won the decision by the margin of one slim *koka*.

Now my injuries were as nothing. I had made *rokudan*! The official was holding out the coveted red and white checkered belt. I reached to take it.

And it faded. "No, no!" I cried, trying to hold it together—but it was all only a dream, and I was falling awake.

*

I opened my eyes. I was sitting up in bed, reaching for the footboard. It was gaily painted red and white, but it was no *rokudan* belt.

I certainly had ambitious dreams. To be the highest ranking white judoka in America, or some such—and I didn't know a thing about judo! As far as I knew, I had never practiced it or any other martial art at all.

Of course, I didn't know much about myself. I had been staggering along the burning edge of a Florida highway, sick and half starved, until a well—intentioned stranger had given me a hand. He had thought I was drunk or spaced out, but when he talked with me he realized I was an amnesiac. So he fed me and gave me a place to stay for several days while we tried to find out who I was. We had no luck; he offered to take me to the police, who might identify me by my fingerprints, but I balked. Suppose I were a criminal? I didn't like that notion at all. I wanted to remember on my own, so I could make my own decision, rather than having it made for me. Suppose, for example, I had been framed and conked on the head? I could find myself in jail with no way to recover the truth.

My benefactor was understanding, but felt he could not ethically do more for me, in the circumstance. I don't blame him. He did help me get a temporary job and a room of my own. So I became the pole man on a survey crew, lining up my pole for the transit man to orient on. Unskilled labor, but I still managed to foul it up a few times. The pay was enough to sustain me, and it really was not demanding work. Just as well, because I was a pretty weak character. I weighed about 130 pounds at the start, which was pretty thin for a man standing over six feet tall.

I seemed to be recovering from some sort of injury or operation. There were scars on my stomach, and at times I suffered dizzy/weak spells. And I had nightmares—inchoate, fevered things, snatches of terror in some deep jungle, of being chased by someone wielding a huge sword, or drowning in a river swarming with crocodiles—that sort of thing.

But this last dream had been different. For the first time it had been pleasant, in a violent, rough-hewn way, and I had been sorry to awaken. True, I had been hard—pressed, even hurt in that experience, but I had felt competent to handle it. I had been a real man.

I'd be willing to go through a lot of pain to have that feeling again, mine to keep awake as well as asleep.

Now all I had was the pain in my back and hand. The dream was false, but my pains were real; they had been with me when I found myself on the street. I had been roughly treated, somewhere, somehow, somewhen. How ingenious of my subconscious to build this into my fleeting dream of glory!

Still, if there was judo in my dream, maybe I had known something about it once. Maybe I should look into that, in case it offered any key to my lost identity. Probably wasted effort, but . . .

So that evening after work I went to the local club whose advertising poster I had seen. It was *Taizo Sone;* they seemed to have two or three clubs in the area, and this was the closest one.

I was in luck. They met in a community center, two or three times a week, and I had come on the right night. Students in pajamalike uniforms were putting mats into place. Someone directed me to the instructor, whose name was Steve. He was a young man, in his early twenties, and not large or muscular or rough-spoken. In fact not at all the way I'd expected a martial artist to be.

"Sure," he said. "Sit down and watch the class. If you want to join, fill out this application form. It costs ten dollars a month."

"Thanks." I sat down and looked at the form—and hit a snag. For the name I filled in the one I had taken to get me by until I found out who I really was: CAESAR KANE. And my current address. But age—I didn't know my age.

"How old do I look?" I asked Steve.

"Maybe thirty five," he said.

"That old?" I was shocked; I certainly did not feel middle aged.

He shrugged. "That entry is mostly for the children. In tournaments they are graded by age and size."

"Oh." So I gritted my teeth and filled in 35, sure it was wrong. But amnesiacs could not be choosy.

"Time for class," Steve said. "Why don't you try it?"

"Why not?" So I stripped myself of liabilities like shoes, wallet and keys, and went to join the line forming for class. Except that I didn't really know where I belonged.

I must have looked as bewildered as I felt, because a cute little girl took me in charge. She had long yellow braids and bright blue eyes, and seemed three sizes too small for her uniform. "You have to stand at the end," she explained. "You don't have a *gi*."

I took her word for it. The others were arranging themselves by size and the colors of their belts, the darker belts seeming to have more authority. The little girl's belt was white, and she was the smallest of that color, so she was at the end, except for me. I towered over her, feeling like the scarecrow of Oz. What was I doing here, anyway?

"My name's Penny," she said brightly. "I'm six."

Introductions, yet! "I'm Caesar. I don't know how old I am." Damned if I'd say thirty five!

She went into a giggle. "Everybody knows how old he is!"

From way down at the far end of the line someone called "RE!" Everybody bowed. Belatedly I bowed too, a stiff little effort from the waist. We were bowing to the instructor, Steve, in his black belt, and a taller friend beside him, a brown belt.

"Move out, spread across the mat," Steve said.

We spread out. I had no idea what I was supposed to do, but at least I could follow the leader.

It wasn't hard. Steve led us, so all I had to do was copy him. First we just sort of jumped around, limbering up. Then we whirled our arms around, twisting at legs and hips. If this were all there was to it, I'd have no trouble.

Then Steve sat and spread his legs out wide. "Grab your right toe, keep your knee straight, touch your forehead to your knee," he said, doing it easily. I tried it with confidence.

It felt as if the back tendons of my thigh were about to rip out. I could almost hear the piano—wire *sproing*! as my head balked a good foot from my knee. Touch? Not in a lifetime!

"Oooo, it hurts so good!" Steve remarked. I could agree only with the first three words.

But my surreptitious glance around reassured me: a number of the others couldn't do it either. Some children, like little Penny, were limber and/or soft—boned, but others were groaning.

At last, after several similar contortions, we proceeded to something different. "On your backs!" Steve cried. "Hit it!" And he slammed one hand into the mat beside him.

I was completely lost. What was the point of this? But in a moment a green belt came over and explained it privately: "These are breakfalls. You hit the mat to take the shock when you fall. Your arm's a lot tougher than your gut. Like this." And he whammed the mat with a sound like a pistol shot.

I copied his position and threw out my arm. It struck with a sound like bubblegum popping, and my hand stung.

"Not like that," he cautioned me with a straight face. "Open your fist, put your palm *down*, not up, and cup your hand. Make the whole arm level." He demonstrated with another detonation.

Somehow, with the green belt's help, I got through the assorted breakfalls, which proceeded from lying-on-back, to sitting-on-mat, to squatting, and finally to standing. But I was bruised, my left elbow skinned, and I wondered how I was going to survive the hour, let alone the course.

"Form two lines for rollouts," Steve cried next.

The students lined up off the mat and took turns doing forward rolls on the main section. These looked like fouled—up somersaults with crash—landings. I went out, put my head down, pushed off as I had seen the others do—and plowed shoulder-first into the mat. Ouch! It felt as though my collar bone had fractured. But I guess it hadn't, because I could still move my arm. After that I lacked the nerve to try it again.

"Tonight we'll start with the *o-goshi*, the big hip technique," Steve announced. "Watch as I throw Paul." And he took hold of his friend the brown belt, whirled around, and heaved him over his back. Paul went tumbling to the mat, striking it with bone—sundering force. I winced; there went one friend! This class was murder, in the most physical sense.

But the brown belt jumped right back up, smiling. Some how he had survived that devastating crash unhurt.

Now Steve went through it slowly, stepping in close, bending his knees, putting one arm around the victim's back and heaving.

Paul went over, landing with less of a smack. I watched every motion, and it was completely clear. Anybody could do it, once he knew how.

Nevertheless, Steve demonstrated it several times, explaining the position of the feet, arms, head and knees, as though such details mattered. I wondered why he went over it so much when it had been obvious the first time.

"Now take your partner and throw it five times each," Steve said.

The others paired off. I didn't know anybody, so I just stood there awkwardly. Then a girl trotted up. She was small, pert, and wore a kind of double pony—tail. The baggy *gi* masked her other attributes, but I judged her to be in her early twenties. "You look lost," she said. "Okay, you can throw me."

Anywhere but in a judo class, that would have sounded funny. "Throw a girl?" It hadn't occurred to me that these exercises were coed. At least, not in the adult division. Obviously they were, however.

"Well, I can't throw you, because you don't know how to take a fall yet."

That seemed to make sense, though how this maybe hundred pound girl would throw a man my size even if he could take a fall was unclear. So I stepped in to throw her, and suddenly discovered that I had no idea how to do it. Steve's demonstration had made it look so easy, as though there were no other possible outcome but a smooth flip to the mat. But *seeing* and *doing* were vastly different things. "I don't know this throw," I confessed.

"I'll show you," she said brightly. "By the way, I'm Vonnie."

"Bonnie?"

"Vonnie—with a V. Everyone confuses it."

"Caeser," I said. "I think."

She laughed without affectation. She was a very pleasant, open sort. "Now you put your right foot across the front—there, that's right—sort of half turn—put your arm around my waist—bring your left foot back more—"

I followed her directions with a certain difficulty. It wasn't that I had any wrong idea about where I was, but my natural inclination when I had my arm about a girl was to draw her in facing me, rather than across my rump. Vonnie was a good deal shorter than I was, so my hand fell mainly across her back up near her shoulders, and I knew that wasn't going to work for a throw.

"Bend your knees," she said. "You have to get down low enough to pick me up. Pull on my sleeve with your left hand. Pull harder, forward. Turn. No, the other way, *away* from me, look to your left—that's right."

That was right? I was twisted up like a corkscrew, with her half sprawled across my side and back. This would never work!

"Now, heave forward," she said. "No, go ahead, put some oompth into it—that's it—straighten your knees as you go around—there!" There was a slap on the mat. "You did it!"

I looked, astonished. She had just landed on the mat in front of me. I had thrown her—and I had no idea how I had done it.

She bounced up. "That was very good. Now try it again, faster. *O-goshi.*"

"Oh, gosh," I echoed.

And about the third time I threw her, I began to catch on to the nature of the throw. Instead of seeming impossibly awkward, it became almost natural. "Wonderful!" Vonnie encouraged me. I had learned the *O-goshi* hip throw!

There was more practice that evening, but I knew the high point had been passed. I was tired, sore and confused by the multiplicity of Japanese names and techniques, but I was actually learning judo.

The class concluded with some practice with the instructors. We formed two lines. Steve faced one line, and Paul the other. The first students went out, bowed, and took hold of the instructors, trying to throw them—whereupon the instructors threw the students instead. I was near the end of Paul's line, so I had plenty of time to watch. The students looked so clumsy I was sure they were faking it, just going down to make the instructors look good. Yet when little yellow—braided Penny hooked Paul's leg and pushed, he went down on his back, slapping the mat, while she clapped her hands for joy. Hmm.

Then my turn came. I stepped up to the edge of the mat and bowed, and from the center Paul bowed to me. A nice formality, this careful judo courtesy; I liked that. But now Paul looked like a giant, there in the splendor of his brown belt, and my confidence evaporated.

Well, nothing ventured, etc. We came together. I grabbed his left sleeve and pulled—and he just looked at me curiously. I couldn't even remember the proper grip.

"Here," he said after a moment. "Take my left lapel in your right hand, like this, and my right sleeve in your left. Right. Now go ahead and try a throw."

Smarting under my embarrassment of ignorance, I turned into the *o-goshi* hip throw Vonnie had taught me.

Paul just stood there, unmoved. "Get down lower," he advised. "Pull on my sleeve."

I bent my knees—I had forgotten that detail—pulled—and fell over backwards. Paul merely shook his head sadly.

I got up and tried it again. I grabbed his lapel, pulled—and he made a little motion with one foot, tapped me on the shoulder, and I crashed down on my back again.

"You need to keep your balance," Paul said mildly, making a little bow of dismissal.

Balance. Yes.

It seemed I still had a way to go for my 6 Dan dream.

Chapter 2:

Strange Conquests

I leaned back comfortably, my belly full of the crude but delicious native repast. The monkey stew had been good, and the roasted termites very tasty. The fermented-corn beer was weak, but there was plenty of it, and of course it was safer to drink than the water.

Dulce had given up cautioning me about indulging; she was fed up in more than one sense and I was half-hypnotized by the flickering fire and the relief of finding help after isolation in the deep jungle.

The small, grizzled Chief spoke a few words in his native language. I turned to Dulce, who had to interpret for me. "He says the tribe wishes to honor the White God," she explained.

"Not by cutting off my head!" I protested, moderately alarmed. "These are headhunters, remember."

"*Reformed* headhunters," she reminded me. Dizzy as I was, I noted again what a voluptuous woman she was, and how pretty her face was when she spoke. There were worse fates than being lost in the jungle with such a companion. And she had taken good care of me in my illness, too. I owed her a lot. "Anyway," she continued, "they don't decapitate friends. Only enemies. It should be safe for a White God like you." She smiled with momentary malice. "See that you *behave* like a god, not a devil."

"What sort of honor is it?"

"I don't know. Probably something they just cooked up, an instant ceremony to suit the occasion. They were quite impressed by your combat performance, you know."

The Chief spoke again, smiling. "He says for you to go with him," Dulce said.

I eased to my feet. "Okay, we'll come."

But the Chief barred Dulce. "It seems this is a stag party," she said, just a bit nettled. "Go ahead, Jason; I'm sure it's safe. I'll relax here." And she settled back with a determined complacency.

Stag party? My alcohol—fogged interest quickened. What would these hospitable primitives have, a dancing native girl bursting out of a nut-flour cake?

I accompanied the Chief, and a dozen warriors fell in behind us. I was certainly glad the natives were friendly.

We came to a large hut on the outskirt of the village, that I had not seen before. Its floor inside was covered by soft brush and dry moss, making a bouncy, fragrant mattress from wall to wall. And on this huge bed were five naked girls.

The Chief spoke, augmenting his words by a pantomime of such suggestive nature that I could not fail to catch his meaning. He made motions of grasping, hugging, kissing, stroking and spreading, and he bucked his groin forward violently several times.

It seemed I was being invited to patronize the royal harem.

"Well, thanks, Chief," I said. "But I'm not really in the mood, and Dulce would be jealous, So if it's all the same to you—"

The Chief grunted firmly, pointing at the nearest girl. The torchlight was not good, but she was evidently the pick of the tribe, maybe fifteen years old with heavy black hair, fine full breasts, nice little buttocks and good legs. Small—she could not have weighed more than a hundred pounds—but all the tribespeople were small. They lacked the advantage of civilized nutrition; in fact they probably went hungry often when the hunting was bad. Regardless, this girl was very comely.

I looked around, squinting to see better in the irregular illumination of the interior brands. “Well, if it’s really that important to you—” I did not regard myself as a promiscuous man, but sometimes protocol requires special activities. “But not in front of a crowd; we Caucasians prefer privacy.”

It seemed they understood a bit of English, or at least my tone, because the warriors shook their heads negatively and crowded closer. They intended to stay. And from their attitude I got the impression that this honor was not exactly voluntary; like the eating of bread together as a sign of friendship, it was a necessary formality. I had to perform in their presence, sharing my hero’s seed with their tribe, in this manner becoming part of them.

Well, there was nothing for it but to humor them. It was an honor: they thought enough of me to wish to perpetuate me within their tribe. And the girl *was* alluring, and I suspected something aphrodisiac had been added to the food, because I felt its effect. Or maybe it was the aroma of the scented torch. Supposedly primitive peoples can be remarkably sophisticated about matters of the flesh.

Okay, if I had to do it, I’d do it right. I’d give them a show to remember. I might have felt otherwise if I had been sober, which is why I normally don’t drink. Alcohol has a very liberating effect on me, to put it politely, perhaps because I am not used to it. But this was a unique situation.

I stripped. After all, I entered judo matches in public; this wasn’t that different. I focused on the girl’s nether bifurcation, tantalizing in the flickering half-light, the shadows as suggestive as the visible portions, and felt my member swelling in response. There was a murmur of satisfaction among the men, then of awe; my member was in proportion to my size, but I was substantially larger than they were. Soon I was turgid as a blocked garden hose.

I almost leaped on that poor girl. No finesse at all; I got down on her, thrusting between her widely spaced legs, holding her shoulders to keep her from sliding out from under. My member found the place and rammed home as her legs clasped about my waist, her ankles crossing and locking behind me. It was well that I wasted no time, for I came explosively the instant I touched bottom, pumping spurt after spurt deep into her body, my hips smacking into her thighs and buttocks with every urge.

There was something very like applause from the watching warriors, as if I'd just performed a beautiful judo technique and won the match with an *ippon*. Well, that was close enough. I'd shown them what the White God could do, all right!

I relaxed, but the girl did not. She must have been hurting inside from the sheer velocity and distention of my production, but she clutched me to her. She hauled my chest down to her breasts, flexing her thighs against me. And you know, my member, that had partially softened after the climax, began to engorge again. Maybe I was an exhibitionist at heart; ordinarily once was enough. But think what an impression I could make if I fired off two rounds in rapid order!

Something shoved against my shoulder, knocking me over to the side. My contact with the girl was broken, and I fell on my back with my tumescent member projecting up. One of the other girls had done it, forcefully intervening.

Now that girl plumped down on my crotch, pausing only to grasp my member and stuff it into her aperture. She was a solid girl, almost fat, with big soft buttocks and bulging tummy but still fairly good looking. She bounced on me, her big breasts slapping audibly with every jerk.

I just lay there on my back, amazed, while she rode me like a horse. The spectators began clapping in unison with her motion—whomp, whomp, WHOMP! She rose so high and came down so hard I was afraid my member would slip out and get crushed under her pile-driving mass. I had a vision of it snapping in half, like a stepped-on stick. In self defense I had to follow her motions, bridging as she rose, keeping my lodging secure.

And slowly I peaked again, my organ filling with liquid, swelling to huge proportion. The climax was not as sharp as before, but overall it was as powerful: like a locomotive steaming into a station, instead of a sport-car squealing to a stop.

So the second girl was satisfied, and I was limp. I nudged her off, and she went.

And a third girl came, short but well endowed. She got down to embrace me, her breasts dangling above my chin.

Now ordinarily such a position would be most stimulating. I'm one of those males who regard naked breasts as natural playthings. But these had arrived on the scene just too late. "Hey, wait!" I protested. "I'm spent!"

But she protested, grabbing hold of my exhausted member as though to knead it back to health and vigor. And the standing warriors raised their spears and made performance-motions.

"Now hold on!" I said, forgetting that the girl was doing that already. "You can't expect me to—"

They persisted. They expected. They had the spears. I was supposed to run the line of all five girls. Some honor!

It seemed that when the White God honored this tribe, he was expected to do the whole job. Or else.

What happened to gods who didn't make the cut? That was no difficult conjecture: obviously they were no longer considered to be gods. A fallen god become a devil, an enemy—and these people were headhunters.

If I failed, it would not be from lack of initiative by the girl. She really wanted that White-God elixir; she was just about pulling the spigot out by the root.

The Chief stepped forward, scowling. He didn't like suffering the embarrassment of presenting a fake god. He raised his hand in an incipient signal of negation. I was in trouble.

Then I felt something strange but wonderful. It was a filling and hardening, something intangible flowing from my *hara*, the seat of my being in my belly, to my external member, suffusing it with new strength and substance and confidence.

It was the *ki*, that mysterious force that imbued me with superhuman power at my greatest need. I had no real control over it, and had never anticipated its manifestation in this situation.

Nevertheless, it was here, and suddenly I was formidable. My member swelled to such proportion and rigidity that it sprang out of the girl's hands, startling her. She gave a little shriek, as of one surprised by a striking snake, though that snake merely looked her in the eye.

I rolled to my knees, caught her about the waist, and bore her back. She fell, her two legs going straight up in the air, and I pressed in from below, skewering her with my hugeness. The fit was tight, in this position, and her legs pressed against my chest and shoulders, pushing me back. But I thrust right on through, reaming out the channel and pumping it full of fluid.

Ippon! Now the applause was deafening.

I didn't wait for the fourth woman; I whipped out of the third one, letting her collapse like a punctured balloon, and dived for the next. Caught by surprise, she was on her stomach. No matter; I grabbed her by a buttock, heaved her up until she bent forward at the waist, and took her from the rear. My *ki* kept me charged; in moments I had filled her up, like a car getting gasoline. And the spectators were staring, awed.

this way, and my supercharged member was simply too big for this child-sized girl.

Then she wriggled and my left hand slipped, depriving her suddenly of support. She dropped hard, with a little scream, and the impalement was complete. I climaxed again, almost fearing that the force of my jets would shoot her through the roof, but of course nothing of the kind happened. I waited until the orgasm had spent its fury, all the greater for its confinement in that tight channel, then gently lifted her off me. My member was still hard.

The tribesmen were exclaiming and slapping each other on the backs. I knew they had never seen anything like this. I stood up, my erection paramount. "Where's the rest of your women?" I demanded.

"Jason!"

It was Dulce, who had forced her way through the throng, alerted by the commotion. Shocked, she stared at me, seeing it all. It wasn't that she was squeamish about sex; she certainly wasn't. But she hated to see me make a complete fool of myself, and she was concerned about my health. With good reason, on both counts.

Suddenly the *ki* drained out of me. My whole body went limp. I felt as if a gallon of blood had been sucked from me, and maybe it had. What had I been filling those five containers with?

I looked at the girls, and was appalled. One was picking lice out of her long black hair and eating them; another had a set of toothmarks on one breast—mine, I was sure!—and a third smiled at me with her teeth filed to points. A piranha-mouth! Had I kissed her? She was not mature, she was old! The fat one was consumptive, hacking up phlegm. And the child-sized one was bleeding profusely from the genital injury I had dealt her. The room looked like a battlefield, complete with fat flies settling on the bodies.

I felt sick, and not merely in the body. I had an awful premonition that I was about to suffer another gallstone attack. Dulce didn't even have to say "I told you so."

I woke, sweating. This time I was glad to see the dull familiarity of my bachelor room. If this episode had been sheer imagination, I needed to find better things to think about. If it was a memory from my past life, I might have good reason for my amnesia. Running a line of willing women in front of a cheering crowd of headhunters? Impaling a childlike girl? It *better* be a dream!

Yet somehow I suspected that it wasn't, even though it had gone like a parody of my prior dream about making the sixth degree black belt. That woman Dulce, for example—it was as though I actually knew her. And the jungle—almost it came back. I had been there, somewhere . . .

No, impossible! Time to return to the real world, like Walter Mitty.

*

The start of the second judo class was not so bad, as I now had some notion how to do the breakfalls and knew better than to attempt the forward roll. My shoulder still hurt, but I was able to function. I had made the plunge and invested in a *gi*; it was huge and stiff and baggy on me, and I felt like a walking sandwich-billboard. "Don't worry, it'll shrink," Steve assured me. I hoped so; it was hard to convince myself that the whole class was not staring at my clown-like aspect. On top of that, it chafed.

"Back to back with your partner," Steve cried after the initial exercises were done.

Huh? This was something new!

People paired off and sat on the mat, leaning back against each other the way kids do at a picnic. Again I lacked a partner, and wasn't really too eager to find one. Suddenly my shoulder seemed to hurt worse; it had gradually intensified as the hours passed, last time; nothing seemed to be broken, but I didn't want to aggravate it.

But again I was approached by a girl—not Vonnie, but a well-constructed black-haired lass. She wore no *gi*; instead she had jeans and a sweatshirt. She looked about twenty-two. Her name, it developed, was Terry, and she had not been to very many classes herself. That gave us a kind of camaraderie; we were both beginners. With so many teen-age green and brown belts sliding so easily through impossible contortions, it was a comfort to know that other beginners existed.

We sat down back to back. "But what do we do?" I asked over my shoulder, my nose banging into her loose long hair. When I started out to learn judo, all of three days ago, the last thing I had anticipated was to find myself sitting in clothing like starched pajamas on a thirty-foot square mattress, leaning into an attractive young woman. This was martial art?

"It's matwork," she explained. "Like wrestling. You try to get a holddown."

"Wrestling?" I thought I'd misheard. But indeed, now all the other couples were going at it vigorously, getting into all manner of tangles, clutching heads to chests, throwing thighs over faces, tearing jackets open, wedging forearms through crotches and lifting, sending belts flying loose, crushing each other to the mat, panting and groaning with effort.

I looked at Terry.

I just couldn't *do* it! First, and least important, I didn't know any holddowns. Second, how could I wrestle with a *girl*? Anywhere I grabbed her . . .

Maybe something similar occurred to her. "Okay," she said. "I'll hold you down and you try to get out of it."

That suited me. Of course she would not be able to hold me down, but at least I could find out what the hold was like.

I lay down on my back, and she put the *kuzure yoko shiho gatame*, or variation of the side four quarter hold on me. No, I didn't master its name until much later. All it was, basically, was her kneeling beside me, leaning over my chest, and wrapping her two arms around my far arm. There was very little weight on me; I was conscious of her two breasts pressing into my torso, but they were hardly burdensome.

Then I tried to break the hold. It was the strangest thing: she had no real weight on me, but I couldn't get off my back. I don't care what others may think, I really was trying. No matter how I squirmed and struggled, she was right there, her hair flying across my face. I had no leverage, no way to sit up or turn over. I thrashed around for about two minutes, wearing myself out, before I finally got a hand against her knee, pushed it *away,* and twisted out from under.

Later I learned that if a judo hold is maintained for thirty seconds, it's an *ippon* or victory for the holder. So I had really lost four times over.

Suddenly I had a whole lot of respect for that hold.

Next we practiced turning over a prone opponent. I still working with Terry. Steve demonstrated several ways to lever someone over, and it really wasn't complicated; anybody could do it.

Then it was our turn. Terry lay down on her stomach, and I tried to flip her onto her back. I started to slide my right hand under her arm and around behind her head in the half-nelson Steve had shown, but she had her arm tight against her side. I couldn't get through without going lower down on her torso, beyond her elbow, and moving up from below, and then I encountered her, er, chest. Jamming my hand through there could be subject to misinterpretation. She was a buxom girl.

So I tried the alternate method Steve had shown, taking hold of her collar and putting my shoulder down against her side to bulldoze her over. I shoved—and she didn't budge. Who would have believed it could be so hard to turn over one feminine-type girl! As with the holddown, I had greatly underestimated the problem.

But I tried. I braced my knees and shoved valiantly—and felt an odd kind of tearing in my left side. It wasn't really painful, just muscles sliding about over my rib-cage, making the area a little numb. So I kept on trying to turn her over, and failing. She was glued to the mat, smiling.

A young brown belt stopped by. The higher belts did this, acting as assistant instructors. "I can't turn her over," I complained.

"Well, you slide your hand around like this," he said, happy to show me the ropes. But he couldn't seem to get his hand in either, perhaps encountering the same complex of problems I had. Terry had her arms tightly clamped in good proper resistive style, and of course she was *supposed* to resist. And a man just doesn't grab a girl by the bust and roll her over. Not in public. (In dreams—ah, in dreams! Jungle, White God, running the line—for shame!) So far, our efforts had only tickled her.

Another brown belt appeared. "What's the matter?"

"We can't turn her," I said.

"No problem." He was a large, husky man. "You just take hold of elbow and knee, like this, and haul her up—" He hauled, lifting Terry abruptly a foot off the mat. She screeched and flailed her arms, understandably startled—but dropped down on her stomach again and clenched her elbows to her sides more tightly than ever.

"Well, you do have to apply a little force," the husky brown belt said calmly, picking her up again and twisting her in the air to flip her on her back as she dropped.

Something in her clothing went SNAP!

"Oops," he said, taken aback. "Are you all right?"

"Quite all right," Terry said quickly, tucking herself back together. Obviously she was unhurt. Woman wear elastic in various places, of course; that's one of the intriguing things about them.

That ended turnover practice. I now had the unenviable distinction of having been unable, even with the help of two brown belts, to turn over one girl—and my increasingly sore side indicated I had injured myself in the attempt. I was some judoka!

*

There were actually two classes, with a five minute break between them. I had entered the beginning class, but as an adult I was eligible for the Seniors class too. "Why don't you try it," Steve suggested. "We go into self-defense techniques, chokes and armlocks that the kids aren't allowed to do."

Well, why not? I wanted to learn judo, and this was a good way, if I didn't tear myself up too much more. So I stayed. The smaller children went home, including Penny who insisted on saying good-bye personally with a hug; but a few more adults appeared, so it was a group of similar size. As usual, I had no partner.

This time a man approached me. He was Mr. Campbell, an orange belt who looked to be about my own age, and he was the club treasurer. He seemed very nice—but the truth was, *all* the people in judo seemed nice, and I knew I would want to continue coming for social as well as physical reasons. Aspects of judo, such the forward rolling breakfall, terrified me, but I liked the people. I had not really expected such friendliness and helpfulness in a martial arts class.

This time Steve demonstrated the *seoi-otoshi* technique, or shoulder drop, in which he turned as in the *o goshi* but kept his right hand on Uke's lapel—I remembered that the thrower was always Tori, the other Uke—and stuck his right leg back. It looked easy—as they all did, when Steve did them.

Mr. Campbell was familiar with the throw, so he threw me first. Over I went, seeing the high ceiling spin by. Wham! right on my hurt side, and I also scraped the skin off my left elbow again and stung my hand and banged my head: a typical fall.

He helped me up. "Sorry—I didn't realize you weren't used to the falls yet. Are you all right?"

"Fine," I said dizzily. "I seem to have landed wrong."

"It takes time to learn," he said. "I'll just load you next time."

"Load me?" That sounded bad.

"I won't complete the throw. Like this." And he went into the throw again. My feet went up sickenly, and I tensed for the worst—and then he set me down gently, upright. Hey, this was much better! After this I would remember the key word: LOAD.

Then it was my turn. Following his directions, I stepped around, turned, and heaved. My right wrist bent backwards painfully, and he did not budge. A complete failure.

"Try it again," Mr. Campbell said. "This time bend your knees.

You have to get down low, to pick me up."

Oh, yes—I always forget that detail. The knees really didn't seem very important. So I humored and spun around, bending my left knee as I threw my right leg down almost to the floor behind him. "Wrist stiff!" he warned, and I jerked my fistful of lapel forward and heaved.

And he went up like a feather, over my shoulder, and landed resoundingly on the mat.

"Beautiful!" he cried, getting up. He wasn't hurt at all. I wished I had that secret of safe landing!

"You jumped," I said unbelievingly. I knew I couldn't have done the throw all by myself.

"I didn't jump. You threw me."

So just getting down that extra couple of inches had made all the difference. Another valuable lesson learned. Mr. Campbell was shorter than me, so getting down really counted. And now I really liked this throw, my first successful effort with a partner my own weight. *Seoi-otoshi.*

Steve ended the class with some testing for promotion. He looked down the line. "Angel," he said.

A girl came out. She chose a partner and stood before Steve. "*Ippon seoi nage*," he said.

She took hold of her partner, whirled around, and threw him over her shoulder. *Wham*! In the still hall, the landing was like a crack of thunder. Steve made her do it twice more, and it remained just as impressive.

"*Morote seoi nage*," Steve said.

Angel whirled into a throw that seemed just about like the first one. Slam! The boy struck the mat. I was amazed at the repeated impacts he withstood. *I* would have been crushed to a quivering hulk, yet he took fall after fall without concern. It reminded me of the dwarves bowling on the mountain, and I was Rip Van Winkle watching their game of nine pins. Just one big human in this instance, crashing like thunder again and again. Boom-boom-

boom, seeming to land so hard that bones must splinter, yet without damage.

"*Tai otoshi*," Steve said, heedless of the carnage. "*O soto gari. O goshi.*" How could anyone even remember the horrendous names? Yet Angel performed them all.

I was impressed and dismayed. Here was one nondescript girl selected from the class (later I saw her in street clothes, and she was quite striking; it was the *gi* that made all women sexless), a mere white belt—and she seemed to know all the throws in the book! How could *I* ever master all this? She even did three holddowns I didn't recognize.

Angel made her yellow belt promotion. But I wondered whether there was even any point in my remaining in the class. It would take me years just to master the yellow belt techniques—and I couldn't even take a fall yet!

Chapter 3:

Sword and Stone

I faded in and out as I floated down the Amazon River. At times I was quite lucid, admiring the crocodiles that hopefully paced my raft. At other times the pain was so bad that I wished the reptile's hopes would be fulfilled. I was dying anyway; why prolong the agony?

Something grabbed me. Instinctively I fought, knowing it was useless and pointless; I could never overcome a crocodile in water. But I wasn't *in* the water; human hands were holding me.

They were Indians, jabbering in their own language. I didn't know whether that was good or bad; I didn't recognize them. They might help me—or eat me.

They helped me. They portaged me overland for many days. We could not understand each other, but it hardly mattered, because I did not remember who I was or where I was going. Sometimes I was able to walk; at other times I could only lie and moan. A pretty maiden tended to me then, seemingly amenable to my every need—except the need to be free of pain.

Then I found myself in the city of Manaus. How I got there and how I left there—blanks.

Time, confusion, travel—whom did I meet, who helped me? More blanks—and I was on a tramp steamer, and it must have been in the ocean, for there was no land in sight, and the swelling waves added to my discomfort. You might think that slow undulations would lull me to sleep, but they made me feel seasick. Yet I had to eat. The food was exceedingly greasy and overspiced, but I had suffered illness and hunger on the route and lost much weight, and now that food was plentiful I could not be choosy.

About three AM I woke with a sensation of fullness, heartburn, indigestion, and general malaise. Not seasickness, for it had happened often before I was on the boat, and this was worse. I heard myself screaming. The ship's doctor was a drunk; he gave me some sort of medicine and a shot of morphine, and I relaxed.

But next day it was back, the pain spreading from my right side into my back and stomach. The skin over the region of my gall bladder was swollen and sensitive. My body was turning yellowish, and in the mirror I saw the whites of my eyes becoming yellow too. This horrified me, as it reminded me of the dread addiction to the drug Kill-13, where the whites turned red. I had fought the purveyors of that drug, and thereby lost my fiancee; the whole series of associated memories was anathema. But in this case it was not addiction, but jaundice: the bile from my gall bladder was blocked off, and spreading throughout the body instead of the digestive system. Another symptom was in my stools: dead gray, no brown. An ugly thing to contemplate, in more than one way.

Half delirious with pain and morphine, I lay on my bunk and heard the captain discussing my case with the doctor. "He's going to die. You'll have to operate."

"Cap'n, I *can't* operate! I do not have a proper license or instruments."

"And you're a drunken bum. I know. But we don't have any choice. We're not much as a ship or crew, but we're human."

"We don't have anesthesia."

"We have plenty of rum."

"I never did this kind of surgery before."

"You'd rather just weight him down and dump him over the side? You know he can't live unless you operate. Now. What kind of murder do you prefer?"

They were rough men engaged in illicit trade, but decent in their fashion. And so the doctor agreed to operate, reluctantly. I had no say in the matter, which was just as well. Because as he anesthetized me by forcing me to drink cup after cup of cheap Dark Bacardi Rum, he imbibed a fair quantity of that anesthetic himself, and he told me his life story. It was not reassuring.

He was a slight fellow in his forties, with protruding eyes under rimless glasses. He had a three day beard and a lot of hair around his body, and his breath was bad. "I lived in Cuba," he explained. "When the revolution came, I was in my third year of medical school. I had trouble with the Minister of Agriculture of the new regime, because I had taken his wife away from him, and he had me jailed. I learned the rest of my medicine by practicing in prison." He poured another round. He seemed to be determined to keep pace with me, but I was drinking to get dead drunk so I couldn't feel the knife. Had I been sober, I might have found the situation more alarming. But I *wasn't* sober; that was the point.

"When I was freed," he continued, "I left the country, faked papers, and won a job as ship's doctor. The captain knows this, but he's satisfied, because it means I'll never tell the authorities about his contraband. Where else could I get a job?" He sighed. "But I don't know how I'll get through this time." He poured another round. "I haven't operated on anyone since my prison days, and even then it didn't matter much whether my patients survived. I don't have any instruments, just kitchen knives."

I laughed. I thought that was very funny. Surgery with a kitchen knife! Hilarious! Which meant I was just about drunk enough.

When the time came, four crewmen seized my arms and legs and tied me to a bunk. One of them looked at the doctor and his setup and had to go on deck to heave his own digestion over the side. But I was crazy wild drunk, not afraid at all, thinking it all one big game. After all, I didn't have to do the surgery, or even watch it. But just to be sure, they put a funnel in my mouth and nearly drowned me in more rum. I remembered seeing an old man tortured by being funneled full of water—but then some censor in my brain clamped down and all my past was blank again.

Then I saw the knife, and abruptly I was sober. The doctor was trying to sterilize the thing in the flame of a guttering candle. It was a common vegetable paring knife, not large, but a terrible vision. The doctor's hand was shaking.

But he had guts, because he came at *my* guts. I would have bolted, but I was securely tied down, my abdomen exposed. The blade sliced into my quivering flesh. I screamed and bridged.

"Don't do that!" he exclaimed, backing off as I felt the hot flow of blood down my side. "You'll make me cut up your whole intestine!"

After that I screamed, but did not move my torso much. My mind sheered off into the vivid remembrance of other pains, other tortures, physical and mental. The time Kan-Sen put a thumbscrew on me . . . Illunga half-castrating me with a kick to the groin . . . Mirabal's electrodes shooting current through my chest . . . Chiyako.

Chiyako—that was the worst of all. My beloved Chinese-American fiancée, daughter of Shaolin kung fu, brutally killed before my eyes by the savage Kill-13 addict. That pain never ceased; only its encapsulation had permitted me to function normally.

I had a terrible spasm, and then I was unconscious again. There was blood all over my belly, soaking the sheets beneath me. But there was also a tremendous sense of peace flooding through me, as though that blood were carrying away the horrors trapped in my body. The awful pressure was gone; the gallstone—indeed, the whole gall bladder—had been removed. Dazed-looking crewmen were mopping the blood out of the site of surgery, eyes squinting so that they did not have to look at any more of me than absolutely necessary.

"Thanks, fellows," I said.

"We're not through this yet," the doctor warned me. "You're bleeding like a stuck pig, and I haven't closed the incision."

"Want me to stop the bleeding?" I asked. I didn't seem to be joking.

"*Si, Señor,*" he agreed absently as he prepared his suture materials. Sweat dripped from his forehead into the wound.

I concentrated. The bleeding slowed, then stopped. It was the *ki*, come to help me in my hour of dire need.

The doc stared. "It's the DT's! he exclaimed. "I'm seeing that wound close up by itself!"

"I see it too," a crewman said. "Maybe he's dead."

"Just sew it up," I snapped. "I don't know how long I can do this."

"He doesn't *sound* dead," another crewman said, awed.

Clumsily, the doctor sewed. I don't know what he used—maybe a sail-canvas stitching outfit. But I felt it drawing the wound shut.

At last he was done. The operation was a success! I passed out.

I woke hours later with a raging fever. The surgery had been performed under septic conditions, and infection had set in. I had merely exchanged one doom for another.

The pain of the knife is sharp. The pain of contamination is dull. But the knife is soon finished, while the infection ravaged me for days. I couldn't eat, could hardly move; I hacked weakly on the bunk, lacking the strength to clear my congestion more strenuously. My remaining flesh withered away. I had lost a good deal of blood before my *ki* clamped down, and had little reserve energy. Slowly I spiraled toward the nether terminus. There was nothing the doctor could do; he had no penicillin or wonder drugs.

I saw the four-armed black goddess Kali, the face of death. Then that face shattered like mud-plaster and revealed the skull-like visage of Exu, the Voodoo Satan. He had put a curse on me, and every detail of that curse had been fulfilled. Yet Exu was not my ultimate enemy. The enemy I sought was—blank. That knowledge had been wiped from my brain. Even the incipience of death would not conjure that essential information.

Yet I would not let myself drift into that dark abyss. I had a mission, transcendently important—that I could not remember. I *had* to live, whatever sacrifice it took.

At last the dark tide turned. My fever peaked and dropped, down a little more each day. I recovered some energy and appetite. "I prayed for you," the doctor said. "Don't laugh."

"I'm not laughing." It was still an effort to speak. I knew he had saved my life, however precariously.

"Or maybe it was for myself I prayed. But I didn't think you'd make it."

"You're a good doctor."

He swore vehemently in Spanish. "A foul lie!" But he was pleased. And my statement must have been true, because how could a poor doctor have saved me despite being in an alcoholic stupor?

We neared the coast of America. "We helped you," the captain told me. "It was a favor to one who loves you. I do not know who. But we must not let them find you aboard our ship. There would be questions, a search." He spread his hands apologetically.

"I understand," I said. Indeed I did. A search would turn up their contraband cargo. "I will remember nothing."

We shook hands. "Perhaps we shall meet again," he said, "when memory is feasible."

Delicately put. "I hope so."

So they put me ashore in a small boat without lights, at night, and left me standing on the beach. Silently the craft returned to the night. I waved once, knowing they could not see the gesture. Then my memory faded.

I turned and tramped toward the lights of the nearby city. There was nothing else to do.

*

One evening Mr. Campbell did not show up, and neither did any of the girls. The thing about working with such people was that they were less aggressive and more careful than the strong young men. This meant that I didn't get exhausted to the point of pain, or get hurt taking hard falls. It seemed to take forever for injuries to heal, and it was very easy to re-injure the same places before healing was complete. So my effective choices were either to drop out of judo, or to work with those who didn't hurt me. Because there was so much to learn, and skill took more practice than muscle, I stayed in and practiced carefully. Slowly I was learning to take better falls, though they frankly scared me, and I was mastering the names of the techniques.

Tonight I knew I was in for it. The luck of random selection matched me with a husky yellow belt named Jeff, seventeen or eighteen years old, and we started with matwork. No way could I match his strength; it took him about fifteen seconds to put me in the *kami-shiho-gatame* or smothering hold, and it was aptly named. His chest was pressing my head into the mat, and it was all I could do to breathe. My struggles were useless; he seemed to weigh three hundred pounds, and to be anchored by metal bolts driven into the foundation. Might as well try to lift the building!

"Try to break the hold," Jeff told me, unconsciously adding insult to injury. What did he think I was doing?

After a time he let me go. "You put the hold on me," he said. So I put it on him, sliding my forearms under his shoulders from above and gripping his belt. I shoved my chest down on his face and clung so tight he'd never get out. Let *him* smother a while! "Ready?"

He hadn't noticed my hold? He was teasing me. "Yes."

And he simply rolled over sidewise, and I was on the bottom again. "You didn't spread your legs," he explained. "You had no side stability."

Another forgotten detail! Why did it come so easily to him, and so hard to me? Yet he was only a yellow belt. What did it take to get beyond that?

"Where's Mr. Campbell?" I gasped when I was too exhausted to make even a show of resistance. Oh, the resiliency of youth!

"Didn't you hear? He fell off the roof of his house, sawing a branch from a tree. Broke his arm in three places. He's in the hospital."

"Oh, no!" I exclaimed, almost as concerned for myself as for Mr. Campbell. If I had to work much longer with Jeff, *my* arm would get broken in three places. Or feel like it, anyway.

Right then I decided to undertake a program of exercise, for self defense. Against judo class workouts. I could no longer depend on someone like Mr. Campbell to throw me gently. I had to be able to take a hard fall, or to prevent my opponent from throwing me. At the moment I could do neither.

"Line up," Steve said. "*Uchikomis,* loading practice."

Uh-oh. If there was one thing worse than matwork, it was loading practice. Because we didn't just load one or two times; we'd do twenty five loads in quick succession, then twenty five more with another technique, and so on, until our *gis* were sopping with sweat and we were staggering like drunken folk.

Jeff had to go show a new student the breakfalls, so I was alone again. I had only moments to take any partner available—and the only one free happened to be little Penny.

You'd think it would be an unequal match, a grown man and a six year old braid-headed girl. Yes indeed, but not quite as expected. We loaded *ippon seoi nage,* the one-arm back-carry throw. She just grabbed my arm and leaned forward; no trouble at all for her as she was not tall enough to take any of my weight. But when it was my turn, I had to squat down almost to the mat, in order to get under her arm. She thought it was great fun, by my legs were killing me.

Steve walked by. "It's good for you," he said. Yeah, sure; that's what they used to say about cod liver oil and tetanus shots.

But maybe Steve had mercy, because then he had us change partners. Some more people had come in; I hadn't seen them, but how could I see anything with a face full of sweat and waves of pain radiating from my knees? Penny got someone closer to her size, which pleased her not at all, and so did I.

"*O soto gari*!" Steve announced, and started counting off that impossible rapid Japanese cadence. "*Sho! Ni! San! Yon! Go!*" My new partner swing into it without seeming difficulty while I took my turn as dummy. I mean, as *Uke*. "*Roku! Shi!*" Twenty fine pulls and sweeps, just like that.

"Other partner," Steve called, reminding me of a square dance. Some of those exercises were indeed like dances, especially when we had to move around in semi-randori style and alternate techniques. I imagined music playing, couples circulating, only instead of "swing your partner" it was "throw your partner." Might be possibilities there!

In *o soto gari* you step out to Uke's right side, swing your right foot up behind him, then sweep it back, knocking his right leg out from under while you smack him down with good shoulder contact and a yank on his right arm. It is a very effective throw if you can ever get into position for it. In competition, Uke never lets you get close enough. But in loading practice, he's not resisting, of course; you sweep your foot back to the side of his foot so as not to throw him, and give a good hard shoulder or chest-to-chest thunk.

Well, I tried it. I didn't do everything right the first time, of course; I never do. I stepped across, swung my leg out, looked down to see if I was doing it properly, and saw my partner's belt. Up until now I had just sort of blissfully rested, eyes half closed, while Tori buffeted me. You get that way in *uchikomis* pactice, kind of shell shocked. So I hadn't actually looked at my partner.

The belt was black.

I blinked, faltering in mid effort. The film of sweat over my eyeballs must've distorted my perception of a green belt. Gave me a scare, there for a moment. I looked again, and it was definitely, shockingly black, with a white stripe through it.

Now black belts are rather like the officer corps in the military; they don't mix much with the peons. The only black belt I'd seen was Steve. What was this one doing here? And why the added decoration of the stripe?

Well, I was stuck in the middle of loading practice. I had to carry through. But suddenly I had the shakes, knowing how utterly clumsy I was. Now it was important that I do it *right*, somehow. Step to side, sweep with leg, pull down with left hand, shove with right hand, smack shoulder to shoulder, thunk!

Lo and behold, I did it right. Desperation must have given me temporary skill. Only my shoulder contact was not a hard, bony smack; it was more of a right chest to right chest collision that felt wrong. I tried at again, and again it was wrong, more of a cushiony contact. What was the matter?

I studied the situation, amidst the repeated loadings. Slowly it came to me, despite the present dullness of my mind. I was doing it more or less right, but my partner had a very soft chest under the *gi*. In fact my partner was a woman.

A female black belt? I must be dreaming! I wasn't even sure such things existed, and certainly they didn't do loading practice with male white belts like me!

At last the count stopped; maybe Steven's voice was getting tired. Breathless as I was, I still didn't want it ended. What in the world could I say to my partner—"nice day"? Matter of fact, it *wasn't* a nice day; it was night and it was raining. The water was sluicing down the window panes.

"*O goshi*!" Steve cried. Nope, he hadn't lost his voice. Pity.

There was a crack of thunder almost overhead, and the lights went out. It was a real storm!

Now it was pitch black in the *dojo*. There wasn't much to do except wait it out; no doubt the power would return in a few minutes. I had read that central Florida was the thunder and lightning capital of the nation: more noisy weather here than anywhere else. Could be; here was some evidence.

"How do you do?" my partner inquired. Her voice was low, and for me it had an oddly suggestive quality. It must have been the notion of a female black belt. I had worked out with female white belts and yellow belts, one of each, but they were more or less on my level. A black belt—obviously she had had a hell of a lot of judo experience, though she didn't seem older than I. And a hell of a lot of skill; I had felt her easy competence during the loading, now that I thought back on it. I had in my innocence supposed that only Steve did such things so well they seemed natural, but probably it was a quality of all black belts. The thought of a young woman with all that skill did something funny to me. What *other* skills might she have?

"Are you there?" she inquired with the hint of a smile in her voice. Obviously I was here physically; she had hold of my lapel.

"Uh, hello, I'm Caesar," I mumbled, embarrassed. What was I doing, thinking like that about a woman I hardly knew? Who was like an officer, while I was a lowly recruit.

"So it's Caesar, now," she murmured.

"What?" It almost seemed as if she knew me.

"I'm Susan."

Even a female name! Yet what had I expected, a Martian name? Now I was aware of her presence in more subtle ways. She was hot, too, after the exercise, but she wasn't drippingly sweaty as I was. She gave off a gentle glow of warmth, and she smelled nice. The darkness prevented me from looking at her, so I was more aware of the non-visual aspects. Somehow they made her seem twice as feminine as before. Of course I hadn't even noticed her gender at first.

Still the lights did not come on. There were noises of impatience around the hall, but I was hardly aware of them. Underneath all my amnesia and inexperience I discovered that I was still a male. This warm closeness in the dark, this alarming but exciting concept of a female black belt who just might have known me from somewhere before—no, I must have misheard or misinterpreted. I tried to keep my thoughts in line, but I kept remembering the feel of those *o soto gari* chest contacts, too soft.

"Let's finish the *uchikomis*," she suggested.

"In the dark?" I asked dully.

"Judo is balance and feel. You don't need to see." And she stepped into me, put her arm around my waist, leaned forward and lifted me off my feet.

Startled, I almost flailed the air. But she set me dawn again with complete control. Then she swing into another *o-goshi*. At first I was amazed at her strength, then I became aware of the fine balance and limberness of her body. She could lift me because she was doing the technique correctly, in contrast to my efforts. That way it required very little brute strength.

"You try a few," she murmured.

"Okay." What else was there to do? I stepped into her, too close, in the dark. She was almost as tall as I. "Sorry."

She did not deign to acknowledge my obvious clumsiness, which made me feel even more awkward. If only this was some other venue than judo!

I backed off and tried again. I stepped across, slid my right arm around her waist, bent my knees, turned away, and lifted. Up she came; she was feather light.

"Very good," she said. It was a verbal pat on the head. Had I been a dog I would have wagged my tail. I felt like doing it anyway.

What do you know: I could do *o goshi* in the dark. Maybe better than in daylight. I put her down, then tried it again. That gave me a chance to note other details, such as the pleasing swell of her hip as my hand slid across, and the supple accommodation of her body to my effort. I had been able to lift her because she cooperated perfectly. A white belt would not have known how, especially in the dark. The lack of loading sounds elsewhere in the dojo suggested that the yellow and orange belts were similarly challenged.

I lifted her again—and it didn't work. "You have to bend your knees," Susan reminded me.

Damn! I always forgot one of those details when I didn't concentrate. She had corrected me exactly in the manner of any other instructor. Right when I wanted to think of her in some other vogue. I was probably blushing, hoping the light did not come back on right now.

I tried once more, bending my knees—but this time my balance was all off, and instead of drawing her up, I fell back into her, my head banging into her chest. Fortunately it was not a hard landing; she was female, all right.

"Let me show you," she said, unperturbed. She must have had eons of practice dealing with duffers like me. "Draw on Uke's right lapel, bringing him off-balance. Duck down low, bring him close across your hip, then straighten your knees." She demonstrated, her posterior rising to catch me across the crotch.

The complete darkness made me dependent on touch, and hyper-aware of bodily contact. There was something about that smooth lifting pressure in that area by that pneumatic derriere. I knew it wasn't supposed to happen in Judo, but I suffered a specific reaction. It was necessary that we stop this practice before that reaction became rigidly evident. I opened my mouth—

The lights came on. "*O goshi*!" Steve called immediately. And Susan proceeded to load twenty five *o goshis* in rapid order, every one perfect, every one catching me right where it counted. Ooooh!

*

My exercise program went reasonably well. The first time I did pushups at home, I almost made it to nine, which was better than I expected. Judo must have built me up some already. I found a child's swing in the yard and did chins: the first three weren't bad, but the fourth was uncomfortable, and I barely made the fifth. My arms remained fatigued for an hour or more after each exercise. I also did squat jumps, and fell over after twelve, my legs knotting in agony. And sit-ups—after the twentieth the pain in my stomach was so bad I had to quit.

But my body responded. Every three or four days I found myself able to do another chin, and I recovered more rapidly from the effort. In about six weeks I made it to fifteen, with the other exercises increasing similarly. My weight increased, and it wasn't fat; one day I stepped on the scales and discovered to my amazement that I had gained thirty pounds. I still couldn't match Jeff in matwork, but I could hold my own against women, children, and white belts.

But meanwhile I was still learning things in class. One day I worked with a big brown belt named Bo. We were doing *randori*, but I had absolutely no chance to throw him. Yet he could throw me without seeming effort; in fact, I seemed to throw myself. He didn't actually throw me, knowing I was afraid of falls; he'd just load me.

"How come I have so much trouble, while you do it so easily?" I asked him, frustrated. "I know you outweigh me, and you're a brown belt, but I can't even turn in for a throw unless you let me, and can't perform it anyway."

"*Kuzushi*," he said.

"God bless you."

He smiled. "*Kuzushi.* You move your opponent about, offbalancing him. That way he sets himself up for your technique. Like this." And he guided me around with so natural an imperative that it seemed pointless—until I found myself straddling his leg in an *o uchi gari* reap. He had hardly moved; I had walked right into it.

"*Kuzushi*," I repeated with new appreciation.

One day a new student came: a man about my own age. He had no partner and looked lost in his brand new *gi*. I well remembered the feeling, so I went up to work with him. I showed him some of the breakfalls and talked him through the *ippon seoi nage* throw the way Vonnie had done for me with *o goshi*. He was amazed to discover that it worked; he had actually done a throw! And I was able to take the fall all right because I knew he couldn't throw me hard.

He was Mr. Taylor, and he made his living selling potato chips. He became a regular judo student. I had a partner again.

Chapter 4:

Roofer's Affair

But much of my judo was no longer in the dojo. Because Susan, the black belt, took an interest in me. Why, I had no idea. She had an almost boyish figure, with small breasts and comparatively lean muscular body, large hands and feet, but she was undeniably feminine, with ample posterior and thighs. She was bronzed by the sun and exuded health. A woman like her could have her pick of black belts, and I was a stumbling white belt. But there it was.

Had I known what she had in store for me, I might have walked out the moment she first entered the dojo. Then again, maybe not. I'm a man, after all, and men are traditionally foolish about women. It's in the job description.

She came to the club several times, and always worked with me. Though her demeanor and judo were always proper, there was something entirely female about her that always stimulated me embarrassingly, and she could hardly have been ignorant of the effect. Maybe it intrigued her.

I was a lonely man without a past, only a lot of fantastic dreams. Here was an attractive woman showing an inexplicable interest in me. How would any man in my situation have reacted?

So when she invited me to come help her on a weekend chore, I accepted. It would give me a chance to know her better, and who could say how far it might go? After all the suggestion of the judo practice, I really wanted to find out the reality.

Saturday morning I reported to her address, and a princely estate it was. She was evidently rich. But she didn't invite me in; she had her car out front, a sporty Mercedes-Benz. It seemed that the chore was not at her home. She was wearing a man's shirt, some kind of tight brown riding pants, and boots. She looked good in them; the pants molded the buttocks and the rest just seemed to suit her.

We drove north out of town, the car purring like a contented tiger. Half an hour passed without arrival. "How far are we going?" I inquired.

"That depends on you."

What did she mean by that? I hesitated to ask for a clarification, so was silent another half hour. Now we were well out of town, in fact out of the county, still proceeding north at a good clip.

She pulled into a drive-in eatery. "This is where the chore is?" I inquired dubiously.

"No. This is where we get a bite to eat. It's a long drive."

I shrugged. "Just so long as we're back by dark. My landlady worries."

She gave me a sidelong glance. "We may be. But you're a big boy now. What'll you have?"

"Tell you in a minute." I struggled to get my wallet out of my back pocket, which was hard to do with the seat belt holding me securely down. I wasn't sure how much money I had, but knew it wasn't much.

"My treat," she said with a smile. "I'm well off."

She must be. Her house had been palatial, and the car was an import of luxury, not economy.

The carhop came up. Susan rattled off an order for hot dogs, potato sticks, onion rings, and milk shakes, to go.

So we ate while driving, me handing her things as she needed them. "Uh, if you have so much money," I began, balancing this and that on my knees.

"Why do I gobble cheap food on the run?" she finished. She sucked on her straw, swallowed, then continued. "Because at home I can't get away with this. My cook would die of shock; she's a nutrition nut. I get so tired of formal meals. This is the only chance I have to eat on the run. Fun, isn't it?"

"I guess so. Just where are you taking me? or am I allowed to know?"

"To my little cabin in the wood. To tack down the roof."

"Oh." So she had a satellite estate, as it were. Well, why not? She could evidently afford it.

Susan hummed a tune as she chewed on onion rings that I dipped in catsup for her. Surely an abomination to her fastidious cook! The melody sounded half familiar, but I couldn't place it. Probably it dated from my prior life, wherever that had been.

Then suddenly it came: "To the Woodland!" I exclaimed.

She glanced my way, raising an eyebrow in the way she had. "You remember it?"

I pieced it out. "To the woodland—far away—longs my heart forever. To the woodland longs my heart—This no man can sever. In the woodland far away—there lives my darling loved one."

"Why Caesar, I didn't know you cared!"

I felt the heat of embarrassment coming to my face. "You were humming it, not me."

"You *don't* care? I could have sworn otherwise when we did *o goshi* in the *dojo*."

The bitch. She had been aware of my predicament, and now in perfect judo style had brought me down by pushing in one direction until I resisted, then abruptly reversing. "What is your interest in me?" I demanded, partly to cover my shame. The truth was, I would have liked to do with her as I had dreamed I did with a jungle harem, but such thoughts could never see light. She was playing with me.

"Oh, you remind me of someone I once knew."

Or was it possible that she had known me before? Then why tease me instead of telling me? "Who?"

"All in good time."

I gave it up. She had me pretty much dancing on a string, and knew it. I had to let her play her little game, because she might have at least two things I desperately wanted. The second thing was knowledge of my past.

In due course we entered Citrus County, Florida. The almost-level ground had given way to gentle hills, and now these hills became more pronounced, and I liked that better. I must have lived in hilly county, when I was myself.

At last we turned onto a gravel road, that gave way to sand, then dirt, then grass, and finally to forest leaves. We bumped uphill to a wooden cabin, about twelve feet by twenty four feet, set on concrete blocks. Sure enough, its roof was blank knotty plywood, with only the lower portions shingled.

"I don't think we can finish that today," I said dubiously.

"There are sleeping bags inside."

So I was to spend the night with her. Yet how much did I dare presume?

"Here are the shingles," Susan said, indicating a pile on the north side. "There are hammer and nails inside. Why don't you start in on the roof, and I'll see what I can do about supper."

There was so much domestic suggestion in this setup that I dared not let my imagination roam. I donned the workman's apron she gave me, filled its pocket with roofing nails, took a hammer, set the ladder and climbed up.

"You'll need more than that," she cautioned me. "Better take up the box, and some shingles." So I ferried up the shingles, perching them near the edge of the upper slope, just within reach from the top of the ladder.

The Cabin was fourteen feet tall at the roof-ridge, and it stood from one to two feet above the ground, depending on which side of the hill I looked. That may not sound like much, but I discovered when I reached the upper rungs that I was nervous about heights. The roof had two slopes, like an old fashioned barn; the outer one was steep, so that the ladder leaned against it, and the inner one was only about thirty degrees off the level. But the ladder did not reach quite up to the bend. So I had to go to the very top rung and scramble up over the ridge, onto the slanting upper surface, and it felt precarious as hell. Suppose the ladder slipped out from under? Suppose I lost my balance?

Well, Susan was watching, so I grasped what courage I had and scrambled up.

I made it, but I wasn't sure how I'd get down again. The slant had looked almost level from below, but now it seemed dangerously steep. I could not see beyond the bend in the roof; it looked like a sheer drop-off. Wherever I set my feet and hands—and I dared not get off all fours—that slant seemed to be shoving them and me toward the dread edge.

"Start with the felt," she called from somewhere far below.

"Felt what?" I yelled back. For there wasn't anything to feel up here, except nervous.

"The felt. The roll-roofing material."

Oh. Not felt as in feel, but felt as in hat. The tar paper. I had a pre-cut segment up here with my pile of shingles. It was supposed to go down first, under the shingles. Cushioning them, maybe. I was learning to be a roofer.

I crawled to the end of the cabin with the roll. This was worse yet: fifteen feet straight down. It was a horrifying, dizzy height. If I fell—

Then a little gust of wind passed.

I hugged the roof, sprawled on my belly, my feet straddling the peak. Oh, that wind tugging at me! It seemed like a hurricane blowing me to doom. Oh, sure, I knew it was just a baby wind, a zephyr, nothing to take seriously. But my feeling didn't believe that.

So how did I move about now? Well, I did push-ups. Up, drag

knees along, down; up, knees, down. Suddenly my judo exercise program had relevance to real life.

I flattened an end of the felt and tacked it down with a nail. Ouch! Naturally I hit a finger.

Then I hooked one leg over the roof-ridge to counterbalance the upper part of my body, lest I slide head-first off the roof. I knew there really wasn't that much danger of sliding; had the roof been one foot off the ground, I'd have walked upright readily. But my fear did not abate. I scraped elbows, belly, ad knees doing it the hard way. The *only* way for me.

If I had ever thought to impress Susan, I had certainly managed to torpedo that. But the fact was, if she had been up there with me, naked, I would still have had more concern for the drop-off than for her. This exposed roof really had my number.

At last I got the felt tacked down. Now I started on the shingles. They might look small from a distance, but up close they were yard-long sections impregnated with ground stone on one side, half green, half brown. And they were stuck together. They had dabs of tar in the centers, so as to glue down the roof when the heat of the sun struck them. Oh, yes, there was heat; I felt it now, wafting up from the roof, bathing me, making me sweat.

I wrenched off the first shingle in the pile. It gave way suddenly, giving me one hell of a fall-scare. After that I *pried* them loose, carefully. As with judo, these seemingly simple things had to be done just right, or there were consequences. I went to work laying and hammering, placing each row so that it was staggered, the edges of the shingles lining up horizontally but not vertically. That was so rain could not find a crevice straight past the layers. The job would have been tedious if I hadn't been so scared. I might get this job done, somehow, but I'd never make a professional roofer.

For an hour I laid down shingles, and I got about a quarter of the job done. My right forearm was numbing with fatigue, because I wasn't used to hammering, but I was no good with my left. I made a mental note: practice hammering left handed, just in case I ever needed to do this again, so that one hand could spell the other. I had some scrapes on my knuckles from the sharp bits of rock in the shingles. But I dragged on.

I finished another row, crawled back for the next shingle and a reload of nails—and saw something skitter inside the nail box. A bug of some kind, probably a roach. Something gave me a feeling of *deja vu*; I remembered a roach from somewhere—crawling up a divinely shaped leg? I was peering up under a skirt, seeing that roach, and hearing the weird beat of fantastic music.

Ridiculous! What would I be doing on the floor, looking up some dancing girl's leg? Male erotic fantasy of the kind I already had too much of. I needed reality, not fantasy.

Well, I didn't like roaches. I wanted this one out of my nails. I picked up the box and shook it. Out tumbled a scorpion.

It was only a little one, not much over an inch long. But the sight of it gave me an ugly shock. Suppose I had put my hand on it, grabbing blindly for nails? The sting of a scorpion, I knew from somewhere, could kill. Maybe this little one wouldn't be fatal, but the pain might send me toppling off the roof.

The scorpion hid behind the box. That was no good; I didn't want to share the roof with it at all, and I certainly didn't want it back in the nails. I twisted about awkwardly and shoved the box with one foot.

The scorpion was gone.

Where was it? I hadn't seen it go inside the box, but it wasn't outside either. Had it fallen off the roof? I didn't wish that fate on it, though it probably could survive the fall better than I could. Maybe slid under a shingle? Poor thing; I bore it no malice, I just didn't want its company. Now how could I put my hand in the box, not being *sure*?

"Something the matter?" Susan called. "You stopped hammering."

"Uh, nothing," I called back, ashamed to admit my timidity. "Just tired." That was at least a half truth.

"You sure? You sound shaken."

Maybe the truth would do. "There's a scorpion."

"Ignore it; the local ones are harmless."

That information helped somewhat. "Thanks."

"Better get the felt up over the ridge before it rains," she advised. "Get the crack covered over."

Rain? I looked at the sky. Huge gray/black clouds loomed to the south. A storm, certainly.

I scrambled to unroll the felt. I still had a few nails in my apron; they would do to tack it down. I bent the felt lengthwise across the ridge and banged in several nails, then began unrolling.

There was an ominous swishing through the trees, as of a gale approaching. A light spattering of raindrops fell. God, those southern storms blew up fast!

I unrolled some more and hammered feverishly. I had to get it down before the real rain hit.

But as I neared the far end, a big gust came. It whipped across the roof, tugging at me, making me cower spread-eagled across the ridge, my fingers scratching for purchase that wasn't there. I had a mental picture of a mountain climber clinging to a near-vertical face of rock a mile above the canyon, his fingers sliding as the hurricane force wind savaged him. Sure my situation wasn't anywhere near that bad, but that was the image. Imagination is marvelous stuff.

The felt I had just tacked ripped out. It sailed past me. My body was weighting down one part of it, but somehow I got off it. I didn't want to be carried along with it. The whole roll rolled off the roof. There was a pause, and then I heard the solid thunk as it hit the ground. There, but for the grace of God—

Now the rain sluiced down in earnest. The entire roof became slick. The wind buffeted me, not satisfied with the roll of felt. I couldn't stay up here, but how could I get down? I couldn't even see the ladder, assuming it remained in place. If I started down to find it, and it wasn't there, I might not be able to halt my slide down the steeper outer roof. I'd got to the ground with or without the ladder.

"Over here!" Susan cried. She stood outside, getting splendidly wet. She was not a large breasted woman, but her soaked blouse clung to what she had, giving it perfect definition. A view to remember. But I was *here*, and she was *there*, and I had another concern at the moment: protecting my body.

"I can't get down!" I cried despairingly, knowing I lied; if this storm got any worse I'd come down regardless, maybe headfirst.

"The ladder's here," she yelled, pointing. "Slide your feet down toward it."

"I can't see it!"

"I'll tell you where. Trust me."

Shivering with more than cold, I twisted around and let my feet slide over the bend. My fingers had no purchase; my whole body began an inexorable slide, exactly as I had feared.

"Go right!" she cried. "Right!"

I pushed over my right foot, and felt nothing. My hands were leaving the ridge, slipping in water. No traction; I could not return.

"It's right below you! Another inch!"

I dropped that inch—I had no choice—and my toe felt the top of the ladder. It began to slide sidewise under my thrust. "Hold it in place!" I screamed.

She held it. The ladder firmed. I slid down, my left foot finding the second rung. Now I had support. But not until I got down far enough to put my hand on the rung did I relax, and then not much.

I stepped to the ground at last, and Susan was there, and we fell into each other's arms. She was cold and wet, like me, and her once elegantly coiffured hair straggled in dark rat-tails, but to me she was warm and lovely and wonderful to hold.

"Let's get the hell inside," she said.

That was right: it was still raining. I had forgotten for the moment, secure in her embrace. We disengaged and got inside. Now the rain abated somewhat, having done its damage.

"This will never do," Susan said. "Get your clothes off."

"But—"

"Think I want you dripping all over the furniture?" she demanded. Actually there was no furniture to speak of, just piles of building supplies and boxes of this and that, and drips were descending from the rafters. But it seemed to make sense at the time. A lot of things make sense when you're shivering wet and nervous, that don't add up when you're warm and dry and confident.

Still, I dawdled a bit. Susan gave a little sniff of disgust and unbuttoned my shirt, stripped it off me, and wrung it out over a bucket. I took off my shoes and poured them into the same container. A lot of water had descended from the cloud in those few minutes.

"Now the pants," she insisted.

"You're wet too," I pointed out.

"So I am." And she called my bluff by emerging from her own blouse and skirt. She was slender, but fairly solid around the hips, with firm thighs. The higher grades of judo tend to have strong legs.

I took down my trousers, still feeling awkward as hell, and stood in my underpants. I remembered the *o-goshi* loading, fearing a similar embarrassment, and of course the very thought mad it start to happen.

"Oh, come *on*," Susan said, unsnapping her wet bra. "Everything's soaking."

Her breasts, like the height of the roof and the force of the wind, were more impressive up close. Some generous-busted women are overly padded elsewhere; Susan was lean enough so that nothing detracted from what she did have. In fact, a slender woman can be the very essence of sex appeal. It was certainly true in this case. Her judo practice and skill gave a her a certain healthy grace even when she was standing still. Despite my discomfort, I found the situation extremely suggestive.

I didn't dare take off my underpants.

She fetched a towel from somewhere and began to dry me off.

"You've certainly lost a lot of weight, Jason," she murmured as she rubbed my shoulders. "What happened to you?"

Actually I had gained weight recently, but I must have had more before my amnesia. "I'm don't know. I'm an amnesiac; my life dates back to only a few days before I started class. I think I had an operation or something. There's a scar on my body, and I was pretty thin."

"You don't remember anything?"

"Well, sometimes I think I remember, but the stuff is so fantastic it makes no sense at all. Once I dreamed I was a black belt in judo."

"Well, it happens." She dried my legs. Her touch in that region did nothing to alleviate my condition.

"Another time I dreamed I was making love to—" I broke off, and not only because of the delicacy of the subject. Susan had just tugged down my underpants, without warning.

She eyed the result, which was impressive at this stage. "It happens," she repeated, seeming pleased rather than shocked. She brought up the towel to dry the remainder, paying special attention to what was most in evidence. If I had thought *o goshi* was bad . . .

Abruptly she stopped. "There's sleeping bags in the loft. Come."

I had been about to, but perhaps not the way she meant. Then again, maybe that *was* what she meant.

She climbed the ladder to the loft, and I followed, getting an excellent view of that comparatively plush posterior of hers. No view in the world like that! Again I had a fleeting memory of looking up such legs. Had it been anticipation instead?

She glanced down at me, catching me looking. "Let's do it," she said as she cleared the ladder.

There were, indeed, sleeping bags spread out. She lay on top, sunny side up, and I grabbed her, burying my face in those breasts. Then I slid up to get on top of her. Nature took over; I climaxed before I had even completed entry, which subtracted somewhat from the experience.

She squinted at me. "Where'd you practice lovemaking? In the Amazon jungle?

Amazon jungle! *Could* that have been where? It almost seemed so. But I didn't say that. "Sorry. Did I hurt you?" Yet she was clearly no virgin.

"That's not the point. As with a judo throw, you have to consider your partner too."

I paused, not knowing what she meant. But she showed me. She talked with me for a little while, explaining that women, too, had sex drives, but that their expressions of them differed from that of the male. More care had to be taken, the preliminary moves done correctly, like turning in, placing the feet and hands, bending the knees, and lifting for an *o goshi*. Art, rather than force, or it fouled up. It was a good discussion, and I realized I had blundered. Just as I did so often in judo.

But she was not condemning me, merely educating me. She made her points delicately, without affront. Then she showed me how. She stroked me, just so, and I turned on. Then I stroked her similarly, getting it right, and despite the classroom nature of the lesson, I saw that she was turning on too. Do a thing right, and it works, regardless. She turned to her side, her back to me, and guided my body and hand. Oh, that posterior! And so I remembered that there was more than one direction from which to approach a given destination, and that some positions are better than others, when both parties are considered.

Because I had shot my wad the first time, there was less urgency about the rerun. I was able to stimulate her in the way she needed, as long as she required, and when she slowly worked into her own climax I was ready to match it. *Had* to match it; her pulsing interior would not be denied. And you know, it was much better this time, not only for her but for me. I had learned something valuable.

And in retrospect, my dream of the jungle harem seemed ludicrous, for a whole new set of reasons. I had never even thought of how the girls might feel about the matter. I had supposed I was performing heroically, when in fact I had short-circuited the real potential of the act. I hoped I would remember this lesson, next time I dreamed of a harem.

*

We had cold bean sandwiches for supper; the rain had made an outdoor fire impossible, and there was no electricity or gas. When this rich girl roughed it, she went all the way, so to speak. But I was hungry, and beans and milk from a thermos were delicious.

We took an evening walk out in the forest, marred only by the barbed sandspurs that kept sticking to our legs. Our clothing was still wet, so we went naked, like true children of nature; there was no one here to see. And what is so indecent about such exposure? There is nothing so beautiful as the unadorned human body in good health. If you ask me, the indecency is merely in the minds of those who scream about indecent exposure. But of course my opinion wasn't worth much; I had, pretty close, been born yesterday.

About a quarter mile to the east there was an old railroad cut, with three tracks running through a man-made chasm forty feet from top to bottom. Much higher than the cabin roof, but it didn't bother me despite the steepness of the slope. All in the perspective, I suppose. We climbed down and up the other side, scrambling four legged like animals, and I flipped down a little clod of dirt that hit her on the left breast, and she chased me until we both got grounded by the ubiquitous sandspurs. By then it was all the way dark, and we limped back to the cabin.

We slept naked in the bag. I was so tired I conked right out, believe it or not, before my hand got much farther than her left breast. (She had washed the dirt off it.) As with everything else, multiple sex sounds great from a distance, but in practice it becomes too difficult to be worthwhile. I know that's not the way the male magazines would have it, but I wonder how many of their writers and editors have actually tried it? An endless hunger is generally endless because it is unsatisfied, not vice versa.

The last thing I remember before I faded out was belated confusion: what was the name she had called me, earlier, as we undressed? She had told me I had lost weight, which meant she must have known me before. *What had she called me?* My fogged brain would not bring it back, and I didn't care to inquire directly. I feared she would get angry at the slip, and refuse to make love again. I did not want to risk that. Tonight I was sated, but what of tomorrow? Whereupon I slept.

In the middle of the night it rained again. I had not gotten the felt to stay over the ridge, and so the roof leaked. Drip, drip—right onto our double sleeping bag.

Susan woke up and said something unladylike. She scrambled out and found a poncho in the dark; I felt her body sliding past me. We spread the poncho over the sleeping bag so that the drips ran off.

Now I had been recharged somewhat by sleep, and my interest in her body was renewed. I ran my hands over her breasts, stomach, and thighs, growing more excited. She murmured appreciatively. Slow and mutually fulfilling—yes, that was the way.

And would you believe, I fell asleep again before coming to the point. I think I heard her chuckle in my dreams. The white belt had muffed another technique despite the cooperation of the black belt. That's one thing that really gets me, in retrospect. There was absolutely no excuse!

I woke before dawn, needing to relieve myself outside. I slid out, found the ladder, went down quietly, and opened the door. The night air was chill on my bare skin, but not too bad. I moved out from the cabin, looked up between the trees, and saw the stars.

They were magnificent. They shone like diamonds in the cleared, washed sky, so many there was no counting them. I saw the three bright lights of Orion's Belt, and up to the north the Big Dipper. That exhausted my knowledge of the constellations, but I must have stood for ten minutes admiring the splendor of the heavens. It was an experience that reached right into my being. I almost forgot to do what I had come to do.

When I returned, Susan was awake. "Now you hold the fort while I go out," she said. Which set me back a bit; like many men, I had sort of thought that women got along without natural functions. It's that pedestal we put them on; we want them to be sexy but nothing else.

As dawn came, I tried to get a fire going in the crude stone hearth outside, but the wet wood made the effort as frustrating as my latter sexual ones. So we had cold cereal and milk, and it was really quite adequate.

"Oops, I forgot!" she said. "I have a bag of charcoal. Pour a little kerosene on it from the lamp and get it started; we need a fire to dry out our clothes."

So we had a fire of sorts after all, an almost flameless one that we shrouded in hung clothing. With luck the sun would also be out soon, and would help.

Meanwhile, that roofing job remained unfinished. I took a look at the ladder, and realized that I had lost the courage to go up again. Oh, I tried, but the moment I put a hand on the rung, I thought of Mr. Campbell, falling from his roof and breaking his arm in three places. If I went up again—

I went back inside, disheartened. "I haven't got the nerve," I said, expecting to get bawled out. She had, in a fashion, already paid me, and now I was reneging on the job. "I can't go up again. I know the roof needs doing."

"Take it easy," she said. "When that felt thunked down last night in the storm, for a moment I thought it was you. I could never have forgiven myself. I was just glad to get you safely down."

"I'm a coward," I said glumly, not much cheered by her understanding attitude. "I came here to help you do a job, and I can't do it."

"You did a job," she said, smiling.

"Damn it, I'm going up!" I exclaimed, turning about. I went to the ladder, put hands and feet on it, ascended—and balked at the second run from the top. The nerve was drained out of me; fifteen feet was too long a fall to contemplate. The stupidity of it made me almost as mad as the fact of failure.

Then I had a small inspiration. I descended and approached Susan. "Throw me," I told her.

"What?" She was washing dishes with a sponge and Kleenex—another thing her cook would have bawled her out for.

"Three feet to a mat is nothing compared to fifteen feet to the ground. I'd much rather take a controlled judo fall than an uncontrolled roof fall. Throw me."

Bemused, she spread out the sleeping bags and threw me. I took an imperfect fall, and bounced up. "It didn't hurt me!" I exclaimed, rubbing my shoulder where it hurt, some. "Throw me again."

"Here he has me alone in the woods," she muttered, "naked, miles from help, and what does he want? To be thrown."

I had forgotten: we were still naked. But it didn't matter. She threw me again with the *ippon seoi nage*, one of the few throws that will work naked, and it was evident that I had lost much of my fear. Whenever I started to worry, I visualized that roof, and that made it all right. I had conquered another hurdle, of a sort.

After that I made myself useful working on the foundations, mixing concrete and troweling it into the stacked concrete blocks on which the cabin perched. The work was tedious but worthwhile.

Susan washed me off when I finished. Her attention caused me to react again. "You know, I wish I'd been less sleepy in the night," I said ruefully.

"You lost your turn," she agreed. "Now it's my turn."

"Your turn?"

"To do you. Passive mode. Lie down."

"By daylight?"

She laughed. "I love your naïveté!"

I lay on the impromptu mat, and she addressed me with slow strokes and kisses. Before long she had me worked up to a fever pitch, but she wouldn't let me act. Instead she spread herself on me, tantalizing me, keeping me from taking any initiative, and at her leisure took me in and milked me with her body. When I finally came, it felt like a volcano erupting. What an experience!

She got up, having done me, and looked out the window. "There was supposed to be a delivery by now. Must be late."

"Someone was coming?" I asked. "Suppose it had happened when—"

She half smiled, and I realized with a certain chagrin that this had been part of her game: the excitement of possible discovery. It was just as well I hadn't known.

Near noon the clothes were dry and we made ready to drive back after dressing. At that point a pickup truck pulled up. It was a man from a lumber company, bringing a load of interior paneling for the cabin. So the delivery had made it after all.

"Better get that roof shingled before it rains," he observed. "Water will ruin this stuff."

"It already rained," Susan said. "Our ladder's really too short."

"That so? I've got a larger one."

"You know how to roof?" Susan asked.

"Sure. It's part of the business. But I have to unload this stuff and tack it in and get back to the shop."

Susan delved into her purse and came up with a hundred dollar bill. "Can they spare you a couple more hours? We could use the help."

"We already been paid for the paneling job. Gotta do it."

"In addition."

"Lady, roofing labor ain't worth—"

She tucked the bill into his shirt pocket. "It is to us." She smiled persuasively.

He melted. "You've got a deal!" And he took his ladder off the truck, leaned it against the cabin, put a heavy bundle of shingles on his shoulder, and proceeded right up. "Come on," he called to me. "We can polish this off in an hour."

Seeing him so casual about it, there was nothing I could do but mount the ladder. I hesitated at the top, and he put out a strong hand to steady me. I crossed over to the roof—the thing I thought I'd never do again.

"Lay out the shingles; I'll nail them down, soon's I get the felt laid." He was down the ladder and back with the felt, and in a few minutes accomplished what I had failed to in much longer time. Then he started in on the shingles, holding with the soft side of his fingers up so that a hit would not hurt as much, striking each nail four time with perfect aim. I had had to strike a dozen times, and I had lost numerous nails from bending or flipping out when they struck impervious knots. Here was a real professional, every bit as skilled in his area as the judo black belts were in theirs.

In his presence, surrounded by his confidence and competence, I found my own fear of the roof diminished. I moved about on hands and feet rather than by crawling, and I didn't even notice the wind. I laid out shingles and he hammered in the nails. And in an hour we had finished the whole top section of that roof.

"Thanks," I said. "You have no idea how relieved I am to have that done."

"Glad to help. Not just for the money." He winked. "Girl like that—you're lucky."

We descended the ladder, and as my foot touched the ground I realized that I had been relieved of the charge of cowardice, and had done what had terrified me before. All I had needed was a longer ladder and a confident companion.

How many seemingly insuperable obstacles of life could be overcome by just that formula? The proper tool and proper approach. What of my worst one, the amnesia? My memory of my past remained closed, but somehow I felt I was closer to the breakthrough now.

The man finished the paneling with the same efficiency and

drove off. Probably the extra money had contributed to his positive attitude; he could have a considerable party with that.

Soon we followed. It had been quite a weekend, and I had a lot to think about.

CHAPTER 5:

EIGHTY PER CENT

Every month or so our *dojo* had a team tournament with one of the other *Taizo Sone* dojos in town. Half a dozen of our students would be matched with their students, and each winner got a medal or ribbon. After the tournament there would be testing for promotions.

I had watched these little tournaments with fascination, seeing how different competition judo was from normal *randori* practice. I had not entered any matches, however, knowing that would be utter folly. Now I had learned the basic throws and holds, and felt I was ready to try for the lofty eminence of Yellow Belt. So I was present and garbed in my *gi*, and nervous as hell.

The students of the other *dojo* were there, with their instructor Tom, a *sandan* or third degree black belt. Black belts didn't compete in these affairs, but served as coaches and referees.

Tom and Steve got together and picked out one child from each class, little white belts. They were carefully matched up by size and skill, to make it fair. The idea was to give them experience in matches, without the outcome being certain. Then two more, larger boys, yellow belts. And so on up, sometimes matching yellow belt with a larger white belt so that it was skill against size. In real tournaments, I understood, it was pot luck, and white belts frequently came up against black belts, almost certainly doomed. But here the emphasis was on good matches, or at least fairness.

"Caesar," Steve said.

Huh? I looked at him. Steve indicated a place on the mat where the other contestants were sitting. Already a white belt my size was coming from the other side.

I was going to compete in a match.

My mouth went dry. My knees felt rubbery. How could I go out there and actually fight? I didn't know anything! I glanced wildly around.

And caught Susan's eye. She was one of five black belts who had shown up for the tournament. I remembered the cabin roof, and the cabin loft. And I was more afraid of being a coward in her eyes than I was of being a coward in fact.

I walked to the mat area and sat down beside my teammates. It was amazing how deadly serious this innocent little meet had become, merely because I was now a participant rather than a spectator. I guess a lot of life is like that. A person pays a whole lot more attention when his own neck is on the block.

Jeff came to sit beside me, and after him a green belt. *They* didn't seem worried; why was *my* gut squeezed and squished like a Rorschach blob? We were seven all told, and opposite us were sever from the other *dojo.*

Nervously I watched the first match. Our boy was smaller than his opponent, and that was bad, because size does count in judo when skill is equivalent. The lighter player has to work harder to lift the heavier one, and can more readily be lifted himself. Our champion tried hard, attempting an *o soto gari* leg throw to the rear, but the other boy pushed him back, grabbed him around the neck, and fell on the floor. No art to it at all, and the referee, a large black belt named Shawn, gave no score, but now the larger boy got the *kesa gatame* or scarf hold. This was clumsily applied—

even I could see that—but decisive. In thirty seconds it was over. The outlook was bleak; we were behind one match to nothing.

But lo! We won the second match, and the third, then lost the fourth. It was two to two—and suddenly I was up.

I was scared stiff, which may have been just as well, because otherwise my knees might have buckled. My opponent was smaller than I, and a good deal younger, but he might as well have been a giant. I only hoped I would not lose too quickly.

I grabbed his left lapel and right sleeve in approved manner, and looked into his eyes—and realized that he was just as scared as I was. It didn't help; now I was afraid we'd *both* make fools of ourselves.

We moved around, neither daring to try anything. All my confidence in the techniques I had practiced was gone; I knew nothing would work. "Attack! Attack!" someone yelled, and I didn't know which one of us he meant.

Shame, not courage, drove me to it: I attacked. I tried to turn into an *o goshi* hip throw, but he had hold of my sleeve and I couldn't turn. That never happened in practice throws. So it was nothing, not even a spoiled attempt, as far as anyone could see. But he had felt my effort. So he jerked me forward, and I stiff-armed him, not meaning to but simply unable to make my arms bend. That, as it turned out, was a good defense. At least at this level. So all we did was move a little more.

We were both getting tired. I was panting, and so was he, and his handsome long hair was getting in his face and God knows how I looked—*and we hadn't done anything.*

Time was running out. I realized it was not going to end with a bang but a whimper, a draw, and indecisive match. No credit to either of us, no medal or ribbon. People on either side were yelling up a storm of encouragement: "Throw him, Caesar!" "*O soto gari*, Alan!" "Attack!" "Take him to the mat!" But we were stuck in a morass of inability. We were too evenly matched, too inexperienced. Never again would I watch someone else's match and think myself superior; fatigue and uncertainty changed the whole picture. Sure we had been taught the techniques—*but this was real.*

I saw the brown belt with the stopwatch lift the beanbag he used to signal the end of the match. When he threw it onto the mat, it would be over. A hell of a poor showing.

This couldn't be tolerated. One of us had to win, or we'd both lose. I wrenched about and dropped into a *seoi otoshi*, the throw Mr. Campbell had taught me, my last attempt. But I didn't have my balance, hadn't used *kuzushi* to break *his* balance, and had my right elbow in the wrong position. As a result the attempt was a disaster. Alan resisted, hauling me back. His counter was better than my effort; I fell backwards, my feet going up in the air—and I came down on the back of my head, hard.

The room spun. I felt no pain. Just shame.

When my head cleared, Susan was mopping my face with a wet paper towel. "Some breakfall, Caesar," she muttered disgustedly.

I sat up and stared at her. "Susan! When did you get your black belt?"

Her eyebrow raised. "Beg pardon?"

"You were a brown belt in my class."

Now she stared at me. "Uh-oh. You remember?"

I looked down. "What the hell am I doing in a white belt?" But as I asked, I remembered. I was a white belt—but also a black belt. I had two sets of experiences, and for the moment I wasn't sure which was real.

"What is your name?" Susan asked me.

"Jason Striker, of course." I paused. "No, Caesar Kane. No, both."

"That blow to your head," she said. "It brought you back!"

"Did it? I still seem to have a gap. Between leaving my own *dojo* up north and coming to this one. What happened?"

"If you don't know, no one else does," she said. "You disappeared there, and reappeared here, months later. Emaciated and amnesiac."

Alan came over. He had won the match, but didn't look happy. "I'm sorry," he said. "I didn't mean to—"

"'Sall right," I said, shaking hands with him. "It was a fair match. I have to learn how to take a better fall, is all." Yet maybe I had gained a hundred times more than I had lost, for now I had my past back. A significant part of it, anyway.

I shook my head, trying to get it settled. I saw Jeff doing throws in the main area. *Uchimata*, for an *ippon*—was it only the next match? No, the tournament was over; he was testing for promotion, going for his green belt, skipping right over orange. No wander he had been so tough. *Tomoe nage*, the stomach throw. Combinations. Kids really had to work for their belts here.

Jeff made it, and I was glad for him. I wondered how he had done in his tournament match while I was out. He must have won, for it would have taken two victories to overcome my defeat and put our team ahead—and there was the trophy cup, on our side. I had missed some good matches. But you have to expect to miss something if you insist on getting knocked out before the tournament is over.

Now the black belts went out for some *randori* or free practice among themselves: Steve and Tom, Shawn and Mike.

"Come on," Susan said. "Get your system going."

"*Randori*? I asked. "I can't go out there with all those black belts."

"That depends," she murmured, "on who you think you are."

"Who?" I asked, not getting her drift.

"Are you Caesar Kane, who just lost a match to a fourteen year old boy—or are you Jason Striker, 5 *Dan*?"

I pondered. "You know, I'm not sure. I've got both memories, and always before I have woken up to find that—"

"So let's find out," she said, drawing me to my feet. "You're going to throw me, or get thrown. Hard."

We moved out onto the mat. I saw some students staring at me; obviously I should be home soaking my head, not going out for *randori* after my injury. But the fact was that I had suffered much worse bashes in the past, and fought through; this one was nothing in comparison. I did want to know, as Susan put it, exactly who I thought I was.

Susan wasn't fooling; she spun into a *moroto seoi nage*, lifting so hard I would ordinarily have flipped right over her and whomped into the mat on my barely-healed side. But I merely stood firm. "How many times have I told you," I reprimanded her gently, "*kuzushi.* You didn't break my balance." And I turned and swept her feet out from under with a perfect *okuri ashi barai* assisted foot sweep. "Timing and balance," I concluded as she struck the mat.

"Just like old times," she muttered as she got up. "You made me look like a white belt, you prick."

I smiled graciously at her. "You asked for it."

She nodded. "I was glad to get it, Jason."

Then I walked over to Mike and Shawn. "Mind if I cut in?" I inquired.

They looked askance at me, not having seen my action with Susan, or perhaps assuming she had been teaching me an effective counter. But they did not protest.

I took Mike, who had recently made his black belt by placing high in the high school nationals, and moved him about. He was young but highly skilled, probably destined to be a leading competitor on the national scene in a few years. He thought, naturally enough, that he was working with a white belt, so he didn't even try to throw me. No black belt needs to prove himself against a white belt; instead he acts as a teacher, helping the novice to improve his skill.

So I lifted him with a *hane goshi* spring hip throw, not putting too much force into it. He went over, but put his right hand down and turned out neatly so that my throw counted for no score. A very nice recovery on his part. He had a supple, smooth manner about his *randori* that I liked. We resumed motion.

Now he was on guard. A white belt does not catch a black belt twice, especially with the same throw. So I did another *hane goshi*, a hard one this time, too fast and accurate for him to resist. My right leg swept up his legs and he flipped over, this time taking a perfect fall.

He sat up and stared at me. What I had done should have been impossible, even for another black belt of his rank. He had never before encountered efficiency like that, and was trying to decide whether it had been a fluke. I made a little bow and went on to the next: big Shawn.

Shawn was another high school prodigy. He had earned his black best at age 15 by coming in second in the high school nationals. He might have been first, but his opponent had fouled him, and he had gotten mad and fouled him back—and the referee had caught only Shawn's action. He was huge and strong, a natural wrestler. Most people tried to avoid getting into matwork with him—so I took him down with a *sumi gaeshi*, rolled over as he started to get up, and flipped him into the *jigoku jime* hell strangle. He had strong arms and a good neck, but I knew exactly what I was doing, and he had to tap out before his lost consciousness. It is considered very classy to take a man with his own specialty, but as it happened, *my* specialty was matwork too.

Three down, two to go. Why did running a line of five black belts seem so familiar?

Tom and Steve had stopped their *randori* and were staring at me, as well they might. Susan might have let me throw her, and Mike might have taken one fall for me. But Shawn would never have gone voluntarily into the hell strangle, and a white belt hardly knew how to apply it properly.

I bowed to Steve. He returned the bow, and came to meet me. He hardly knew what to make of this, having seen me in all my white belt inadequacy for several weeks, but he was not about to take a fall for me. He found it difficult to take falls for any of his students, perhaps fearing that they would lose respect.

I took hold of him—and had him almost helpless. I was no stronger than I had been as a white belt, but now I had all the skill of a *godan*. I knew precisely how to make my strength count, nullifying his. It was similar in its way to holding a bird in one's open palm and preventing it from flying away by countering its balance in subtle ways. Before, Steve's skill had toyed with mine; now mine toyed with him—and we had not even moved. There is as big difference between a *godan* and a *shodan* as there is between a *shodan* and a *rokkyu*. That is, 5 *dan* is to 1 *dan* as 1 *dan* is to a white belt.

I eased up enough to let him attempt a throw, and he spun into a *tsuri komi goshi* lift-pull hip throw But I kept my balance, and as he went down low I stepped forward so that my legs straddled him, holding him down and voiding the effort. He had to break and scramble out from under. Next time we closed I threw him with an *uchi-mata*. And went on to Tom.

Tom was a *sandan*, a third degree black belt who could probably have made fourth degree any time he wanted to. He had been given his belt by the club founder, Taize Sone, and valued it as such. He was a skilled competitor, interested in making the national Olympic team. His mode of action was deceptive; he wasted no effort or motion in superfluous style. He took it so easy it seemed he wasn't really trying. But just try to throw him or get him in a holddown!

I moved him about, and he moved with me, retaining his balance. I tried my *uchi-mata*, but couldn't get him over. So I did a takedown and clamped an armlock on him—and he calmly braced himself and lifted me clear of the mat, voiding my hold. This time I had my work cut out for me, though Tom hadn't yet even tried any techniques of his own.

"Now I recognize you," he said. "Only one person does *uchi-mata* like that. Jason Striker. What are you doing here in a white belt?"

"It's a long story," I said. "I'm wondering about it myself."

We stopped the *randori*; it had become pointless. "This is Jason Striker," Tom said to the others. "*Godan*, former national champion. I thought he looked familiar, but I couldn't believe it."

I understood, however. I had not faked any clumsiness as a

white belt; it had been quite genuine. My transformation had been remarkable.

But I did have a headache. It was time to go home and recover. Past time.

*

I was sad to leave the Taizo Sone judo clubs, but it was urgent that I sort out my memories and get my affairs in order. I had been out of circulation entirely too long, for all that I had needed that time to fully recover my physical health. So my amnesia had its silver lining.

First I phoned Ilunga, back at my own *dojo*. "Where you been, White Master?" she inquired as though I'd merely checked in an hour late. I visualized her strong black face; she was one hell of a woman, this karate mistress. She was in charge in my absence, quite competent, and probably smarter than I was. She *had* emotion, but didn't show it.

"Florida," I said succinctly. "Where was I going?"

"South America," she said. "Maybe you better talk to Luis."

"Senor," Luis said immediately. She must have put him on the extension. "Are you well?" He was a Cuban exiile, not at all like the drunken doctor of my vision, but a 5 *dan* in judo. I had no concern about the welfare of my judo classes while they were in his hands. With Ilunga for karate and accounts, and Luis for judo, I was superfluous, which thought did not please me quite as much as it might have. Evidently they had managed just fine without me.

"Well enough," I said, deciding not to go into the whole story. Susan had loaned me a set of weights to enhance my exercise, and I was recovering my optimal condition. "I lost my memory, only just got it back, most of it. Ilunga said I was headed for South America; that part's still blank, except for some visions of the Amazon River. Do you know anything about it?"

"Only that it is dangerous, *Señor*," he said. "You received word from your enemy Kan-Sen that the lord of the ninjas needed you, and you departed. I urged against it, and Ilunga called you—pardon the term—a honky fool."

"That's her way of saying that she loves me," I said, only half joking.

"*Si.* But you went, and we have heard nothing more, until this moment. We feared very much you were dead."

"Close enough," I agreed. "Obviously *someone* wants me dead. But I have the feeling it's more important than that. I'd better run it down before *it* runs *me* down. So don't let on that I'm alive. This call is strictly private."

"Honky fool!" Illunga repeated vehemently.

"I want them to believe that I'm dead," I explained. "That way I can catch them by surprise."

"Catch who by surprise?" Luis inquired.

"I wish I knew."

Illunga gave a derisive snort, but I knew she and Luis would protect my secret. They both loved me, in their fashions, and would keep the faith.

So I resigned from my survey job and cleaned out my room. I had planned to sneak out alone, but Susan intercepted me. Women have a knack for such things. "I know I'm less interesting now that your memory's back," she said. "But there are still things I can do for you."

She was more or less right on both counts. There had been many women in my life, and I valued the memory of most of them, especially my dead fiancée Chiyako. Susan when I knew her had been no more than a promising brown belt student. I did not as a rule date my students, though some had made that rule difficult to honor. But Susan had left my dojo two years ago and I had not seen her since. Evidently she had kept up with her judo and retained an interest in me, so that when she discovered me as a white belt . . . Well, she was no longer my student, and she had made her point. I liked her more than somewhat, and she had helped me considerably. I really knew her better now than I had before, and not just socially. I had had no idea she was rich, not that it would have made a difference. She had merely been one brown belt among many, almost anonymous. She must have preferred it that way.

"I have a motor home," she continued. "I can take you where you're going, privately. I have money. I can shop for you. Alone, you're just going to get yourself killed, as you almost did before."

Nobody seemed to have any confidence in my abilities outside the dojo—especially those who knew me best. That was another irritation, in part because it might be warranted. Obviously I had fouled up badly, somewhere between here and South America. "If you come with me," I pointed out, "you may get killed too."

"Yes. Isn't it exciting?"

I wasn't certain whether she was joking. There are things about women I have never understood. They are *not* merely soft men. This one had seduced me on the cabin floor in broad daylight, knowing that a delivery man was on his way. Evidently she had a hankering for innocent danger. But what I faced was ugly danger. "I'll think about it," I said. Maybe I could sneak out alone.

"You'll think about it with me along," she insisted. "I want you to tell me to my face, not copping out on the phone the way you did with your *dojo*."

That was another thing: why did women always fathom *me* so much better than I fathomed *them*?

Thus I found myself in her motor home. It was a Cruise-Air—after a moment I fathomed the pun—looking like a yellow striped box with oblong windows, small-seeming wheels, and a door in the middle of the left side. But inside it was a luxury apartment twenty two feet long, with padded couches, a dinette, kitchen, bathroom, and whatever. No need to pay hotel or motel bills with this; all the comforts of home traveling right along with you. All except—

I looked at Susan, who avoided my gaze. That was a signal. *All* the comforts of married life, really. That made me a bit nervous. Just what designs did she have on me?

"I have credit cards for everything," she said brightly. "It can all be done in my name, keeping you anonymous."

That was exactly the way I wanted it. Because I remembered more than I had told Luis. It wasn't just the long journey down the Amazon River, it was the background. Kan-Sen was my enemy, true, but now he worked for Fu Antos, lord of the ninjas, who was building his new Black Castle somewhere in the Amazon jungle. My connection with Fu Antos went way back. He had saved my life, and I had helped him reincarnate in youthful form.

I had assumed that if my enemy worked for my friend, he became my friend, even if I didn't want it. Now it occurred to me that my friend might have become my enemy. If that were so, I was free to kill Kan-Sen, and there was nothing I'd rather do. For he had killed my fiancée Chiyako. But maybe I was rationalizing, trying to find a way to justify the vengeance I craved.

I might kill Kan-Sen. But first he would have to be interrogated. For surely he knew what I needed to know about Fu Antos. Someone had left me for dead in the Amazon. Had it been the ninja, or someone who had tried to stop me from reaching the ninja? I had to be sure, before I acted.

Because if Fu Antos was now my enemy, I had one hell of a job cut out for me. Fu Antos was perhaps the most formidable warrior of all time, and he had conquered death itself. I would never have suspected him of turning against me, but he was the only one I knew who had the power to wipe out a man's memory. He could do astonishing things with his fantastic power of *ki*.

"I think I smell wood burning," Susan remarked. "Is it really such an awful chore, traveling with me?"

I had to laugh. "I was remembering things I had forgotten, trying to figure them out."

"You forgot our weekend in the woods? I can explain that very simply. I loved playing with you when you didn't know who you were. When I could be the instructor."

I had to laugh again. "Yes you were, and I appreciate it. This was something else."

"You must tell me all about it. Maybe I can figure that out too, for you."

I realized that it might really help to have her input, for my question was intractable. *Why*? Why would Fu Antos summon me to the Black Castle—to kill me? Or to wipe out my memory? That made no sense at all. I had meant him no harm, and would not have known he had left Japan had he not sent the aikido *sensei* Hiroshi—armed with a bag of diamonds—to summon me. Fu Antos surely had enough enemies, without wiping out his friends. "Maybe you can," I agreed.

"I'm glad that's settled."

I hardly heard her. I would have to assume that one of the ninja's enemies had intercepted me before I reached the Black Castle. A powerful enemy, with brainwashing facilities—for surely *something* had been done to my mind—but who still did not dare to kill me openly. Maybe he had held me prisoner while he destroyed my mind, and I had somehow escaped before the job was quite complete. So now I had recovered maybe eighty per cent of my memories, including all my prior life. Just the twenty percent or less that related to the last several months remained lost.

In any event, I had a score to settle. I would have to make my own investigation to discover why my real enemy was. And hope that that enemy did not discover me first.

"Where to, sir?" Susan inquired with a smile. She was driving; it was her vehicle and I had no license. I had been driving recently of course; I didn't like breaking the law, but to get a license I would have had to verify my identity, and I hadn't *had* an identity. Now I had one, but my wallet and all its papers had been lost along with my memory.

"Miami," I said.

*

We drove east, leaving the Suncoast. We passed some of the non-tourist artifacts, such as a monstrously ugly phosphate mine.

Phosphate was the backbone of Florida industry, but its byproducts destroyed the local soil and landscape and lead to increasing incidence of cancer, and of course big money talked, preventing reform. That was the ubiquitous shame of mankind, always putting short range self interest before the welfare of the larger society or the land itself.

"Reminds me of your attitude," Susan said, looking at the desolate landscape.

"What?"

"Brooding. Ugly. Silent."

She had me there. "I'll try to reform."

"You'd better. This hasn't been much of a date so far."

"This is no date!" I protested. Then I realized that she was teasing me. I was being socially clumsy, as usual.

We passed a sign advertising a large amusement park. "Let's go there," Susan said.

"This is serious business, not a holiday."

"But it has to *look* like a holiday," she pointed out. "You don't want anyone to know your real mission."

"Nobody's watching me now!" I snapped.

"Right," she agreed, turning into the park.

I tried to fathom the logic, but could not. Had I made a mistake, traveling with her? If all she had in mind was distracting me from my mission—

"They turned too," Susan said.

"Who?"

"The car that's been tailing us the last twenty miles."

"Who would want to follow me?" I demanded.

"Maybe we should find out. I'd guess the news of your return spread pretty quickly. Why did you run the line at Taizo Sone?"

"*You* told me to—"

"It was a foolish feminine idea. You should have ignored it."

No arguing with that. I had destroyed my privacy at the outset. I suspected that our alleged tail was coincidence, merely someone headed for this park at our speed. But if it were not—

Well, it would not be hard to verify the matter. If anyone was after us, they'd have to keep pretty close, because it would be almost impossible to keep track in the hustle and crowding of the park. Once we were sure we were not being followed, we could resume our journey. Probably Susan had made it up, as an excuse to have a good time. I evidently had not impressed her sufficiently with the urgency of my mission.

"If we park and leave the vehicle, and somebody is after us, they could plant a bomb in it," I said, hoping to shake her up so that she would change her mind about stopping here.

"It's got a security system and a loud alarm," she said. "If anyone breaks in, the whole neighborhood will know."

Sigh. She had countered my ploy without even trying.

We bought tickets at the grand entrance. It was a good thing Susan had money to burn, because they weren't cheap. I felt a bit like a gigolo, having her pay for everything. Maybe that was the way she wanted it. Before, I had been short of memory, dependent on her for judo knowledge. Now I was short of money. The feeling was similar.

Park personnel challenged us at the ramp to the interior. "Any food in that bag?"

Susan frowned. "No food." She turned to me. "Must be they don't want any wrappings littering the premises."

"Must be," I agreed. I had thought it was an inspection for weapons, like the checkout for boarding an airplane. Which showed how a person can overreact to the mere notion of being followed.

But inside there was food being hawked everywhere. Paper cups, straws, and similar items littered the walks and lawns. We passed a stream, and it was so gray with pollution that most of the trash in it was hidden beneath the murk. "Why did they try to stop us from bringing in any food?" I marveled.

"Because we'd never pay their prices if we had any alternative," Susan said. "They need a captive market."

I glanced at their prices. They were sky-high. "I'll starve first," I said, disgusted. "What kind of tourist trap *is* this?"

"An efficient one. Don't grump; food's on me."

That didn't help. "Are we still being tailed?"

"Yes."

*

[Not yet written sequence here: it rains, and half the attractions are shut down so that Jason and Susan can't use up their tickets, and get soaked. They use the distraction of the rain to get behind the men who are following them, and there is a fight scene in a closed attraction. They demolish the thugs, but learn nothing, as they are merely hirelings. Except for one name: Mirabal. That triggers some more of Jason's missing memory. Susan, turned on by the excitement, seduces Jason before they leave the site. His extreme nervousness at the prospect of discovery in such a public place delights her.]

*

It was late by the time we got out of the park, and I was tired. But it was necessary to get well away from the scene of the action, so that this mysterious Mirabal would not be able to trace our whereabouts. He surely knew what our vehicle looked like, so even being on the road was no guarantee of security.

"Hey!" I exclaimed. "I know a place near here. A friend of mine has a *dojo*."

"First place your enemies would look," Susan said. "I like adventure, but we're getting more than I bargained on this soon."

"I doubt it. It's a small *dojo*, and I've never been there. I knew him up north several years ago, and promised to drop in if I were ever in the area. I know people all over the country, so nobody'd be able to guess that I'd visit this particular place. He can keep his mouth shut, and would give us a place to hide the vehicle. By the time they figure out where we are, we'll be gone."

"In short, you want to see him again, just as I wanted to go to the park."

I sighed. "I guess so. The camaraderie of judo—"

"Well, no one can say I'm not fair about these things. What's his address?"

So we pulled into the little *dojo* of *Sensei* Josef Fuentes, 3 *dan*. He was a dark haired Cuban of about 40. There were a lot of Cuban judokas in Florida, because of the sizable Cuban exile population.

It was late, and no class was in session. But my friend welcomed me with a big Latin smile, and opened his *dojo* to us. So we had a little workout of three. It may sound funny, doing active judo practice when we were tired, but judo isn't work for me, its *life*. I feel better after doing good *randori* than I do after taking a nap.

After a while I sat down at the edge of the mat and let Susan work with Josef. They did *randori* that was almost like a *kata*, or judo playlet, alternating throws. It was very nice, almost *too* nice. I began to grow restive. I was the one she was traveling with, after all.

Then I caught myself. Was I getting jealous about a woman I hadn't wanted to travel with anyway? Because of standard judo courtesy? What was the matter with me?

I knew the answer: Susan had set out to impress me, and had succeeded. I had always had a soft spot for female martial artists, and I did like a relationship with an attractive and amenable young woman. She had baited me like a fish, and the hook was halfway set. I had to school myself to accept what she offered without letting her lure me into a commitment I couldn't legitimately make. Not while part of my life was missing. So she was working well with Josef, and smiling at him, giving him pleasure. I should be happy for him, not resentful. It was just a passing interaction.

Then we sat down and talked, reminiscing about old times. We soon discovered that Josef had a serious concern of his own. "Last month this man—I do not dignify him by naming him—came and told me that whenever I hosted a tournament in my *dojo*

I must pay eighty per cent of the money to the Judo Federation. I asked him why, and he said because otherwise my people would never get promoted. My *ikkyus* would not make *shodan*, my *shodans* would not make *nidan*, and I myself—!" He shook his head, bewildered.

I frowned. "That's impossible. Promotions are handled by the Board and they are based on merit. No one pays for his belt; that would be completely contrary to everything judo stands for."

"So I thought," he said. "I showed that man the door in a hurry. But last week my best student went for his promotion, well qualified, and they turned him down. And I talked with other *senseis*, and they say the same. They don't like it, but they pay, and then they have no trouble. I did not agree to pay, and—shall I show you my student? Do you want to see what he can do?"

"No, I believe you," I said, troubled. I was privately certain that he had overrated his students. It is a measure of an instructor's success how his students perform, and naturally he believes in them—sometimes unrealistically. But to try to blame the promotions board—that was an ugly tactic, and it disturbed me fundamentally to see my friend do this.

Josef perceived my skepticism, and said no more. The evening concluded on a subdued note.

Back in the motor home, Susan spoke up. "That man was serious, Jason," she said. "He's caught between honor and the welfare of his students."

"He can't be," I snapped. "Judo doesn't work that way. I've been in it long enough to know, and I've never seen such a thing."

"Maybe you just don't want to hear of it," she said. "I've seen things happen, like tournament dates fixed to coincide so that each tournament loses half its contestants to the other, and preferential treatment by referees, bad calls—"

"Listen, I don't let *anyone* badmouth judo!" I said, whirling on her.

She didn't budge. "So I notice. But if you want the truth—"

I was so angry I stomped out of the vehicle. But as I walked alone in the dark, the doubt loomed larger. There are bad apples in any profession, even, alas, judo. *Could* someone have tried this kind of thing? The more I pondered it, the more it upset me.

Finally I returned to Susan. She was sitting up in bed in the convertible dinette, looking so beautiful in her nightclothes that I was sorry I had ever argued with her. "I need some change for a pay phone," I said.

Wordlessly she handed me a fistful of quarters.

I phoned the secretary of the United States Judo Federation, whom I knew only by reputation. I did not give my name. "I just want to verify something," I said, and quickly sketched out the situation as Josef had presented it.

There was a pause. "Who are you?" he demanded. "Who is making this complaint?"

I started to answer, but froze. If I gave my name, the whole judo world would quickly know where I was, and I already had enough trouble. I had to keep my secret and get going on my private mission before word spread further. Most especially, I didn't want anyone knowing I was headed south. It might mean my life. "I can't tell you," I said lamely.

"Well, what *dojo* was threatened?"

Again I could not answer, lest I give myself away.

"You expect me to believe an anonymous complaint?" the secretary inquired, his voice cold.

Worse and worse! He was reacting exactly as I had, and I couldn't blame him. "I just want to verify that—"

"There is nothing anonymous about my response," he said firmly. "I state categorically that no ranks are bought in judo, directly or indirectly. Not in America, not anywhere in the world. Not in Kodokan judo. The situation you describe would not be tolerated by the USJF. If anything of the kind were to come to my attention, I would investigate and take appropriate action immediately. I speak for myself and the USJF president. Send me a letter providing al the facts—the names and dates—and you will see how rapidly we satisfy you, if there is merit to your charge. But I will not accept anonymous denigration of our fine martial art."

"Uh, thank you," I said, somewhat at a loss, but at the same time rather proud. This was the sort of response I subscribed to.

In the morning I would tell Josef exactly how to resolve his dilemma. One letter with the facts to the secretary, and the whole sordid thing would be investigated. There would be a paper trail, what tournament money went where, and they would rout it out. Judo is an honest martial art; it cleans its own house. No 80% payoff can be tolerated, ever. No payoff of any amount.

Meanwhile, Susan was waiting in that bed . . .

*

[Unwritten sequence: Jason and Susan go on to Miami, where they get faked up papers and changed appearances and head for Brazil, sneaking out of the USA so that enemies can't trace them.]

CHAPTER 6:

TWO PICTURES

Our Catalina flying boat landed in the river near the city of Manaus. I saw the jungle close by, encroaching on river and city.

"Jog your memory?" Susan inquired.

"Not enough," I said. "I think I passed through here after the critical part, after my memory had been erased, and I wasn't here long, so it really doesn't count."

[Enemy pursuit develops.]

We fled up the Rio Negro, the Black River. I did not recognize the area, but since sections of my journey down had been overland, and much of my river travel had been while unconscious, that indicated nothing.

[An airplane flies low to strafe them. The enemy is pulling out all the stops. They dive into the crocodile or piranha infested water and swim to shore, managing to make it through to an Indian tribe they befriend with gifts.]

The Indians were wonderfully half primitive. The men had some modern western clothing, but not enough to go around. One wore trousers, with the top half of his body bare. Another had a soiled shirt, with the bottom half of his body bare. Some had loincloths, and most had tattoos in many colors covering many parts of torso, limbs, and head. Red paint was dabbed to beautify their genitals. They wore feathers in their hair.

The women, in contrast, were big-eyed, innocent, and bare. The hair of their heads was long and black; they had no hair elsewhere. They were not old in years, but age comes rapidly to primitives. Women of 20 or so were already saggy of breast. Only the dawningly nubile girls of thirteen or so were pretty.

Could this be the tribe whose harem I had—? No, impossible; I didn't recognize any of them, and they didn't recognize me. Probably the episode had never happened. I *hoped* it had never happened! Yet it was one of my few leads to the Black Castle.

[But Mirabal's men soon catch up and invade the village, indiscriminately slaughtering men, women, and children. In the melee they save the life of a half-breed Indian who speaks English; grateful, he leads Jason and Susan to shelter in a house in the village of a secret tribe he knows, where no intruder can penetrate. It seems that the only reason these two white fugitives are accepted there, for now, is that it is clear that the military men want them dead. The enemy of their enemy just might be a friend. If not—it will be easy to kill the two. So the danger is hardly over.]

"This is horrible!" Susan exclaimed. "They don't care who they hurt!"

"This is the way it has always been," the guide said grimly. "It is what we expect from the white man."

"But you have a white parent," I said, perhaps tactlessly. "If the natives hate the white raiders—"

He glanced briefly at me. "Such liaisons are not always voluntary on the part of the natives."

"Not—?"

"Rape," Susan murmured.

Oh. Unable to figure out anything to say, I turned and looked at the wall. There were two pictures on it, and they immediately compelled my attention.

The first picture showed a young man with regular features,

handsome, distant eyes, in the uniform and helmet of a Brazilian military officer. I was a amazed to see such a representation here, obviously well cared for.

The second picture showed two ancient Indians seated side by side with sunken eyes, deeply wrinkled faces, similar in their piercing gaze.

"What do you make of them?" the guide inquired. Now there were several armed natives with him. They seemed expectant, but I wasn't sure about what. Something was in the offing, and I hoped it wasn't a brutal game of turnabout, with Susan suffering the rape. We could fight if we had to, but we were both tired, and would be unable to find our way out of the jungle even if left alone. We needed the support of these people, not their enmity.

Yet the Indians did not seem menacing, just waiting. I realized that this was some kind of a test, and my reaction might have serious repercussions, for good or ill. I had to say the right thing—and I had no idea what that might be.

Honesty seemed to be the best policy. So I confessed my ignorance. "I don't understand," I said. "The first could be one of the soldiers who hunts you, rapes your women, burns your villages. Though he has some Indian blood, I think. While the second—" I broke off. "Wait, there is something—" I squinted at the second picture. "Something familiar about one of the—he's part white, isn't he! And he—the physique, the lines of the face—that old man is the same as the young soldier!"

The Indians relaxed. They might not speak my language, but they understood that I had made a key connection. That, it seemed, was good.

"Marshall Candido Rondon," the guide agreed. "The greatest man of the western hemisphere. In youth—and age."

I had never heard of him, and found myself embarrassed. But I soon learned, for this man in the pictures had probably just saved my life and Susan's freedom. Because I, an ignorant outsider, had in my fashion recognized him.

Rondon was a half-caste Indian, born in 1865, died in 1958,

founder of the Service for the Protection of the Indians, SPI. He came from the Mato Grosso, a huge jungle section next to Bolivia, served by the twin Amazon tributary rivers, the Xingu or River of Gold, and the Tapajos, River of Fevers, and bounded on the east by the *Rio das Mortes*, the river of Death. Gold, fever, and death—apt terms!

Rondon's father had been a gold seeker, his mother a Guanas Indian. Both died by the time he was two, and he was raised by the Indians until adopted by his white uncle. He obtained an excellent education. As an adult he undertook to plant telegraph poles through the wilderness, so as to bring a measure of civilization there. This was a formidable undertaking; they had to carve paths through the jungle, and men died from disease.

But the worst threat was from the Indians. "My people had been betrayed so often by the white man," the guide explained. "It was safest to kill him on sight."

"But that would only bring more white men with guns," I protested.

"Yes. But at least we died fighting."

But Rondon instituted a radical new policy. "Don't kill the Indians," he said. And he enforced it. His men killed no Indians—even though Indians killed his men. He tried to pacify them with gifts and with great oaths of friendship. "I bring you peace," he said. And gradually his sincerity registered, and the Indians trusted him. He was, after all, partly of their blood.

In the process Rondon traversed twenty thousand miles of jungle, learned ten Indian dialects, discovered fifteen new rivers, and became known as one of the greatest explorers of all time. The American president Teddy Roosevelt joined him in one adventure, and the two became friends.

Rondon was a genuinely good man, revered by both the Indians and the Brazilian Congress. He founded the SPI.

"The SPI!" another Indian spat, with the guide translating. "Service for the Prostitution of Indians!"

I turned to him, confused. "If such a good man organized it, why do you hate it?"

They told me: almost from the first, without Rondon's knowledge, the SPI was perverted from its original purpose. Instead of protecting Indians, it became the apparatus for destroying them. Its three great principles were exploitation, starvation, and murder—all under the guise of legitimizing, of helping the Indians.

*

[The text ends here, written December 7, 1975, with notes for coming scenes of torture, rape, and massacre as Mirabal's troops continue their pursuit. Jason Striker had not believed that mass killing continued to the present day, but he sees it happen. This was to be another example of honest history and sociology, included as background for these adventure novels. But our research stopped at this point.]

SUMMARY OF THE REMAINDER:

Slowly, with much intrigue and violence, Jason Striker zeroes in on the dread Black Castle. The ruthless but politically powerful Mirabal has teamed up with the ninjas to monopolize the vast oil deposits located in the Amazon, and so the ninja influence now permeates both the jungle and the government of Brazil. In short, Jason faces a thoroughly formidable complex of enemies. The closer he gets to the Castle, the less his life is worth. Yet he persists.

When he arrives, his memory becomes complete, and he knows at last what has been done to him, and the gigantic treachery that has been fashioned against modern civilization itself. For Fu Antos means to destroy contemporary society and reduce world population to the medieval level, subservient to the ninja castle. This project is well on its way to success. The Black Castle has been built on the site of ancient ruins; there is evidence of alien visitation from space, millennia ago. There are strange things here, and Fu Antos is reconstructing the secret science of these aliens, augmenting his own weird physical and mental powers fantastically. But Jason arrives just before the arrangements are complete, and now he knows Fu Antos to be his enemy, the one he must destroy.

The timing is very bad for Fu Antos, who has been preoccupied with other matters. Yet the ninja master, so young in appearance, has remarkable powers in his own right, and a shrewd four hundred year old mind. The code of the ninjas requires him to meet the man he has wronged in single combat to the death. But it is no ordinary combat. Fu Antos uses his *ki* to evoke the finest martial artists of all time to oppose Jason. They are mere simulations, but their threat is genuine, for of course behind these images is the highly skilled martial art of the ninjas. Jason must prevail in the most formidable challenge of his career, for these are not his equals but his superiors in combat. Only imagination, savage determination, and his own erratic but powerful *ki* get him through. Indeed, Jason's *ki* is one reason Fu Antos wants him dead, because Fu knows its potential.

Balked on this level, Fu Antos pulls out all the stops. He evokes Jason's lost fiancee, the only woman he ever loved in his prior life. She tempts him and lies to him, unmanning him. And in separate but devastating nonphysical ways Fu Antos destroys Jason's more recent romantic interests, proving that they also have been deceiving him. For example, Dulce sold herself to Fu Antos. She did it to save Jason, whom she loves, but now it seems like a betrayal. And Susan, who befriended and seduced him during his amnesia, didn't tell him that she is a married woman, merely out for illicit adventure. She likes him, but she was always playing a game with him. They never had any future together, just dalliance that he would never have agreed to, had he known. Faced with these seeming betrayals, there seems to be no point in Jason's competing against this monstrous mentality.

Now, in Jason's stunned confusion, Fu Antos deprives him of his *ki* and all his black belt skill. He reverts him to Caesar Kane, in effect, and has him completely at his mercy—and there is no mercy in him. But he still must meet Caesar in physical combat; Dulce insists on that, and she does have considerable influence, as she closely resembles the one woman Fu himself loved. Nevertheless the case seems hopeless for Jason. But Fu Antos makes one fatal oversight: he forgets that Jason now has completely separate white belt judo skills, learned during his amnesia in Florida. Even a white belt can be dangerous, especially against an overconfident opponent. Caesar overcomes Fu Antos by surprise. Then the subjugated Indians rise up and destroy the Black Castle and all its secrets. The curse of the ninja, like the curse of the voodoo god that operates in this area, has been abated—but its scars will remain as long as Jason Striker lives.

AUTHOR'S NOTE:

When the authors entered into this Ninja subset of the series, they made it clear to the editor that the series should not be cut off at this point, because there would be no proper conclusion. The editor said there was no problem, because the series was selling well. But then he moved on, and a new editor took over—and it seems the first thing he did was decide that the series was *not* selling well, and he cut it off. This is typical of the behavior of editors; it's like the new ape male killing the offspring of the old male, so that all the cubs by this female will be his own. In this case there was more to it than that; the new editor had a grudge against Piers Anthony, and bounced everything of his he could reach, not caring about its quality or market potential. That attitude finally caught up with him, and cost him his position, but the damage was done.

Thus this novel was cut off, and never published. Piers Anthony went on to best-sellerdom with Xanth and other fantasies, and Roberto Fuentes went on to became an insurance salesman in Miami. Now, more than a quarter century later, thanks to the Internet and electronic publication, this portion of *Curse of the Ninja* finally is available for readers.

Elements of the novel were drawn from our own experience, adapted to the need. Jason's gall-bladder surgery derived from

Roberto's surgery of the time, except that Roberto's was a good deal more sanitary. The roofing job was from Piers' experience; when the roll of felt struck the ground, his wife thought it was *him* falling off the roof. The white belt sequences were Piers', and the instructors and other students were real people. For example, Piers was the one who was unable to turn over the white belt girl, even with the help of two brown belts. Piers' daughter Penny was in the class, and played herself in the novel. Susan was from Roberto's side, rather liberally adapted for story purposes; she never came to that Florida class.

There was a lot of research for both of us. Here is an example of a note Piers wrote to Roberto: "You want Manaus in the novel, and I know why. Good place to show. But it is not on the Xingu river, which is where you want the Black Castle. While reading *Green Hell* [a research text on the area] I narrowed down the likely locations for the Castle to two: up the Xingu, and in the Acre province of Brazil. There are still-wild Indian tribes in each area. But the Xingu has unavigable rapids, so our boat convoy could not have approached the Black Castle as we described [in *Amazon Slaughter*] unless the Castle was downriver, or on some other river. Question is, is the Amazon/Jurua river navigable? There may be *no* navigable rivers penetrating into the deep hinterland. But my main reason for preferring the Jurua River is that up here, in Acre, not only are the remaining Indians more numerous and savage, it is also closer to the oil region and to the von Daniken *Gold of the Gods* region. Daniken says that in Equador, near the Santiage River—which is a tributary of the Maranon, which in turn flows into the amazon—is a system of monstrous squared-off caves that seem to have been fashioned by sobe ancient alien civilization. Other research indicates that von Daniken must be taken with a shovelful of salt; he never went to some of the places he claimed. So we could conjecture similar tunnels, perhaps interconnecting ones, that Fu Antos has discovered, and he has built the Black Castle over the entrance to this system. Also, our scene with the water flooding, in the last novel—there had to have been a higher source, with a steep incline, for that water to be dammed up and rush down. Near the Andes is best for that. So I argue for Acre." This shows the way we hashed over settings and scenes throughout the series; none of it was careless writing.

The question of the corruption of Judo by the demand for most of tournament money was, unfortunately, a real one, accurately described here. We made an unofficial query about it to the American Judo headquarters, and got a response of exactly the nature described. But those who were being dunned were nervous about making a formal complaint, because justice is not always served by those in charge, as politics demonstrate the world over, and there could be serious consequences for any whistle-blower. We hoped that publication of this novel would help blow the lid off that scandal, but it didn't get published.

We tried various other notions, doing chapter and summary, but none of them were accepted for publication. Accordingly, we are filling out this partial-novel volume with those other projects, in this manner completing our collaborative enterprises. Thus it least will give readers an idea of what *doesn't* get published. Editorial whim governs far more than most readers perhaps understand.

The first of these, "Ki" is a short story featuring Hiroshi, the little aikidoist, in the time before the first novel, *Kiai!*, started. It was published in the June 1974 issue of VERTEX, a science fiction magazine. The second, "Beast of Betelgeuse," was accepted for publication by GALAXY, another science fiction magazine. But then the magazine was sold, a new editor took over, and of course the story was dumped.

KI

Clap two hands, Hiroshi thought, *and there is sound.* He clapped once, precisely, with two hands. There was sound.

But what is the sound of one hand clapping? He made the motion with one open hand. There was no sound.

But one hand with ki *extended . . .*

Was there a ghostly sound?

Hiroshi listened carefully. No, that was not the clap of one hand he heard. It was more distant, more urgent. It was the call of imperative need.

0-Sensei, I go, he said in his mind. He stood, stepping into his wooden sandals at the edge of the tatami. He let the pleats of his black *hakama* skirt straighten, and walked serenely out of his *dojo.* His students did not even turn from their exercises, for the ways of their honored teacher were at times inscrutable.

He walked down the narrow street, his sandals making no sound on the cobblestones. The houses were wooden, two and three stories high, gay and clean and individual. Some resembled pagodas, and here and there were small, pretty gardens with dwarf trees and oddly shaped shrubbery. The way was crowded now; the majority of the men and women hurrying by wore kimonos, but perhaps two in five were in the ugly new Western dress. Street vendors hawked their wares with piercing cries, selling fish, shrimp and octopus.

He arrived at the Tokyo airport ten minutes before the great jet was scheduled to take off. Most of the passengers had already boarded. A phenomenally fat man was just emerging from a rest room.

Hiroshi walked down the passage to the door to the airfield. "Ticket, sir?" the guardian of the gate inquired.

Hiroshi shrugged. "I travel to New York City, in America."

"I know where New York is!" the man said testily. "But you have to have a ticket! And you'll have to take another flight; this one is sold out."

Hiroshi shook his head gently, touching his wispy beard. "This flight is necessary."

"Not without a ticket!"

The huge man came up behind Hiroshi. The man was not actually tall, but he dwarfed the little teacher, who stood just five feet high and weighed one hundred pounds. "Kindly step aside, sir," the ticket-taker said abruptly to Hiroshi. "You are interfering with our last passenger, and the schedule—"

"I regret I can not," Hiroshi said politely but firmly.

"Old man—" the ticket-taker began ominously, not showing the deference due to age. Then a massive arm reached over Hiroshi's shoulder, and a fat hand oily with sweat balked the ticket-taker's action.

"One moment, sir," the last passenger said.

Hiroshi turned to face him. The man's bulk was vast—perhaps three hundred pounds—but he carried himself with power. He wore a kimono to accommodate his gross musculature, and sturdy sandals on his feet. He was in his middle or late twenties, with long black hair tied in a topknot.

"I am Kiyokuni, sumo wrestler," he said.

"Hiroshi, aikido."

They bowed to each other formally, the large and the small. "I *thought* I recognized you, *O-sensei,* but I did not expect to find you in such a place as this," Kiyokuni said. "I have long wished to meet a teacher of your eminence."

"On the contrary," Hiroshi demurred. "It is an honor to address an esteemed young member of the *Yokozuna*, the very highest league of wrestling. I have admired your career."

"Sir, you must board!" the ticket-taker said urgently to the wrestler. "See, the fuel line has already been taken from the wings of the plane."

They ignored him. "No career compares with yours, greatest of teachers," Kiyokuni said, deeply flattered. "I am bound for Hawaii, to give a sumo exhibition. But I would cancel it instantly to visit with you."

"I regret I must travel to New York," Hiroshi said. "But another time—"

There was the growing sound of the jet motors warming up. "Sir!" the ticket taker cried desperately. "The flight will leave without you!"

"This airplane continues to America," Kiyokuni said. "My ticket is only to Hawaii, but if you would accept it—"

"This is most kind of you," Hiroshi said, accepting it.

"But your exhibition!" the ticket-taker cried over the roar of the engines.

"Let it wait! I will take the next flight!"

Hiroshi presented the ticket-taker with the ticket and went out to board the plane, cutting off further discussion. He found his seat and was strapped in just as the machine began to taxi down the strip.

*

They were airborne. He peered out of the window, intrigued by the view of the city. The plane circled, gaining altitude, then oriented east and moved out over the ocean.

"This—this is a skyjack!" a nervous voice said.

Hiroshi looked down the aisle. It was a Korean University student, a short chubby swarthy peasant-type in a Mao jacket, holding a Nambu automatic pistol. The gun shook, but it was no less dangerous because of that.

"Tell the pilot to take it to North Korea!" the hijacker said in bad Japanese. The side of his face twitched.

The stewardess, pale but composed, turned. "Wait!" the man cried. He looked about wildly, and his gaze fell on tiny Hiroshi. "You, old man! You're my hostage! If they don't turn the plane, I'll—I'll *shoot—stand up here!"*

Gravely Hiroshi stood up and sidled past the man on the adjacent seat, a horrified Caucasian tourist. Hiroshi was the least impressive figure of a man on the plane, physically, yet there was an aura of serenity about him that gave him stature. The gunman should have noticed.

"You all see?" the hijacker cried, as though playing to an audience. "I'll shoot—I'll kill this feeble old man! So you just tell the pilot—and don't use the radio! North Korea!"

The stewardess walked slowly toward the pilot's compartment. The gunman gestured violently to Hiroshi. "Right here in front of me! Closer!"

Hiroshi came to stand facing him, looking very small and frail. He extended his *ki,* but the student's deathwish was so strong that no control was feasible at the moment. "It would be better not to do this," he said gently.

"Shut *up!"* The gun jabbed at Hiroshi's chest.

"Innocent people could be hurt," Hiroshi said as though establishing a point of order. "And I regret that I am unable to visit Korea at this time."

"I'll shoot!" the man cried, jabbing again.

So swiftly that no one saw his hand move, Hiroshi placed the fingers of his left hand on top of the pistol, pushing the barrel back. It was a slide-action weapon, and could not be fired in this position. Almost simultaneously his right hand shot forward, fingers stiffly extended. They struck the man's solar plexus with a force few would have believed.

The watching passengers gasped as the hijacker crumpled, unconscious. The pistol was now miraculously in Hiroshi's hand. "I regret the necessity," he said to the others. "Please take this weapon to the pilot for safekeeping, and ask him to resume his scheduled route. We shall have to make this unfortunate youth comfortable."

Someone took the gun, gingerly. Hiroshi squatted to attend to the injured man. He placed his hand on the hijacker's chest and extended his *ki.* "The pain of dying is more than this," he murmured.

The eyes opened. "Then I don't want to die!"

Hiroshi nodded wisely. "You will remain in Hawaii. I have need of your ticket."

The youth fumbled in his pocket and brought out his ticket. It was to New York. "I—I never really wanted to go to Korea! It was *life* I hated, and I thought I would get killed. But now even jail seems sweet! Something inside me . . ." He touched his chest where Hiroshi's hand had rested. "Some strange power—you made me well!"

"I merely showed the way," Hiroshi said. He returned to his seat as the ex-hijacker got up. There was a kind of glow on the face of each, reflected in the faces of the passengers.

The copilot came down the aisle. "Who broke up the hijack?" he demanded. "There'll he a reward."

People gestured to Hiroshi. "Please see that he is not punished unduly," Hiroshi said. "He needs medical attention, and is sorry for the misunderstanding."

The copilot looked down at him. "So you're the one!" he said, not concealing his surprise. "Well, I can't promise, but I'll try. What's your name?"

Hiroshi handed him his original ticket. "Kiyokuni," the pilot read from the envelope, making a note. "This name will make headlines all over the world, tomorrow!"

But Hiroshi was already entering meditation. *I am hanging by my teeth over an abyss,* he thought, *looking down into the level water far below.* He looked, and saw the ocean. *"What is Zen?" a seeker inquires. What shall I answer?*

*

But long before he had the answer the smoggy spires of New York, America, appeared. He put aside the problem with infinite patience and stepped down to wintry Kennedy Airport.

"Your passport, sir," an official said in English.

"It is very kind of you to inquire," Hiroshi replied in the same language, and walked on.

The official chased after him, blocking his way. "I must check your passport!"

"I much appreciate the offer," Hiroshi replied with consummate courtesy. "But I shall not put you to this trouble. I possess no passport."

The man's mouth turned dour. "Then you'll go right back where you came from, old-timer!"

Perceiving the man's distress, Hiroshi put a gentle hand on his white wrist. He extended his *ki.* The officer's belligerent countenance smoothed. Now he was at peace.

Hiroshi took Route 78 west, walked across the Brooklyn Bridge, and went north on Broadway. He admired the glittering signs and imperative traffic. *How like Japan!*

People stared at him, for it was a bitterly cold October afternoon, with a cutting wind swooping down the street, and he wore only his light shirt, dark skirt, and open wooden sandals. But the *ki* was about him, making him impervious.

After three hours of walking, he turned into an alley. In America, he remembered, men did not relieve themselves on the public streets. It was always best to honor the foibles of the natives.

Garbage cans overflowed, broken glass littered the path, and a stench rose from puddles of greasy water. This was a dark canyon between tall buildings. The alley was restful after the continuous blare and flash of the main street. And—his *ki* awareness guided him this way.

A large black man jumped out from the shadow of a doorway. His hands closed about Hiroshi's thin neck.

The little teacher calmly reached up and grasped the mugger's two thumbs, one in each hand. Very gently he turned his hands outward, carrying the thumbs along and breaking the choke. The mugger swore fiercely and fought, but the pressure was inexorable. In a moment the two thumbs broke.

The man screamed, but Hiroshi extended his *ki* again and made the hands go numb. "Violence is unfortunate," he murmured regretfully. "It is an insufficient response to the prior wrongs done you and your people. Go to the police; they will treat your injury and confine you until your drug addiction is gone. Do not accept the first probationary position you are offered, or the second, for they will lead you into inadvertent temptations. The third will seem intolerable, a thing of no pride, but that is the one you must take. In three years we shall meet again, in better circumstances."

He walked on down the alley, the mugger staring after him. Hiroshi's students sometimes came to him by devious routes, but he had not before recruited in a New York alley.

At dusk an hour later he reached the southern fringe of Central Park. He entered it through the "Artist's Gate," passing under the gaze of Simon Bolivar, to whom he made a little bow of greeting.

Inside he turned right, admiring the trimmed hedges near the path like any other tourist. Despite the cold, there were some blue and pink flowers. The lights were coming on in the buildings adjacent to the park, giving the effect of a Chinese Wall of immense proportion surrounding this lush valley, with illuminated mountains beyond. There was not a prettier spot this instant in all Japan, he thought appreciatively.

Now he came to the Pond, where great flocks of birds abounded. He was thirsty after his hours of travel, so stopped to drink of its water. There was no refreshment available to man to match that of water after thirst!

A policeman riding a horse saw him. "Don't drink from that, mister!" the officer bawled, alarmed. "It's polluted!"

Hiroshi stood up and made a bow. "I thank you for your gracious warning. But there is no danger."

The policeman looked at him a moment. "Hey—don't I know you from somewhere?"

Hiroshi spread his hands. "I am a visitor to your fair city."

The officer shook his head as if trying to nail an elusive memory, then decided this was a harmless nut. He rode on, his beautiful horse snorting in the chill.

Hiroshi had been aware of the toxicity of the water. But his *ki* protected him, neutralizing the adverse bacteria and pollutants. He would not suffer.

He continued on around the Pond, then north, not hurrying. He passed the small zoo, now closed for the night, and came to the Mall. He inclined his head to the bust of each famous man beside it, politely. He came at last to the Lake, skirting it to reach the Ramble, a wooded hill to the north. The night was now advanced, and few people remained in the park. The aimless, hidden paths of the Ramble were forbidding in the heavy shadows, but he walked quickly into the thick of it, following his *ki.*

There was a feminine scream near at hand. Hiroshi stepped toward it, unsurprised. Two white men were holding a struggling black girl under a lamp. They wrestled her down as Hiroshi approached, one sitting astride her head and pinning her arms while the other pried at her legs.

"Please free the girl and depart in peace," Hiroshi said.

The man on her head looked up at Hiroshi, startled, then contemptuous. "Get outa here you little queer before we do the same to *you!*"

"I regret I must insist," Hiroshi said. "The young lady does not wish to participate."

The other man got his hands on her panties and pulled

them down. The girl twisted her body desperately, and the top man slapped her hard across the face. "Don't give me no trouble, nig—"

Hiroshi had drawn alongside, extending his *ki.* He seized the hair of the speaking man and turned the head upward. The rapist's mouth opened involuntarily. Hiroshi delivered a knuckle blow to the nerve center between the ear and the upper hinge of the jaw. The man screamed in agony and fell away.

The other man jumped up, drawing a knife from a leg sheath. He was naked below his flapping shirt, but that hardly inhibited him. He lunged, the knife held low, going for the gut.

Hiroshi's left hand moved like the head of a striking snake, sweeping the knife-arm outwards. His right hand, dangling open and loose, whipped against the man's exposed anatomy. It was a devastating strike that knotted the rapist into a ball of agony. It would be a long time before he recovered either the ability or the will to rape again.

The girl scrambled up, wide-eyed. Hiroshi bowed, unruffled. "I regret I employed excessive violence in the presence of a lady. I shall have to meditate upon that flaw in my nature. But I trust you are well?"

She looked at his sandals, his skirt, and his oriental countenance. She was terrified. "Please—let me go!"

Hiroshi extended his *ki* once more. "I am Hiroshi, humble teacher of aikido, a system of meditation and self defense. This is my practice costume, the *dogi.* I heard your distress and came to help. I do not mean to alarm you; as you can see, I am an old man and quite harmless."

That last seemed laughable. Hiroshi was sixty, but hardly harmless. The leading specialists of the world's leading martial arts—karate, judo, wrestling, kung-fu and others—had encountered the little *sensei* in past decades and departed with thoroughgoing respect for his physical and mental prowess. Aikido was no mean discipline, and he was the leading practitioner of his time.

Nevertheless, what he said was true. He was a man of peace,

and considered himself primarily a teacher. When force was required, he employed it, but only as a necessary resort, and then with genuine regret.

The girl had no way of knowing this. But his *ki* reached out, pacifying her, and her fear abated. "I—I'm sorry," she said. "I was driving across the park on the transverse road, and my motor quit. I—these men offered to help, but before I knew it—"

"We shall go to your car," Hiroshi said. "Perhaps it is feeling better now."

It did not occur to her to argue. They walked north toward the road. "I had to deliver some important papers, and my apartment was just across the park," she said, her tension making her speak rapidly. "They were for tomorrow's session—I work at the UN—I just don't know what happened to my car—it wasn't out of gas. You're Japanese, aren't you?"

"I am." Her car was just past one of the underpass tunnels employed to keep transverse traffic clear of the park proper.

"It just stopped," she repeated. "And wouldn't start. I ran down the battery trying to—"

Hiroshi put his hand on the hood. He extended his *ki,* seeking rapport with the needs of the motor. "Please try once more," he said.

"I *told* you—the battery's dead!" But she tried the starter.

Some power had regenerated during her absence. The motor struggled over, once, twice—and caught.

"It's running!" she cried unnecessarily.

The sound of horse's hooves approached. The mounted policeman came up. "Lady, don't park here!" he cried. "The park's dangerous at night—don't you know that?"

She began to laugh, hysterically. Hiroshi walked around the car and put his hand on hers, and she calmed. "It's all right, officer!" she said. "It stalled, but he fixed it somehow. And—"

"Merely coincidence," Hiroshi said. "I know nothing of motors."

The policeman squinted down at him. "You again! If you're molesting this woman—"

"No, no!" she cried. "He's my friend! Let me give you a ride, Mr. Hiroshi!"

"I am most grateful," Hiroshi said. "But this is not the favor I require from you. Please go your way."

"Get moving, lady!" the officer brayed.

She drove off.

The policeman stared at him. "Hiroshi, she called you. I know that name! *Thought* I placed you! Aikido!"

Hiroshi bowed. "It is of no importance."

The man jumped down from his horse. "I'm taking you into the station! Come along now—"

Hiroshi's motion was so slight as to seem insignificant, but it was the policeman's arm that ended in the submission lock, not the little teacher's.

"Hey—do that again!" the man exclaimed as Hirosbi released him. "Slow motion!"

He reached for Hiroshi's arm again, slowly, and the *sensei* made his move again, slowly. "You must use your opponent's *ki* against him," Hiroshi explained. "Then he defeats himself."

"You *are* him! That's what I wanted to know! I saw your picture in the book when I studied the comealongs. The top man since the founder died! But we have so many kooks around here, I just had to check. How come you're in New York?"

"I have minor business here," Hiroshi said. "I am glad you have profited from my book."

"Hey, the chief'll want to meet you! You're just about the toughest fighter in the world, aren't you?"

"The mental discipline is far more important than the physical, and the peaceful solution is always best."

"Not around here it isn't!" the officer said jovially. "These muggers and perverts—oh, you mean the *ki.* Well, I never did understand about that, much. But I heard you can do things with your mind, like telepathy. That right?"

"I do no more than you could do, with proper training," Hiroshi said. "*Ki* is inherent in everyone. I regret I can not visit your chief at this time."

"Okay," the policeman said regretfully, remounting. "I sure won't try to tell *you* what do do! But watch yourself around the park, will you? It's a rough beat!"

Hiroshi bowed. "I shall do so, sir."

The man trotted off with a friendly wave. Hiroshi walked south along the pleasant paths.

He came again to the little zoo, and climbed over its wall. Inside was a large plaster whale with a wide-open mouth. Goldfish swam in a glass aquarium inside it. He climbed in and curled up on the whale's tongue, sheltered from the bitterly cold wind, and relaxed.

I am hanging over a pit of wild tigers, he thought. *Only the rope about my waist sustains my weight. A beaver is gnawing on that rope. I see some wild berries growing on the fringe of the pit, just within reach. I pick one as the last strand parts . . .*

His eyes closed and he felt warm all over as he drifted to sleep. *How sweet it tastes!*

*

The sweet taste of the berry remained in his mouth as he woke. Dawn was near; attendants would be arriving soon. He climbed out of the whale, turned to make a formal bow to it, then climbed nimbly out of the zoo.

He was hungry, despite the berry. He had not eaten since leaving the airplane. But his business was now too urgent to permit further loss of time, and fasting was good for the spirit. He drank again from the Pond and proceeded on out of the park, south on Fifth Avenue, admiring the glittering stores, then east on 42nd Street.

First he saw the massive Secretariat Building, with its phenomenal expanse of glass. Then he saw the wide plaza and the row of flags of all the member nations; Japan's was the most beautiful.

He entered the General Assembly Building's main lobby, locating the Information Desk.

There was the girl he had saved from a fate worse than rape. "Mr. Hiroshi!" she exclaimed, her dark face lighting. Then her mouth tightened, for she did not want her employers to know about the park incident.

"If it is not too much to ask," Hiroshi said, inclining his head politely, "I should like to attend the General Assembly meeting."

"No trouble at all, Mr. Hiroshi!" she said, flustered. "We have regular tours!"

"I do not wish the visitor's tour. I must attend with the delegates."

"You don't understand, Mr. Hiroshi!" she protested. "No visitors are allowed on the assembly floor during a business session. You would have to have a special pass." She paused. "Or is that what you mean?"

Hiroshi nodded. "It is necessary."

She bit her lip. "After what you did look, I—please don't tell anyone! I wouldn't do this for anyone else in the world, but—here's a pass for the guest of a delegate. I'm sure this one won't be used today. I'd lose my job if—"

"This is most kind of you," Hiroshi said, accepting.

He entered the main assembly hall with the delegates, his pass clearing the way past the guard. It was like an amphitheater inside, with many rows of chairs. He peered up at the huge, tall dome admiringly. "What a magnificent *dojo!" he* murmured, thinking of his own small practice hall.

He made his way to the Cuban delegation. "Please," he said to the delegate in Spanish. "May I speak to the exile?"

The man faced him, displeased. "There is no Cuban traitor here, señor! Only true Revolutionaries. And I do not believe I know you."

"I must apologize for the misunderstanding," Hiroshi said humbly. "I thought perhaps the man entered as your guest."

"No guest! If someone is using my pass—"

Hiroshi laid down his guest pass. The delegate's face became grim. "This is mine! Who—?"

"I fear he means mischief. Would you be so kind as to contact your office and ascertain—?"

"I shall certainly check it out!" the man said angrily, picking up the pass. "This should never have been issued!"

Now Hiroshi moved to the Japanese delegation and took a seat. The delegate looked at him and did a doubletake. "Are you not Hiroshi, the aikido *sensei?"* he asked in Japanese. "What brings you here?"

"This is not readily explained."

The man frowned. *"Sensei,* I have the utmost respect for your motives. But you can not remain here. This is the United Nations, and an important session is about to begin. If you will go to my office in the Secretariat Building, I will speak to you as soon as I can."

Hiroshi only smiled—and remained. Seeing that he would not be moved, the delegate put the best face on it and let him be.

The President of the General Assembly called the meeting to order.

A wild-haired man barged in, pursued by two guards. He charged toward the Speaker's rostrum. Suddenly he stopped, whirled about, and gestured at the guards. "Killers!" he cried in high-pitched Spanish. "Shoot! You can't touch me!"

Both guards drew their guns and fired. The noise was deafening. But the bullets went up into the dome—shot after shot, until the guns were empty.

Then there was silence. Astonishment and dismay showed on the faces of the two guards, and in the assembly.

The Speaker was furious. "What is the meaning of this?" he cried in French. Hiroshi heard the English translation in his earpiece.

"Shut up!" the intruder cried, still in Spanish.

More guards rushed in. "Remove this man!" the Speaker said.

It was obvious that neither he nor the intruder understood the other, but their tones made their meanings clear.

One of the first two guards hurled his pistol at the Speaker. The missile missed, crashing into the glass-enclosed floor where the press and translators worked with such force that it cracked the unbreakable glass. Spiderwebs ran in all directions from the center of impact.

The intruder climbed to the Speaker's rostrum. "Shut up, all of you!" he cried again. "I am Mario Garcia! I am a slan, a clear, and the true President of Free Cuba, and now you all *listen to me!"*

The delegates, shocked, listened to their earpieces, hearing his words in one of the five official languages. But many did not get the word, because the strike at the translators' booth had brought a number of the translators to their feet, gaping. The six reinforcement police stood unmoving, while the President and his staff quietly cleared out. Only the news-hungry television camera crew kept operating, broadcasting it all.

"I am the only sane man in the world!" Garcia cried into the mike. He was a tall, thin, nervous young man with very light hair and reddish white skin, almost albino. His eyes were blue and seemed weak, not tracking properly, though he was not wearing glasses. "I am the only one fit to rule, so you'll have to make me King of the world!"

No one answered. Everyone seemed to be waiting for someone else's initiative, with many shaking their heads in bewilderment. Even the English translation was out of commission now; but that made no difference to Hiroshi. He watched the wild young man closely, studying his every move.

"I am a Doctor of Scientology!" Garcia cried. "And a black belt in judo! And founder of the SLF! Now elect me King of the world—or I'll destroy you along with the Communists!"

Still no one replied, and the guards remained strangely inactive. There was an increasing murmur among the delegates. Hiroshi rose and walked toward the Cuban delegation.

"See, I'll show you!" Garcia said, gesturing with both his arms.

"I control metal. I have telekinesis! I have telepathy! I am a slan! You are powerless against me!"

The Cuban delegate spied Hiroshi and gestured him close. "Señor, you were right!" he whispered, tapping his scribbled notes. "I called my office, and we have a file on this madman. His mother was a santera, that espiritismo cult. His mind became unhinged when his family lost its ill-gained fortune, and he became a traitor to his country and left Cuba. How did you know he was here?"

"The *ki* led me," Hiroshi said, not quibbling about definitions. To the Castro government of Cuba, anticommunist was interchangeable with traitor. "Please—more information?"

"You can do something?" The delegate paused, alarmed, as the remaining guards fired a volley into the dome. "The madman I comprehend; he is mad! But what is the matter with guards?"

"It is necessary first to understand Garcia," Hiroshi said gently.

"Yes!" The delegate brushed back his dark hair. "I made notes from the telephone. Garcia is from a volatile family, but he is highly intelligent. Good marks at Havana University, but he left in midterm to study something called 'Scientology' and seems to have done well there too. And judo, despite a sickly nature and bad eyesight. First degree black belt, before dropping out. Some experience with LSD, but he doesn't seem to be a drug addict. Apparently he has tremendous drive, but little staying power—apart from his madness."

Hiroshi nodded. "So the credits he claims are accurate. But what is this 'SLF' he names?"

"There's something about that too. He is a science fiction enthusiast—a 'fan.' He founded a club—" he leafed through his notes, finding the place. "Here: 'Slans Lunatic Fringe,' devoted to the works of A. E. van Vogt, L. Ron Hubbard, and others of the type. Nonsense."

"On the contrary, señor!" Hiroshi said warmly. "This is relevant. You have told me that he is honest, and has studied aspects of the occult powers of the mind. Mad he may be, but his power is real."

He moved up the aisle between the chairs, toward the dais, leaving the confused delegate behind.

Garcia was still demonstrating his control. "All metal! All the world runs on metal, doesn't it? So I am master already!" He glared about. "You!" he cried, pointing at the delegate from Holland. "You are convinced now?"

Someone whispered a translation. The man shook his head scornfully.

"Your metal watch!" Garcia said. "I lift it, thus:" The man's left hand jerked up. "And over—thus!" The man's fist smashed into his own jaw. He fell back in his seat, his lip bleeding. *"Now* do you believe?" Garcia yelled triumphantly.

The man looked at his watch, then back at Garcia. The shock in his face was answer enough.

"I can as readily make the guns of the guards kill you!" Garcia continued. "I can rip out the metal girders of this building and bring the vault down about your heads! There is no limit to my power! I am the world's first true Clear!"

Hiroshi extended his *ki.* It met the powerful, aberrant force of the Cuban, related to *ki* but lacking its restraint. *Ki* was akin to the force and goodness of the human spirit, while Garcia's variant derived from frustration and insanity. In a more devious respect, the two complemented each other as evil complemented good.

"Now make me King of the world!" Garcia cried again to the group. "Before I destroy you all!"

Hiroshi approached him, knitting his fingers in the *kuji-kiri* exercise. "I regret this is impossible," he said politely. "Please desist and come with me."

"You dare?" Garcia demanded with a quiver, his eyes watering as he focused on the little man. "I'll bash your head in with your own watch!"

Hiroshi held up his wrists, continuing the hypnotic *kuji-kiri* motions. He wore no watch, no bracelet, no ring.

"I'll shoot your own coins into your eyes!"

Hiroshi shook his head. "I have no money." He was very close now, his fingers working in marvelously intricate patterns.

Garcia tore his gaze away from those fingers. "You'll still die!" He gestured to a guard, and the man's gun leveled.

Hiroshi extended his *ki.* This was why he had saved it, using the finger-hypnotism instead. He could not use his *ki* in two ways simultaneously, and could not match the sheer raw power of the youth. But he could begin to rein in Garcia hypnotically, while using his *ki* to interfere with the man's paranormal control. Just a little jog of the gunman's elbow, as it were, as he fired . . .

The gun went off. The shot went wide. It had worked! "I, too, am a kind of clear," Hiroshi said softly. He was not familiar with the term, but that did not matter.

Garcia stared—into the winding fingers. "You lie, you little Jap!" But he must have felt the *ki* interference, and he sounded uncertain.

One of the thrown pistols lay in the dais. Hiroshi picked it up. "I control this metal. Take it—if you can."

Challenged specifically, Garcia concentrated. His force leaped out, surrounding Hiroshi, tearing at his control. If he *could* take over, Hiroshi was lost. But that power was untrained and unruly, not focused to best advantage. Hiroshi hung on, his *ki* extended to the utmost. He had never before braved an attack such as this!

The gun quivered, but did not leave his hand. He had withstood the storm.

"Now *I* shall move it," Hiroshi said, as though he had never felt the struggle. His hand flicked. The gun flew off to the side, and struck the lifting weapon of another guard. Both guns dropped to the floor.

With an incoherent scream, Garcia jumped at Hiroshi, his hands stiffened for deadly blows. That was his mistake. No man who knew Hiroshi would have tried such an attack.

The little *sensei* caught one arm, lifted it, and hit under Garcia's armpit with his thumb. Then he applied a submission lock on the man's arm.

Garcia screamed with pain. Guns, coins and watches flew up all over the room, but Hiroshi's *ki* was spread out in a thin interference pattern that prevented accurate attack from that quarter. He held the grip.

All fight left the would-be king of the world. "You *are* a clear!" he muttered brokenly.

"Merely proper discipline," Hiroshi said modestly, maintaining the grip.

In a moment a crowd formed about them. "Congratulations!" the President of the General Assembly exclaimed, an interpreter standing beside him and rendering it into English almost simultaneously. "You subdued the madman!"

Hiroshi shook his head. "Not mad, merely misunderstood. He has no power over metal. Only over people. He did not realize that himself, or he would have had far more power than he showed. Still, it is a wonderful *ki* he employs, deserving of scrupulous study. I shall see that this occurs."

"We'll throw the book at him!" a guard cried. "Making us shoot up the assembly hail—"

But the Cuban and Japanese delegates interceded, Communist and Capitalist standing shoulder to shoulder on this issue. "This man deserves whatever reward he asks," the Cuban said. "He saved our lives!"

"He is Hiroshi, the world's leading aikido *sensei,*" the Japanese said. "No lesser man could have stopped Garcia—and no police can control Garcia now. Let Hiroshi take this man wherever he wishes; what jail could hold him?"

No one could argue with that. "It was I who borrowed your visitor's pass," Hiroshi confessed to the Cuban. "I regret the necessity, and fear the information girl will be blamed."

"I shall demand her promotion!" the man said earnestly. "That madman's plan was full of holes. He could never have been king of the world, but he could have killed many of us and complicated the international situation perilously, if you hadn't been here!"

There was the clamor of Babel as everyone tried to question and congratulate simultaneously in scores of languages. The President was trying to reestablish order, futilely. In the confusion, Hiroshi escaped with his charge.

The trip to Japan was simplified by the complete cooperation of governments and airlines, but complicated by Hiroshi's need to maintain surveillance over Garcia. If the man ever realized the extent of his power and used it effectively, he would never again be confined. Only one place was secure, and that was where Garcia had been destined from the moment Hiroshi responded to the message of *ki,* could he have known.

They went to the Japanese Isle of Hokkaido, into chill mountainous wilds. Fierce Ninjitsu warriors watched, but recognized Hiroshi, and did not challenge him.

Inside an ancient castle, in a bleak bare chamber, a long-bearded, emaciated man of about ninety sat cross-legged. The eyes were shrunken and sightless, the ears deaf, the movements so slow as to suggest idiocy, and an odor of putrefaction rose from the shriveled body.

Hiroshi bowed. *"O-Sensei* Fu Antos, I have answered your call," he said with unfeigned respect, though his action and words were superfluous. "Here is a talent for study."

Ki reached out from the ancient, far more powerful than Hiroshi's own. Garcia stiffened and looked about, frightened—and the pressure of his containment eased. The blind dumb head inclined. The talent was worthy.

Hiroshi bowed again and backed away, alone. The relief was vast. What would he have done, had Fu Antos not acceded? Now his mission was done.

A day later, still exhausted, he returned to his *dojo.* His students crowded about, forgetting themselves in their eagerness to learn of his adventures. They were powerful athletes and ranking practitioners of the martial arts, but before him they were like children.

"A few necessary errands," was all the weary *sensei* would say as he sat on the floor in his accustomed spot.

One student held a newspaper whose headline screamed of New York and paranormal talents. He looked at Hiroshi and shook his head, resigned. Would any student ever master even a tiny fraction of the spirit and power and humility this wizened little mystic possessed? What was *ki,* after all?

It was a question Hiroshi himself longed to have answered. *Clap two hands,* he thought, *and there is sound . . .*

BEAST OF BETELGEUSE

If a tree falls in the forest, and no one hears, what sound does it make?

Hiroshi sat in the Lotus posture, meditating—on the daily newspaper. The bold strokes of the Japanese symbols slashed down the page, telling of the recent wave of crime. Illegal gambling, prostitution, and narcotics were flourishing, and in seeming response the stock market was roaring. What did it mean?

His eyes focused beyond the printed page, peering at the cause behind the effect. For crime was an effect, the result of a chain of indignities to the human condition, rooted ultimately in a seeming defect in the nature of man. Hiroshi had meditated many times on the paradox of imperfection flowing from perfection, a perfect Supreme Deity creating imperfect man, and had come to no conclusive answer. Perhaps man was put on Earth to *earn* his redemption, as a good sword was tempered by the fire. If so, the effort seemed to be failing.

But this was more than the usual corruption. Crime was becoming powerful, organized, disciplined, imaginative. Where was the guiding force?

Hiroshi perceived it now. It was the *Yakuza*, the long-time criminal gangs of Japan. Somehow one of the gangs had multiplied its power in the last few months, emerging paramount. Now it was extending its sticky fingers into formerly legitimate enterprises, investing its ill-gotten profits in solid commercial ventures. This process was already so far advanced that the *Yakuza* was on the way to the financial domination of Japan itself—something no gang had ever been able to do before. The takeover was proceeding so swiftly, smoothly, silently, and efficiently that no one had sounded the alarm.

Hiroshi was not a politician or business man, but he cared about basic rightness and proportion. This was part of his philosophy of Zen. Meditation was good, but sometimes it became necessary also to act.

So he acted. He opened his mind to commune with his ancient master of martial arts, Fu Antos, Lord of the Ninjas.

COME. The summons rang like the clarion of temple bells inside Hiroshi's mind.

And so Hiroshi came. North from the great metropolitan area of industrial Japan. He journeyed by fishing boat to the port city of Sapporo, then by mule cart to the northern wilds of the interior of the island Hokkaido. He was a little old man with a serene countenance who paid scant attention to obstacles, to the perplexity of those he encountered along the way. He walked through the wilderness, climbing ever higher, his bare feet relishing the earth and grass beneath. He wore only a thin black silk kimono with trousers underneath; he had removed his *geta* or wooden sandals lest they be damaged in the roughening terrain.

As he ascended, the warm fall weather became cold, the sky darkened, thunder sounded, and a freezing rain started to fall. Yet he continued, his lightly bearded face tranquil; his interior power of *ki* kept him warm. He arrived, in a remarkably short time, at the ancient, rundown Black Castle of the Ninjas.

It was a ruin, its cyclopean stones tumbled in disarray, its once-proud moat half filled in. He negotiated the difficult causeway through the surrounding marshes, entered the collapsing main gate, and passed through the hoary dark halls until he penetrated to the nethermost chamber.

Here the light of a single taper high on a wall cast a dim radiance across the bleak dank stone. In the center, on a simple *tatami* or reed mat, sat the incredible old Lord of the Ninjas, Fu Antos. His legs were withered and useless; he had not walked in twenty years, or moved from this self-imposed prison. He looked and smelled somewhat like a week-old corpse. Yet there was an amazing aura of power about him that made him the most remarkable man of recent centuries. Hiroshi could actually perceive a faint luminous field around the hunched figure, startlingly like the haloes in Christian pictures of saints. Yet Fu Antos was no Christian, and certainly no saint.

"O-Sensei," Hiroshi said respectfully.

Fu Antos acknowledged with twitches of his skeletal fingers in the ninja *kuji-kiri* hypnotic pattern. Hiroshi entered the trance willingly, for it was the old man's only remaining means of specific communication. The chamber seemed to change, becoming darker, as though night had fallen and deprived it of even the smallest leakage of outside light. The lone candle glimmered low. That was all, for a time; the decrepit man sat with his sunken orbs turned upward as if staring through the massive walls and indeed the entire castle to the stars beyond. Now those lights appeared, at first a faint patina on the rough ceiling, then the full night sky. The stars in their myriad glory bathed the chamber, and the great Milky Way stood out bright and clear: so many stars, so distant, that they became no more than a pale white wash. What secrets lay beyond that awesome firmament?

Fu Antos contemplated the oneness of the universe, the great nothingness. He had achieved *Satori*, or enlightenment, a oneness with Buddha, and was immersed in the sheer beauty of it.

Suddenly a bright streak developed, much more than a shooting star, much closer, like a bolt of lightning yet more disciplined. This dazzling display illuminated the room as if it were day, though there was no window. Immediately it faded, and there was a tremendous impact that shook the castle and the entire mountain range within which it stood. A sonic boom as of thunder passed deafeningly. The few attendant ninjas woke in alarm.

Tanaka, in charge of the castle, also Fu Antos' chief jailer, rushed down to check on his lord. "Yes I remain alive," Fu Antos said through his fingers, irritably. "Almost I thought the bolt from heaven had come to release me from this prison of a body in which you hold me, but the joy of transformation is not yet."

Relieved, Tanaka made as if to bring food and a sanitary facility (an old pot) for his master, but Fu Antos stopped him with the peremptory lift of one little finger. "This is a thing of awful import. Take three men and investigate."

"A meteorite," Tanaka protested, for he had had an education in the outside world. "Impossible to locate at night—and for what reason? It will not fly away again."

"Do you debate with me?" Fu Antos' fingers demanded. "It is no meteorite. Go, before—"

There was a second burst of light, brighter than before, and again the castle shook. A stone dislodged from the corner of the ceiling and crashed to the floor, throwing off a spark of its own. The sound of a colossal explosion reverberated through the castle chambers.

"Too late," Fu Antos signaled. "Go, then, in the morning."

Tanaka bowed and hurried off to check the shaken castle. It had been well constructed in Fu Antos' youth, almost four hundred years before, but such jarring was not good for it.

*

Next day Tanaka led his three ninjas through the mountain forest below the snow-line in search of the meteorite. It was fall, all the more lovely for its brevity. The men walked silently, and their fierce dogs were quiet too; they had reverence for both the living and the dead. They had known much of each, for the ninjas of Japan had been among the most effective agents of the medieval world. Ninjas had excelled as spies and assassins, but the technological age had reduced the need for their services. These days a lone rifleman in a tall building could kill a President in a crowd, and never even stand trial. Who had need of the lifelong training and specialization of a ninja? The fine art of assassination had come upon hard times. There were too many do-it-yourselfers in the business.

Yet Fu Antos lived, and with him his diminishing cadre. The world had forgotten the ninjas, and the ninjas had shut out the world. Now that contact was in danger of being renewed, owing to the intercession of an alien presence.

Tanaka's party found the meteorite on the far side of the mountain range. It was a strange one, not round but bullet-shaped, with a charred but basically smooth outline. One end of it terminated in a half-melted tangle of metals. The explosion had destroyed what must have been a large segment. Congealed drops of alloy were spattered across the landscape like tektites, and lingering heat still emanated from the remaining mass. The earth and rock of the mountain had been gouged by both the impact and the explosion, making a double crater.

They explored the fringes and discovered large, strange, hooflike depressions that marked a kind of trail, as though a huge boar had passed. But there were no pigs in this region; the ninjas had hunted them out long ago, not from any aversion to the species but to ensure that this prey attracted no civilized hunting parties that might discover the Black Castle. In any event, there were no pigs on Earth with hoofs exactly like these. They seemed to be in pairs, not fours, as if this pig were traveling upright: an obvious impossibility.

The prints pointed away from the meteorite cavities, and led downhill into the deepest forest. A peculiar aroma was associated with them, that made the dogs whine and growl nervously, and where the trail crossed over rock there were droplets of some kind of oil.

In a forest glade they found it: like a standing pig with a porcine snout and cloven hoof and formidable tusks, about seven feet tall and six hundred pounds heavy. Any notion that this was an ordinary boar was dispelled by the manifest intelligence of the face. The snout was mobile despite the tusks, and the round eyes possessed uncanny comprehension. The creature wore a bright, tight suit over much of its torso, emblazoned with a design like that of the Japanese flag, but with a bigger sun. The rest of the beast was covered by hair, with very thick, stiff bristles, obviously good protection.

It made an inquiring grunt and stepped forward, its nose questing. Its manner was not aggressive; rather, it seemed curious about the men, and unafraid, mirroring the ninjas' own attitude. But the half-wild dogs laid back their ears, growled nervously, and then in the fury of desperate fear, charged.

A metallic tube appeared in the creature's hand-hoof. A thin beam speared from it to touch the lead dog. The animal gave a yelp of surprise and pain and dropped, a disk-shaped spot smoking on its forehead. Twice more the beam flashed, and the two other dogs died. Then the death tube swung to cover the ninjas.

Tanaka's unerringly thrown *shuriken*, or small metal star, flashed quicker than thought, knocking the tube from the thing's grip. The pig-man squealed with frustration and dropped to all fours, reaching for it. But the four ninjas were already loosing their arrows. They had been trained to act without taking time to plan, when the need arose.

The first shaft struck the creature on the flank, but only pricked it despite being well-sent. The second clung momentarily to its shoulder before dropping. The hide was like leather armor, almost invulnerable to light weapons, and the clothing seemed to be missile-proof. The third arrow winged toward an eye, but the head ducked down and it bounced harmlessly off the impervious skull.

Now the ninjas charged, closing the gap before the beast could recover the laser tube. Two went to the right side, one to the left, and one came head-on with a *bisento*, a spear-like halberd. The weapon struck first, but the monster hunched its head down and took the thrust on the shoulder. The creature seemed to have uncanny anticipation of ninja moves, nullifying their attacks even as they started.

Then the head thrust forward and up. The left tusk drove into the ninja's belly, snagged on his backbone, and swept him off his feet. The mighty neck muscles hurled him into the branches of a tree at the edge of the glade, where he hung, broken and dripping.

Now Tanaka, on the left, delivered such a powerful thrust to the pig-man's gut that the point penetrated the softer armor of the underside. With a roar of pain the thing's head swung about, jaws gaping. The teeth closed on Tanaka's right arm and crunched together irresistibly. The head twitched back—and Tanaka's arm was ripped off. The ninja, his pain blocked off by shock, merely stared in astonishment before collapsing.

Meanwhile, one of the remaining ninjas was attacking with a *kusari-gama,* a chain with a sickle on one end and an iron ball on the other. He swing the sickle at the beast, but somehow the pig-man avoided it and the chain wound around Tanaka's just-severed arm instead. The beast then hauled the ninja in on his chain and used the bloody arm to smash in the man's head.

The last ninja was working with a *yoketsu shagi* double-bladed knife, one blade straight, the other curved. He plunged it into the exposed neck, but there was only gristle and muscle, and the neck was so thick that not much damage was done. The beast scooped up a fallen spear between its teeth, actually employing its head in preference to its hand-hoof, and shoved it through the ninja's chest. Then its sharp rear hoofs finished off the fallen Tanaka.

"I begin to comprehend," Hiroshi said. "The beast-man—he was an alien creature from another planet circling another star. From—he paused to read the moving fingers carefully. "From Betelgeuse, the red giant, six hundred and fifty light years from here. He crashed, but he was suspended in a special bath of oil with an oxygen mask, an impact-chamber. So he survived, and to cover his traces he blew up the remains of the ship. Which suggests that he was a criminal among his kind, a fugitive from justice. And now he is among us."

But that was not all. The ninjas had covered up the site of the crash because it was too close to the Black Castle. Hiroshi was not in complete sympathy with the ninjas' single-minded determination to protect the secret of their stronghold, but he honored their ways, and so was trusted by them.

But now the Beast posed a real problem. It was from an advanced interstellar culture and possessed some sophisticated technological devices. It craved power, so it was setting out to establish an empire here on Earth before its irreplaceable devices wore out or malfunctioned beyond the point of repair. It was no scientist or craftsman; it could not duplicate what it had saved from the ship. So it had to use all its resources now to achieve its ambition.

This was the cause of the current crime wave. The Beast had succeeded in making contact with a *Yakuza* gang, and had quickly made it a far more formidable organization, and used it to control the others of that ilk. It had either eliminated or absorbed all the moneymaking rackets in rival hands, and would soon be a political force to be reckoned with. In fact, the day was not far off when it would take over the government itself.

"This must not be," Hiroshi murmured. "The Beast of Betelgeuse must be nullified."

Fu Antos' hoary head nodded almost imperceptibly. He did not care about the world, but he respected Hiroshi's humanitarian concerns. Hiroshi was one of his few liaisons with civilization, and one year Hiroshi would facilitate events that would enable the ninja lord to free himself of this hulk of a body. Also, the Beast had killed four of his ninjas and three good dogs, and that required an accounting. He signaled again with his fingers. "Take Mario and those ninjas you require. Bring the body to me. Do not let the authorities know what has happened." Because, to Fu Antos, privacy was more important than the welfare of the world. If news of the Beast, alive or dead, got out, it might complicate the ninja's secrecy.

"Surely it is not necessary to kill the Beast," Hiroshi protested. "It must possess secrets of immense value to the world."

Fu Antos dismissed that with a disdainful crook of one little finger. "It is criminal—and telepathic."

Then Hiroshi realized what he was up against. But the job had to be done. "I will deal with it—my way."

Fu Antos responded with the mere shrug of one withered knuckle.

*

Mario and the three ninjas closed in on the lair of the Beast of Betelgeuse. This was a condominium in a quality residential district of Tokyo. Criminals occupied every apartment, but they behaved with such law-abiding decorum that they were a credit to the neighborhood. It was amazing how little difference there was between them and legitimate businessmen.

Then there were sophisticated electronic devices protecting the building, for it is often the criminal mind that most fears crime. Not merely the best equipment that the technology of Japan could produce—which of course was the best in the world—but also clever little robots constructed from plans the Beast had salvaged—perhaps stolen—from its home system. They could lock onto the life emanations of a given person, track him down relentlessly, and destroy him with a laser beam to a vital area. the ninjas' misgiving about the decline of the fine art of assassination were misplaced, at least in this instance; the little robots were quality killers. They were also good guards, incorruptible—and once the gang gained control of a major electronics company, those machines would be mass-produced. Then the Beast would be invulnerable. But at the moment there were only three of them.

This was where Mario Garcia came in. He was a tall albino lad with whitish blond hair, thin and nervous, a half-crazed Cuban exile and self-styled "Slan" who had tried to destroy the United Nations. He was also telekenetic—a freakish psi talent. He could fix on metal objects with his mind and move them about. Because he had used his talent wildly, and tried to hurt people, he had been taken in charge by Fu Antos, the only man who could control him. It would not be safe to expose him to the temptations of the world long, as his mind was not yet completely pacified, but this mission required his unique skill.

Mario's mind spread out to infiltrate the locks and alarms and booby traps of the building and nullify them. All had vital components of metal, so all were vulnerable. The little robots were largely metal too. They were more of a challenge, being of alien conception, but still subject to his domination. One, two, three, they went dead. The young man nodded to his companions.

Now the ninjas infiltrated. Disdaining the usual entrance, they employed their metal tigers-claws to scale the walls; they pried open high windows with special tools. Silently they entered. An internal sentry spotted one; the ninja silenced him with a strangling cord and tied him up, unconscious. He did not kill, for Hiroshi had forbidden it, and the ninjas obeyed him implicitly despite his absence. This was the problem about working with a humanitarian; he imposed unrealistic restrictions and reduced the pleasure, not to mention the effectiveness, of the mission. A few little killings would have done so much for morale.

The ninjas obeyed, but in Mario's mind was barely-suppressed contempt for the little Aikidoist. He knew Hiroshi could fight, for the man had originally subdued him and brought him captive to the dank dull Black Castle. But he also knew that Hiroshi's vaunted power of *ki*, that mysterious inner force that some martial artists possessed, had only barely prevailed over Mario's own telekinesis. Had the little ascetic not had Fu Antos to back him up—in fact, Mario had learned enough during his bondage to overcome Hiroshi's *ki*. But he couldn't make his break while Fu Antos lived, for Fu had *ki* like the faith to move mountains, and toughness of mind to match. Fortunately the Lord of the Ninjas was very old; he could not survive much longer. Even that awesome *ki* could not maintain life in a body rotting out from under it. Not indefinitely.

So for now Mario would do the jobs that the ninja master assigned him, like the elimination of the pig-man. It should be no problem, with the ninjas to do the physical chores, and Mario to control the metals.

But the raiding party had reckoned without the telepathy of the Beast. Deep in the heart of the building the alien was well aware of the raid. It dispatched thugs to engage the ninjas and to close in on Mario. This would take a little time, for now nothing mechanical or electronic was operative, including the elevators and intercom system, and the ninjas were expert fighters, and he wanted Mario alive. Mario could be very useful to the Beast! There would be no problem obtaining Mario's cooperation, after the ninjas were out of the way, because the Beast could offer Mario exactly what he wanted: power and freedom. Victory was sure, for neither Mario nor the ninjas knew what they were up against. Their thoughts were open books.

Alone, the Beast waited, monitoring the progress of both thugs and raiders. This was a challenge, because its telepathy was short-range; it faded rapidly beyond a few feet, and was diluted by multiple foci. As a man has difficulty distinguishing anything when several people talk at once, so it had to work to make sense out of any single mind in the jumble. But the Beast was of a telepathic species, long adapted to this type of problem; it enjoyed the challenge in much the same fashion Mario enjoyed the challenge of disabling alien machinery. It skipped from mind to mind as a man tunes a radio when looking for a weather forecast, catching tantalizing snatches here and there, pausing occasionally, then moving on during commercials.

Then the Beast became aware of something strange and alarming. There was a dead spot nearby, a presence that was alive but did not seem to think. Close, too close. In fact *it was in this room.*

The Beast cast about, using its physical senses that it had necessarily tuned out to avoid interference with the telepathy. So it saw and smelled the mental ghost: a small, whiskery old man

"How do you do?" Hiroshi inquired politely in Japanese, making one of his little bows.

Amazed, the Beast reacted involuntarily. It charged the intruder. But the little man moved with remarkable alacrity, avoiding the ripping tusk.

The Beast, no fool, desisted at the physical level and concentrated on the mental. Normally it scored accurately with its weapons because it was aware of the intentions of its opponents. In this manner it had killed four ninjas in the forest while still shaken from the crash-landing. The ninjas had reacted almost without thinking, so that they had been able to wound it, but ultimately they had had to plan their attacks, and that had been their undoing. Now—

The Beast paused, dismayed. *This man had no mind!*

"It is the *ki*, and my Zen mind training," Hiroshi explained helpfully. "I can not duplicate your talent, but I can nullify its application to me. You can not read my mind."

The Beast tired. To it, a person without a mind was like an animal without a smell: baffling. But Hiroshi's *ki* surrounded him, making him opaque to the creature's mind-probe. This was why he had been able to sneak in here, under cover of the distraction created by Mario and the ninjas, who did not know Hiroshi had preceded them. Without that feedback, the guidance of the prey's own mind, the alien was in effect blinded. It emitted a frustrated blast of emotion as red and hot as its native star, Betelgeuse, two hundred and fifty times as large as Earth's sun and three thousand times as luminous.

"Ah, so you can broadcast too," Hiroshi remarked. "You are very talented. Why do you abuse your powers?"

THINK YOU CAN BALK ME?! the savage thought came through, piercing Hiroshi's aura of *ki* and entering his mind like a spear through froth. Yet thought alone could not hurt the tough little man, and that same froth so fuzzed his own emissions of thought that they were meaningless to the Beast. *I KILL!*

But it was an empty threat. On the purely physical level, without mind contact, the Beast was a clumsy monster, while the man was a finely trained combat specialist. The martial art of Aikido was recognized the world over as one of the most effective modes of self defense known. Policemen used it to control criminals, and even experts in karate, judo, and kung fu respected it. Hiroshi was the leading figure in Aikido. Old and feeble as he seemed, he could not be touched by the Beast—as long as he was on guard.

Of course, if the Beast kept him occupied long enough, the thugs would have time to eliminate the ninjas—probably at great loss, for ninjas were deadly in close quarters, like weaponed ghosts—or get to Mario. When the machines resumed functioning, Hiroshi would be caught in this trap. Then—!

"It would be better to talk," Hiroshi said mildly, seeming to be unaware of the plots fulminating in the Beast's brain. His *ki* did not interfere with his spoken voice, so the Beast could understand him well enough. "You could do so much good in this world, if you would. But you associate with criminals."

Sorry the Beast projected contritely. It could not speak physically, as its snout and palate were not formed for this. *I thought you were an assassin, come to kill me. I must protect myself.*

"I may be your assassin," Hiroshi agreed. "But not if I can find a better way. My purpose is to save my world from disaster, for there remains much good in it. If I can persuade you to use your powers to facilitate that good instead of for your personal power, then we shall have no quarrel."

Something like a sneer rippled through the Beast's brain. A do-gooder! It had dealt with this kind before, in its home-system. Too bad the home authorities had caught on.

Now the Beast projected its sad story. It was, it explained in regretful mental tones, a refugee from a distant planet, no criminal but a victim of circumstance. It had publicly criticized the criminal government of its planet, and had had to flee that region of space to avoid execution. The civilization of Betelgeuse was a marvelous thing, with miracles of science, art, and philosophy, but the wrong element had somehow managed to get into power. Much as, it pointed out obliquely, had happened not so long ago in the

Earthly nation of Germany, precipitating global war, and even more recently in America, and might conceivably happen in a more civilized nation such as Japan itself some day. So the Beast—no beast, but an important person, like a noble, had fled. But its ship had malfunctioned six hundred light years out, and it had barely made it a scant fifty more light years to a habitable planet. It survived the crash, but when it tried to make contact with the nearby ninjas, they had attacked it. So it had had to fight.

Hiroshi frowned. "True. You did not initiate hostilities. The dogs could not be restrained."

So the Beast/Noble had avoided that type of savage and trusted no one. Instead it had made contact with people it need have no compunction about controlling: Japan's criminal element. The Beast had made these criminals into good citizens. If it could rehabilitate hardened thugs, think what it could do for ordinary citizens!

"Yet you are forming an empire based on crime," Hiroshi pointed out gently.

Only to start, the Noble Beast explained. When it had taken over all the criminals and made them honest, productive citizens, it would proceed to the politicians and financiers and industrial barons and make *them* honest. Then there would be good government and good economics and the world would become a better place for everyone.

"This is intriguing," Hiroshi admitted. "Yet I must mistrust any person or thing who seeks such absolute power for itself, however excellent the objective. Power tends to corrupt."

Not for myself, the Beast projected with strong emanations of sincerity. This fool was taking the bait! Mario's thought had been correct: Hiroshi was not really so much. He was an altruist, therefore gullible. There were no mind readers on this planet to spill the Betelgeuse beans. *I will install the best possible man in the world as Emperor, to rule wisely and well. It will be an iridium age.*

Hiroshi shook his head, half convinced. "No man could do it, especially not as your puppet."

No man but one, the Beast projected, stepping closer. *The one I have chosen is—you.*

"Me!" Hiroshi exclaimed. "I am no—"

You are genuinely incorruptible, no figurehead. You care about the world. You must be Emperor. The Beast nudged up another foot. Its left tusk was now very near Hiroshi's head. The powerful neck muscles tensed.

And Hiroshi flicked one finger at a spot on the Beast's forehead. It was a hard strike, for the finger was braced by *ki* and years of training to be like an iron bar. The Beast fell, numbed. Hiroshi had scored on its one vulnerability, that spot where the juncture of the two sutures of the skull bones conducted even the lightest shock to the sensitive brain.

What gave me away? it projected weakly.

"Your assumption about the basic corruptibility of man," Hiroshi replied sadly. "You thought every man had his price, and you tried to bribe me with the promise of power. This betrayed the ultimate nature of your thinking. No fire will temper bad metal into a good sword, alas. I am sorry I was unable to persuade you."

So am I the Beast projected. Then a black hole opened up, as of a giant red star collapsing into nothingness, and its life expired.

A great tree has fallen in the forest, Hiroshi thought sadly. *What sound might it have made, had it stood?*

KIAI!—HOW IT BEGAN

Piers put his arm around Roberto's neck and slowly applied pressure. Roberto's breathing became harsh and his eyes bulged as the blood was cut off. It was the *hadaka jime*, or naked strangle. Then Roberto applied a crushing *ude gatame* armlock, a submission hold that can readily dislocate an elbow, making Piers yelp with pain . . .

It all started almost five years ago with an irate post card.

Things often get violent in science fiction fandom, where professionals and amateurs spar in a perpetual free-for-all. Novelist Piers Anthony had skirmishes with several fanzines, which are small-circulation amateur magazines published for personal satisfaction. One of these printed a letter by a critical reader, Roberto Fuentes: "Piers Anthony is not my favorite author . . ."

Fighting words! But Piers, adept in his fashion at the principle of *ju*, or yielding to gain an advantage, sent Roberto a card: "Are you Spanish? I used to live in Spain . . ."

No, Roberto was Cuban. And soon the two collaborated on a science fiction novel, *Dead Morn*, centered around the 1962 Cuban Missile Crisis. It was a major work, that should have made both authors famous.

That was in 1970—and the novel remains on the market. Perhaps its 115,000 word length scares off publishers. Or the graphic sex and violence. Or the authentic detail exposing the manner Fidel Castro came to power. Or the new thinking in time travel. One publisher has taken a year considering the manuscript, and has not yet made a report. The editor says he is still reading it. Another publisher was interested—but then fired 200 employees and returned the novel. Publishing, actually, can be considered as a form of martial art; writers have to be tough.

In 1971 Roberto brought his wife Graciela and seven year old son Robertico to visit Piers in Florida. Piers lives in an old Spanish-style house with his wife Cam and daughters Penny and Cheryl. Roberto took Piers to see a judo class in Tampa. Roberto was 2 Dan, a second degree black belt in judo; Piers had never seen judo in action. The instructor was Ed Maley, 5 Dan.

Piers sat and watched—and started writing a story, "Kiai!" It featured a 5 Dan judo instructor who looked a bit like Ed Maley, but was called Caesar Kane: Kane as in Kano, the founder of judo. Roberto provided the judo action for the story, and the team was launched in a new field: martial arts fiction.

"Kiai!" never sold. The world was not ready for competent martial arts fiction. Undaunted, we built it into a novel, *Kiai!*, incorporating a notion that intrigued us both: competition between different martial arts, to discover once and for all which was best. Naturally judo came out on top—but we feel this is more than empty vanity, for judo incorporates the strikes of karate and armlocks of aikido, making it the broadest barehand martial art in the world. We believe that judo should win such a tournament.

Half a dozen publishers rejected the novel. Oh, it was well enough done—but they said there was no reader interest in martial arts. Who cared about judo or karate—and who had even heard of kung fu or Thai kick—boxing? Forget it!

Then *Kung Fu* appeared on TV, a well-done martial art series, and suddenly publishers were scrambling for martial art. *Kiai!* was snapped up, and other publishers put their hack stables to work turning out kung fu imitations. Our hero's name had to be changed to Jason Striker; after all, who would believe we had "Kane" before

Kung Fu had "Caine"? But a typical editorial foulup allowed a couple of references to Kane to slip through to confuse readers.

Roberto started as the judoka, Piers the author. But this collaboration changed the lives of both. Roberto is becoming an author, doing reviews and articles for JUDO TIMES and collaborating with magazine editor Steranko on an *atemi* article and martial arts poster. Piers has taken up judo, making his yellow belt and having his first competition match at age 40. It was against a 14 year old boy, another yellow belt, and yes, Piers lost: *waza ari*, a half point decision.

Who can say that the time will not come when Roberto is an individual novelist and Piers a black belt? We all have to start somewhere. At any rate, it was in this fashion that the two came to the friendly practice described in our opening scene. Roberto was showing Piers how to apply strangles and armlocks, and also what they felt like. That knowledge would in due course be translated into a scene in another book.

We are not unduly modest. We'll stack our collaborative fiction up against anything else in the genre. In fact, much of the competition does not seem to be written with much literary or martial authority. You can't simply read a book on kung fu or karate, go to a few practice sessions, and be an instant black belt! We are prepared to defend that statement against the challenge of any rival authors either on the judo mat or in the literary arena. Roberto is the former black belt champion of Cuba, who retired undefeated. He was for many years a teacher of judo with his own dojo, and is the present Metropolitan Master champion. He recently made 3 Dan, third degree black belt or San Dan, as a competitor. Piers, a former English teacher, has sold 16 science fiction and fantasy novels, several of which have been in contention for best-of-year awards. His major novel *Macroscope* will have its sixth printing in 1975.

Our four collaborative martial arts novels, *Kiai!*, *Mistress of Death*, *The Bamboo Bloodbath* and *Ninja* (the one-word titles are ours; the others are the publishers, so don't blame us) exploit our respective skills. We have also had one fantasy/martial art story published, "Ki," and are working on a factual history of judo. We do a great deal of research, so as to make our work authentic, and try to avoid formula plotting end stereotyped characterization.

But we are limited. Most editors have little notion of the meaning of martial art. To them, it is just a current fad, a way to sell a few more books. We have to compromise with this attitude, or we will not be published. We were turned down by one publisher for not having an oriental hero. So there is some junk in *Kiai!*, and more in the sequels. Still, we feel that some of the other books in the genre are fantastic and unreal. Some are entertaining and decently written; some aren't. But the fact is, even the greatest fighter in the world can not go barehanded against five men armed with guns and come out alive. Even one armed novice is dangerous, and as for machine-guns in the open—frankly our martial artist would be cut to pieces. We do have group fights and gun scenes, but we have tried for some credibility. A couple of our characters *have* gone up against impossible odds—and died in the process. Jason Striker is extremely wary of guns and other weapons, though it makes him seem like a coward at times.

We have incorporated as much genuine martial art as we could. We made our protagonist into a real man in today's world. He's 5 Dan in judo, 3 Dan in karate, with training in kung fu (actually that's a misnomer for the entire complex of Chinese physical exercise; it would make as much sense to talk about a black belt in American PhysEd) and aikido. This is not extreme; there are a number of 5 Dan judokas in America, such as our model Ed Maley, and any one of them could match Jason Striker in competition, if they are not too old. Many martial artists study several systems, and hold black belts in each. In one novel Striker has a friendly match with a lame Cuban judoka, and loses. That judoka, Luis Guardia, is real. So Striker is not superhuman. He fights well, but he gets tired, and he makes mistakes.

Sometimes Striker "runs the line" contesting with every student in the class, one after the other. This can be devilishly difficult, because the instructor has no respite, while every student is fresh and eager to pull an upset victory. This is drawn from experience: Roberto visited the Gulfport, Florida Judo Club and ran the line. One of the eager students he casually threw was Piers. Fortunately Roberto made it through in good form: dead tired but victorious in every match. It *can* be done, even by a man of forty. Other episodes in the series are also drawn from real life, such as accidentally strangling a too-ambitious student into unconsciousness, or getting an arm broken in competition. Roberto's arm never has mended completely.

Striker is also uncertain in love. More than one woman has found him a bit naive, even stuffy. One kicked him in the crotch, putting him in the hospital. He encounters all kinds: white, yellow, black, Indian, slender, voluptuous, mild, murderous. Sometimes it is romance, sometimes combat, or both at once. Yet here too there is reality, for most of the women are drawn from life, as are the love scenes. Roberto had a varied education before settling down to marriage.

Many of the characters, while fictional, are representations of real people. There is an American boxer modeled after Mohammed Ali, who we feel was wronged by the political deprivation of his world boxing title some years back; a karateka like Mas Oyama, and aikidoist like Morihei Uyeshiba. Striker's arch-enemy Kan-Sen in real life is Mockansen, no villain but a Cuban/Chinese master of Kung Fu who instructed Roberto more than twenty years ago, before that mode became popular here. The names of some real people, like Diago, are used with fictional identities. The leading fictional character, Fu Antos, lord of the ninjas, derives from the authors' names: FUenteS and ANThOny.

The locales, too, are authentic. When Striker goes to Havana, the city is described as though by someone who lived there, as Roberto did. He also lived in others we use: Managua, Nicaragua; Miami, Florida; even New York City, in many ways the strangest of all. When Striker is in the jungle or Everglades, one of us has been there before him, and we have supplemented our observations by extensive research. Roberto was a Cuban exile commando in the same Central American jungles that are described in our novels. When there is a bomb, we know how to build it, for Roberto was active in the anti-Castro underground as an urban terrorist and guerrilla, and he did make bombs and set them off.

But more important, we try to put something in our books that is worth having. Judo is more than a system of combat; it is a philosophy, even a way of life. Striker is hardly the perfect judoka; there is blood on his hands, thanks to the demands of the genre. But he believes in the ideals of judo, and tries to practice them, and when he falls short he suffers. In that aspiration and failure we try to show what judo is and should be.

We tackle significant issues. We analyze the drug problem as it applies to martial arts, not as a plotting device (Superman come quick! There's a shipload of heroin docking in Miami!) but to show the harm drugs do, and what contemporary efforts are being made to rehabilitate addicts. No, we *haven't* been hooked on drugs in real life, but we have known those who were. Piers actually walked into a juvenile drug rehabilitation center, telling them frankly why he wanted information: that he was doing a book with an addict character, and that one recommended treatment for his own hyperactive daughter was to put her on speed. So he had both professional and personal motive to learn about drugs. The interview in which they refused to cooperate appears in *The Bamboo Bloodbath*, except that Striker does, after all, get in. We don't think much of outfits that preach love but operate in secrecy. Abuse is too easy, not only of drugs, but of human civil rights.

We tackle racism: our criminal/heroine is a black karateka, raped by white men, with vengeance in her soul yet justice in her motive. While we can't claim to know what it is to be black, one of us has mixed ancestry and both of us are immigrants from foreign countries. One of us was raised in a society remarkably free from prejudice, especially in boy-girl relations; the other resides in the South. It does provide a hint.

We tackle pollution, as our ninja sets out to rid the world of it.

And history, with actual events adapted to our purpose.

In short, under the veneer of physical and emotional violence and sex, we have a serious philosophy of creation. Roberto reads English, Spanish and French, so that he can do more varied research. (Piers knew Spanish as a child, but forgot it.) We have assembled a martial arts library including expensive books and backfiles of rare martial arts magazines, such as the French/English JUDO KODOKAN REVIEW, and we read them.

It hasn't shown up much yet in the series—after all, there are only so many pages to a commercial novel—but both authors are in their separate fashions health nuts. Piers is a vegetarian who uses massive doses of vitamin C to abate colds. It works, though he spends about $100 a year on C. He stays clear of sugar and refined foods, preferring breakfasts of rolled oats with milk, spiked with wheat germ and nutritive yeast, and lunches of raisins, nuts and cheese, plus salads from his own garden. He has cleaned the debris from his neighborhood to make compost for the garden; the neighbors are trained to dump their brush on his lot. Even complete trees. There will soon be a natural foods and cheese connoisseur in the series.

Roberto is a sun worshiper, frustrated by New Jersey climate. He has his poor wife cooking odd stuff like hearts, brains and kidneys all the time. He gives his son Robertico (who also appears in *Ninja*) so much milk to drink (instead of soft drinks, which are taboo) that some say the boy will one day urinate white.

Neither author smokes, both are extremely moderate drinkers, and both go for high-protein, high vitamin and mineral diets. Both believe in exercise, much of which is provided by judo. It is hardly surprising that Jason Striker has similar attitudes.

Despite all this agreement, at times we work at cross purposes. Roberto prefers big, hefty, hourglass-shaped women like the Cuban girl Dulce, while Piers tries to slim them down to more petite dimensions. Generally we compromise by including both types. Sometimes things get fouled up in the course of negotiations, and we find ourselves in print with a Chinese girl with a Japanese name, such as Striker's fiancee Chiyako. Alas, we were paying more attention to the size of her bust than to her locale. We'll have to make a rationale for that error in a later novel.

In our actual writing, we discuss notions first in a general way, then hammer out a plot to carry the elements we want to include. There is always much more than we can use; both of us have fertile imaginations, and the problem is always to cut it down to manageable size. Sometimes we just split the idea into smaller segments; that's how *Ninja* spread into four ninja novels now being written. Generally Roberto dictates the story line; just about the whole of *Mistress of Death* was his notion, except for the moderate bosom of Chiyako, and the detail of what happened to that bosom in a broken-bottle fight.

This preparation is slow by mail, and sometimes dangerous. We once lost two weeks work via the mails. (Fortunately there was a carbon. ALWAYS KEEP A CARBON COPY!) Since we meet every year or so, we enter into hours-long dialogue a bit like judo *randori* or free practice, bouncing ideas off each other, fitting them together, amplifying, integrating characters with action. In a few hours we can thrash out what might take months by letter, In August 1974, sitting on the beach (Roberto edging toward the sun, Piers toward the shade), we worked out four novels and the judo history book—one day apiece. Of course, much remained to be done, but the framework was set, so that we knew where we were going, and were assured that there would be no major snags. Not at our end, anyway; we are never assured that publishers will take a given novel.

Roberto then goes to work on research, summarizing relevant material and mailing it to Florida. Often he sends whole books. Piers then does a first draft in pencil, integrating research notes, outline, and theme in a readable narrative. This is his special skill as a writer; lots of people have ideas and information, but few can translate these into readable prose. When he has a chapter or so, he types it in second draft, with parenthetical remarks set off by brackets. These brackets can be one word or several hundred, and they can trigger off pages of discussion by Roberto. [Hey, I'm stuck for a good illustrative example here. Any ideas?]

"About the example: Do not forget mentioning my commando days in Nicaragua. I lived in Managua for 6 months. Amalita, the girl in the first two novels, was alive and well in Managua, at least up till the earthquake, she and I used to go to her house and—"

[Roberto, I can't put *that* in print; they'd have to censor it out. Anyway, I've already typed past that place in this piece.]

"Well, what about the time I was in jail, Cabanas Fortress in Cuba, *paredon* the death wall, etc.—we could tie that into the Brazilian prison scene we are working on. But we'll have to explain about political prison, so the readers don't think I was a criminal."

And so it goes. When Piers hits a snag, he brackets it for Roberto to sweat and goes on. No doubt these letter/manuscripts will make fascinating reading for scholars at Syracuse University library, where Piers's papers are eventually collected. Perhaps in the twenty—second century A.D., when books are no longer written and the science of writing has become a lost art. This article was done the same way, so represents a capsule case-history of our system.

Roberto goes over the manuscript and remarks on both the brackets and any other points that strike him. The result is a letter of comment about the same length as the manuscript itself. Piers plugs in all these corrections—a slow, tedious job, more like piecing together broken pottery than creating—then types the submission manuscript. After that the changes stop, for the publisher's deadline is upon us and the book must get there immediately.

Unfortunately, some errors slip through. For example, in *Mistress of Death* Roberto typoed "crowd" as "crow." Piers didn't question it; he thought it was a nice touch. Thus we have crows clustering around the shops in Chinatown. May the Chinese Americans forgive us!

The truth is that collaboration is hard work. Each of us puts about as much effort into a book as he would writing the whole thing alone, yet each gets only half the money. And the result is necessarily a compromise between our viewpoints. But we don't argue much, not even about bosoms. It will be a long time, if ever, before Piers can tell a judo black belt how to perform a given technique, and perhaps as long before Roberto educates any English teacher on the nuances of the subjunctive mood. In the vast majority of cases we see eye to eye. And why not? We are both college educated married males with a number of common interests.

Oh yes, we can be set off by outsiders. Once a bully started in on a smaller man in a post office, making ethnic slurs, and Roberto stepped in ready to fight. A version of that episode leads off our fourth novel, *Ninja*. If anyone goes after Piers' little girls, he comes running and ugly. The girls carry a whistle, just in case. But we regard these as natural provocations; we try to get along, and the last thing we want is trouble with each other. So we have none. Which seems to be half the secret of successful collaboration.

But why bother to collaborate at all? Because we have complementary skills, so that together we can produce material that neither could alone. We don't care enough about the money to turn out cheap work. We try to do our best, even when it is straight adventure. We like to think that readers of discretion will recognize and appreciate a superior product, even if many editors don't. In the long run we believe that will pay—but even if it doesn't in terms of money, it will in satisfaction. As this article shows, we stand by what we do.

AUTHORS' NOTE: This article was published in the magazine THE DEADLY HANDS OF KUNG FU, June 1975 issue. In the ensuing quarter century some things changed, dating the piece somewhat. Piers' daughters are no longer children, and the novel *Dead Morn* did find a publisher, for a good price. Piers' 16 novels became 116 and counting. Both authors now live in Florida, Roberto in the Miami area, Piers in the backwoods, actually a tree farm.

WINDBREAKER

ANTH

Chapter 1:

Cry For Help

Jose woke alertly. The clock said 6 a.m., but it was already too late. The door was opening, its warning buzzer expertly shorted out, and a Beretta was trained on him. This was a professional call.

He sat up in bed, drawing the sheet up to cover his bulging naked belly. Jose was a dark, swarthy man with a slight Chinese look. "To what do I owe the pleasure of this visit, Señors?" he inquired.

"Don't play cagey with me, spic," the gunman snapped. Two large, grim men trooped in behind him. "The details—now."

Jose turned on him a gaze of bewildered innocence. He had black eyes in a fat face that enhanced the effect. "Señor, I have no comprehension!"

The man glanced at his gun. It was a .32 automatic with a silencer attached. Then he used it to gesture to one of his companions. That one drew a stiletto and approached Jose. The needle point touched the fat of the belly through the sheet.

Jose sweated. He had an oily skin that made the sweat show up rapidly. He scratched nervously at the pimple on his nose. He smiled ingratiatingly, showing his prominent front gold tooth.

"Not the pot," the gunman said. "We don't have time for the fine points. Make him talk fast."

The knifeman looked disappointed. He made a little gesture with the knife. Jose got the message. He stood up, a dribble of blood emerging from his navel where the point had lodged. The sheet fell away, and he was naked.

The stiletto moved down to the exposed crotch. "First balk, one ball," the gunman said. "Second balk, other ball. After that it will get uncomfortable—but you *will* talk."

Jose knew they were not bluffing. These were professionals, and the man with the knife was a sadist. The eagerness to carve shone in his face. He wanted his victim to balk.

Jose smoothed back his greasy black hair. "Señors, the police are on their way," he said, "The alarm is under the bed. It went off when my weight lifted. If you leave right now—"

The third man bent quickly to check the bed. Neither of the others moved; they watched suspiciously.

"Bastard's right," the man said. "There's a spring-release contact under the front bedleg. Hand cutoff he didn't use. He suckered us."

"I'll take his ears for that!" the knifeman snarled,

But the gunman shook his head, smiling. "We heard you were sharp, spic. I'd have been suspicious if you *hadn't* pulled something like this, You know we can't kill you and run, because we don't have the info out of you yet. And you'd like us to try to haul you out of here, with all your friends watching. We can't move you, dead or alive." He looked out the window, sighting down the alley. "And there's the police now, coming in quiet. One blocking off the back exit. Very neat." He paused momentarily. "But I think we'll bluff it out, this time." He nodded to the knifeman.

The knifeman straightened, reversed his blade, and expertly sapped Jose above the ear. Jose pitched forward, his face crashing into the floor, and lay still.

Then, rapidly, the men tied and gagged him. They did a competent job of both, putting tape over the gag so that he was barely able to breathe; his wrists and feet were tied together, with a cord stretching up into a noose around his neck. If he tried to kick, the motion would tighten the loop and strangle him.

As the heavy footfalls of the police came down the hall, they propped Jose in the solid clothes closet, the hanging suits further muffling him. There would be no sound from him.

Sergeant O'Brien entered. The three hoods were comfortable, drinking Jose's rum over a hand of poker. Two sat in chairs, the third on the bed. The radio played a jangly tune, a little too loud.

"What's the story?" O'Brien demanded, It was an impressive opening, for he was a solid six-two with a red face, and spoke with the authority of twenty years on the force.

All three looked up, startled, "You can't break in here!" the leader exclaimed righteous indignation. "This is a private apartment!"

"Where's Juan Jose?" O'Brien snapped,

"He stepped out to fetch some girls," the gunman said. "About ten minutes ago. He'll be back soon. This is his place, you know."

"I know. We got the alarm signal and I answered it personally. What did do with him?"

"Do? Us? Officer, we're his friends, just in for a game of cards and some fun." The man bounced on the bed. "He promised me a real Chicano girl, know what I mean? I can hardly sit still."

Sergeant O'Brien looked at him, realizing that such bouncing could have triggered the alarm, especially if Jose were not there to neutralize it. Was this a false alarm?

For a moment the policeman stood perplexed. He didn't have time to waste waiting around, and he didn't want to make a scene for nothing. The alarm *had* gone off, but Jose *did* have many odd friends, some distinctly thug-like. The chances were that this was legitimate.

He turned—and heard a faint cry. "Help!"

Immediately his gun was in his hand, cautioning the three men to silence and immobility. They were professionals in their business—but so was he. No one moved. The outside policeman came in to help while O'Brien walked around the apartment, listening, He turned off the loud radio.

Again it came, more distinct this time. "He-e-lp!" The voice was raspingly hoarse, and ended in a staccato croak, but the word was plain.

The gunman went for his gun. It was a mistake. The officer's bullet caught him in the shoulder.

O'Brien yanked open the closet door. There was Jose's posterior under the suits. In a moment they had him out.

The sergeant got to work on the bonds, cutting the choke-rope and freeing the hands and feet. Then he removed the tight gag and tape. Jose was purple from slow suffocation, and there was blood on his lip where the edge of the gag had sawed in. He gasped for air, then rubbed the circulation back into his hands and feet. "Thanks, Mick!" he grunted. "I was on the verge of suffering discomfort."

"You were on the verge of ending all suffering," O'Brien said. "You should have better taste in friends."

"Amigo, I shall heed your advice. Tomorrow."

The three hoods stared. "He was still tied and gagged," the knifeman said, "He *couldn't* have called!"

"Sure he couldn't!" O'Brien agreed heartily. "Good thing I imagined I was hearing a cry for help."

"But I heard it too!" the third thug said, "But how could he have—?"

"All right, you three. March!" the policeman said. But there was a brief delay while he saw to the bullet wound in the shoulder.

O'Brien drooped the banter and looked at Jose with concern. "You okay now, Juan?"

"Fine—now," Jose said.

"Why were they after you? Or can you tell me that?"

Jose shook his head. "Amigo, I do not know. If I had anticipated company, I would surely have been better prepared." He gestured apologetically at his nakedness. "I was merely reposing between assignments."

"God, the spic even lies to his friends!" the wounded gunman said.

Jose looked at him. "Not at all, senor. I do not lie to my friends—or my enemies. I did not lie to you. I do not know what you wanted of me—but now I shall do my best to find out."

"Hey, none of that here!" O'Brien cautioned. "They're in police custody now, and one's wounded."

Jose smiled. "Certainly, amigo. I meant only that I shall investigate. If this man and I should meet again, after he is free on bail, perhaps then I shall question him a trifle more firmly."

The gunman sneered. "Fat chance, fat boy!"

"The name is Juan Jose." Jose pronounced it the Spanish way, 'Wan Hosay,' "Kindly remember it, for I shall remember you."

"Hah! Flabby coward like you—"

But the policeman was already herding them out.

"How *did* he call for help?" the third hood echoed plaintively as they left.

Chapter *2:*

Assignment

Juan Jose rubbed his head where the butt of the knife had struck. He had not been knocked out, but it had seemed best to play dead. Amateurs could be tricked and overpowered, but he would have been shot if he had tried anything fancy on these operators.

Well, perhaps not if he had moved quickly enough and neutralized the gun first. But that would have been a calculated risk that did not appeal. A man did not survive in this business long if he took unnecessary risks—especially when the solution to this particular problem had been so easy. One little cry for help!

Still, the blow had hurt, and the bonds had not been comfortable Those men had really known how to tie a man so he stayed.

He went to the bathroom and mopped his face in cold water. His fingers brushed over the wart on his cheek. It was smaller than it had been a couple of weeks before; he would have to work on it.

He looked at his body in the full-length bathroom mirror. Bad, bad—he was getting too lean and muscular. He would have to do something about that, too. Another half inch of blubber on his belly, some fat under the jaw—if he cocked his head back he could still make a nice double chin, but it didn't look quite natural.

Jose sighed. There was no way around it: he would have to go on a diet. Minimum of five thousand calories a day, mostly in sweets and pastries, until he regained his proper rotundity.

Meanwhile he had dirt on his ass. He stepped into the shower and rinsed it off in lukewarm water. Then he hefted himself on the bar over the stall, doing pull-ups one-handed: six with the right, six with the left. Sure enough, it was too easy; the solid muscle was sheathed by only a thin layer of fat.

He shook himself dry like a dog, feeling his entire gut swing back and forth with the motion. Then he stepped on the scale.

Two hundred and thirty pounds. He shook his head sadly. This was sloppy as hell! At this rate his feet would hardly stay flat.

He dressed. His undershirt had five gold buttons, and he left his topshirt halfway open so that those precious buttons would show. He put an identification bracelet on his wrist, briefly polishing the $5,000 diamond set into it. Two enormous rings graced his fingers. He was now a well-dressed Latin American.

He slicked his hair back until it was a glistening black mass, made sure the welt over his ear didn't show, and stepped out of the apartment. A block away there was a small Mexican-American family restaurant that was excellent for weight-gaining. It was time for breakfast.

Jose settled himself in a corner table with his back to the wall and commenced his diet. His appetizer was a quart of sweet orange juice. Then he had a double order of ham and bacon with toast, with six eggs on the side. He washed these down liberally from a jug of *cafe-con-leche*, a mixture of coffee and milk in 50-50 proportions. He then consumed a one-pound long loaf of Cuban bread with plenty of butter by forming it into sandwiches with round creamy yellow cheese and dunking these into the *cafe-con-leche* for every bite.

After the initial edge of his hunger had been blunted, he signaled the waiter, "Señor—the telephone, if you please." The waiter smiled and brought the phone on a long extension cord. This was a fairly regular ritual.

First, a business call. He dialed the local police station. "Señor Sergeant O'Brien, if you please, señorita," he said to their switchboard operator.

"Right, Mr. Jose," she said, recognizing his voice.

In a moment Sergeant O'Brien was on the line, "Thought I'd be hearing from you, Juan. How's your digestion?"

"The sound of your voice sweetens it considerably, señor." Then Jose got down to business. "Is there any information from my visitors of the morning? I am wondering why they called on me so imperatively . . ."

"Juan, they've all got records a mile long," O'Brien said. "But that's not what you mean, is it? You'll be glad to know that they haven't spilled a word about your mission. Won't say who hired 'em or why. But they must have been well paid."

"Señor, I *have* no mission!" Jose protested.

There was a trace of annoyance in the officer's voice. "Juan, you don't have to tell *me* anything! I know you get private international assignments, and I'm not prying. I'm just reporting on what these hoods—"

Jose raised his free hand and waved a *chorizo*, a thick Spanish sausage, expressively before stuffing it into his mouth. "Señor, you misunderstand! You are my friend! You save my life every day of the week and twice on Sundays! I do not lie to you, I do not accuse you. I have no mission!"

There was a pause. "Sure, Juan, that's true," 0'Brien said at last. "Sorry I was edgy. We'll try to get something more for you, but it looks as if they *think* you have a mission. Or their boss thinks so. Unless it's some old enemy—"

"These did not come for revenge, señor. They came for information. Which I sadly lack. It is a mystery,"

"Well, you're good at mysteries, Juan!" He disconnected.

Jose pondered for a full minute while he masticated his sausage. It *was* a mystery. Finally he shrugged and dialed a long distance number, assigning the charge to his home phone. "St. Thomas Military Academy," a secretary answered.

"Robertico, please, Señora," he said.

"Right away, Mr. Jose!"

In a moment Robertico was speaking. "Hi, Papi! Can I come home this weekend?"

"Hijo, I think not," Jose said regretfully. "A matter of business seems to have intruded itself,"

"Aw, Papi, I'll help you fight the thugs! I'm doing real good in judo class, I could—"

"Judo is not always enough," Jose said seriously.

"Well, sure, you could pulverize my teacher with your vis—vis—"

"Visceral control," Jose said. "I probably could—but do not forget I also know and respect the martial arts, judo among them. There is much for you to learn."

"But I could learn much better from you, Papi!"

"It is more than that, Robertico. I may be away for a few days, and it is not good for a young boy to be alone."

"Papi, I'm nine years old! I can take care of myself!"

"Flesh of my flesh, *you* know that and *I* know that. But the child welfare authorities, *they* don't know that! That is why I have to leave you in that hole of a school—"

"Why don't you get married again, Dad? So I'd have—"

"'Dad'? What is this word?"

The boy ignored the interruption. "So I'd have a mother, and I could stay at home all the time—" There was a tremor in the young voice. Robertico really wanted a home.

"This is no life for a woman, Son. She would—"

"'Son'? What is this word?"

Jose smiled privately. Robertico Jose was becoming a real infighter! "She would soon grow bitchy and jealous."

"No she wouldn't! I could pick you a real good-looking wench, sort of stupid, who—"

"Hijo!" Jose snapped. But his grinning face belied his voice.

ANTH

"It is not right for any woman, even a stupid one, not to know where her man is, what trouble he is in. And you—you need a mama, not a wench! A woman who can cook and make beds and sing songs and sew and teach you manners."

"Yuck!" Robertico exclaimed. "I'm better off at school!"

"I will visit you soon," Jose said, smiling again. "Take it easy on the poor teachers, hellion. They are only trying to earn a living."

"Adios, Papi," the boy said sadly.

Jose had spoken to his son sensibly, with many a Latin gesture and smile. Now he was sober, and there was a shine in his eyes that was not joy. He *did* want his boy with him—but marriage was too complex. What would have happened this morning, had those thugs found a woman in his apartment? Or his son? Jose himself would not have told the hoods anything even if he had known what they wanted. But if they tortured his only child—

He shook his head. If only he *could* be a sensible family man, with regular hours and secure income. But he had tried that once, ten years ago, and now what did he have to show for it?

He had Robertico. That made it all worthwhile. But he did not care to go that route a second time. No more marriages, no more serious involvement.

He had one more call, to his answering service. "Yes, señor," the girl said. "One just came in. I think it's an assignment. Call 555-5837 and use the code name 'Windbreaker.'"

"Thank you, señora." Jose put down the receiver and let out a bellow of laughter that startled the other diners.

The waiter rushed up. "Are you well, sir?"

"Very well, despite your abominable *chorizo*," Jose chuckled. "Bring me another link. One more call, señor–then I shall return your poor tired telephone." The waiter left, perplexed.

Jose dialed the number the answering service had given him. "Windbreaker," he said.

"Who?"

"Windbreaker. Warm sport jacket. Strong man who leads the

way into the storm. Hedge or wall to break the—"

"Enough, Jose!" the gruff male voice said. There was no other introduction, no formality, and no questions, "You're our man. Five thousand dollars plus expenses. You'll receive advance payment and instructions by registered mail, Agreed?"

"No."

Now there was a pause. "Seven-five, then,"

"Negative. It is not the money, señor. I do not work for an anonymous employer. Or one who lacks proper confidence."

"We have confidence! We know you're the best in the business. Our type of business."

"Yet you tested me," Jose said flatly.

"No, Windbreaker. There was a leak."

"I do not work for leaky people. It is bad for my health."

"Not exactly a leak. We let slip to a certain party that we had hired the most capable international agent available. We did not identify him. In this manner we verified a suspicion, and located the best man. The leak has been fixed—permanently—and we now propose to hire the man. You. If our competition calls you the best, that's good enough for us. And we rather like your style."

"Señor, my style stinks."

"Yes indeed!"

"Still, I must know you."

"Very well. Fifteen minutes from now, alone." The man reeled off an address. "You have eidetic memory, don't you? See that you are not followed."

Jose was not partial to either the man's attitude or his assumptions. As though any professional would allow himself to be followed! "Señor, I am not finished with my breakfast. You come here to the La Campana restaurant, and we shall talk."

"Listen, I'm paying you a lot of money."

"Señor, wad that money into a roll one inch in diameter and insert it in your—"

"All right! I'll meet you there. This time."

"And be prompt," Jose said. "See that you are not followed."

There was a stifled sound before the connection broke, Jose smiled broadly. Presumption deserved what it received.

Still, he rather thought he would take the job. His prospective employer had a devious and ruthless mind, and a certain arrogant honesty. Jose liked that. He understood that type of mind.

The code—name had been the signal, of course. It was the man's way of telling him that he knew about the contretemps of the morning, and how Jose had summoned help. Hence the man knew something of visceral learning.

Few people realized that the so-called involuntary reflexes and systems of the body could become voluntary—with proper training. Fewer still could actually practice such control. Hardly any were adept at it. Juan Jose was one of these fewest.

It had been an elementary matter to disrupt his own digestive processes so that gas formed. Then it was merely a matter of ejecting it with sufficient force to create a noisy vibration, while bringing certain muscles into play to shape the sound. The result: a crude cry for help.

The resultant code name: Windbreaker.

But this was not an ability Jose normally chose to advertise. It was not merely that many people found the notion objectionable, but that it was one of a complex of unusual abilities whose main virtue was surprise. Had the hoods known he could make that cry, they would have made sure he was all the way unconscious.

Fortunately, they *hadn't* known, and O'Brien hadn't told them. It seemed that his prospective employer had had the discretion to keep his mouth shut on that matter, also.

Juan Jose finished his meal, burped contentedly, and waited for the man to arrive.

SUMMARY OF REMAINDER:

Juan Jose's employer turns out to be an American gangster who once operated a nightclub, hotel and casino in Havana. He had four partners with whom he theoretically split the proceeds evenly—but he cheated on them so that he actually amassed a considerable fortune. There were no real taxes in Cuba, and he had been adept at "skimming." Thus he amassed about five million dollars "retirement money" in thousand dollar bills and diamonds, buried in small watertight metal containers under a tree in his garden.

But Castro came to power so suddenly that he was caught short—and probably a suspicious partner betrayed him. He was arrested, his apartment searched, and his worldly goods confiscated: about half a million dollars worth of loot was taken over by the state. They then deported him without realizing that they had missed the main portion. But he had no chance to recover the riches himself.

Now about fifteen years have passed, and things have cooled off. The gangster has succeeded in eliminating his erstwhile partners, but his type of business has not been as good in America as it was in Cuba, and he needs that lost money. He can not trust any criminal hirelings to recover it for him, and they would betray him for it without qualm. He dares not show his own face in Cuba, of course. So he is making a legitimate offer to Jose, who is known to be scrupulously fair to friends and enemies alike (though not to people who fit neither of these categories).

Jose is to go into Cuba, dig up the hidden treasure, and bring it back. Perhaps a week's work, with all expenses paid, plus a fee of $7,500. Juan turns it down contemptuously; he has more enemies than friends in Cuba, and the government there does not like him, and the fee offered is a pittance. He bargains for half the loot, and settles for twenty percent: one million dollars. He doesn't need to trust the gangster; he will merely turn over all the money in excess of his million. With that money, Jose can retire and take proper care of his child.

The mission, despite the gangster's description, is more than a week's work. It is possible to get into Cuba, but it can be fatally difficult to get out again, especially with five million dollars. Jose must arrange it so that no one suspects his mission. He obtains false papers and goes to Mexico, where he joins a guerrilla group. This is no picnic; he must prove himself to the tough and suspicious guerrillas by participating in a raid on a railroad station. He does, but other guerrillas get drunk and kill a number of people. They end up seizing the whole town and looting it, withdrawing only when government troops come. Jose, not yet fully trusted, is left to escape on his own. He does so by hiding in a refrigerator truck. He is able to lower his body temperature to survive the freezing interior.

The guerrillas then follow Jose's subtle suggestion and hijack an airplane going to Mexico City, and take it to Havana. True revolutionaries still are welcomed in Cuba. But they are not taken on faith; they must prove themselves. This group is given a fair choice: work in the cane fields, or undertake more training for revolutionary activity in other countries. So they "volunteer" for the training. Jose uses his visceral control to pass a lie detector test. Actually, this training is exactly what he wants, because the training camp is near Havana, and Havana is where the gangster's cache is buried.

They are taught how to use special C-3 grenades. One explodes prematurely and the instructor's head is blown off. The entire party is badly wounded. Jose gets shrapnel his arms; his right hand is wounded, and an artery in the left is cut. He can't apply a tourniquet, so controls the rain and bleeding through his unique talents and walks five miles to the militia post to get help. Then he lets the blood flow and collapses—in the arms of a beautiful Cuban girl—so that the authorities will not suspect his powers.

He is hospitalized in Havana, and touted as something of a hero, because the help he summoned saved the lives of several injured men. He cultivates the association of the girl, Perla, who seems happy to be cultivated. Jose can be quite charming when he puts his mind to it, and his sexual talents are remarkable because of his visceral control. Perla thinks he likes her mind; the others are sure it is her body he likes. The truth is that she lives in the woman's dormitory that has been set up on the former estate of the gangster, and to which he needs unobtrusive entry.

Actually, Perla does have a mind, and talents of her own. The government has researched Jose's background and discovered his real identity and abilities; the girl has been assigned to learn the nature of his current mission. Jose, adept at reading body language, suspects that she is a counterspy, but goes along with her for several reasons. First, her mission means she can be very helpful to him, because they can't find out what he is up to unless he is granted some leeway; second, he is not out to assassinate Fidel, so is innocent of their prime concern; third, he believes he can subvert her to his side if he has to.

Perla catches him as he digs up the treasure. Now he has to deal with her. It would be awkward to kill her, and he has a strong aversion to that anyway. So he tells her the truth and offers to take her out of the country with him if she will join him. She agrees. Of course this may be part of her job as a counter-agent, but it gives him a chance to get moving efficiently.

Unfortunately these negotiations take too long, and the other girls of the dormitory discover them. Now there are no subtleties; the two have to fight their way out and flee to the jungle. Castro's troops pursue with much shooting. The two hide in the swamp. Jose alone could have gotten away easily, but Perla's presence makes it a narrow thing. They manage to board a patrol boat, naked and dripping. They get rid of the occupants and take the boat to sea, eluding further pursuit—only to run into a storm.

They take refuge at Cay Sal, a small island in the Bahamas near Cuba that Cuba claims. The Cubans follow and there is a battle between the gunboats, while the British, who have the authority but not the will to break it up, look the other way. Jose's boat, undermanned, is no match; it begins to sink. He jumps off and swims with the money underwater. Such is his control, he is able to stay underwater some ten minutes, avoiding discovery. But once he is clear he reconsiders, drops the money in the deeps and goes back to rescue Perla.

They escape—but the mission is now a failure. Jose reports this to the gangster employer, who is furious; he does not believe the money is really lost, and thinks he has been double-crossed. So he kidnaps Jose's son Robertico, supposing this will make Jose yield the fortune.

Jose has to raid the gangster's estate, which is well guarded by sophisticated protective devices: vibration-sensitive attachments to doors and windows, anti-intruder screens, pressure-sensitive wires under carpeting, and electric-eye booby-traps. It requires all of Jose's ingenuity to get through, and some help from Perla and Robertico himself. He finally does prevail, though the gangster gets killed in the process.

Now Jose has to sweat out the most difficult problem of all: that of Perla, who naturally expects him to marry her. He is determined not to remarry, especially not without money. But even Robertico is against him on this issue. So Jose is in trouble again, and as the novel ends his sweating is unfeigned.

[This is the first novel of a projected series of adventures featuring the Windbreaker. Others will concern diamond mines in Brazil, Amazonian Indian slave exploitation, and voodoo and blood selling in Haiti.]

AUTHORS' NOTE: Remember, a quarter century has passed since this piece was crafted. Today the corded phones have been replaced by cell phones. Real numbers have also been replaced by 555 numbers, so we did update that. This project found no favor with publishers; perhaps they didn't like the notion that a leading character could break wind.

SORCEX

Sone is the bastard son of Togo, a veteran Samurai warrior. In June, 1281, the two are practicing Kendo, with Sone employing his fine sword against his father's staff. The old man fends off the attack easily, his long wooden pole blocking every thrust of the sword. "Are you a weakling? Strike harder! Harder! " he cries. Sone, an extremely powerful young man, aims a devastating blow at Togo's head, knowing that the sheer force of it will rock the man back and impress him. But the staff, though reinforced with iron, snaps in two, and the blade cleaves Togo's brain, killing him instantly.

Togo's legitimate son Kato charges in and spies the disaster. He has little love for Sone, but it is plain that the killing was unintentional. Thus they argue, not about Sone's guilt, but about the diabolical cause of the accident. Kato claims that some magician has put a spell on Togo's weapons, so that they betrayed their master; Sone concludes that *all* weapons are innately perverse and not to be trusted.

Both youths make oaths on the spot: Kato swears he will not settle down to his father's estate until he has avenged Togo's murder, while Sone swears never again to use a weapon. Kato demands that Sone join the vengeance quest, but Sone refuses, saying there is no one to wreak vengeance on. Kato is furious: "Not only are you a bastard, you are too cowardly to avenge your own father, even when your own arm was ensorcelled for murder," he shouts. "Traitor! Get out of this house!" And Kato draws his own sword, forgetting all Samurai ethics and caution, and charges upon Sone with the blade uplifted. Sone, unarmed, defends himself by employing what in later centuries will be described as a judo shoulder throw, *ippon seoi nage*, and unfortunately snaps his brother's arm.

After this second disaster there is nothing for Sone to do except depart his sire's estate forever. "'When I recover, I will seek you out and kill you!" Kato screams, and Sone, shamed, can not even reply. He moves into a hut some distance away and sets about farming turnips, choosing the lowliest of occupations to expiate his grief and disgrace. But he is so strong that he accomplishes much in a short time, and his turnips sprout in days as if magically fertilized.

Soon a beautiful girl approaches him, saying she is Miho, traveling from a distant land, who needs a place to rest for a few days before going on. This is suspicious, as she could obviously find much superior lodging; but Sone, mindful that his unknown mother might have been just such a visitor to his father's house twenty years ago, shares his hut. Miho shortly seduces him: no difficult task, as he is as lusty as he is muscular, and she has remarkable expertise. He obligingly marries her thereafter.

Next day she goes into the village and buys a baby boy, whom she intends to adopt as their son. Sone is dismayed at the speed and nature of his progression into marriage and paternity, but she explains that it is all right: the baby is cursed with an incurable disease and will soon die. It occurs to Sone that fate is generously assisting him in his effort to expiate his shame through misery, so he shuts up and makes the best of it.

Fate is indeed generous. Sone returns from a hard day's labor in the field to discover the bloody carcass of his new son. Miho is incoherent and can tell him nothing—but huge tiger tracks lead away from the corpse. Sone sees his duty and sets off after the animal. He carries only his pitchfork that he had been using to farm, together with a resin torch and fire case so that he can travel by night. The region is mountainous and the tracks head toward the chill (even in summer) upper reaches, so he wears a thick cotton jacket with leather underpadding: sturdy and warm.

The trail is a strange one: terror, horror and grief remain where the creature has passed, but reports of its nature are inconsistent. Some call it a tiger, others a mad ape, still others a terrible snake. And the tracks vary accordingly. Sone suspects it is a demon creature, that can change its form. He can certainly do the world a favor by eliminating it.

He finally runs it down and brings it to bay, and his suspicion is confirmed: it is a creature of hell. It assumes the form of a dragon and charges him. Instantly Sone fires his torch and jams the brightly flaring end into one of the dragon's eyes. Then be stabs it in the underbelly—its only vulnerable place—with the pitchfork. It changes into a tiger, breaking off the tines of the fork in the process. Sone fends it off somewhat using the handle, then gets on its back and applies a neck lock. The creature then changes madly into a variety of awful shapes, but Sone will not let go, and finally its struggles weaken and he breaks its neck, killing it.

Another man would be joyful at his success, but Sone is grim. He has used torch and pitchfork as weapons; never again will he take up these things, for his oath forbids it. He must find his way home in darkness, and use some other tool for farming. And because his arms and hands were used to choke the creature, they too are weapons to that extent: be will not choke anything again.

He makes it home, but alas, his lovely wife is gone, and in her place is a grossly ugly hag. She is able to tell him only that she is his wife, but placed under a spell; she will not regain her natural beauty until he has seduced a hundred beautiful women, each of whom has to know he is married and each of whom must undertake this humiliation because of envy of that wife. An impossible mission: who in Japan would envy such a wife, and who would yield her virtue to a married man who could not take any new wives?

Sone has been misfortunate, but he is not stupid. He now realizes that magic *is* involved, that has cost him his son and his wife's beauty. So maybe magic *did* kill his father, and Kato was right all along. In which case Sone must try to apologize to his brother, and seek out the guilty magician. The same sorcerer could have put a spell on his wife's tongue, so that she could not tell all she knew.

Sone is slow to anger, but now he is angry, and even considering his vow against the use of weapons he is a formidable antagonist. If there is a magician behind all this trouble, that magician is very likely to be sorry, once located. Sone seeks his brother, but Kato has by now mended enough to start his own quest for vengeance, and though each brother is looking for the other, they miss each other.

Sone heads for the Emperor's palace, hoping the court magician can give him some clues. The Regent of Japan at this time is Hojo Tokimune, and his magician is so powerful he was able to repulse the Mongol invasion of 1274 by summoning the demon Typhun to the aid of the Japanese. A good place to start.

The journey to the capital is an eventful one, as Sone encounters a number of demons, aggressive warriors, and beautiful women, dealing with each as seems expedient. Sone doesn't much like magic, and avoids it when he can; but hostile magic can be difficult to nullify. And each time a warrior attacks him, Sone has to become more ingenious, defending him self with some tool or article never before used as a weapon. In this way a number of the unusual weapons of the later martial arts are invented. And Sone tells each girl that there is none in all the world quite like his wife, and a number of those girls rise to the challenge with excitingly novel techniques of seduction. Thus the so-called Hercules position of love, and others. One samurai warrior even gets a notion, and Sone is hard put to it to dissuade the man from his unfortunate amours. And at one point Kato shows up, and immediately goes after Sone with his sword, refusing to listen to any explanations. Sone is unable to clarify the matter, and gets away only by seeming like a coward.

Finally Sone wins through to Regent Hojo's court, but the court magician is too busy to investigate his problem. The Mongols are making ready to attack again, already sailing for Japan with a huge armada and 165,000 warriors—and Kublai Khan's magician has somehow chained the demon Typhun so that he cannot save Japan this time. It will take a phenomenal effort of sorcery to loose the demon in time, and of course the Mongol magician is constantly making countermoves to prevent that. "Talk with Oichi," the magician snaps, dismissing Sone.

Oichi turns out to be the daughter of one of the Emperor's wives. In the course of having his way with her—a perilous procedure, because of the alert palace guards—Sone learns that she is acquainted with much palace gossip. Her mother's closest friend, another wife of the Emperor, once told a strange story of how she had gone to visit her home-kingdom in Mongolia, for she was a princess in her own right. She had been attacked by thieves, her retinue slain, and she had barely escaped herself. But local villagers would not help her, because she was Mongol and did not speak their language. The nearby Samurai spotted her, half dead, and carried her to his estate where she received help. But there was a price on that help, and she had neither the power nor the inclination to decline, as her host was a most impressive man. She remained to bear his child, then had to hurry back to the Emperor's palace with a made-up story of her marvelous visit home. If Hojo had ever learned the truth, he would have slaughtered that bold Samurai warrior, and the princess, and the bastard baby, and all the household and maybe the nearby village too, bringing fire and shame upon the entire region. So the secret had to be kept—but before she died in a mysterious knife accident the princess confessed all to her friend. That was only a few weeks ago, and Oichi had overheard it, and now told Sone because he very much resembles that dead princess.

Sone is not slow to grasp the import; that princess was surely his mother, and now he knows his own lineage. And she died at the same time and in a similar manner to Togo—as if the same magician had struck. This is a strong hint where he should search next. So he gets off Oichi and proceeds to Mongolia, having more adventures on the way. He is in a hurry now that the trail is hot, so enlists the aid of some mermen who haul him rapidly across the sea. But he yields to the temptation to add a mermaid to his wife-redeeming tally, and the situation gets ugly. He is lucky to win through to the mainland with no more than some wounds and some waterlogging.

When he reaches the Mongol kingdom—a land vassal to Kublai Khan—he learns that this minor court had an extremely powerful magician who served Kublai in war. This magician had a strikingly beautiful and talented daughter—but both vanished not long ago. They may have gone to the old Mongol capital of Karakorum to aid in some top-secret magic related to the war effort against Japan . . .

Sone conjectures that that magician, Mifune, had been so busy serving Kublai Khan over the years, contributing to the Khan's enormous success, that only recently had he thought to check into the princess' situation and learned through his arts of her adultery. Outraged, Mifune must have set out to kill all the guilty parties. Naturally he would have kept the matter quiet, so as not to bring shame upon his kingdom and perhaps incur the wrath of Kublal Khan. That would explain the deaths of Toga and the princess.

But why hadn't Mifune killed Sone too? Because the magician's specialty was enchanting weapons—and Sone had forsworn the use of weapons! Still, Mifune could have sent a demon to do the mischief for him. Sone realizes that this is what happened; the hell-tiger had come and killed his son, before Sone searched it out and killed it in turn.

So it all fits—yet mysteries remain. Where did Miho come from, and why was she transformed? Why the hundred-seduction mandate? That was hardly doing the job of getting Sone killed! It was necessary to run down Mifune and get the truth from him—before killing him to avenge Togo and the princess. Maybe he could make Mifune explain Miho's transformation, or even undo it, if he was more powerful than whoever had done that to her.

There is no problem about traveling across China and Mongolia; the Mongols have so pacified the entire continent that there is no violence or robbery apart from that practiced by the conquerors themselves. Unfortunately, the Mongols do protect their women, especially against handsome wandering Japanese! Soon Sone is in trouble again, and the Mongol pursuit is grim indeed. Nevertheless Sone wins through to Karakorum—only to discover that Mifune has removed to Kublai's summer capital of Xanadu (actually Shangtuho). Sone finally does locate Mifune in one of the special palace retreats the Khan has set up, and finds the magician quite ready to talk to him. Thus the full explanation:

When Mifune spotted that long—ago shame of the princess, he did indeed set out to rectify the matter privately. But he was very busy chaining the demon Typhun and countering the Japanese magician's efforts to free that demon, so could only spare a limited amount of energy for this private project. When Sone's no-weapons oath saved him, Mifune sent the hell-tiger. But Mifune's daughter Miho, a distressingly self-willed girl, learned what he was doing and decided it was unfair to punish the innocent child of the illicit union. (Sone—innocent? They both have a laugh over that.) So she flew to Japan to warn him, beating the demon by several days. But Mifune in turn discovered what she was up to, and laid a spell on her so that she couldn't betray any of his secrets to any outside party. Thus she couldn't warn Sone that the tiger was coming for his blood, that it had to taste before being freed. But Miho found Sone such an attractive specimen that she refused to give him up, so got him to marry her.

That was significant, for it made Sone Mifune's son-in-law. Mifune, honorable to a fault (by his own admission), could not murder his own relatives. So he was forced to tell his erring daughter how to balk the demon: by providing it with the blood of

Sone's blood line, or his son. A technicality the demon was too stupid to fathom, so it was satisfied.

But then Sone had gone after the demon himself. That didn't bother Mifune unduly; if Sone got himself killed on his own initiative, well and good! The problem was solved. Then Sone killed the demon, and the problem was unsolved. Mifune, still preoccupied with the ticklish Typhun situation, decided that he could not accomplish anything useful in regard to Sone before breaking up that marriage. To force a divorce from Miho, so as to get Sone *un*related and therefore killable, Mifune transformed her and set the terms of alleviation. If Sone didn't balk at her ugliness, Miho would balk at his infidelity. A beautiful plan—except that it didn't work.

Sone, knowing the facts, can now kill Mifune. But there is a hitch: he, too, is honorable in his fashion, and he can't kill a relative either. He realizes he is balked, and must leave his father unavenged. But then half-brother Kato catches up, and Sone manages between dodges of the sword to explain some of the situation to him. Kato eagerly heads off to slay the magician. Both die in the ensuing struggle. This takes place on August 15, 1281. The moment Mifune dies, the storm demon Typhun is released, and Typhun proceeds to destroy the Mongol fleet, saving Japan after all. Thus Sone, through no special intent of his own, is his country's benefactor.

Miho, too, is freed of the enchantment, though Sone has not yet (quite) completed the roster of 100 women. She is prepared to be tolerant about her father's demise, since she will inherit his wealth and power, and transports herself to Xanadu to reassure Sone. About to embrace her, Sone, who is not after all so smart about certain things, confessed that the spell on her wasn't really so bad. He rather enjoyed working it off with all those lovely girls, and is a bit sorry he didn't get to go the full hundred.

Miho blacks both his eyes and bites a chunk out of his ear before he gets her down and wrestles her into a turbulent lovemaking. It is a very satisfying reunion.

AUTHORS' NOTE—Novels can be marketed on the basis of a straight summary, as this one was. To bad it didn't sell.

BIOGRAPHY OF A TERRORIST

(Chapter 2, "Three Misses," appeared as an article in the magazine THE DEADLY HANDS OP KUNG FU, May 1976.)

AUTHORS' NOTE: This presentation was written in 1976, so is dated by a quarter century. But though the details have changed in 25 years, the essence hasn't.

INTRODUCTION

There is a rising tide of terrorism around the world. We see it in Europe, Africa, Latin America, Asia—everywhere. The Irish violence has made headlines for years, and so have the Arab-Israeli exchanges between outright wars. There is the Basque separatist movement in Spain, and the "Death Squads" are practically an institution in Brazil. U.S. NEWS & WORLD REPORT estimates that 1,000 people have been killed in the world by acts of terrorism in the past ten years. Terrorism is big business.

America is safer than most parts of the world, but it is hardly immune. From 1975 terrorism has been ravaging southern Florida, with rape, killing and destruction of property proceeding with seeming impunity. Recently a train carrying deadly chlorine and propane was derailed by sabotage. The Patty Hearst case was an example of another kind of terrorism, and so were the airline hijackings. Our political history was changed when President Kennedy was assassinated by a lone terrorist (though there may have been a Cuban connection there), and changed again when President Nixon engaged in the more subtle terrorism eventually exposed by the Watergate investigation.

In fact, there are so many examples that individual cases are hardly news. Terrorism is endemic. It costs us far more than lives and property. It gnaws at one of the basic freedoms we believe in:

freedom from fear. The terrorist is not out for money or sexual gratification or notoriety; his interest is in frightening the average man into giving the terrorist power.

Why isn't it stopped? It isn't that no one cares. It isn't that the police don't try. Terrorism is an insidiously difficult thing to control. Any person can take a gun and shoot at the symbol of his ire. He can take gasoline and a soft-drink bottle and fashion a devastating bomb. Or he can simply make a telephone call to the police, tipping them off about the massive bomb supposedly hidden in a major airport, and chuckle in the comfort of his home while havoc ensues. He has done almost as much damage to the system as a real bomber could have, without real cost or risk to himself.

Terrorism: it takes many forms. Its practitioners range from do-it-yourselfers to complete professionals. No one is safe from it. The only way to begin to alleviate its menace is to understand it. Blindly oppressive measures will not do the job. What motivates a terrorist? How does he operate? Who helps him? What would deter him?

Only one type of person knows the answers. That person is the terrorist himself. He is not necessarily a criminal, or even a violent man; he may be a fun-loving family man with a strong moral code and an unshakable belief in the rightness of his cause. In fact, he may *be* right, by the verdict of history, and the regime he opposes may be wrong. The selfish or casual destroyer is a criminal; the dedicated destroyer is a different and superior type, far more dangerous because of the resources, intelligence, and motivation he brings to his craft. A criminal is basically an amateur; a terrorist is basically a professional. He has committed his life to his cause. Idealism, not mere money, causes him to act.

The successful terrorist of today may be the respected statesman of tomorrow. The Irgun terrorists who fought the British rulers of Palestine entered the government of the new state when the British departed; their last chief of operations became a member of the Israeli cabinet. The Arab PLA terrorists who oppose Israel are now treated with honor by the UN. Former terrorists now govern the nation of Cuba. Oh, yes—the rewards of victory are great!

But these are long shots. For the average terrorist, the practical outlook is bleak. He knows he is likely to wind up in prison, or dead. Why does he choose to subject himself to the roulette that this profession is?

Here is the story of a genuine terrorist. Roberto Fuentes, former terrorist, has worked with Piers Anthony, writer, on five successful novels of martial arts and several shorter pieces. The vast reservoir of experience on which Mr. Fuentes drew for the realistic detail of those books came from his other life—a life that entailed privation, fear, torture, imprisonment, nightmare, execution and sex for the former judo champion of Cuba.

His story illustrates another facet of the trade. The terrorist may be an intellectual, at first reluctant to act despite the wrongs he sees about him. His conviction that he is right and that *someone* has to act draws him into a life he never anticipated or wanted. He comes to the difficult conclusion that there is no recourse remaining except violence; the orderly process of justice has broken down. And so, with mixed emotions, he does act, hating the necessity.

Then, once he has tasted the water of violence, he becomes addicted to it. He develops a perverse fascination for this life outside the law, the sheer challenge of it. He is like nice Dr. Jekyll turning into evil Mr. Hyde, trying to swear off but always doing it again because of the fundamental human need he has tapped. His original ends are distorted as he indulges in greater violence for smaller reason. Sometimes, even, *the means become the end.*

He is now committed to the sheer excitement of the forbidden life, the elite camaraderie he discovers there. His cause may be lost—but he continues, finding another cause, unable to give up this very special existence. The life he had before, as a staid law-abiding citizen, has entirely lost its flavor. Innocent Dr. Jekyll has been absorbed by the stronger personality he unwittingly loosed.

Actually, this is just a theory about one type of terrorist. There are many motivations. The people involved are a highly mixed bag. Many of them hardly comprehend their own drives. But Roberto Fuentes fits this description. He is a member of MENSA. the high IQ society, and he cares about human rights while also loving the decadent good life. A study of his descent into terrorism should provide an insight into the complex nature of this beast.

This biography has been fictionalized to a certain extent, necessarily. Names have been changed to protect the identities of friends who might still be subject to reprisals. The details of certain events have been modified similarly; in some cases the accurate details would void any pretense of anonymity for the participants. Some material remains confidential for military reasons. The United States government has on occasion sued persons who reveal certain types of information too specifically. Therefore this biography must be considered about 25% fiction, with a number of deliberately planted errors. But the essence, and particularly the spirit, are correct. This is the only way it can be done; as will be evident, terrorism is not a gentle employment. Many of Mr. Fuentes' friends are dead, and more are dying violently as time passes; he does not wish to add himself to that total. He is already under sentence of death by the Castro government of Cuba, for one of the exploits covered in this book.

To deal with an enemy, one must first know him. The essence of terrorism is similar wherever it occurs. Though the origins and original incentives of terrorists are diverse, once they are committed they are brothers under the skin. Roberto Fuentes was a Cuban terrorist, but he operated in much the same fashion as a Communist or fascist or splinter-group terrorist would in the United States. In fact, he was trained in the U.S.A. A bullet or a bomb knows no language but its own; it will do its job wherever it is directed.

Roberto Fuentes' progress into terrorism began with idealism. The background political situation is documented in some detail here, to show that it was no casual whim that moved him into such a life.

On January 1, 1959, Fidel Castro came to power in Cuba.

The seven year dictatorship of Fulgencia Batista had collapsed abruptly, and the revolutionists were victorious. It was a time of great expectations. At last the people of Cuba had thrown off oppression and taken the reins of government into their own hands, much as the people of America had done in 1776. There would be a new age of democracy and individual liberty in the island nation; Fidel had promised! The bearded charismatic leader stood for everything that was decent in government, and the people believed in him passionately.

The Constitution of 1940, a model for good government, was going to be restored, and its precepts fully applied for the first time. No more political prisoners, no more unjust confinements. The death penalty was to be abolished. There would be justice for all. The wealth of the nation would be shared among the people. There would be a full and just Agrarian Reform, in which the idle land would be turned over to the working peasants. There would be complete personal freedom. Everyone would get a good education. There would be free elections within six months, just as soon as Fidel got things organized.

The Constitution? Once he was in power, Castro decided Cuba didn't need it after all.

Political prisoners? Their heyday came in Castro's regime, with hundreds of thousands of people locked away in old fortresses.

Executions? Well, first there were a few necessary trials of war criminals—that is, those who had opposed Fidel by force of arms. These trials were very efficient, and there was no foolishness about the verdicts; they quickly justified the execution of the defendants. Sometimes the sentence of death was posted even before the trial was complete. In fact it became a blood bath, with people dying in virtual assembly-line precision—more than three thousand within six months as the result of trials. Somehow these "temporary" executions stretched out over the years, and never did stop. For a number of offenses, such as "crimes against the security of the state," which was a marvelous catch-all, the death penalty became mandatory.

But this was only the formal aspect. Informally it was worse. As early as January 3, 1959, two days after Castro's victory, eighty members of the Batista armed forces together with a number of civilians were simply machine-gunned to death in Sto. de Cuba.

Justice for all? Castro had promised the armed forces of the prior administration that only those guilty of war crimes would be punished. Otherwise these troops might not have surrendered, and the war would not have been over. But consider the case of the 43 airmen. Most Batista airmen escaped the country—easy enough to do, since they had the planes—and so the few on trial included transport pilots and mechanics who had not seen actual combat. The prosecutor could not find evidence against then, since they had committed no war crimes, so they were acquitted.

Acquitted? Fidel was outraged. He denounced the verdict in an inflammatory television broadcast, and had them tried again. This time the judges got the message; 29 airmen were given prison terms of twenty years or more, and twelve received lesser sentences. The presiding judge of the first trial, the one who had blundered so badly as to find the men all innocent merely because there was no evidence, was found dead; the authorities said it was suicide. Perhaps it was.

Another case was that of Major Sosa Blanco, accused of the crimes of another man, Mero Sosa. There was no proof; time and again the government's case against him was shown to be fallacious. Finally they had to stop televising the proceedings because the whole thing was "a Roman circus," making the government look ludicrous. But the case was not thrown out; it had gone too far for that. So the Major was convicted and sentenced in decent privacy.

Sharing the wealth? True, assets were taken away from the rich, and the poor applauded. But somehow that wealth did not filter down to the poor people, and a precedent was set that in the end was ruinous. First the possessions of the remaining Batista supporters were confiscated. Very well, that's called the spoils of war, and it is customary around the world. It had not been Cuban policy before, however. Then the very rich were deprived, and the property of foreigners taken, especially Americans. Well, Americans weren't very popular in Latin America anyway; served them right. But after the spoils, and the rich, and the foreigners—who would be next?

Agrarian reform? It became against the law to own more than 3,000 acres of land in Cuba. Then the limits were reduced. In due course all private property—land, business, houses—was taken by the government, and no one could own his own home. With whom, then, was the land and wealth being shared?

Personal freedom? From the outset Castro began to restrict it. He abolished gambling—yet doesn't freedom mean the right to choose for oneself whether to gamble, rather than having the government make the decision? Total press censorship was invoked. It became a crime for any writer to criticize the government, and citizens were sent to jail merely for listening to American radio broadcasts. Political parties were abolished with one notable exception: the Communist party. Unions were taken over, and strikes forbidden. Most Catholic priests were expelled. "Voluntary" membership in militia groups was required, and "voluntary" sugarcane cutting duty, and contributions of salary to the government for special purposes.

As a result, there was a phenomenal exodus from Cuba by anyone able to move—until travel outside the island was prohibited. Doctors, lawyers, University graduates, the rich and middle class exited first; but as repression intensified it became a complete cross section of the population. Fishermen departed in droves, using their boats to cross the channel to Miami, Florida. To date, the number of exiles approaches one million—of a total population of six million at the time of Castro's takeover. In terms of per cent, that is one of the great migrations of modern history. One sixth of a nation, exiled.

Education? First the religious schools were banned, then the private schools. Foreign magazines and newspapers were eliminated. Every child had to attend the government schools where literacy was achieved by studying propaganda texts. But at first the process was subtle. Roberto Fuentes was a law student at the University of Havana in 1959. A small Communist clique tried to take over the University. Two of Fuentes' professors, Tony de Varona and Aureliano Sanches Arango, made comments that they were against Communism. An assembly was called, at which there was an attempt made to drive out these professors. Fuentes and a few others stood to rebut the Communists: "Since when is it a crime to be anti-Communist in Cuba?" he demanded. "If it *is* then you must expel me too, because I am also anti-Communist." The president of the law school, Major Maximo, replied: "Fuentes, it is not a crime." Then many others stood to declare their own anti-Communism, and the expulsion effort failed. But this showed the trend that was developing—and in due course, it did indeed become a crime to be anti-Communist in Cuba.

Free elections? These were "temporarily" postponed, then abolished as unnecessary. In fact, Fidel's government from the start was hardly distinguishable from a dictatorship. He ruled by personal fiat.

Thus it was scarcely surprising that Roberto Fuentes, who had the background and training to appreciate the erosion of ideals and practice that was happening in Cuba, evolved gradually from a moderate skeptic into a confirmed enemy of the government. His father's family properties were confiscated—a manganese mine, tenement houses, and a small hotel in Sto. de Cuba—and his mother's family farm of 1,000 acres. His uncle was jailed. Roberto himself lost his job at the Havana tunnel, and his judo teaching position—for he was the judo champion of Cuba—and was expelled from the University of Havana. Oh, yes, Fuentes had reason to oppose the new order!

But there was no freedom to protest the administration or to vote it out of power. So the idealists who had actually believed in the promises of the Revolution became disillusioned, and some of them gradually hardened into anti-Castro guerrillas.

This is the story told in this book. It could happen to anyone with the courage to stand up for his convictions as he sees his country progressing into an alien philosophy, its traditions and freedoms despoiled stage by stage, while the majority of citizens merely accept it with sheeplike passivity. There are disturbing signs that it could happen in America.

Such resistance is a hard course. Yet there is a certain psychological appeal to terrorism, as Fuentes says: "It is the great Ego booster. You might be a nerd, a failure at everything, but you know you are superior to all those lawyers making $50,000 a year. You can blow up twenty of them with a bomb, or you can change the world like Oswald, Sirhan and so many others. While you are doing it you are no longer a failure, no longer discriminated against, no longer a disappointment. You are the greatest."

The authors hope that this book will help show the way to make the world safe from terrorism. But not *too* safe—so long as oppression remains.

Chapter 1:

Return

We stood on the deck of a small yacht, peering through the night at the forbidden island. I was half-eager, half afraid; I wanted more than anything to destroy the Communist usurpers of my country, but I knew it was just as likely that they would destroy me instead. Already some of my closest friends had been gunned down, and I myself was marked by Fidel Castro's government for death.

It really would have been easier, and a whole lot safer, to stay home. But where was home? In exile in Florida? My heart was in Cuba, so in a very real sense I was coming home.

It was cool in that pre-dawn darkness, but most of the chill was in my mind. Beside me, Tomas and Nilo were impassive, even confident; they did not seem to have any weak-sister doubts. Tomas was to be our guide; I had been assured that he knew every inch of this area, so why should he worry? Nilo, an illiterate peasant, had stolen a gun and joined a guerrilla band the day his father's small farm in Las Villas province had been confiscated for incorporation into a larger "cooperative." If that was the agrarian reform that Castro had promised, Nilo did not want any part of it! When the guerrilla leader, "Black Thorndyke," was surrounded in a cane field by 5,000 militiamen and burned alive, Nilo had led the surviving guerrillas in a daring raid on a government patrol boat and sailed it right into the Miami River with 25 men. He was extremely lucky to have survived at all—yet here he was, once more ready to give his life for his country. Nerve? He had proved he had it!

I tried to keep my face positive, though I knew they could not make out my expression. My heart was racing, not exactly with enthusiasm. Who in his right mind would volunteer for a suicide mission like this? But there would be no backing out now.

I was returning: that was my overriding thought. I had some fear, but as I explored it in my mind, I found it was not entirely for myself, though I knew the danger we faced. About half the missions into Cuba at this time were aborted, because of lights on the coast, the presence of a strange boat, noises or something similar. To my mind, these were flimsy excuses; the real reason was cowardice.

Oh, sure, people get afraid in the presence of danger. That's natural; in fact fear is an essential human emotion. I have been afraid many times. I don't like the sensation, but I don't let it dominate me. So I had vowed to myself that no matter how afraid I might get, I would keep going. If my companions tried to back out, I thought I would pull a gun on them to make them go through with it. Because I was the leader of this mission; it was my responsibility.

Another complication was the fact that I was virtually a newlywed. Just one month before, I had married the redheaded Nurmi. By day I trained in radio operation; by night I—well, it was a very busy time.

Now I was riding high, as if I were drunk or on some drug; I felt like the most *macho* man in the world, the greatest, the bravest. So what if I might be going alone against ten thousand militiamen? Once I passed the test I would be a real man!

We lowered a small fiberglass boat called a "Boston Whaler"

and a rubber raft with a silent outboard motor. Five of us were going in; two would remain with the boat.

Our mission was complex. On one level, it was to train guerrillas and saboteurs on the island. Many people opposed the Communist regime, but few were trained or equipped to act against it effectively. The expertise we brought was vital. Oddly, we were *not* to make contact with existing anti-Castro organizations. We had been warned that they were riddled by Fidel's G-2 Intelligence operatives and could not be trusted.

On another level, our mission was to go in and learn as much as possible about a wild story concerning Russian missiles in Cuba. I was to be alert for railroad tank cars transporting liquid oxygen—"LOX"—which was fuel for large missiles. Of course the Soviets wouldn't dare put offensive missiles in Cuba, so this was a wild shot, probably dreamed up by some CIA man who fell asleep reading science fiction. Nevertheless, I would check it out as well as I could.

And I was supposed to journey on to Havana, and contact some of my old collaborators there, men I could trust, and perhaps bring one of them out secretly for special training.

We got into the rubber raft. My body performed automatically, doing the things it had been conditioned to do. My mind was still riding that high: we were committed, we were on our way at last!

We were heavily laden. Besides the three of us in the raft, there were about 100 pounds of explosives, and two big oil drums containing twenty M-3 machine guns for the guerrillas we were to train. This, after all, was a complete Cuban exile operation for the MRR—Movement for Recovering the Revolution. We felt that Fidel Castro had betrayed the revolution he fomented, and delivered us all into a worse situation than we had before he came. So now we hoped to recover the original purpose. The founders and many members of the MRR had been in Fidel's "26th of July" fight against Batista.

One of these founders was Captain Nino Diaz, who had been

a member of Raul Castro's column, before becoming disenchanted by the ruthless character of Fidel's brother. Another was Jorge Sotus, chief of the uprising against Batista in Sto. de Cuba in 1956, and leader of the first group of reinforcements Fidel received in the Sierra. Another was Sergio Sangenis, an anti-Batista guerrilla in Matanzas province and for a while chief of Fidel's military intelligence. And Manuel Artime, zone chief of INRRA in the Sierra Maestra. And Rogelio Gonzales Corso, once chief of Agriculture under Castro. These men had not intended to make the country a Communist satellite! So now we all worked to reconvert the Revolution into a Christian socialist movement for the benefit of all the people.

We had substantial American help, of course, but no evidence of that was permitted to show. The Americans had their own motives, not necessarily the same as ours. The Bay of Pigs fiasco was still fresh in their memory. But since they also had a hell of a lot of money and equipment and know-how, we weren't in a position to be choosy.

I dipped my hand in the water. It was pleasant, and its blackness made it seem to be immensely deep. Somewhere down below there would be fish, maybe sharks, sleek torpedoes of the sea. But I knew that sharks seldom attacked groups of men. My mind was mainly concerned with larger threats, such as thousands of militiamen waiting on shore to nab us. Better the sharks than that! And, in opposition to that threat, I had a vision of glorious victory: riding into Havana on a white horse, with cheering throngs, beautiful women such as Onelida in her white dress, saved especially for this occasion—of course I was recently married, but I was never much of a monogamist, and I knew some girls in Havana that . . . but right now there was nothing but darkness and water and hope. The real fascination was that these were the waters of home, that I had swum in as a boy, when Cuba was free.

When Cuba was free . . .

A wind came up. "Oh-oh," Nilo said. He was a young man,

short and light but very strong. A killer with nerves of steel. A good partner for a mission like this. "Squall."

He was right. I wish he'd been wrong. The last thing we needed was a storm!

In moments the squall was upon us. These storms are called *Turbonadas* in Cuba, short but violent. Rain pelted down, whipped into our faces by the wind. It was just a little altercation of the weather, nothing serious—to anyone in a closed house on land. Here in an insubstantial rubber raft, overloaded on open water at night, it was like a damned hurricane. The black waves loomed up like traveling mountains, spraying us with their rabid froth, foaming over the sides, soaking us.

Tomas grabbed a bucket. "Bail!" he exclaimed. I joined him, scooping out the water. We couldn't capsize, really, but we sure as hell didn't want to sit in a deepening puddle either. Supposedly everything was waterproof, but you can never be sure. Our weapons might have been damaged, and our maps and code books, and our radio could have corroded.

I was wearing my poncho, but I was cold and miserable as the water sloshed over my ankles and the waves drenched us completely. Suddenly I needed to urinate; the suggestion can become extremely powerful in such a situation. Not that it would have made any difference, wet as my pants were already. I worried about my glasses and my steel calendar watch, necessary to keep track of the date when out of touch with civilization; the proper date was essential to make closely-timed prearranged radio contacts with the U.S.A.

I remembered what a squall had cost me once before. I had been waiting in the Spanish Club in Havana with a BAR—Browning Automatic Rifle—ready to assassinate Fidel Castro as he came to a Chinese Exposition there. But just before Fidel arrived, a squall had struck, and he had returned to the dry Presidential Palace. But for that coincidence, I would now be safe and sound in the city—or snug in a grave. Assassination is a tricky business, even when successful.

So we bailed, while the fury of the tropical storm made our efforts seem futile. At least the exercise warmed us a little. After about fifteen minutes that seemed more like an hour, the squall passed. We had lost some headway, but now resumed forward progress. The Boston Whaler was just ahead. If this were the worst we had to contend with—

Then our motor quit. "*Singao*!" Nilo swore under his breath. He jerked the starter cord, but the thing was dead. The rain had shorted it out. It was a five thousand dollar silent motor, supposedly proof against such malfunction. Yeah, sure! Maybe a little spy mission into the American manufacturing business was in order, to find out who was goofing off in the motor department. We were stalled on the ocean—and dawn was coming. We were running out of time.

We were in the middle of some small keys that separated a kind of bay, with mainland Cuba not far beyond. No help there.

The Boston Whaler realized our problem. It cut back, and Oreja Mocha threw us a tow-rope. That was the purpose in having it along: to make sure we got where we were going despite our dependence on American equipment. I could not pull a gun on a cowardly silent motor to make it perform! So now we were hauled along at reduced speed.

But the delay was too much. It was getting light. Light was our enemy; we would surely be spotted if we tried to go ashore now. "We have to go back," Mario said. He was an old hand, about sixty years old, white haired. He was an intelligent conversationalist, in contrast to Nilo, but he had a yellow streak.

My hand moved toward my special 9mm assassination pistol with the silencer. "No turning back!"

"But the light—"

"We'll hide out for the day in the largest key," I decided. "Tonight we'll go ashore."

That was it. I was the leader, and I had the pistol. We were down to basics. The islet I saw was mostly swamp and mangrove, a good place to hide—except for one thing. It was close to a fishing village.

We had no choice. We pulled in and anchored our two craft amid the huge boles of the mangroves, hidden from view of the mainland. Tomas, our guide, was an old man; we had to trust his experience. He assured us that he had brought fishermen here in the past, and that no one else ever came near.

We had to stay concealed from the air, too; an occasional helicopter patrol could pass. But the overhanging trees seemed sufficient.

Now for the long wait. The sun came up. It would have been nice to bask and get a tan, or at least to play a game of poker. But we had to remain silent and alert. I wished half our number were female; a lot can be done with a woman who has to keep immobile and quiet all day. Instead I leaned against a tree and swatted mosquitoes, snarling inwardly. We hadn't even started our mission, and here we were stalled. I had to watch to see that Mario didn't try to bug out, going back to the yacht.

About mid-morning a boat came by. It contained two fishermen, and it was headed right for our island. We had nothing against fishermen, but if they discovered up it would be disastrous. One report to the authorities would bring Cuban gunboats swarming like flies. Deadly stinging flies!

The boat stopped about 150 feet from where we were hiding and began to fish. If they came no closer, if those men did not see us, all would be well. Otherwise—

Tomas came to me in agitation. "One of the fishermen—he is my nephew!" he whispered.

"Good. He won't give us away," I said.

"Not good! He is a rabid Communist, and the chief of the fishermen's militia!"

Oh-oh. "You know what that means?" I asked him, giving him a hard stare.

He nodded grimly. "He is no relative of mine any more—not since he turned traitor to his people."

A good attitude. Still, I worried. No man likes to contemplate the death of his own blood-kin. Could we trust Tomas now?

The two fishermen kept drifting closer. Apparently the fish were biting better in our direction. Were they Communist fish, trying to betray us? I stood behind a dead tree trunk, nervously fingering my silent M-3 machine gun. How close could they come, without seeing us? If only they would go some other direction!

Suddenly one of the fishermen turned. He gestured urgently to his companion. He had seen something!

They started their motor and headed directly for us. There was no question now; they had spotted one of our boats and were coming to investigate.

I lifted my rifle and aimed, feeling a cold necessity. Was there any alternative? I had experienced Fidel's prisons, and I had lost friends to Paredon, the wall of death. In the hands of the militia, my life would endure only long enough for their torturers to extract the dregs of my information. After me, my friends—those friends who were now waiting in Havana to help me. Some of them were young women—oh, the G-2 would like to learn their identities! Those sadists seemed to get an extra thrill from making a pretty girl scream . . .

My rifle fired. The silencer worked perfectly; there was only the noise of the gun carriage going back and forth. It was as though the weapon had a mind of its own, and I was a bystander. First the Communist nephew fell, then the other. But the rifle wouldn't stop. The entire clip of twenty five bullets emptied into their jerking bodies. Blood spurted and stained the water. There were messy discharges from their bodily orifices. There is nothing pretty about violent death!

It takes a special discipline to kill a human being. I had done it before, so I was hardened somewhat—but the first time brings nightmares for months. Those who like to watch violence on TV, or read about killings in comic books, have little appreciation of the real nature of it. It is not fun to take a man's life! But when it is his life or yours, and you know that from bitter experience, it happens. That's part of what combat is all about.

The other part, for me, was this: now at last the shades of Virgilio and Antonino could rest in peace.

Virgilio: April 13, 1961, the second day of the Bay of Pigs invasion. I was having breakfast in the house of Graciela, an elderly lady who had given me shelter for the night, and I was looking at headlines in the newspaper. Twenty-five counter revolutionaries had been shot in the Cabanas prison, and among them were Virgilio Campaneria and Alberto Tapia Ruano. They were former companions of mine in the resistance movement, and very good friends. I had broken down and cried over that newspaper, and in the grief and fury of impotence I swore to avenge them. Somehow, somewhere, sometime . . .

Antonino: six months later, in my first retraining camp run by the DRE in Key Largo, I heard on the radio how my good friend and fellow student of law, Antonino Diaz Pou, had been shot in Matanzas prison. He had said goodbye to me a year before, leaving for the U.S.A., but had returned to Havana as a radio operator before the invasion. So we were both in Cuba again, but had not met. He had entered the Venezualan embassy for sanctuary, but left when the Movement needed him to maintain radio contact with Miami. He was waiting on a Matanzas beach to be picked up by friends—but was surprised by the enemy, wounded, captured, and given *Paredon*, execution.

By my logic, I had now avenged my friends.

There was no place to bury the bodies on the key, as it was mostly swamp and tree trunks. But we had to dispose of them somehow, for the corpses could give us away as surely as the living men.

Nilo had an idea: "Send the cadavers back with Mario and Oreja. They can tow the fishing boat to the yacht after we land, then have the Cuban Exile radio report that the two fishermen defected and reached Miami safely in their small boat. No one will know the difference."

Excellent notion! So we set it up that way. We were fortunate that Tomas had recognized them, so we could give their full names.

That night we crossed to the mainland without event in the Boston Whaler, leaving the rubber raft cached in the key. Tomas pointed out the designated landing place: a small beach. In the dark it looked just like a mud hole—but that was why we needed a guide.

I got off the boat—and sank into the mud right up to my armpits. "What the hell kind of a beach is this?" I demanded, not in the best of humor.

I could not move. I was burdened with all my equipment, so was quite heavy—but that is one of the problems on such missions. You have to carry everything you're going to need right along with you. I bore a radio set with batteries and hand generator—and this was not a miniature transistor receiver, but a substantial mass of equipment that covered my whole back, about fifty pounds total. I also had a canteen of water, a submachine gun with silencer and spare clips of ammunition, a .45 pistol, knife, five hand grenades, $30,000 in freshly-minted Cuban 20-peso bills, gold coins (good as gold anywhere!), first aid kit, maps, code books, compass, poncho, hunting knife, food rations, vitamins and personal effects. In short, I was so loaded down I could hardly move even in the best terrain. Now that the supposedly firm beach had turned out to be mush, I was really stuck.

"Well, *move*," Nilo whispered in the dark. "We don't have all night."

"*Cono tu madre*," I snapped. No, I won't translate that; it was an expletive calculated to make the ears of even a hardened terrorist burn.

Nilo chuckled. "How lucky we are that Juan is in a good humor tonight—and so sure of foot." Juan was the name I used for this mission. We always used false names, so that we could not be identified if caught, and could not give away our companions. It also protected our families. I know this precaution saved my own skin once, for the police were combing Havana looking for "Juan"—who did not exist.

After Nilo and Tomas had finished with their unfunny humor, they hauled me out of the gunk and back into the boat. I sprawled, a muddy mess from the chest down. They might have muttered something cute about that, but this was a serious mission where any words might be overheard, so we worked mainly in silence. We were too miserable and scared to engage in much light banter anyway.

We floated further along the coast and landed again about a third of a mile beyond the scene of my accident. This time the ground was reasonably firm. The three men of our mission unloaded. Mario was terrified; he had wanted to turn back as soon as we hit the mud, but we wouldn't let him. Now he perked up; he was finally returning to the security of the yacht. There were no farewells; the boat left quickly.

We were on our own. But our problems were only beginning.

We started walking, following our guide. We tramped and tramped. How far did we have to go to make our rendezvous?

We cached the radio in some forest bushes near the coast. That lightened the load somewhat, but we still had trouble. We had to cross a barbed wire fence. Nilo jumped over, then held up the bottom strand for me to squeeze through. I got hung up on a barb, wouldn't you know it, and had a hell of a time getting unstuck. We passed through a freshly plowed field; that was another mess.

Tomas's age began to tell. He had increasing trouble walking, and finally we had to take his pack and half-carry him. Some guide!

Suddenly Tomas fell on his knees, sobbing. "Kill me! Kill me! I lied, I am no guide, no guerrilla—I only came to bring my own family out! We are lost, I don't know where we are! Kill me!"

No wonder we had landed in muck! Such rage boiled up in me that I grabbed for my gun. I actually put it to his forehead and took the safety off. It was *my* life the son of a bitch had finished.

Lost in enemy terrain—how would any of us survive? But Nilo stopped me. "There will be time for that later!"

Some common sense seeped into my volatile temper. What would another killing gain us? More work to bury the body! It was understandable that a man would do anything to get his family out of Cuba, after all. Tomas was no traitor, only a desperate fool. So we let the matter drop, and we plunged ahead, more or less hopelessly.

And for once we lucked out. We stumbled on the only part of the region our fake guide was familiar with—his own farm—so that suddenly we knew where we were. In the process, as we learned later, we had skirted a group of government militiamen on patrol—and we hadn't even known they were there.

I think ninety per cent of the success of such missions as ours is just plain blind luck—and we can't always tell the good luck from the bad. Had my landing in the mud delayed us just the amount needed to make us miss the patrol?

We made our way to a thicket of thorns, a good hideout for the day. These thickets can be massive affairs, impenetrable, that nobody would fool with short of desperation; that was what made this one so good. Nilo and Tomas went to a small farm to contact the owner, who was a friend. I remained in the thicket, guarding our equipment.

I had had a hard night, what with the mud and barbed wire and the weight of the radio and helping Tomas along, and I was tired. I tried to stay alert, but it was so nice being off my feet that soon I found myself nodding. I lay down to sleep. I shouldn't have done that.

Suddenly I heard voices: Nilo and Tomas must be returning, looking for me. It was hard to tell one thorn thicket from another, which was another good thing about this hiding place. I made small clicking sounds that were our recognition code. The group approached—and I saw it was a bunch of militiamen on their rounds.

I froze in terror. Had my confusion brought the enemy down

on my head? But I was in more luck than I deserved. The militiamen had heard the clicking, but they thought it was a cricket. They passed me by.

I had just about used up my quota of good luck. I did not sleep again.

Later my friends arrived, carrying some goat meat and guava paste and fresh soft white cheese and Cuban bread in a bucket. It was a slops pail, so that it looked as if someone were going to feed the hogs—a good camouflage. Everything had to look innocent and natural; our lives depended on it.

So at last we had good food to eat. Maybe guava paste from a slops pail doesn't sound like much, but I'll settle for it any day. Maybe I'm a hog at heart.

We stayed there several days, giving out money and getting information from townspeople we could trust. I recovered my transmitter and sent a message out. It wasn't a bad time, as such things go. I remember walking to the edge of the thicket at night and watching the full moon over the palm trees. By day the heavens were an incredible azure, and the sun beat down on us; by night it was just as pretty.

Of course there were some inconveniences. Natural functions were a problem. Out in the key or in the boat, the entire ocean was one big flush toilet; just poke your posterior over the edge and make your offering to nature, and no backtalk about pollution. But here on solid land it was no picnic. In the dark, amidst the thornbush, with dried mud caking my pants, I could hardly tell what was what. Mosquitoes zeroed in on my exposed anatomy like darts on a bullseye; *they* knew what was what! That forced me to slap on more repellent when I could find it. I had to wipe myself with huge plantain leaves, and let me tell you, toilet paper is much better! I buried my waste the way a cat does, for it was essential that we leave no traces at all.

The routine life of a guerrilla is not exactly James Bond style adventure. In fact, there are times when it hardly seems worth it. Did you ever see James Bond using a plantain leaf?

Than we headed east at night—and stumbled on what we later learned was a Russian missile base. This was just one of those freaks of the trade; we hadn't really expected to find anything like that, despite our orders.

The woods were full of trigger-happy militia. We had blithely walked into a hornets' nest. For this was the secret of the early 1960's: the Soviet emplacement of intermediate-range nuclear-warhead missiles in Cuba. That daring ploy was intended to shift the balance of world power, and of course it was to precipitate a sudden East-West confrontation of greater significance than any other.

I was, I believe, the first American agent to send hard information confirming this fantastic threat. I understand my report was shunted straight up to President Kennedy. Maybe I was the key link in the chain of events that saved the world from nuclear holocaust in 1962.

At least, I like to think so. Call me terrorist, guerrilla or patriot: few of these can claim as much.

Chapter 2:

Three Misses

My father was arrested on July 26, 1960—ironically the seventh anniversary of Fidel Castro's own abortive first uprising and arrest. So the "26th of July Movement" applied about as well to me as to Fidel, for it started us both on our careers of anti-government activism. Only my opposition was to Fidel's government, which I felt was worse than the one he had overthrown in the name of the People.

My father was no guerrilla, no terrorist. He was sixty five years old, a retired lawyer. All he did was pass out leaflets protesting the repression of the Catholic Church in Cuba. Young Communist toughs had attacked the crowd of women and old men leaving the *Jesus de Miramar* church after mass.

It was not that we thought the Batista government that preceded Castro was good; it was notoriously corrupt. But Fidel made so many fine promises, and reneged on most of them as he brought Communism to Cuba. What had become of free speech, the free press? Abolition of the death penalty? Open elections? Restoration of the Constitution? Freedom of religion? My father's literature set the record straight.

But in a totalitarian state, anti-government propaganda is a serious offense, particularly if backed up by facts. Two waiters at the Spanish Club at the Havana beach had seen my father give some of the leaflets to a friend, and they called the G-2, or secret police. The G-2 searched and found some of this incriminating material at his house when they took him in.

For such a heinous offense, the indictment demanded thirty years in prison. Considering his age, this was much the same as a death sentence.

Of course the police were after me too, as I was my father's son, and active in the same movement. They assumed I would be guilty of the same offense. Guilt-by-association is one of the tenets of this type of government. They were mistaken: I was guilty of much worse.

Before they came, I got my gun, gathered all the incriminating papers I could find, and gave the bagful of literature to the mother of a friend of mine for safekeeping. "Don't look inside!" I cautioned her. But she did look—women are that way, curious as cats—and almost had a heart attack, poor thing. Worse than pornography, that addictive literature of freedom!

Of course another time I did worse than that: I left a shoe box containing live hand grenades with a girlfriend. Girls, despite appearances, *are* good for more than one thing. She didn't sleep a wink all night, but she kept them safe!

So now I went into hiding, but all my friends knew where I was. I stayed at another girlfriend's house, of course. Disappearing does have its little rewards.

When I learned the identity of the two informers who had gotten my father arrested, my hot Latin blood boiled up. I headed for the Spanish Club with my gun, determined to shoot those two waiters immediately. But my friends intercepted me and persuaded me to wait until my father's trial. Wise counsel; I might have made things worse for my father.

All right. I waited. But that didn't mean I was letting it rest. I went to the club several times, and such was my temper I would probably have gone after them with my bare hands if I had seen them. I was then a *nidan* in the martial art of judo, a second degree black belt, champion of Cuba. It would have been a gross abuse of my skill, for judo should be used only for self defense, but I was young then, 25, and peril to a member of my family set me off. I'm older now, but I haven't changed. Fortunately the informers always hid in the kitchen when I showed up, except once when I saw one of them serving another customer. I went to him and said: "You know who my father is," and I turned away. He almost soiled his pants.

I sent them a message, gentle enough considering my sentiments. "If my father is condemned, you are dead." I am not a very subtle person. To make sure it sank in, I had a friend burn their lockers with phosphorus. Phosphorous is nasty stuff; it burns so ferociously that nothing will put it out, and it starts suddenly like a Fourth of July sparkler. Very pretty, throwing living sparks in every direction, with white glaring light tinged with green from impurities. It makes clouds of acrid gray smoke, stinking of sulfur. It didn't melt down their lockers, but it destroyed their street clothes and everything else in there.

They got the message. At the trial they recanted and testified that they had not actually seen my father do anything, and that he was a good man. Of course he was a good man—but not in quite the way they implied. So the case against him collapsed, and he went free.

Naturally the authorities soon caught on to my part in the matter. A stenographer of the court who was a friend of our family later reported to me that a prominent member of the five man court had said "Let the old man go—it is the son we want." So? I wanted him, too!

I disagree with Fidel Castro's politics, but I can say this about his ability: he organized one hell of an efficient police state. Because there were powerful opposing forces, like the Catholic Church, dissidents were not taken in as boldly as in Nazi Germany or Russia. A person would be summoned for questioning—

and not return. No noise, no violence, no shooting—nothing anyone could really point to. Nothing to justify a violent protest or uprising.

So when, a week after my father's trial, my friend Pepito told me I had to go to a meeting, I was suspicious. "No thanks," I said. "That's the classic setup for an arrest. An informer sets up a meeting and the police ambush it."

"No problem," he assured me. "This is a small group that always gets together to play dominoes. They know each other. You have to go, because you are SAC's military coordinator."

SAC in this case did not stand for the American Strategic Air Command, but for something even more important—to me. *Salvar a Cuba*, "Save Cuba," a clandestine resistance movement, small but effective for its size. We were planning an attack on a naval base near Havana. We would raid the ten-man garrison and take their weapons to the Escambray mountains, where we would set up as guerrillas. I looked forward to that; I had not yet discovered the hardships of real country warfare. SAC was made up mostly of University students, my kind of people—those that were supposed to be the most ardent supporters of the Revolution. Ha! Did Fidel assume that to be educated was to be stupid?

Pepito was right: I had to brief this group. It was risky—but counter-revolution is a risky profession. I was learning that the hard way.

"We'll go fast, and get out fast," I said.

We went. I was nervous, and I looked all around as we entered the house. There were half a dozen people playing dominoes and drinking beer—an innocent enough setting, but I was not reassured. In fiction, the hero may be supremely confident—but a real-life guerrilla is understandably jittery. He has no series-contract with a publisher to keep him alive indefinitely. I thought I heard noises outside. For a moment I was ready to bolt for it, diving out the window and running. But it was probably just my nerves. Why make a fool of myself?

Then a man entered. He carried a Springfield rifle and ten

militia uniforms we planned to use on our mission. I thought he was our contact—but he was a government man, who had found this incriminating evidence. "The house is surrounded," he announced. "Please come with me, quietly."

We were outnumbered and unarmed. Any attempt to fight would have gotten us shot. The G-2 always brought overwhelming strength to bear in arrests. Why hadn't I thought to bring my gun? In my inexperience I had stupidly walked into the trap, and now there was nothing I could do.

And so I was arrested—in the classic manner.

I still hoped I could bluff it out. After all, we hadn't *done* anything very serious that they could prove, and the main arsenal of six or eight Belgian-made FALS rifles, several revolvers, two sawed-off shotguns, and some cartridges prepared with heavy buckshot and cyanide for assassination attempts—all this was safely hidden in another place. Oh, we might be given token sentences, but nothing serious. I hoped. Provided nobody cracked under questioning.

But when we got to the G-2 offices, the first thing we saw was a long table loaded with weapons. My friend Tony went white. "My God—they found our cache!

Then I knew we had had it.

I was put in the "cold room" where the air conditioning was turned up so high I thought I would freeze to death. Maybe that doesn't sound like so much of a torture, compared to thumbscrews or hot irons or electric shocks through the genitals, but believe me, a week of such cold makes confession seem very attractive. A man can stand pain for a short period, but the long, slow, subtle debilitation of simple cold can wipe out much of his will to resist. I was dressed in only a light short-sleeved sport-shirt and summer slacks, since Havana ranged from 70°F at night to 85° in the day.

I didn't crack. It wasn't that I was tough, it was that I knew that nothing they were doing to me as a suspect would approach what they would do to me as a confirmed enemy of the state. The G-2 is not a backward organization in this respect; if they had thought I was important, they would have trotted out techniques of interrogation that would have made me crack in a hurry. I was better off shivering, and I knew it. Better to freeze as a small fish, than to roast as a big one.

After that I was taken to the *Cabanas*, the fortress prison. It wasn't like an American penal institution, where cells are restricted to two to four inmates each. There were fifteen long *Galeras* or corridors hewn in the stone of the walls, like railroad tunnels, dank and cold at night. Each contained about 90 men in triple-decker bunks when I arrived, but later there were more. They were served by two toilets and wash bowls and showers. We had to turn in our original clothes for prison uniforms with the letter P on the backs. At the door new arrivals were greeted with the shout "*Carne Fresca*!" meaning "fresh meat!"—hardly reassuring.

Meals were simple. They didn't starve us, but one time the meat was bad, spoiled. Our Galera was overcrowded then, and 150 men had to use the two toilets all at once. Many had such indigestion they could not wait, and had to relieve themselves where they stood. The stench was terrible.

The prison was a community in itself, with all sorts of ups and downs and personal interactions. Much of the life was brutal; some had its humorous aspects. One thing you have to realize about political prisoners: they do not consider themselves to be criminals, but men of conscience. They are the high officials who happened to back the wrong side, the reformers whose good works were not appreciated by the evil State, the innocent who were drawn in by random arrests or mistaken information. Or so they claim.

The truth is that some are criminals, but many more are not. Some of the very best resources of a nation are in the political prison. A lot of political opportunists, too—counting on a change of government to provide high office for them on the strength of their imprisonment. It is a unique atmosphere, completely different from the conventional penal institution.

When I was there, roughly one third of the prisoners were ex-

Batista soldiers, another third were ex-Castro men, and the rest were civilians: lawyers, engineers, students, doctors, artists, Cuba's leading astrologer, the heavyweight boxing champion of the country, University professors, jewelers, chess players, and of course me, the judo champion. In short, an elite society, eclectic as it was.

We tried to entertain ourselves with chess, checkers, dominoes, poker, Parcheesi, Monopoly, and exercises in the yard. Practice in self defense or martial art was of course forbidden. But interesting as these diversions may seem for a few weeks or months, the notion of continuing that life for twenty years or so was appalling.

Yet even the short haul was no picnic. There were fights and beatings and riots, with virtual warfare between the Batista men and the Revolutionists. Yes, each group carried its loyalties right into prison. And always the awful pall of the approaching trials. We knew many of us would die at the wall, *Paredon*, but always hoped selfishly that it would be someone else.

Actually, my experience was far from unique. In Latin America, political prison is often a stepping stone for political power. Perhaps half the leaders are graduates of this type of school. Fidel himself served two years in Batista's prisons, and Batista's predecessor in power had also been in prison. Batista himself had the wit to skip the country fast with his money when his regime toppled, or he would have been in prison too—for the little while until he was executed.

My watch was stolen. My two friends, Eduardo Bringas and Juan Pla, let it be known that if my watch were not returned in one hour, they were going to take action. Such was their reputation, even in prison, that my watch reappeared within the deadline.

Another friend, Ricardo Cruz, started beating up an informer. There are informers inside as well as outside, and they can make a lot of trouble. Once we made a tunnel through the wall of the prison, from the infirmary. We were almost through, when an informer spilled the news. Potential freedom, wiped out just like that. So tempers can flare when an informer is discovered.

When I got to that fight, the soldiers were just coming to break it up. I got in the way, not exactly accidentally, and saved Ricardo from getting struck by a rifle butt, and it ended with Ricardo and me both getting arrested. Technically we were already under arrest, since we were prisoners—but as I said, this was like a community, and we were left pretty much to our own devices if we stayed out of trouble.

We were taken to Teniente Manolo, the chief of the prison. He hated us, because he thought students were supposed to be more in favor of the Castro Revolution than the average citizen. Those of us who opposed Castro were thus doubly traitors, in his eyes. He was so furious I thought he was going to strike me across the face. I'm no hero, but my temper was ragged, and if he had touched me I would probably have thrown him against the wall and tried to beat him to death. You can do a lot of damage to a man in a very short time, if you know how, and I happen to know how. But that would have been the end of me, of course. Such heroics are much safer in fiction.

Manolo must have heeded my expression and thought the better of it. He had much more to lose than I did. Instead he sent us to the *Capillas*. These were dark, cold, barren stone tunnels under the castle, a kind of solitary confinement cell-complex. Prison was bad, but the *Capillas* were worse! I would certainly be more careful in the future; I didn't want to be sent there again.

Back in the main prison a week later, I found the mood changed, tense, ugly. The prison authorities feared that mood, so they started having sudden trials. Five people would be summoned at a time, and only one would return. "They gave me thirty years!" that one would cry joyfully. "Thirty years! Thank God!" This was not a strange reaction—for the other four had gone to the execution wall.

We were all sweating now. They could shoot us all if they wanted, just to clear the cells. Justice in Cuba was at such a state in

Fidel's brave new order that all they needed were the bullets. In three short hours thirty men were condemned to death, including many of my friends. All but one of those were commuted to thirty years, however. Excellent psychological strategy: the black mood lightened, now that the axe had fallen, and there was no riot.

But the single one who was shot was my friend Ricardo Cruz, my companion of the *Capillas*.

When my own trial came, I was convinced I would get at least three years to nine years, while a part of me hoped for a lighter sentence, and another part carried the awful vision of *Paredon*. Oh God, not the Wall! Yet Ricardo had gone . . .

My trial was around three in the afternoon, but the results were not announced right away, and at six we were returned to our cells. We did not know how long it would be; maybe in a couple of hours, maybe in a week. There was no point worrying about it, though of course we *did* worry; how could we stop it? I went to sleep early, around eight, my emotions played out—and at nine-thirty they gave the results over the speaker system.

The names of three of my friends were called out for release. Lucky bastards! Then someone woke me up: "Roberto, get dressed. You are free!"

But I knew about that cruel joke. Wake someone, tell him his name has been called for release. A dream come true! His hopes rise sky high, he runs to the gate—and there he learns the truth. Everyone laughs heartily. Ha ha! Excruciatingly funny. For everybody but him, with his dashed hope. Maybe next day he goes to the Wall. How nice that his last day was brightened by this humor.

So I didn't believe this news. But the chief of the galley in our cell told me it was true, and he wished me luck. Then I believed.

And so I went home, incredibly, a free man.

Death had missed me, once.

*

Some people might have given up counterrevolution after that experience. But I had tasted the water, and had been through too much. The blood of my friends was on the hands of the *Fidelistas.* I was more determined than ever to overthrow the Castro regime in Cuba. Maybe I would have been wiser to leave the country for Miami, as my friend Pepito did—to return four months later as a parachuter in the Bay of Pigs invasion. Ah, well, hindsight . . .

The day after I got home, I went into hiding and started contacting my former associates. We were involved in terrorism—at least that was what the government called our activities. But for us, what we did was the first step in the process of freeing Cuba. A year and a half before, our pursuers had been doing exactly the same thing; then *they* were the terrorists. They had been the ones doing the bombings and shootings, trying to assassinate high government officers and averting disaster only very narrowly. Strange, isn't it, how last year's terrorist becomes this year's law-and-order man. Maybe next year *I* would be a high government official of Free Cuba, on my fine white horse, adored by lovely young girls, trying to suppress the nefarious Communist counter-counter-revolutionaries! I, the patriot! Ah, dreams . . .

There was to be a patriotic dance in a small town near Havana, *Guira de Melenas.* If there was one thing I was *not*, right now, it was patriotic. Not for the Castro regime! So I welcomed the chance to break this up.

A local boy knew the key electric post: the one that, if destroyed, would blacken the entire town. Beautiful! Just let them try to hold the dance, without any electric power. No light, no radio, no music—nothing that depended on the current. Maybe it wouldn't do much to topple Castro, but what a satisfaction to mess it up!

Maybe James Bond type agents deal exclusively with world-shaking missions—but I was merely a garden variety protester. Later my horizons broadened. But at this time, darkening a village dance was my level of expertise. We all have to start somewhere, you know.

The boy did not have the nerve to plant the bomb himself, and there was no one else with the critical knowledge, so it fell to me. We went in a car painted like a taxi, with Jorge, another friend of mine, driving. Friends are a great comfort to a terrorist. We got to the entrance of the town, and saw about ten militiamen with rifles stopping the incoming traffic.

"God, they are searching the cars!" I exclaimed. There I was, in the front seat, with the bomb in my lap like a picnic basket. It consisted of five pounds of C-3 plastic explosive wrapped in newspaper. Five pounds may not sound like much, but it was equivalent to ten sticks of commercial dynamite: enough to destroy a house, let alone our carfull.

I was eating *Pan de Caracas*, a dry cornbread, and my mouth got so parched the stuff stuck in my throat. The Chinese used to have a test of guilt: if a handful of rice held in the mouth remained dry, the suspect was guilty. I would have failed that test, for sure!

I clutched my gun under my shirt. I looked out at the militiamen in front of the car. I will never forget his mustached face or the FAL rifle he carried. *If he asks me what I have in the newspaper, or makes me get out of the car,* I thought, *I'll shoot him in the stomach and make a break for the woods*! I was not being brave; I was terrified, but I knew I would never get out of prison alive a second time, because *all* of those caught with explosives were sent to *Paredon.* My temperament was such that I preferred to die fighting; I did not have the nuts to stand before the firing squad bravely defiant to the end.

But Jorge, thank God, had a face of iron. "Companero," he said to the militiaman, "want me to open the trunk?"

The man nodded. "Yes, please." This was routine, for him; he didn't expect to find any plastic explosive wrapped in newspaper like fresh fish.

Jorge opened the trunk—and of course it was empty.

"All right—go on," the militiaman said, bored. We were

through—but I'd had the worst scare of my life.

We continued on into town. We found the pole with the transformers, wrapped the bomb around it (you can shape plastic explosive; it is very versatile, the bomber's best friend), tightened it with a belt, and touched a match to the three minute fuse.

The fuse would not light.

Of all the—! We tried again—and again. Once it started to burn, but it was only the outer casing, not the powder trail, and nothing happened. I had to go back, cut off the end, and try with a much shorter piece. I swear it took five excruciating minutes to ignite that thing, with us sweating all the time. Any chance discovery by the militia—

Finally it caught. Now all we had to worry about was getting blown up! We piled into the car and took off. I know we made it out of town within three minutes, because as we left we heard the explosion behind us and saw the lights go out. Success!

Later I learned that one man, Tomas, who had helped us, had been caught and sentenced to 30 years. I had been tried *in absentia* and sentenced to death. That didn't bother me much; the sentence was meaningless so long as they didn't catch me. But how well I still remember that mustached militiaman who stopped our car: my second miss with death.

*

Berty Andino, the MRR Action and Sabotage chief, called me one day; he had 20 pounds of C-3 explosive already made into bombs, and he wanted me to test a new kind of detonator. Would I do it?

"Sure," I said. I like bombs. Watching a real blast is almost like a religious experience. "But can I keep the bombs until tomorrow? My brother is Christening his second son this afternoon, and I'm to be the Godfather."

He paused. "No, it can't wait. I'll get another person." I knew he thought I was going to die soon—after all, I had been condemned to death, and my luck couldn't hold out indefinitely—and he wanted me to have this one moment. This nice little family ceremony might well be my last.

Maybe Berty would not have been so nice about it if he had known my other reason for begging off: I had lined up three luscious girls for a party with two friends that night. One was Hilda, one of the most beautiful black girls I have known: petite with lovely silky shoulder-long hair; another was her friend Toby, and I have forgotten the name of the third (a rose by any name would smell as sweet), but she had soft cloudy black hair and other attributes best left to the imagination.

Terrorism has a strong effect on the personality, because of the constant threat of death. Some people turn religious; others develop an inordinate craving for sex. I was not religious.

So I did not go on the bombing mission. Instead I attended my nephew's Christening, and my private party. My friend Enrique went to pick up our third man, Barreto, and for one whole glorious hour I was *alone with all three girls.* What a party!

Suddenly we heard a tremendous explosion, that shook the buildings in a wide area. That would be Berty's crew, doing the job; for a moment I was sorry I was not in on it. But there are other things in life than bombs, and I was enjoying three of them right now; my regret was minimal.

Next day I learned: the new detonators had been faulty. The two men had put the stuff in a car and driven toward their mission—and the plastic had gone off prematurely. Twenty pounds of C-3! Pieces of men and car were scattered across a hundred yards of street, so mangled that nothing could be identified.

Except for the Christening and my hot party, that bang would have been Enrique and me. My third miss with an appointment for death, because I was too busy making time with three lovely misses . . .

SUMMARY OF REMAINDER:

The following chapters will detail the life/death crises and complications of the protagonist, gradually filling in more of the background of the Cuban situation and clarifying the motives and philosophy of the terrorist.

Roberto Fuentes was involved in several secret missions for Cuban exiles and the United States, and twice escaped Cuba by seeking refuge in a foreign embassy. Even that was not the sanctuary some might imagine; the Castro government knew how to bring a lot of pressure to bear to get him out, even trying to remove him by force. He was the only one to receive asylum from Castro twice in different embassies, those of Mexico and Uruguay.

Several times he tried to kill Fidel Castro. One attempt was foiled by a sudden storm; another by Fidel's last-moment change of plane. He blew up a hotel Fidel was to visit, the Hilton-Havana Libre, almost catching an occupant who was later to become his wife, Grace. Another occupant was one of his best friends, counter-revolutionary leader Manolito Baro. Roberto also tried to kill two of Castro's top officers, again being balked by freak luck, such as a shotgun misfiring at point-blank range.

He was involved in the Bay of Pigs fiasco, as a leader of the Cuban underground ready to start a concurrent insurrection in Havana. He shows why that effort failed, owing to incredible mismanagement. Had he followed the fouled-up script, he would have been dead—again.

He tells how the assassination of President Kennedy stopped the next major effort to free Cuba. It is not known whether Fidel Castro had any part in the assassination—but the CIA tried to kill Castro, and Fidel was not a man to take that sort of thing lightly, and was himself an expert in such matters. Later, Bobby Kennedy was reviving part of the anti-Castro plan—when be too was killed. A grim coincidence—perhaps.

Roberto also had a varied sex life, sleeping with white, black and brown women both pro and anti-Castro. One of them was the sister of a major in Castro's escort. Another was the wife of a major in Batista's army, and another the wife of a Cuban baseball star, and still another was a beauty queen. He shows how he turned from an apolitical intellectual hedonist who cared more about his next girlfriend than who was ruling his country, into a dedicated counter-revolutionist, a fanatic man of action. The kind of man the modern terrorist elsewhere in the world is all too likely to be, who will not be stopped by repressive measures.

Roberto became one of that small minority who does the really dirty work and pays the penalty—if caught. He underwent deep psychological changes that still affect him today. His accomplices underwent similar changes; some of them remained active in America, and were among the original number whose arrest sparked the Watergate investigation that finally toppled the Nixon presidency. One of these men, Rolando Martinez, had taken Fuentes to Cuba several times on secret missions, risking his life many times. In this manner it is shown how the foreign exploits of the United States returned to make mischief in its own government.

Another way in which these U.S.-trained killer-chickens have come home to roost shown in the recent rash of killings in Miami; done by professionals, they leave no hints for the police. But the Cuban community knows. Today some of these terrorists are turning to drug traffic; they are good at that too. The drug problem will not be solved until the terrorist problem is solved.

Thus the story of Roberto Fuentes campaign to free Cuba shows the devious but enormous ramifications that have affected not only Cuba, but all Americans. Patriots of other nationalities have similar modes of operation, and hardly a day passes without news of their actions. If we do not want the assassination of one American President and the resignation-in-disgrace of another to be merely the beginning of a wave of real terrorism, it would be wise to understand the message Mr. Fuentes brings.

Printed in the United Kingdom
by Lightning Source UK Ltd.
2606